Frances Power Cobbe

Life of Frances Power Cobbe

In Two Volumes. Vol. II

Frances Power Cobbe

Life of Frances Power Cobbe
In Two Volumes. Vol. II

ISBN/EAN: 9783744713306

Printed in Europe, USA, Canada, Australia, Japan

Cover: Foto ©Raphael Reischuk / pixelio.de

More available books at **www.hansebooks.com**

LIFE OF
FRANCES POWER COBBE

BY HERSELF

IN TWO VOLUMES

VOLUME II.

BOSTON AND NEW YORK
HOUGHTON, MIFFLIN AND COMPANY
The Riverside Press, Cambridge
1894

CONTENTS.

VOL. II.

CHAPTER XIV.

ITALY. 1857—1879.

I VISITED Italy six times between the above dates. The reader need not be wearied by reminiscences of such familiar journeyings, which in my case, were always made quickly through France (a country which I intensely dislike), and extended pretty evenly over the most beautiful cities of Italy. I spent several seasons in Rome and Florence, and a winter in Pisa; and I visited once, twice or three times, Venice, Bologna, Naples, Perugia, Assisi, Verona, Padua, Genoa, Milan and Turin. The only interest which these wanderings can claim belongs to the people with whom they brought me into contact, and these include a somewhat remarkable list: Mr. and Mrs. Browning, Mrs. Somerville, Theodore Parker, Walter Savage Landor, Massimo d' Azeglio, John Gibson, Charlotte Cushman, Count Guido Usedom, Adolphus Trollope and his first wife, Mr. W. W. Story, and Mrs. Beecher Stowe. Of many of these I gave slight sketches in my book "Italics;" and must refer to them very briefly here. That book, I may mention, was written principally at Villa Gnecco, a beautiful villa at Nervi on the Riviera di Levante, then rented by my kind friend Count Usedom, the Prussian Ambassador, and his English wife. Count Guido Usedom — now alas! gone over to the majority — was an extremely

cultivated man, who had been at one time Secretary to
Bunsen's Embassy in Rome. He was so good as to
undertake what I may call my (Italian) Political Education; instructing me not only of the facts of recent
history, but of the *dessous des cartes* of each event as
they were known to the initiated. He placed all his
despatches for many years in my hands, and explained
the policy of each nation concerned : and even taught
me the cryptographs then in diplomatic use. His own
letters to his King, the late Emperor Wilhelm I., were
lively and delightful sketches of Italian affairs; for, as he
said, he had discovered, that to induce the King to read
them they must be both amusing and beautifully tran-
scribed. From him and the Prefects and other influential men who came to visit him at Villa Gnecco, I gained
some views of politics not perhaps unworthy of record.

One day I asked him, " Whether it were exactly true
that Cavour had told a distinct falsehood in the Cham-
bers about Garibaldi's invasion of Naples ? "   Count
Usedom replied, " He *did ;* and I do not believe there
is a statesman in Europe who would not have done the
same when a kingdom was in question."   He obviously
thought (scrupulously conscientious as he was himself)
that, to diplomatists in general and their sovereigns,
the laws of morality and honor were like ladies' brace-
lets, highly ornamental and to be worn habitually, but
to be slipped off when any serious work was to be done
which required free hands. He said: " People (especially women) often asked me is such a King a *good
man?* Is Napoleon III. a *good man?* This is non-
sense. They are all good men, in so far that they will
not do a cruel, or treacherous, or unjust thing *without
strong reasons* for it. That would be not only a crime
but a blunder. But when great dynastic interests are
concerned, Kings and Emperors and their ministers are
neither guided by moral considerations or deterred from
following their interests because a life, or many lives,
stand in the way." He adduced Napoleon III.'s *coup*

d'état as an example. Napoleon was not a man to in-
dulge in any cruel or vindictive sentiment; but neither
was he one to forego a step needed for his policy.

The year following these studies under Count Usedom I was living in London, and met Mazzini one evening by special invitation alone at the house of Mr. and
Mrs. James Stansfeld (I speak of Mr. Stansfeld's first
wife, sister of Madame Venturi). After dinner our
hosts left us alone, and Mazzini, whom I had often met
before and who was always very good to me, asked me
if I would listen to his version of the recent history of
Italy, since he thought I had been much misinformed on
the subject. Of course I could only express my sense
of the honor he did me by the proposal; and then,
somewhat to my amazement and amusement, Mazzini
descended from his armchair, seated himself opposite
me cross-legged on the magnificent white rug before
Mrs. Stansfeld's blazing fire, and proceeded to pour out
— I believe for quite two hours — the entire story of
all that went before and after the siege of Rome, his
Triumvirate, and the subsequent risings, plots and battles. If any one could have taken down that wonderful
story in shorthand it would possess immense value, and
I regret profoundly that I did not at least attempt,
when I went home, to write my recollections of it. But
I was merely bewildered. Each event which Mazzini
named — sitting so coolly there on the rug at my feet:
— "I sent an army here, I ordered a rising there," appeared under an aspect so entirely different from that
which it had borne as represented to me by my political
friends in Italy, that I was continually mystified, and
asked: "But Signor Mazzini, are you talking of such
and such an event?" — "*Ma sì Signora*" — and off he
would go again with vivid and eloquent explanations
and descriptions, which fairly took my breath away.
At last (I believe it was near midnight), Mrs. Stansfeld,
who had, of course, arranged this effort for my conversion to Italian Republicanism, returned to the drawing-

room; and I fear that the truly noble-hearted man who had done me so high a favor, rose disappointed from his lowly rug! He said to me at another time: "You English, who are blessed with loyal sovereigns, cannot understand that one of our reasons for being Republicans is, that we cannot trust our Kings and Grand Dukes an inch. They are each one of them a *Rè Traditore!*" One could quite concede that a constitutional government under a traitor-prince would not hold out any prospect of success; but at all events Victor Emanuel and Umberto have completely exonerated themselves from such suspicions.

To return to Italy and the men I know there. Count Usedom's reference to Napoleon's *coup d'état* reminds me of the clever saying which I have quoted elsewhere, of a greater diplomatist than he, Cavaliere Massimo d'Azeglio. Talking with him, as I had the privilege of doing every day for many months at the *table d'hôte* in the hotel where we both spent a winter in Pisa, I made some remark about the mistake of founding religion on histories of miracles. "Ah, les miracles!" exclaimed D'Azeglio; "je n'en crois rien! *Ce sont des coups d'état célestes!*" Could the strongest argument against them have been more neatly packed in one simile? A *coup d'état* is a practical confession that the regular and orderly methods of Government *have failed* in the hands of the governor, and that he is driven to have recourse to irregular and lawless methods to compass his ends and vindicate his sovereignty. A *coup d'état* is like the act of an impatient chess player who, finding himself losing the game while playing fairly, sweeps some pieces from the board to recover his advantage. Is this to be believed of Divine rule of the universe?

D'Azeglio was one of those men (of whom I have met about a dozen in life) who impressed me as having in their characters elements of real *greatness:* not

being merely clever or gifted, but large-souled. When
I knew him he was a fallen statesman, an almost forgotten author, a General on the shelf, a Prime Minister
reduced to living in a single room at an hotel, without a
secretary or even a valet; yet he was the cheeriest
Italian I ever knew. His spirits never seemed to falter. He was the life of our table every day, and I used
to hear him singing continually over his water-color
drawing in his room adjoining mine at the *Gran' Bre-
tagna,* on the dull Lung-Arno of Pisa. The fate of Italy
which still hung in suspense was, however, ever near
his heart. One day it was talked over at the *table
d'hôte,* and D' Azeglio looked grave, and said : " We
speak of this man and the other ; but it is God who is
making Italy ! " It was so unusual a sentiment for an
Italian gentleman to utter, that it impressed the listen-
ers almost with awe. Another day, talking of Thackeray and the ugliness of his school of novelists, he observed : " It is all right to seek to express Truth. But
why do these people always seem to think *qu'il n'y a
rien de vrai excepté le laid ?* " The reason — I might
have replied — is that it is extremely difficult to depict
Beauty, and extremely easy to create Ugliness ! Beauty
means Proportion, Refinement, Elevation, Simplicity.
How much harder it is to convey *these* truly, than Dis-
proportion, Coarseness, Baseness, Duplicity ? Since
D' Azeglio spoke we have gone on creating Ugliness and
calling it Truth, till M. Zola has originated a literature
in honor of Le Laid, and given us books like " Assom-
moir " in which it is perfected, almost as Beauty was of
old in a statue of Praxiteles or in the Dresden Madonna.

One day that M. D' Azeglio was doing me the honor
of paying me a visit in my room, he narrated to me the
following singular little bit of history. It seems that
when he was Premier of Sardinia and Lord John Russell of England, the latter sent him through Lord
Minto a distinct message — " that he might safely

undertake a certain line of policy, since, if a given
contingency arose, England would afford him armed
support." The contingency did occur; but Lord Russell was unable to give the armed support which he had
promised; "and this," said D' Azeglio, "caused my
fiasco." He resigned office, and, I think, then retired
from public life; but some years later, being in England, he was invited to Windsor. There he happened
to be laid up with a cold, and Lord Russell and Lord
Minto who were also guests at the castle paid him a
visit in his apartments. "Then," said D' Azeglio, " I
turned on them both, and challenged them to say
whether Lord Minto had not conveyed that message
to me from Lord Russell, and whether he had not
failed to keep his engagement. They did not attempt
to deny that it was so." D' Azeglio (I understood him
to say) had himself sent the Sardinian contingent to
fight with our troops and the French in the Crimea, for
the express and sole purpose of making Europe recognize that there was a *question d'Italie* (or possibly he
spoke of this being the motive of the Minister who did
so.) Another remark which this charming old man
made has remained very clearly on my memory for a
reason to be presently explained. He observed, laughing: "People seem to think that Ministers have
indefinite time at their disposal, but they have only
twenty-four hours like other men, and they must eat
and sleep and rest like the remainder of the human
race. When I was Premier I calculated that dividing
the subjects which demanded attention and the time I
had to bestow on them, there were just *three minutes
and a half* on an average for ordinary subjects, and
eight minutes for important ones! And if that be so in
a little State like Piedmont, what must it be in the
case of a Prime Minister of England? I cannot think
how mortal man can bear the office!"

Many years afterwards I told this to an English

statesman, and he replied — with rather startling
gaieté de cœur, considering the responsibilities for Irish
murders then resting on his shoulders : — "Quite true;
it is all a scuffle and a scramble from morning to night.
If you had seen me two hours ago you would have
found me listening to a very important despatch read
to me by one of my secretaries while I was dictating
another, equally important, to another. All a scuffle
and a scramble from morning to night!" Count Usedom told me that at one time he had been Minister of
War in Prussia, and that he knew a great battle was
imminent next day, the Prussian army having just
come up with the enemy. He lay awake all night
reflecting on the horrors of the ensuing fight; remembering that he had the power to telegraph to the General in command to stop it, and longing with all his soul
to do so, but knowing that the act would be treachery
to his country. Of this sort of anxiety I strongly
suspect some statesmen have never felt a twinge.

It was at Florence in 1860 that I met Theodore Parker for the first time. After the letters of deep sympathy and agreement on religious matters which had
passed between us, it was a strange turn of fate which
brought him to die in Florence, and me to stand beside
his deathbed and his grave. The world has (as is natural) passed on over the road which he did much to
open, and his name is scarcely known to the younger
generation; but looking back at his work and at his
books again after thirty years, and when early enthusiasm has given place to the calm judgment of age I still
feel that Theodore Parker was a very great religious
teacher and confessor, — as Albert Réville wrote of .
him: "*Cet homme fût un prophete.*" That is, he received the truths of what he called "Absolute Religion" at first hand in his own faithful soul, and spoke
them out, fearless of consequences, with unequalled
straightforwardness. He was not subtle-minded. He

did not at all see obliquely round corners, as men like
Cardinal Newman always seem to have done; nor estimate the limitations which his broad statements sometimes required. It would have been scarcely possible
to have been both the man he was, and also a fine critic
and metaphysician. But his was a clear, trumpet voice,
to which many a freed and rejoicing spirit responded;
and if he founded no sect or school, he did better. He
infused into the religious life of England and America
an element hardly present before, of natural confidence
in the absolute goodness of God independent of theolo-
gies. No man did more than he to awaken the Protestant nations from the hideous nightmare of an Eternal
Hell, which (within my own recollection) hovered over
the piety of England. As he was wont himself to say,
laughingly, he had "knocked the bottom out of hell!"

I will copy here some notes of my only interviews
with this honored friend and teacher, to whom I owed
so much: —

"28th April. Saw Mr. Parker for the first time. He
was lying in bed with his back to the light. Mrs. Parker brought me into the room. He took my hand tenderly and said in a low, hurried voice, holding it: 'After
all our wishes to meet, Miss Cobbe, how strange it is
we should meet *thus*.' I pressed his hand and he turned
his eyes, which were trembling painfully and evidently
seeing nothing, towards me and said, 'You must not
think you have seen *me*. This is not *me*, only the
wreck of the man I was.' Then, after a pause he
added: 'Those who love me most can only wish me
a quick passage to the other world. Of course I am
not *afraid* to die (he smiled as he spoke) but there
was so much to be done!' I said: 'You have given
your life to God and His truth as truly as any martyr
of old.' He replied: 'I do not know; I had great
powers committed to me, I have but half used them.'
I gave him a nosegay of roses and lily-of-the-valley.

He smiled and touched the lily-of-the-valley, saying it was the sweetest of all flowers. I begged him, if his lodgings were not all he desired, to come to Villa Brichieri (a villa on Bellosguardo, which I then shared with Miss Blagden), but he said he was most comfortable where he was. Then his mind wandered a little about a bad dream which haunted him, and I left him.

"April 29th. I was told on arriving that Mr. Parker had spoken very tenderly of my visit of the day before, but had said, 'I must not see her often. It makes my heart swell too high. But you (to his wife) must see her every day. Remember there is but one Miss Cobbe in the world.' Afterwards he told Dr. Appleton that he wanted him to get an inkstand for me as a last gift. [This inkstand I have used ever since.] He received me very kindly, but almost at once his mind wandered, and he spoke of 'going home immediately.' He asked what day of the week it was. I said: 'This is the blessed day; it is Sunday.' 'Ah yes!' he said. 'It is a blessed day when one has got over the superstition of it. I will try to go to you to-morrow.' (Of course this was utterly out of the question.) Then he looked at the lily of Florence which I had brought and told him how I had got it down from one of the old walls for him, and he smiled the same sweet smile as yesterday, and touched the beautiful blue Iris, and soon seemed to sleep."

I called after this every day, generally twice a day, at the Pension Molini where he lay; but rarely could interchange a word. Parker's friend, Dr. Appleton of Boston, who was faithfully attending him, sent for another friend, Professor Desor, and they and the three ladies of the party nursed him, of course, devotedly. On the 10th May I saw him lying breathing quietly, while life ebbed gently. I returned to Bellosguardo and at eight o'clock in the evening Professor Desor and Dr. Appleton came up to tell me he had passed peacefully away.

Parker had, long before his death, desired that the first eleven verses of the Sermon on the Mount should be read at his funeral. Whether he intended that they should form the only service was not known; but Desor and Appleton arranged that so it should be, and that they should be read by Rev. W. Cunningham, an American Unitarian clergyman who was fortunately at the time living near us on Bellosguardo, and who was a man of much feeling and dignity of aspect. The funeral took place on Sunday, the 13th May, at the beautiful old Campo Santo Inglese, outside the walls of Florence, which contains the dust of Mrs. Browning, of Arthur Hugh Clough, and many others dear to English memories. It was the first funeral I had ever attended. The coffin when I arrived was already lying in the mortuary chapel. My companions placed a wreath of laurels on it, and I added a large bunch of the lily-of-the-valley which he had loved. Then eight Italian pall-bearers took up the coffin and carried it on a sidewalk to the grave. When it had been lowered with some difficulty to the last resting-place, my Notes say : —

"Dr. Appleton then handed a Bible to Mr. Cunningham. I was standing close to him and heard his voice falter. He read like a man who felt all the holy words he said, and those sacred Blessings came with unspeakable rest to my heart. Then Desor, who had been pale as death, threw in one handful of clay. . . . The burial ground is exquisitely lovely, a very wilderness of flowers and perfume. Only a few cypresses give it grandeur, not gloom. All Florence was decorated with flags in honor of the anniversary of the Piedmontese Constitution. We said to one another : 'It is a festival for us also — the solemn feast of an Ascension.'"

Of course I visited this grave when I returned to Florence several years afterwards. The cypresses had grown large and dark and somewhat shadowed it. I had the violets, etc., renewed upon it more than once, but I heard later that it had become somewhat dilapidated, and I was glad to join a subscription got up by an American gentleman to erect a new tombstone. I hope it has been done, as he would have desired, with simplicity. I shall never see that grave again.

Two or three years later I edited all the twelve volumes of Parker's works for Messrs. Trübner, and wrote a somewhat lengthy preface for them; afterwards reprinted as a separate pamphlet entitled the "Religious Demands of the Age." Three biographies of Parker have appeared; the shortest, published in England by Rev. Peter Dean, being in my opinion the best. The letters which I received from Parker in the years before I saw him are all printed by my permission in Mr. Weiss' "Life," and therefore will not be reproduced here.

That venerable old man, Rev. John J. Tayler, writing to me a few years later, summed up Parker's character I think as justly as did Mr. Jowett in calling him a "religious Titan."

I read lately with much pleasure your preface to the forthcoming edition of Theodore Parker's works. I agree cordially with your estimate of his character. His virtues were of the highest type of the hero and the martyr. His faults, such as they were, were such as are incident to every ardent and earnest soul fighting against wickedness and hypocrisy; faults which colder and more worldly natures easily avoid, faults which he shared with some of the best and noblest of our race — a Milton, a Luther, and a Paul. When freedom and justice have achieved some conquests yet to come, his memory will be cherished with deeper reverence and affection than it is, except by a small number, now.

I remain, dear Miss Cobbe, very truly yours,

J. J. TAYLER.

At the time of Parker's death I was sharing the apartment of my clever and charming friend, Isa Blagden, in Villa Brichieri on Bellosguardo. It was a delightful house with a small *podere* off the road, and with a broad balcony (accommodating any number of chairs) opening from the airy drawing-room, and commanding a splendid view of Florence backed by Fiesole and the Apennines. On the balcony, and in our drawing-rooms, assembled regularly every week and often on other occasions, an interesting and varied company. We were both of us poor, but in those days poverty in Florence permitted us to rent fourteen well-furnished rooms in a charming villa, and to keep a maid and a man-servant. The latter bought our meals every morning in Florence, cooked and served them; being always clean and respectably dressed. He swept our floors and he opened our doors and announced our company and served our ices and tea with uniform quietness and success. A treasure, indeed, was good old Ansano! Also we were able to engage an open carriage with a pair of horses to do our shopping and pay our visits in Florence as often as we needed. And what does the reader think it cost us to live like this, fire and candles and food for four included? In those halcyon days under the old *régime*, it was precisely £20 a month! We divided everything exactly and it never exceeded £10 apiece.

Among our most frequent visitors was Mr. Browning. Mrs. Browning was never able to drive so far, but her warm friendship for Miss Blagden was heartily shared by her husband and we saw a great deal of him. Always full of spirits, full of interest in everything from politics to hedge-flowers, cordial and utterly unaffected, he was at all times a charming member of society; but I confess that in those days I had no adequate sense of his greatness as a poet. I could not read his poetry, though he had not then written his most difficult pieces, and his conversation was so playful and light that it never occurred to me that I was wasting precious time chatting frivolously with him when I might have been gaining high thoughts and instruction. There was always a ripple of laughter round the sofa where he used to seat himself, generally beside some lady of the company, towards whom, in his eagerness, he would push nearer and nearer till she frequently rose to avoid falling off at the end! When we drove out in parties he would discuss every tree and weed, and get excited about the difference between eglantine and eglatere (if there be any), and between either of them and honeysuckle. He and Isa were always wrangling in an affectionate way over some book or music; (he was a fine performer himself on the piano), and one night when I had left Villa Brichieri and was living at Villa Niccolini at least half a mile off, the air being in some singular condition of sonority, carried their voices between the walls of the two villas so clearly across to me that I actually heard some of the words of their quarrel, and closed my window lest I should be an eavesdropper. I believe it was about Spirit-rapping they were fighting, for which, and the professors of the art, Browning had a horror. I have seen him stamping on the floor in a frenzy of rage at the way some believers and mediums were deceiving Mrs. Browning.

Thirty years afterwards, the last time I ever had the privilege of talking with Robert Browning (it was in Surrey House in London), I referred to these old days and to our friend, long laid in that Campo Santo at Florence. His voice fell and softened, and he said: "Ah, poor, *dear* Isa!" with deep feeling.

At that time I do not think that any one, certainly no one of the society which surrounded him, thought of Mr. Browning as a great poet, or as an equal one to his wife, whose "Aurora Leigh" was then a new book. The utter unselfishness and generosity wherewith he gloried in his wife's fame — bringing us up constantly

good reviews of her poems and eagerly recounting how
many editions had been called for — perhaps helped
to blind us, stupid that we were! to his own claims.
Never, certainly, did the proverb about the "*irritabile
genus*" of poets prove less true. All through his life,
even when the world had found him out, and societies
existed for what Mr. Frederic Harrison might justly
have called a "culte" of Browning, if not a "latria," he
remained the same absolutely unaffected, unassuming,
genial English gentleman.

Of Mrs. Browning I never saw much. Sundry visits
we paid to each other missed, and when I did find her
at home in Casa Guidi we did not fall on congenial
themes. I was bubbling over with enthusiasm for her
poetry, but had not the audacity to express my admiration (which, in truth, had been my special reason for
visiting Florence), and she entangled me in erudite discussions about Tuscan and Bolognese schools of painting,
concerning which I knew little and, perhaps, cared less.
But I am glad I looked into the splendid eyes which
lived like coals, in her pain-worn face, and revealed the
soul which Robert Browning trusted to meet again on
the threshold of eternity.[1] Was there ever such a testimony as their *perfect* marriage — living on as it did in
the survivor's heart for a quarter of a century — to the
possibility of the eternal union of Genius and Love?

I received in later years from Mr. Browning several
letters which I may as well insert in this place.

19, Warwick Crescent, W., December 28th, 1874.

Dear Miss Cobbe, — I return the Petition, for the
one good reason, that I have just signed its fellow forwarded to me by Mr. Leslie Stephen. You have heard
"I take an equal interest with yourself in the effort to
suppress vivisection." I dare not so honor my mere

---

[1] "Then, soul of my soul! I shall meet thee again,
     And with God be the rest!"

wishes and prayers as to put them for a moment beside your noble acts, but this I know, I would rather submit to the worst of deaths, so far as pain goes, than have a single dog or cat tortured on the pretence of sparing me a twinge or two. I return the paper, because I shall be probably shut up here for the next week or two, and prevented from seeing my friends; whoever would refuse to sign would certainly not be of the number.

Ever truly and gratefully yours,

ROBERT BROWNING.

19, WARWICK CRESCENT, W., July 3d, 1881.

DEAR MISS COBBE,— I wish I were not irretrievably engaged on Monday afternoon, twice over, as it prevents me from accepting your invitation. By all I hear, Mr. Bishop's performance must be instructive to those who need it, and amusing to everybody.[1]

Thank you very much,

Ever truly yours,

ROBERT BROWNING.

---

[1] This refers to an afternoon party we gave to witness poor Mr. Bishop's interesting thought-reading performances. He was wonderfully successful throughout, and the company, which consisted of about thirty clever men and women, were unanimous in applauding his art, of whatever nature it may have been. I may add that after my guests were departed, when I took out my cheque-book and begged to know his fee, Mr. Bishop positively refused to accept any remuneration whatever for the charming entertainment he had given us. The tragic circumstances of the death of this unhappy young man will be remembered. He either died, or fell into a death-like trance, at a supper party in New York, in 1889 ; and within *four hours* of his (real or apparent) decease, three medical men, who had been supping with him, dissected his brain. One doctor who conducted his autopsy alleged that Bishop had been extremely anxious that his brain should be examined *post mortem*, but his mother asserted, on the contrary, that he had a peculiar horror of dissection, and had left directions that no *post mortem* should be held on his remains. It was also stated that he had a card in his pocket warning those who might find him at any time in a trance, to beware of burying him before signs of dissolution should be visible. In a leading article on the subject in the "Liverpool Daily Post," May 21st, 1889, it is stated that by the laws of the United States "it is distinctly enacted that no dissection shall take place without the fiat of the

19, Warwick Crescent, W , October 22d, 1882.

Dear Miss Cobbe, — It is about a week ago since I
had to write to the new Editor of the " Fortnightly,"
Mr. Escott — and assure him that I was so tied and
bound by old promises " to give something to this and
that magazine if I gave at all " — that it became impossible I could oblige anybody in even so trifling a matter.   It comes of making rash resolutions — but, once
made, there is no escape from the consequence — though
I rarely have felt this so much of a hardship as now
when I am forced to leave a request of yours uncom-
plied with.   For the rest, I shall indeed rejoice if that
abominable and stupid cruelty of pigeon-shooting is put
a stop to.   The other detestable practice, vivisection,
strikes deeper root, I fear ; but God bless whoever tugs
at it !

Ever yours most truly,

Robert Browning.

Another of our most frequent visitors at Villa Bri-
chieri was Mr. T. Adolphus Trollope, author of the
" Girlhood of Catherine de' Medici," " A Decade of
Italian Women," and other books.   Though not so suc-

coroner, or at the request of the relatives of the deceased ; so that some
explanation of the anxiety which induced so manifest a breach of both laws
and custom is eminently desirable.   A second examination of the body at
the instance of the coroner, has revealed the fact that all the organs were
in a healthy state, and that it was impossible to ascribe death to any spe-
cific cause or to say whether Mr. Bishop were alive or dead at the time of
the first autopsy."   Both wife and mother believed he was "murdered ;"
and ordered that word to be engraved on his coffin.   His mother had herself experienced a cataleptic trance of six days' duration, during the
whole of which she was fully conscious.   The three doctors were proceeded
against by her and the widow, and were put under bonds of £500 each ;
but as the experts alleged that it was impossible to decide the cause of
death, the case eventually dropped.   Whether it were one of "*human
vivisection*" or not can never now be known.   If the three physicians
who performed the autopsy on Mr. Bishop did not commit a murder of
appalling barbarity on the helpless companion of their supper-table, they
certainly *risked* incurring that guilt with unparalleled levity and calous-
ness.

cessful an author as his brilliant brother Anthony, he
was an interesting man, whom we much liked. One
day he came up and pressed us to go back with him and
pay a visit to a guest at his Villino Trollope in the
Piazza Maria Antonia — a lovely house he had built,
with a broad veranda behind it, opening on a garden of
cypresses and oranges backed by the old crenelated and
Iris-decked walls of Florence. He had, he told us, a
most interesting person staying with him and Mrs.
Trollope ; — Mrs. Lewes — who had written "Adam
Bede," and was then writing "Romola." Miss Blagden
alone went with him, and was enchanted, like all the
world, with George Eliot.

Mr. Trollope told me many curious facts concerning
Italian society which, from his long residence, he knew
more intimately than almost any other foreigner. He
described the marriage settlement of a nobleman which
had actually passed through his hands, wherein the
intending husband (with wondrous foresight and pre-
caution!) deliberately named three or four gentlemen,
amongst whom his future wife might choose her *cavalier
servente!*

We had several other *habitués* at our villas ; Dall'
Ongaro, a poet and ex-priest ; Romanelli, the sculptor ;
and Miss Linda White, now Madame Villari, the charming authoress and hostess of a brilliant *salon ;* wife
of the eminent historian who was recently Minister of
Education.

Perhaps the most interesting of our visitors, after Mr.
Browning, was Mrs. Beecher Stowe. She impressed me
much, and the criticisms I have read of her "Sunny
Memories" and other books have failed to diminish my
admiration for her. She was one of the few women, I
suppose, who have actually *felt* Fame, as heroes do who
receive national triumphs ; and she seemed to be as
simple and unpretentious, as little elated as it was possible to be. She had even a trick of looking down as if

she had been stared out of countenance; but this was
perhaps a part of that singular habit which most Evangelicals of her class exhibited thirty years ago, of shy-
ness in society and inability to converse except with the
person seated next them in company. It was the verification, after eighteen centuries, of the old heathen
taunt against the Christians, recorded in the dialogues
of Minucius Felix, "*In publicam muta, in angulis gar-
rula!*" I have recorded elsewhere Mrs. Stowe's remark when I spoke with grief of the end of Theodore
Parker's work. "Do you think," she said, suddenly
looking up at me with flashing eyes, "that Theodore
Parker has no work to do for God *now?*" I must not
repeat again her interesting conversation as we sat on
our balcony watching the sun go down over the Val d'
Arno. After much serious talk as to the nearness of the
next life, Mrs. Stowe narrated a saying of her boy on
which (as I told her) a good heterodox sermon *in my
sense* might be preached. She taught the child that
anger was sinful, whereupon he asked: "Then why,
Mamma, does the Bible say so often that God was
angry?" She replied (motherlike): "You will understand it when you are older." The boy pondered seriously for awhile and then burst out: "Oh, Mamma, I
have found it out! God is angry, *because God is not a
Christian!*"

Another of our *habitués* on my first visit to Florence
was Walter Savage Landor. At that time he was, with
his dear Pomeranian dog, Giallo, living alone in very
ordinary lodgings in Florence, having quarrelled with
his family and left his villa in their possession. He
had a grand, leonine head with long white hair and
beard, and to hear him denouncing his children was to
witness a performance of "Lear" never matched on any
stage. He was very kind to me, and we often walked
about odd nooks of Florence together, while he poured
out reminiscences of Byron and Shelley, some of which

I have recorded (Chap. ix., p. 235), and of others of the older generation whom he had known, so that I seemed in touch with them all. He was then about eighty-eight years of age, and perhaps his great and cultivated intellect was already failing. Much that he said in wrath and even fury seemed like raving, but he was gentle as a child to us women, and to his dog whom he passionately loved. When I wrote the first "Memorial" against Prof. Schiff which started the anti-vivisection crusade, Mr. Landor's name was one of the first appended to it. He added some words to his signature so fierce and contemptuous that I never dared to publish them!

We also saw much of Dr. Grisanowski, a very clever Pole, who afterwards became a prominent advocate of the science-tortured brutes. When I discussed the matter with him he was entirely on the side of science. After some years he sent me his deeply thought-out pamphlet, with the endorsement "For Miss Cobbe — who was right when I was wrong;" a very generous retraction. We also received Mr. Frederick Tennyson (Lord Tennyson's brother), Madame Venturi, Madame Alberto Mario, the late Lord Justice Bowen (then a brilliant young man from Oxford,) and many more.

By far the best and dearest of my friends in Florence however, was one who never came up our hill, and who was already then an aged woman — Mrs. Somerville. I had brought a letter of introduction to her, being anxious to see one who had been such an honor to womanhood; but I expected to find her an incarnation of science, having very little affinity with such a person as I. Instead of this, I found in her the dearest old lady in all the world, who took me to her heart as if I had been a newly-found daughter, and for whom I soon felt such tender affection that sitting beside her on her sofa, (as I mostly did on account of her deafness) I could hardly keep myself from caressing her. In a letter to Harriet St. Leger I wrote of her: "She is the very ideal of an

old lady, so gentle, cordial and dignified, like my mother; and as fresh, eager and intelligent *now*, as she can
ever have been." Her religious ideas proved to be
exactly like my own; and being no doubt somewhat
athirst for sympathy on a subject on which she felt
profoundly (her daughters differing from her), she
opened her heart to me entirely. Here are a few notes
I made after talks with her : —

" Mrs. Somerville thinks no one can be eloquent who
has not studied the Bible. We discussed the character
of Christ. She agreed to all I said, adding she thought
it clear the Apostles never thought he was God, only the
image of the perfection of God. She kissed me tenderly
when I rose to go and bade me come back at any hour
— at three in the morning if I liked! — *May* 18*th*.
Mrs. Somerville gave me her photograph. She says she
always feels a regret thinking of the next life that we
shall see no more the flowers of this world. I said we
should no doubt see others still fairer. 'Ah! yes,' she
said, 'but *our own* roses and mignonette! I shall miss
them. The dear animals I believe we *shall* meet. They
suffer so often here, they must live again.' — *June* 3*d*.
Wished farewell to Mrs. Somerville. She said, kissing
me with many tears, 'We shall meet in Heaven! I
shall claim you there.' "

I saw Mrs. Somerville again on my other visits to
Italy, at Genoa, Spezzia and Naples; of course making
it a great object of my plans to be for some weeks near
her. In my last journey, in 1879, I saw at Naples the
noble monument erected over her grave by her daughter.
It represents her (heroic size) reclining on a classic
chair — in somewhat the attitude of the statue of
Agrippina in the Vatican.

Mrs. Somerville ought to have been buried in Westminster Abbey. When I saw her death announced on
the posters of the newspapers in the streets in London,
I hurried as soon as I could recover myself, to ask Dean

Stanley to arrange for her interment in the Abbey. The
Dean consented freely and with hearty approval to my
proposition, and Mrs. Somerville's nephew, Sir William
Fairfax, promised at once to defray all expenses. There
was only one thing further needed, and that was the
usual formal request from some public body or official
persons to the Dean and Chapter of Westminster. Dean
Stanley had immediately written to the Astronomer
Royal to suggest that he and the President of the Royal
Society, as the representatives of the sciences with
which Mrs. Somerville's fame was connected, should
address to him the demand which would authorize his
proceeding with the matter. But that gentleman *refused*
to do it — on the ground that *he* had never read Mrs.
Somerville's books! Whether he had read one in which
she took the opposite side from his in the sharp and
angry Adams-Le Verrier controversy, it is not for me to
say. Any way, jealousy, either scientific or masculine,
declined to admit Mary Somerville's claims to a place
in the national Valhalla, wherein so many men neither
intellectually nor morally her equals have been welcomed.

From the time of our first meeting till her death in
1872, Mrs. Somerville maintained a close correspondence
with me. I have had all her beautifully-written letters
bound together, and they form a considerable volume.
Of course it was a delight to me to send her everything
which might interest her, and among other things I
sent her a volume of Theodore Parker's Prayers, edited
by myself. In October, 1863, I spent a long time at
Spezzia to enjoy the immense pleasure of her society.
I was then a cripple and unable to walk to her house,
and wrote of her visits as follows to Miss Elliot : —

"Mrs. Somerville comes to me every day. She is
looking younger than three years ago and she talked to
me for three hours yesterday, pouring out such stories
of recent science as I never heard before. Then we
talked a little heresy, and she thanked me with tears in

her eyes for Parker's Prayers, saying she had found them the greatest comfort and the most perfect expression of religious feeling of any prayers she has known."

Another time I sent her my "Hopes of the Human Race." She wrote, three weeks before her death, "God bless you, dearest friend, for your irresistible argument for our Immortality! Not that I ever doubted of it, but as I shall soon enter my ninety-third year, your words are an inexpressible comfort."

Mary Somerville was the living refutation of all the idle, foolish things which have been said of intellectual women. There never existed a more womanly woman. Her "Life," edited by her eldest daughter, Martha Somerville (her son by her first marriage, Mr. Woronzow Greig, died long before her), has been much read and liked. I reviewed it in the "Quarterly" (January, 1874), and am tempted to enclose a letter which Martha Somerville (then and always my good friend) wrote about it:

FROM MISS SOMERVILLE TO F. P. C.

22d January, Naples.

MY DEAR FRANCES, — I have this morning received the "Quarterly Review" and some slips from newspapers. What can I say to express my gratitude to you for the article — so admirably written, and giving so touching a picture of my Mother — as you, her best friend (notwithstanding the great difference of age) knew her? Also I received lately the "Academy" which pleased me much, too. The Memoir has been received far more favorably than I ventured to expect.

A long time after this, I paid a visit to friends at St. Andrews and stopped from Saturday to Monday, on my way, at Burntisland. Writing from thence to Miss Elliot about her own country, and countrymen, I said: —

"I came here to look up the scene of Mrs. Somerville's childhood, and I have found everything just as she described it; — the Links; the pretty hills and woods full of wild flowers; the rocky bit of shore with boulders full of fossil shells which excited her childish wonder when she wandered about, a beautiful little girl, as she must have been. If ever there were a case of —

"'Nourishing a youth sublime,
    With the fairy tales of science and the long results of Time,'

it was surely hers. Very naturally I was thinking of her all day and wondering whether she is *now* studying the flora of Heaven, of which she used to speak, and pursuing Astronomy among the stars; or whether it *can* be possible these things pass away for ever! I wanted very much to make out where Sir William Fairfax's house had been, and finally was directed to the schoolmaster who, it is said, knew all about it. I found the good man in a large school-house where he has 600 pupils; and as soon as he learned my name he seized my hand and made great demonstrations; and straightway proceeded to constitute himself my guide to the localities in question. The joke however was this. Hardly were we out of the house before he said, 'I'll send you a pamphlet of mine — not about science, I don't care for science, I care for Morals; — and I've found out there is only *a very little thing to be done to stop all pauperism and all crime!* You are just the person to understand me!' The idea of this poor schoolmaster in Burntisland compressing *that* modest programme into a 'pamphlet' seems to me deliciously characteristic of Scotland."

A college for ladies was opened some years ago at Oxford and named after Mrs. Somerville. I greatly rejoiced at the time at this very fitting tribute to her memory; and induced my brother to send his daughter, my dear niece, Frances Conway Cobbe, to the Hall. I ceased to rejoice, however, when I found that a lady bearing a name identified with vivisection in England was nominated for election as a member of the Council of the College. I entered (as a subscriber) the most vigorous protest I could make against the proposed choice, but, alas! in vain.

One of our visitors at Villa Brichieri was a very pious French lady, who came up to us one day to dinner straight from her devotions in the Duomo, where a Triduo was going on against Renan; and, as it chanced, she began to praise somewhat excessively a lady of rank whose reputation had suffered more than one serious injury. My English friend remarked, smiling, in mitigation of the eulogy : —

" Elle a eu ses petits délassements!"

The answer was deliciously XVIII. Century : —

"C'est ce qui m'occupe le moins. Pourvu que cela soit fait avec du bon goût! D'ailleurs on ne parle sérieusement que de deux ou trois. Le Prince de S., par exemple. Encore est-il mort celui-là!"

It was during one of my visits to Florence that I saw King Victor Emanuel's public entry into the city, which had just elected him King. This is how I described the scene to Harriet St. Leger : —

" Happily we had a fine day for the king's entry on Monday last. It was a glorious sight! The beautiful old city blossomed out in flowers, flags, garlands, hangings and gonfalons beyond all English imagination. In every street there was a triumphal arch, while *boulevards* of artificial trees loaded with camelias, ran from the railway to the gate and down the via Calzaioli. Even the mean little sdrucciolo de' Pitti was made into one long arbor by twenty green arches sustaining hanging baskets of flowers. The Pitti itself had its rugged old face decked with wreaths. I had the good fortune to stand on a balcony commanding a view of the whole procession. Victor Emanuel, riding his charger of

Solferino, looked — coarse and fat as he is — *a man* and
a soldier, and more sympathetic than Kings in general.
Cavour has a Luther-like face, which wore a gleam of
natural pleasure at his reception. The people were
quite mad with joy. They did not cheer as we do, but
uttered a sort of deep roar of ecstasy, flinging clouds of
flowers under the King's horse's feet, and seeming as
if they would fling themselves also from their balconies.
Our hostess, an Italian lady, went directly into hysterics,
and all the party, men and women, cried and kissed and
laughed in the wildest way. At night there was a
marvellous illumination, extending as far as the eye
could reach, in every palazzo and cottage down the Val
d' Arno and up the slopes of the Apennines, where
bonfires blazed on all the heights."

In Florence my friends had been principally literary
men and women. In Rome they were chiefly artists.
Harriet Hosmer, to whom I had letters, was the first I
knew. She was in those days the most bewitching
sprite the world ever saw. Never have I laughed so
helplessly as at the infinite fun of this bright Yankee
girl. Even in later years when we perforce grew a
little graver, she needed only to begin one of her descriptive stories to make us all young again. I have not
seen her now for many years since she has returned to
America, nor yet any one in the least like her; and it
is vain to hope to convey to any reader the contagion
of her merriment. Oh! what a gift, beyond rubies,
are such spirits! And what fools, what cruel fools, are
those who damp them down in children possessed of
them!

Of Miss Hosmer's sculpture I hoped, and every one
hoped, great things. Her Zenobia, her Puck, her
Sleeping Faun were beautiful creations in a very pure
style of art. But she was lured away from sculpture
by some invention of her own of a mechanical kind
over which many years of her life have been lost.

Now I believe she has achieved a fine statue of Isabella
of Spain, which has been erected in San Francisco.

Jealous rivals in Rome spread abroad at one time a
slanderous story that Harriet Hosmer did not make
her own statues. I have in my possession an autograph
by her master, Gibson, which he wrote at the time to
rebut this falsehood, and which bears all the marks of
his quaint style of English composition.

Finding that my pupil Miss Hosmer's progress in
her art begins to agitate some rivals of the male sex, as
proved by the following malicious words printed in the
" Art Journal " : —

" Zenobia — said to be by Miss Hosmer, but really
executed by an Italian workman at Rome " ;

I feel it is but justice on my part to state that Miss
Hosmer became my pupil on her arrival at Rome from
America. I soon found that she had uncommon talent.
She studied under my own eyes for seven years, model-
ling from the antique and her own original works from
the living models.

The first report of her Zenobia was that it was the
work of Mr. Gibson. Afterwards that it is by a
Roman workman. So far it is true that it was built up
by my man from her own original small model, according to the practice of our profession; the long study
and finishing is by herself, like every other sculptor.

If Miss Hosmer's works were the productions of
other artists and not her own there would be in my
studio two impostors — Miss Hosmer and myself.

JOHN GIBSON, R.A.

ROME, November, 1863.

Gibson was himself a most interesting person ; an
old Greek soul, born by hap-hazard in a Welsh village.
He had wonderfully little (for a Welshman) of anything like what Mr. Matthew Arnold calls Hebraism

in his composition. There was a story current among us of some one telling him of a bet which had been made that another member of our society could not repeat the Lord's Prayer; and it was added that the party defied to repeat it had begun (instead of it) with a doggerel American prayer for children: —

> "Before I lay me down to sleep,
> I pray the Lord my soul to keep."

"Ah! you see," said Gibson, "he *did* know the Lord's Prayer after all!"

Once he sat by me on the Pincian and said: "You know I don't often read the Bible, I have my sculpture to attend to. But I have had to look into it for my bas-relief of the Children coming to Christ, and do you know, I find that Jesus Christ really said a good thing?"

I smothered my laughter, and said: "Oh, certainly, Mr. Gibson, a great many excellent things." "Yes!" he said in his slow way. "Yes, he did. There were some people called Pharisees who came and asked him troublesome questions. And he said, — he said, — well, I forget exactly what he said, but 'Deeds not words,' was what he meant to say."

The exquisite grace of Gibson's statues was all a part of the purity and delicacy of his mind. He was in many respects an unique character; a simple-hearted and single-minded worshipper of Beauty; and if my good friend Lady Eastlake had not thought fit to prune his extraordinarily quaint and original Autobiography (which I have read in the MS.) to ordinary book form and modernized style, I believe it would have been deemed one of the gems of the original literature, like Benvenuto Cellini's, and the renown of Gibson as a great artist would have been kept alive thereby.

A merry party, of whom Mr. Gibson was usually one, used to meet frequently that winter at the hospitable table of Charlotte Cushman, the actress. She had, then, long retired from the stage, and had a handsome house in the via Gregoriana, in which also lived her friend Miss Stebbins and Miss Hosmer. Our dinners of American oysters and wild boar with agro-dolce-sauce, and déjeuners including an awful refection menacing sudden death, called "Woffles," eaten with molasses (of which woffles I have seen five plates divided between four American ladies!), were extremely hilarious. There was a brightness, freedom and joyousness among these gifted Americans, which was quite delightful to me. Miss Cushman in particular I greatly admired and respected. She had, of course, like all actors, the acquired habit of giving vivid outward expression to every emotion, just as we quiet English ladies are taught from our cradles to repress such signs, and to cultivate a calm demeanor under all emergencies. But this vivacity rendered her all the more interesting. She often read to us Mrs. Browning's or Lowell's poetry in a very fine way indeed. Some years after this happy winter a certain celebrated London surgeon pronounced her to be dying of a terrible disease. She wished us farewell courageously, and went back to New England, as we all sadly thought to die there. The next thing we heard of Charlotte Cushman was, that she had returned to the stage and was acting Meg Merrilies to immense and delighted audiences! Next we heard that she had thus earned £5,000, and that she was building a house with her earnings. Finally we learned that the house was finished, and that she was living in it! She did so, and enjoyed it for some years before the end came from other causes than the one threatened by the great London surgeon.

One day when I had been lunching at her house, Miss Cushman asked whether I would drive with her in her brougham to call on a friend of Mrs. Somerville, who had particularly desired that she and I should meet, — a Welsh lady, Miss Lloyd, of Hengwrt. I was, of course, very willing indeed to meet a friend of Mrs.

Somerville. We happily found Miss Lloyd, busy in her sculptor's studio over a model of her Arab horse, and, on hearing that I was anxious to ride, she kindly offered to mount me if I would join her in her rides on the Campagna. Then began an acquaintance, which was further improved two years later when Miss Lloyd came to meet and help me when I was a cripple, at Aix-les-Bains; and from that time, now more than thirty years ago, she and I have lived together. Of a friendship like this, which has been to my later life what my mother's affection was to my youth, I shall not be expected to say more.

On my way home through France to Bristol from one of my earliest journeys and before I became crippled, I had the pleasure of making for the first time the acquaintance of Mlle. Rosa Bonheur. Miss Lloyd, who knew her very intimately and had worked in her studio, gave me an introduction to her and I reported my visit in a letter to Miss Lloyd in Rome.

" Mlle. Bonheur received me most cordially when I sent up your note. She was working in that most picturesque studio (at By, near Thoméry). I had fancied from her picture that she was so much taller and larger that I hardly supposed that it was she who greeted me, but her face is *charming ;* such fine, clear eyes looking straight into one's own, and frank bearing ; an Englishwoman's honesty with a Frenchwoman's courtesy. She spoke of you with great warmth of regard ; remembered everything you had said, and wanted to know all about your sculpture studies in Rome. I said it had encouraged me to intrude on her to hope I might persuade her to fulfil her promise of stopping with you next winter, and added how very much you wished it, and described the association she would have with you, sketching excursions, *bovi,* and Thalaba " (Miss Lloyd's Arab horse). "She said over and over she would not go to Italy without going to see you ; and

that she hoped to go soon, possibly next winter. . . .
Somehow, from talking of Italy we passed to talking of
the North, which Mlle. Bonheur thinks has a deeper
poetry than the South, and then to Ireland, where she
wishes to go next summer (I hope stopping at my
brother's *en passant*) and of which country she said
such beautiful, dreamy things that even I grew poetic
about our '*Brumes*' — to which she quickly applied the
epithet 'grandiose' — and our sea, looking, I said, like
an angel's eye with a tear in it.   At this simile she was
so pleased that we grew quite friends, and I can only
hope she will not see that sea on a gray day and think
me an impostor!   Nothing I liked about her, so much,
however, as her interest in Hattie Hosmer, and her
delight in hearing about her Zenobia [1] (*triumphans*) in
the Exhibition; at which report of mine she exclaimed :
'That is the thing above all others I shall wish to see
in London!   You know I have seen Miss Hosmer, but
I have never seen any of her works, and I do very
much desire to do so.'   . . .   Her one-eyed friend sat
by painting all the time. She is not enticing to look at,
but I dare say, not bad.   I said I always envied friends
whom I caught working together and that I lived alone ;
to which she replied '*Je vous plains alors!*' in a tone
of conviction, showing that, in her case at all events,
friendship was a very pleasant thing.   Mlle. Bonheur
showed me three or four fine pictures she is painting,
and some prints, but of course I was as stupid as usual
in studios and only remarked (as a buffalo might have
done), that Roman *bovi* were more majestic and like
Homeric Junos than those wiry little Scotch short-
horns her soul delighteth to honor.   But Oh! she has
done a Dog, *such* a dog !   Like Bush in outward dog,
but the inner soul of him more profoundly, unutterably
wise than tongue may tell! a Dog to be set up and

---

[1] A statue of Miss Hosmer exhibited in London, purchased by an American gentleman for £ 1,000.

worshipped as Anubis.   Certainly Mlle. Bonheur is a
finer artist than Landseer in this, his own line.   I wish
she would leave the cattle, and 'go to the dogs.'"

My last journey but one to Italy was taken when I
was lame; and, after my sojourn at Aix-les-Bains, I
spent the autumn in Florence and the winter in Pisa;
where I met Cav. D' Azeglio as above recorded.   Miss
Lloyd rejoined me at Genoa in the spring to help me to
return to England, as I was still (after four years!)
miserably helpless.   We returned over Mont Cenis
which had no tunnel through it in those days; and, on
the very summit, our carriage broke down.   We were
in a sad dilemma, for I was quite unable to walk a
hundred yards; but a train of carts happily coming up
and lending us ropes enough to hold our trap together
for my use alone, Miss Lloyd ran down the mountain,
and at last we found ourselves safe at the bottom.

After another very pleasant visit together to her
friend Mlle. Rosa Bonheur, and many promises on her
part to come to us in England (which, alas! she never
fulfilled) we made our way to London; and, within a
few weeks, Miss Lloyd — one morning before breakfast
— found, and, in an incredibly short time, *bought* the
dear little house in South Kensington which became
our home with few interruptions for a quarter of a century, No. 26, Hereford Square.   It was at that time
almost at the end of London.   All up the Gloucester
Road between it and the Park were market-gardens;
and behind it and alongside of it, where Rosary Gardens and Wetherby Place now stand, there were large
fields of grass with abundance of fine old lime trees and
elms, and one magnificent walnut tree which ought
never to have been cut down.   Behind us we had a
large piece of ground, which we rented temporarily and
called the "*Boundless Prairie*," (!) where we gave afternoon tea to our friends under the limes, when they were
in bloom.   On a part of our garden Miss Lloyd erected

a sculptor's studio. The house itself, though small, was very pretty and airy; every room in it lightsome and pleasant, and somehow capable of containing a good many people. We often had in it as many as fifty or sixty guests. In short, I had once more a home, and a most happy one; and my lonely wanderings were over.

CHAPTER XV.

For some time before I took up my abode in London
I had been writing busily for the press. When my
active work at Bristol came to an end and I became for
four years a cripple, I naturally turned to use my pen,
and, finding from my happy experience of "Workhouse
Sketches," in "Macmillan's Magazine" that I could
make money without much difficulty, I soon obtained
almost as many openings as I could profit by to add to
my income. I wrote a series of articles for "Fraser's
Magazine," then edited by Mr. Froude, who had been
my brother's friend at Oxford, and whom from that time
I had the high privilege to count as mine also. These
first papers were sketches of Rome, Cairo, Athens, Jerusalem, etc.; and they were eventually reprinted in a
rather successful little volume called "Cities of the
Past," now long out of print. I also wrote many
papers connected with woman's affairs and claims, in
both Macmillan and Fraser; and these likewise were
reprinted in a volume, "Pursuits of Women." Beside
writing these longer articles, I acted as "Own Correspondent" to the "Daily News" in Rome one year, and in
Florence another, and sent a great many articles to the
Spectator, Economist, Reader, etc. In short, I turned
out (as a painter would say) a great many *Pot-Boilers.*
These, with my small patrimony, enabled me to bear
the expense of travelling and of keeping a maid; a
luxury which had become indispensable.

I also at this time edited (as I have mentioned) for Messrs. Trübner, the twelve volumes of Parker's works, with a preface. The arrangement of the great mass of miscellaneous papers was very laborious and perplexing, but I think I marshalled the volumes fairly well. I did not perform as fully as I ought to have done my editorial duty of correcting for the press; indeed, I did not understand that it fell to my share, or I must have declined to undertake the task. Mr. Trübner paid me £50 for this editing which I had proposed to do gratuitously.

I had much at heart — from the time I gave up my practical work among the poor folk at Bristol — to write again on religious matters, and to help so far as might be possible for me to clear a way through the maze of new controversies which, in those days of Essays and Reviews, Colenso's "Pentateuch" and Renan's "Vie de Jésus," were remarkably lively and wide-spread through all classes of society. With this hope, and while spending a summer in my crippled condition at Aix-les-Bains, and on the Diablerêts, I wrote to Harriet St. Leger: —

"I am now striving to write a book about present controversies and the future basis of religious faith. I want to do justice to existing parties, High, Low and Broad, yet to show (as of course I believe) that none of them can really solve the problem; and that the faith of the future must be one not *based* on a special History, though corroborated by all history."

The plan of this book — named "Broken Lights" — is as follows: I discriminate the different sections of thinkers from the point of view of the answers they would respectively give to the supreme question, "What are the ultimate grounds of our faith in God, in Duty and in Immortality?" First, I distinguish between those who hold those grounds to rest on the *Traditional Revelation;* and those who hold them to be the

Original Revelation of the Divine Spirit in each faithful soul. The former are divided again, naturally, into those who take their authoritative tradition from a *Living Prophet,* a *Church,* or a *Book.* But in Christian times we have only had a few obscure prophets (Montanus, Joseph Smith, Swedenborg, Brother Prince, Mr. Harris, etc.), and the choice practically lies between resting faith on a *Church,* or resting it on a *Book.*

I classify both the parties in the English Church who rest respectively on a Church and on a Book, as *Palæologians;* the one, the *High Church,* whose ground of religious faith is: "The Bible authenticated and interpreted by the Church;" and the other the *Low Church,* whose theory is still the formula of Chillingworth: "The Bible, and the Bible only, is the religion of Protestants."

But it has come to pass that all the distinctive doctrines of Christianity (over and above Theism) which the Traditionalists maintain, are, in these days, more or less opposed to modern sentiment, criticism and science; and among those who adhere to them, one or other attitude as regards this opposition must be taken up. The Palæologian party in both wings insists on the old doctrines more or less crudely and strictly, and would fain *bend modern ideas* to harmonize with them. Another party, which is generally called the *Neologian,* endeavors to *modify or explain the old doctrines,* so as to harmonize them with the ethics and criticism of our generation.

After a somewhat careful study of the positions, merits and failures of the two Palæologian parties, I proceed to define among the Neologians, the *First Broad Church* (of Maurice and Kingsley), whose programme was: "To harmonize the doctrines of Church and Bible with modern thought." This end it attempted to reach by new readings and interpretations, consonant with the highest modern sentiment; but it remained of course obvious that the supposed Divinely-inspired Authorities had failed to convey the sense of these interpretations to men's minds for eighteen centuries; indeed, had conveyed the reverse. The old received doctrine of an eternal Hell, for example, was the absolute contradiction of the doctrines of Divine universal love and everlasting Mercy, which the new teachers professed to derive from the same traditional authority. This school emphatically "put the new wine into old bottles:" and the success of the experiment could only be temporary, since it rests on the assumption that God has miraculously taught men in language which they have, for fifty generations, uniformly misinterpreted.

The other branch of the Neologian party I call the *Second Broad Church* (the party of Stanley and Jowett). It may be considered as forming the Extreme Left of the Revelationists; the furthest from mere Authority and the nearest to Rationalism; just as the High Church party forms the Extreme Right; the nearest to Authority and furthest from Rationalism. I endeavor to define the difference between the *First* and *Second Broad Church* parties as follows: —

"The First Broad Church, as we have seen, maintains that the doctrines the Bible and the Church can be perfectly harmonized with the results of modern thought, *by a new, but legitimate exegesis of the Bible and interpretation of Church formulæ.* The Second Broad Church seems prepared to admit that, in many cases, they can only be harmonized *by the sacrifice of Biblical infallibility.* The First Broad Church has recourse (to harmonize them) to various logical processes, but principally to that of diverting the student, at all difficult points, from criticism to edification. The Second Broad Church uses no ambiguity, but frankly avows that when the Bible contradicts science the Bible must be in error. The First Broad Church maintains that the Inspiration of the Bible differs in *kind* as well as in *degree* from that of other books. The Second Broad Church appears to hold that it differs in degree, but *not* in kind."

After a considerable discussion on the various doctrines of the nature and limitations of Inspiration, I ask, p. 110, 111 : —

"Admit the Inspiration of Prophets and Apostles to have been substantially the same with that always granted to faithful souls — admit, therefore, the existence of a human element in Revelation, can we still look to that Revelation as the safe foundation for our Religion ?

"To this question the leaders of the Second Broad Church answer unhesitatingly : 'Yes. It has been an egregious error of modern times to confound the Record of the Revelation with the Revelation itself, and to assume that God's lessons lose their value because they have been transmitted to us through the natural channels of human reason and conscience. Returning to the true view, we shall only get rid of uncounted difficulties and objections which prevent the reception of Christianity by the most honest minds here in England and in heathen countries.' "

But in conclusion I ask : —

"'What influence can the Second Broad Church exercise on the future religion of the world ? What answer will it supply to the doubts of the age, and whereon would it rest our faith in God and Immortality ?' The reply seems to be brief. The Second Broad Church would, like all the other parties in the Church, call on us to rest our faith on History ; but in their case, it is History corroborated by consciousness, not opposed thereto. In the next chapter it will be my effort to show that under *no* conditions is it probable that History can afford us our ultimate grounds of faith. Meanwhile, it must appear that if any form of Historical faith may escape such a conclusion and approve itself to

mankind in time to come, it is that which is proposed
by the Second Broad Church, and which it worthily
presents — to the intellect by its learning, and to the
religious sentiment by its profound and tender piety."
— "Broken Lights," p. 120.

These four parties, two Palæologian and two Neologian, thus examined, included between them all the
members of the Church of England, and all the Orthodox Dissenters.   There remained the Jews, Roman
Catholics, Quakers, and Unitarians, and of each of these
the book contains a sketch and criticism ; finally con-
cluding with an exposition (so far as I could give it) of
Theoretic and of *Practical Theism.*

The book contains further two appendices. The first
treats of Bishop Colenso's onslaught on the Pentateuch ;
then greatly disturbing English orthodoxy. The second
appendix deals with the other most notable book of
that period : Renan's " Vie de Jésus." After maintain-
ing that Renan has failed in delineating his principal
figure, while he has vastly illuminated his environment,
I give with diffidence my own view of Christ, lest Traditionalists should, without contradiction, assume that
Renan has given the general Theistic idea of his character. After referring to the measureless importance of
the *palingenesia* of which Christ spoke to Nicodemus, I
draw a comparison between the New Birth in the individual soul, and the historically-traceable results of
Christ's life on the human race (p. 167).

" Taking the whole ancient world in comparison with
the modern, of Heathendom with Christendom, the general character of the two is absolutely analogous to that
which in individuals we call Unregenerate and Regen-
erate. Of course there were thousands of regenerated
souls, Hebrew, Greek, Indian, of all nations and languages, before Christ, and of course there are millions
unregenerate now. But, nevertheless, from this time
onward we trace through history a *new spirit* in the

world; a leaven working through the whole mass of souls." . . .

The language of the old world was one of *self-satisfaction,* as its Art was of *completeness.* On the other hand : —

"The language of the new world, coming to us through the thousand tongues of our multiform civilization, is one long cry of longing *aspiration :* 'Would that I could create the ineffable Beauty! Would that I could discover the eternal and absolute Truth! Would, oh, would it were possible to live out the good, the noble, and the holy!'" . . .

"This great phenomenon of history surely points to some corresponding great event whereby the revolution was accomplished. There must have been a moment when the old order stopped and the new began. Some action must have taken place upon the souls of men which thenceforth started them in a different career, and opened the age of progressive life. When did this moment arrive? What was the primal act of the endless progress? By whom was that age opened?"

"Here we have really ground to go upon. There is no need to establish the authenticity or veracity of special books or harmonize discordant narratives to obtain an answer to our question. The whole voice of human history unconsciously and without premeditation bears its unmistakable testimony. The turning point between the old world and the new was the beginning of the Christian movement. The action upon human nature which started it on its new course was the teaching and example of Christ. Christ was he who opened the age of endless progress."

"The view, therefore, which seems to be the best fitting one for our estimate of the character of Christ, is that which regards him as the great Regenerator of Humanity. *His coming was to the life of humanity what Regeneration is to the life of the individual.* This is not a conclusion doubtfully deduced from questionable biographies, but a broad, plain inference from the universal history of our race. We may dispute all details; but the grand result is beyond criticism. The world has changed, and that change is historically traceable to Christ. The honor, then, which Christ demands of us must be in proportion of our estimate of the value of such Regeneration. He is not merely a Moral Reformer inculcating pure ethics; not merely a Religious Reformer clearing away old theologic errors and teaching higher ideas of God. These things he was; but he might, for all we can tell, have been them both as fully, and yet have failed to be what he has actually been to our race. He might have taught the world better ethics and better theology, and yet have failed to infuse into it that new Life which has ever since coursed through its arteries and penetrated its minutest veins." .

"Broken Lights" proved to be (with the exception of my "Duties of Women") the most successful of my books. It went through three English editions, and I believe quite as many in America; but of these last all I knew was the occasional present of a single specimen copy. It was very favorably reviewed, but some of my fellow Theists rather disapproved of the tribute I had paid to Christ (as quoted above); and my good friend, Professor F. W. Newman, actually wrote a severe pamphlet against me entitled "Hero-Making Religion." It did not alter my view. I do not believe that our *Religion* (the relation of our souls to God) can ever properly rest upon History. Nay, I cannot understand how any one who knows the intricacies and obscurities attendant on the verification of any ancient History, should for a moment be content to suppose that God has required of all men to rest their faith in him on such grounds, or on what others report to them of such grounds. In the case of Christianity, where scholars like Renan and Martineau — profoundly learned in ancient and obsolete

tongues, and equipped with the whole arsenal of criticism of modern Germany, France, and England — can
differ about the age and authority of the principal *pièce
de conviction* (the Gospel of St. John), it is truly pre-
posterous to suggest that ordinary men and women
should form any judgment at all on the matter. The
Ideal Christ needs only a good heart to find and love
him. The *Historical* Christ needs the best critic in
Europe, a Lightfoot, a Koenen, a Martineau, to trace his
footsteps on the sands of time. And *they* differ as regards nearly every one of them!

But though History cannot rightly *be* Religion or the
basis of Religion, there is, and must be, a "History of
Religion;" as there is a history of Geometry and Astronomy; and of that History of the whole world's Religion the supreme interest centres in the record of

> " The sinless years
> That breathed beneath the Syrian blue."

Yet, as regards my own personal feeling, I must avow
that the halo which has gathered round Jesus Christ
obscures him to my eyes. I see that he is much more
real to many of my friends, both Orthodox and Unitarian, than he can ever be to me. There is nothing, no,
not one single sentence or action attributed to him of
which (if we open our minds to criticism) we can feel
sufficiently certain to base on it any definite conclusion,
and this to me envelopes him in a cloud. Each Christian age has indeed (as I remark in my "Dawning
Lights") seen a Christ of its own; so that we could
imagine students in the future arguing that there must
have been "several Christs," as old scholars held there
were several Zoroasters and several Buddhas. Just as
Michael Angelo's Christ was the production of that
dark and stormy age when first his awful form loomed
out of the shadows of the Sistine, in no less a degree do
the portraits of "Ecce Homo" and the "Vie de Jésus"
belong to our era of sentiment and philanthropy. We

have no sun-made photograph of his features; only
such wavering image of them as may have rested on the
waters of Galilee, rippling in the breeze. I must not
however further prolong these reflections on a subject
discussed to the best of my poor ability in my more
serious books.

After "Broken Lights", I wrote the sequel: "Dawning Lights," just quoted above. In the first I had endeavored to sketch the "Conditions and Prospects" of
religious belief. In the second I speculated on the
Results of the changes which were taking place in
various articles of that belief. The chapters deal con-
secutively with Changes in the Method of Theology,
— in the Idea of God; in the Idea of Christ; in
the Doctrine of Sin, theoretical and practical; in the
idea of the Relation of this Life to the Next; in the
idea of the Perfect Life; in the Idea of Happiness; in the Doctrine of Prayer; in the Idea of
Death; and in the Doctrine of the Eternity of Punishment

This book also was fairly successful, and went into a
second edition.

Somewhere about this time (I have no exact record),
I edited a little book called "Alone to the Alone," consisting of private prayers for Theists. It contains contributions from fifteen men and women, of prayers,
mostly written for personal use, before the idea of the
book had been suggested, under the influence of those
occasional deeper insights and more fervent feelings
which all religious persons desire to perpetuate. They
are all anonymous. In the "Preface" I say that the
result of such a compilation —

"'Is necessarily altogether imperfect and fragmen-
tary, but in the great solitude where most of us pass
our lives as regards our deeper emotions, it may be
more helpful to know that other human hearts are feeling as we feel, and thinking as we think, rather than to

read far nobler words which come to us only as echoes of the Past.' The book is 'designed for the use of those who desire to cultivate the feelings which culminate in prayer, but who find the rich and beautiful collections of the churches of Christendom no longer available, either because of the doctrines whose acceptance they imply or of the nature of the requests to which they give utterance. Adequately to replace in a generation, or in several generations, such books, through which the piety of ages has been poured, is wholly beyond hope; and the ambition to do so would betray ignorance of the way in which these precious drops are distilled slowly, year after year, from the great Incense-tree of humanity.' "

The remainder of the " Preface," which is somewhat lengthy, discusses the validity of prayer for the attainment of *spiritual* (not physical) benefits. It concludes thus (p. xxxvi.) : —

" And, lastly, if Religion is still to be to mankind in the future what it has been in the past, it must still be a religion of prayer. Nothing is changed in human nature because it has outgrown some of the errors of the past. The spiritual experience of the saintly souls of old was true and real experience, even when their intellectual creeds were full of mistakes. By the gate through which they entered the paradise of love and peace, even by that same narrow portal of Prayer must we pass into it. No present or future discoveries in science will ever transmute the moral dross in human nature into the pure gold of virtue. No spectrum analysis of the light of the nebulæ will enable us to find God. If we are to be made holy, we must ask the Holy One to sanctify us. If we are to know the infinite joy of Divine Love, we must seek it in Divine communion."

This book was first published in 1871; one of the years of the rising tide of liberal-religious hope. A third edition was called for in 1881. when the ebb had set in. In a short preface to this third edition I notice this fact, and say that those hopes were doubtless all too hasty for the slow order of Divine things.

"Nay, it would seem that, far from the immediate aurora of such a morning, the world is destined first to endure a great 'horror of darkness,' and to pass through the dreary and disaster-laden experience of a night of materialism and agnosticism. Perhaps it will only be when men have seen with their eyes how the universe appears without a thought of God to illumine its dark places, and gauged for themselves where human life will sink without hope of immortality to elevate it, that they will recognize aright the unutterable preciousness of religion. Faith, when restored after such an eclipse, will be prized as it has never been prized heretofore. . . .

"And Faith *must* return to mankind sooner or later. So sure as God *is*, so sure must it be that he will not finally leave his creatures, whom he has led upward for thousands of years, to lose sight of him altogether, or to be drowned for ever in the slough of atheism and carnalism. He will doubtless reveal himself afresh to the souls of men in his own time and in his own way — whether, as of old, through prophet-souls filled with inspiration, or by other methods yet unknown. God is over us, and Heaven is waiting for us all the same, even though all the men of science in Europe unite to tell us there is only Matter in the universe, and only corruption in the grave. Atheism may prevail for a night, but faith cometh in the morning. Theism is 'bound to win' at last; not necessarily that special type of Theism which our poor thoughts in this generation have striven to define; but that great fundamental faith — the needful substructure of every other possible religious faith — the faith in a righteous and loving God, and in a life for man beyond the tomb."

The book contains seventy-two prayers; half of which refer to the outer and half to the inner life. Among the former are noon and sunset prayers; thanksgivings for the love of friends, and for the beauty of the world; also a prayer respecting the sufferings of animals from human cruelty. In the second part some of the prayers are named: "In the Wilderness;" "On the Right Way;" "God afar off;" "Doubt and Faith;" "Fiat Lux;" "Fiat Pax;" "Thanksgiving for Religious Truth;" "For Pardon of a Careless Life;" "For a Devoted Life;" "Joy in God;" "Here and Hereafter."

I never expected that more than a very few friends would have cared for this book, and in fact printed it with the intention of almost private circulation; but it has been continuously, though slowly, called for during the twenty-three years which have elapsed since it was compiled.

I wrote the essays included in the volume, "Hopes of the Human Race," in 1873-1874. This has run through several editions. The long introduction to this book was written immediately after the publication of Mr. Mill's "Essay on Religion;" a most important work of which Miss Taylor had kindly put the proof sheets in my hands, and to which I was eagerly anxious to offer such rejoinder from the side of faith as might be in my power. Whether I succeeded in making an adequate reply in the fifty pages I devoted to the subject, I cannot presume to say. The pessimist side taken by Mr. Mill has been gaining ground ever since, but there are symptoms that a reaction is taking place, beginning (of all countries!) in France. I conclude this preface thus (p. 53) : —

"But I quit the ungracious, and, in my case, most ungrateful, task of offering my feeble protest against the last words given to us by a man so good and great, that even his mistakes and deficiencies (as I needs

must deem them) are more instructive to us than a
million platitudes and truisms of teachers whom his
transcendent intellectual honesty should put to the
blush, and whose souls never kindled with a spark of the
generous ardor for the welfare of his race which flamed
in his noble heart and animated his entire career."

The book contains two long essays on the "Life
after Death" contributed originally to the "Theological Review." In the first of these, after stating at
length the reasons for supposing that human existence
ends at death, I ask: "What have we to place against
them in the scale of Hope?" and I begin by observing
that all the usual arguments for immortality involve at
the crucial point the assumption that we possess some
guarantee that mankind will *not* be deceived, that
Justice will eventually triumph, and that human affairs
are the concern of a Power whose purposes cannot fail.
Were the faith which supplies such warrant to fail,
the whole structure raised upon it must fall to the
ground. Belief in Immortality is preëminently a
matter of Faith: a corollary from faith in God. To
imagine that we can reach it by any other road is vain.
Heaven will always be (as Dr. Martineau has said) "a
part of our Religion, not a branch of our Geography."
But in addressing men and women who believe in God's
Justice and Love, I hope to show that, not by one only
but by many *convergent* lines, Faith uniformly points
to a Life after Death; and that if we follow her
guidance in any one direction implicitly, we are invariably conducted to the same conclusion. Nay more:
we cannot stop short of this conclusion and retain
entire faith in anything beyond the experience of the
senses. Every idea of Justice, of Love, and of Duty is
truncated if we deny to it the extension of eternity;
and as for our conception of God himself, I see not
how any one who has realized the dread darkness of
"the riddle of the painful earth" can call him "Good"

unless he can look forward to the solution of that problem hereafter. The following are channels through which Faith inevitably flows towards Immortality : —

1st. The human race longs for Justice. Even "if the Heavens fall," we feel Justice ought to be done. All literature, from Æschylus and Job to our own time, has for its highest theme the triumph of Justice, or the tragedy of the disappointment of human hope thereof. But where did we obtain this idea ? The world has never seen a Reign of Astræa. Injustice and Cruelty prevail largely even now in the world; and as we go back up the stream of time to ruder ages where Might was more completely dominant over Right, the case was worse and worse. Where then did Man derive his idea that the Power ruling the world — Zeus, or Jehovah, or Ormusd — was Just ? Not only could no ancestral experience have caused the "set of our brains" towards the expectation of Justice, but experience, under many conditions of society, pointed quite the other way. It is assuredly (if anything can be so reckoned) the Divine spirit in man which causes him to love Justice, and to believe that his Maker is just, for it is inconceivable how he could have arrived at such faith otherwise. But if death be the end of human existence this expectation of justice has been only a miserable delusion. God has created us, poor children of the dust, to love and hope for Justice, but He Him-self has disregarded it, on the scale of a disappointed world. After referring to the thousands of cases where the bad have died successful and peacefully, and the good — like Christ — have perished in misery and agony, I say "boldly and so much the more reverently : *Either Man is Immortal or God is not Just.*"

2d. The second line of thought leading us to belief in Immortality is — that if there be no future life, there are millions of human beings whose existence has answered no purpose which we can rationally attribute to a wise and merciful God.　He is a *baffled* God, if His creature be extinguished before reaching *some* end which He may possibly have designed.

3d.　The incompleteness of the noblest part of man offers so strange a contrast to the perfection of the other work of creation that we are drawn to conclude that the human soul is only a *bud* to blossom out into full flower hereafter.　No man has ever in his life reached the plenitude of moral strength and beauty of which his nature gives promise.　A garden wherein all the buds should perish before blooming would be more hideous than a desert, and such a garden is God's world if man dies for ever when we see him no more.

4th.　Human love urges an appeal to Faith which has been to millions of hearts the most conclusive of all.

"To think of the one whose innermost self is to us the world's chief treasure, the most beautiful and blessed thing God ever made, and believe that at any moment that mind and heart may cease to be, and become only a memory, every noble gift and grace extinct, and all the fond love for ourselves forgotten for ever — this is such agony, that having once known it we should never dare again to open our hearts to affection, unless some ray of hope should dawn for us beyond the grave.　Love would be the curse of mortality were it to bring always with it such unutterable pain of anxiety, and the knowledge that every hour which knitted our heart more closely to our friend also brought us nearer to an eternal separation.　Better never to have ascended to that high Vita Nuova where self-love is lost in another's weal, better to have lived like the cattle which browse and sleep while they wait the butcher's knife, than to endure such despair.

"But is there nothing in us which refuses to believe all this nightmare of the final sundering of loving hearts?　Love itself seems to announce itself as an

eternal thing. It has such an element of infinity in its
tenderness, that it never fails to seek for itself an
expression beyond the limits of time, and we talk, even
when we know not what we mean, of "undying
affection," "immortal love." It is the only passion
which in the nature of things we can carry with us
into another world, and it is fit to be prolonged,
intensified, glorified for ever. It is not so much a joy
we may take with us, as the only joy which can make
any world a heaven when the affections of earth shall
be perfected in the supreme love of God. It is the
sentiment which we share with God, and by which we
live in Him and He in us. All its beautiful tenderness, its noble self-forgetfulness, its pure and ineffable
delight, are the rays of God's Sun of Love reflected in
our souls.

"Is all this to end in two poor heaps of silent dust
decaying slowly in their coffins side by side in the
vault? If so, let us have done with prating of any
Faith in Heaven or earth. We are mocked by a fiend."
— "Hopes," p. 52.

5th. A remarkable argument is to be found in Professor F. W. Newman's "Theism" (p. 75). It insists
on the fact that many men have certainly loved God and
that God must love them in return (else Man were better than God); and we must reasonably infer that
those whom God loves are deathless, else would the
Divine Blessedness be imperfect, nay, "a yawning gulf
of ever-increasing sorrow."

6th. The extreme variability of the common human
belief that the "soul of man never dies" makes it
difficult to discern its proper evidential value; still it
seems to have the *Note* of a genuine instinct. It begins
early, though (probably) not at the earliest; stage of
human development. It attains its maximum among
the highest races of mankind (the Vedic-Aryan, early
Persian, and Egyptian). It projects such varied and

even contrasted ideals of the other life (*e.g.* Valhalla
and Nirvana) that it cannot well have been borrowed by
one race from another but must have sprung up in each
indigenously. Finally the instinct begins to falter in
ages of self-consciousness and criticism.

7th, lastly. The most perfect and direct faith in
Immortality belongs to saintly souls who personally
feel that they have entered into relations with the
Divine Spirit which can never end. "*Faith in God and
in our eternal Union with Him*," said one such devout
man to me, "*are not two dogmas but one*." "Thou wilt
not leave my soul in Hades. Thou wilt guide me by
thy counsel and afterwards receive me to Glory."

"Such, for a few blessed souls, seems to be the perfect 'evidence of things not seen.' But can their full
faith supply our lack? Can we see with their eyes and
believe on their report? It is only possible in a very
inferior measure. Yet if our own spiritual life have
received even some faint gleams of the 'light which
never came from sun or star,' then, once more, will our
faith point the way to Immortality; for we shall know
in what manner such truths come to the soul, and be
able to trust that what is dawn to us may be sunrise to
those who have journeyed nearer to the East than we;
who have surmounted Duty more perfectly, or passed
through rivers of affliction into which our feet have
never dipped. God cannot have deluded them in their
sacred hope of His eternal Love. If their experience
be a dream all prayer and communion may be dreams
likewise."

In conclusion, while commending to the reader's consideration what appears to me the true method of solv-
ing the problem of a Life after Death, I point to the
fact that on the answer to that question must hang the
alternative, not only of the hope or despair of the human race, but of the glory or the failure of the whole
Kosmos, so far as our uttermost vision can extend.

" Lions and eagles, oaks and roses, may be good after their kind; but if the summit and crown of the whole work, the being in whose consciousness it is all mirrored, be worse than incomplete and imperfect, an undeveloped embryo, an acorn moulded in its shell, a bud blighted by the frost, then must the entire world be deemed a failure also. Now, Man can only be reckoned on any ground as a *provisionally* successful work; successful, that is, provided we regard him as *in transitu,* on his way to another and far more perfect stage of development. We are content that the egg, the larva, the bud, the half-painted canvas, the rough scaffolding, should only faintly indicate what will be the future bird and butterfly and flower and picture and temple. And thus to look on man (as by some deep insight he has almost universally regarded himself) as a 'sojourner upon earth,' upon his way to 'another country, even a heavenly,' destined to complete his pilgrimage and make up for all his shortcomings elsewhere, is to leave a margin for believing him to be even now a Divine work in its embryonic stage. But if we close out this view of the future, and assure ourselves that nothing more is ever to be expected of him than what we knew him to be during the last days of his mortal life; if we are to believe we have seen the best development which his intellect and heart, his powers of knowing, feeling, enjoying, loving, blessing and being blessed, will ever obtain while the heavens endure — then, indeed, is the conclusion inevitable and final. Man is a Failure, the consummate failure of creation. Everything else — star, ocean, mountain, forest, bird, beast, and insect — has a sort of completeness and perfection. It is fitting in its own place, and it gives no hint that it ought to be other than it is. 'Every lion,' as Parker has said, 'is a type of all lionhood; but there is no Man who is a type of all Manhood.' Even the best and greatest of men have only been imperfect types of a single phase

of manhood — of the saint, the hero, the sage, the
philanthropist, the poet, the friend — never of the full-
orbed man who should be all these together.   If each
perish at death, then — as the seeds of all these varied
forms of good are in each — every one is cut off pre-
maturely, blighted, spoiled.   Nor is this criterion of
success or failure solely applicable to our small planet;
a mere spark thrown off the wheel whereon a million
suns are turned into space.   It is easy to believe that
much loftier beings, possessed of far greater mental and
moral powers than our own, inhabit other realms of
immensity.   But Thought and Love are, after all, the
grandest things which any world can show; and if a
whole race endowed with them should prove such a
failure as death-extinguished Mankind would undoubtedly be, there remains no reason why all the spheres
of the universe should not be similar scenes of disappointment and frustration, and creation itself one huge
blunder and mishap.   In vain may the President of the
British Congress of Science dazzle us with the splendid
panorama of the material universe unrolling itself 'from
out of the primal nebula's fiery cloud.'   Suns and
planets swarming through the abysses of space are but
whirling sepulchres after all, if while no grain of dust is
shaken from off their rolling sides, the conscious souls of
whom they have been the palaces are all for ever lost.
Spreading continents and flowing seas, soaring Alps and
fertile plains are worse than failures, if we, even we,
poor, feeble, sinful, dim-eyed creatures that we are, shall
ever 'vanish like the streak of morning cloud in the
infinite azure of the past.' "

The second part of this essay discusses the possible
conditions of the Life after Death.   I cannot summarize
it here.

The rest of the volume consists of a sermon which I
read at Clerkenwell Unitarian Chapel, in 1873, entitled
"Doomed to be Saved."   I describe the disastrous

moral consequences to a man in old times who believed himself to have sold his soul to the Evil One, and to have cast himself off from God's Goodness for ever; and I contrast this with what we ought to feel when we recognize that we are *Doomed to be Saved* — destined irretrievably to be brought back, in this life or in far future lives, from all our wanderings in remorse and penitence to the feet of God.

The book concludes with an essay on the "Evolution of the Social Sentiment," in which I maintain that the primary human feeling in the savage which still lingers in the Aryan child is *not* sympathy with suffering, but quite an opposite, angry, and even cruel sentiment, which I have named *Heteropathy;* which inspires brutes and birds to kill their wounded or diseased companions. Halfway after this comes *Aversion;* and last of all, *Sympathy* — slowly extending from the mother's " pity for the son of her womb," to the family, the tribe, the nation, and the human race; and, at last, to the brutes. I conclude thus : —

" Such is, I believe, the great hope of the human race. It does not lie in the progress of the intellect or in the conquest of fresh powers over the realms of nature; not in the improvement of laws, or the more harmonious adjustment of the relations of classes and states; not in the glories of Art, or the triumphs of Science. All these things may, and doubtless will, adorn the better and happier ages of the future. But that which will truly constitute the blessedness of Man will be the gradual dying out of his tiger passions, his cruelty and his selfishness, and the growth within him of the god-like faculty of love and self-sacrifice; the development of that holiest sympathy wherein all souls shall blend at last, like the tints of the rainbow which the seer beheld around the great White Throne on high."

Beside these theological works I published more recently two slight volumes on cognate subjects : " A

Faithless World," and "Health and Holiness." I wrote
" A Faithless World" (first published in the "Contemporary Review") in reply to Sir Fitzjames Stephen's
remark in the "Nineteenth Century," No. 88, that
"We get on very well without religion." . . .
"Love, friendship, ambition, science, literature, art,
politics, commerce, and a thousand other matters will
go equally well as far as I can see, whether there is or
is not a God and a future state." I examine this view
in detail and conclude that instead of life remaining (in
the event of the fall of religion) to most people much
what it is at present, there would, on the contrary, be
actually *nothing* which would be left unchanged by
such a catastrophe.

I sent a copy of this article when first published (as
I was bound in courtesy to do), to Sir James, whom I
had often met, and whose brother and sister were my
kind friends. He replied in such a manly and generous
spirit that I am tempted to give his letter.

32, De Vere Gardens, W.,
December 24.

My Dear Miss Cobbe, — I am much obliged by your
note and by the article in the "Contemporary," which is
perfectly fair in itself and full of kind things about
myself personally.

The subject is too large to write about, and I am
only too glad to take both the letter and the article in
the spirit in which they were written and ask no further
discussion.

It seems to me very possible that there may be a
good deal of truth in what you suggest as to the nature
of the difference between the points of view from which
we look at these things, but it is not unnatural that *I*
should think you rather exaggerate the amount of suffering and sorrow which is to be found in the world. I
may do the opposite.

However that may be, thank you heartily for both your letter and your article.

I am sure you will have been grieved to hear of poor Henry Dicey's death. His life had been practically despaired of for a considerable time.

I am, ever sincerely yours,

J. F. STEPHEN.

Several of these books of mine, dealing with religious subjects, were translated into French and published by my French and Swiss fellow-religionists, and also in Danish by friends at Copenhagen. "Le Monde Sans Religion;" "Coup d'œil sur le Monde à Venir;" "L'Humanité destinée au Salut;" "La Maison sur le Rivage;" "Seul avec Dieu" (Geneva Cherbuliez, 1881), "En Verden uden Tro," etc., etc.

But all the time during the intervals of writing these theological books, I employed myself in studying and writing on various other subjects of temporary and durable interest. I contributed a large number of articles to the following periodicals :—

"The Quarterly Review" (then edited by Sir William Smith).

"The Contemporary Review" (edited by Mr. Bunting.)

"Fraser's Magazine" (edited by Mr. Froude).

"Cornhill Magazine" (edited by Mr. Leslie Stephen).

"The Fortnightly Review" (edited by Mr. Morley).

"Macmillan's Magazine" (edited by Mr. Masson).

"The Theological Review" (Unitarian organ, edited by Rev. C. Beard).

"The Modern Review" (Unitarian, edited by Rev. R. Armstrong).

"The New Quarterly Magazine" (edited by W. Oswald Crawford).

One collection of these articles was published by Trübner in 1856, entitled "Studies New and Old on

Ethical and Social Subjects" (1 vol., crown 8vo., pp. 466). This volume begins with an elaborate study of "Christian Ethics and the Ethics of Christ" ("Theological Review," September, 1869), which I have often wished to reprint in a separate form. Also a very long and careful study of the "Sacred Books of the Zoroastrians," which brought me the visits and friendship of a very interesting Parsee gentleman, Nowrosjee Furdoonjee, President of the Bombay Parsee Society, and of another Parsee gentleman resident in London. Both expressed their entire approval of my representation of their religion.

These "Studies" also contain a long paper on the "Philosophy of the Poor Laws," which, as I have narrated in a previous chapter, fell into fertile soil on the mind of an Australian gentleman and caused the introduction of some of the reforms I advocated into the poor law system of New South Wales.

There were also in this volume articles on "Hades ;" on the "Morals of Literature ;" and on the "Hierarchy of Art," which perhaps have some value; but I have not of late years cared to press the book, and have not included it in Mr. Fisher Unwin's re-issue of 1893 on account of the paper it contains on "The Rights of Man and the Claims of Brutes." This article, which appeared first in "Fraser's Magazine," Nov. 1863, was my earliest effort (so far as I know, the first effort of anybody) to work out the very obscure and difficult ethical problem to which it refers, in answer to the demands of vivisectors. I am not satisfied with the position I took up in this paper. In the thirty years which have elapsed since I wrote it, my thoughts have been greatly exercised on the subject, and I think I see the "Claims of Brutes" more clearly, and find them higher than I did. But, though I believe that I expressed the most advanced opinion *of that time* on the duty of man to the lower animals, and of the offence of cruelty towards them, I here enter my *caveat* against the quotation of this article (as was lately done by a zealous Zoöphilist) as if it still represents exactly what I think on the subject after pondering upon it for thirty years, and taking part in the anti-vivisection crusade for two entire decades.

I have mentioned this matter especially, because it is of some importance to me, and also because I do not find that there is any other opinion which I have ever published in any book or article, on morals or religion, which I now desire to withdraw, or even of which I care to modify the expression. It is a great happiness to me at the end of a long busy literary life, to feel that I have never written anything of which I repent, or which I wish to unsay.

A collection of minor articles, with several fresh papers of a lighter sort — an "Allegory," "The Spectral Rout," etc. — was also published by Trübner in 1867, under the name of "Hours of Work and Play."

In 1872, Messrs. Williams & Norgate published a rather large collection of my essays, under the name of "Darwinism in Morals and other Essays." The first is a review of the theory of ethics expounded in Darwin's "Descent of Man." I argue that the moral history of mankind (so far as it is known to us) gives no support whatever to Mr. Darwin's hypothesis that Conscience is the result of certain contingencies in our development, and that it might, at an earlier stage, have been moulded into quite another form, causing Good to appear to us Evil, and Evil Good.

"I think we have a right to say that the suggestions offered by the highest scientific intellects of our time to account for its existence on principles which shall leave it on the level of other instincts, have failed to approve themselves as true to the facts of the case. And I think, therefore, that we are called on to believe still in the validity of our own moral consciousness, even as we believe in the validity of our other faculties; and to rest in the faith (well-nigh universal) of the human race, in a fixed and supreme Law, of which the will of God is the embodiment and Conscience the Divine transcript." — "Darwinism in Morals," p. 32.

In this same volume (included in the re-issue) are essays on "Hereditary Piety" (a review of Mr. Galton's "Hereditary Genius"); one on "The Religion of Childhood," on Robertson's "Life;" on "A French Theist" (M. Pécaut); and a series of studies on Eastern Religions; including reviews of Mr. Fergusson's "Tree and Serpent Worship" (with which Mr. F. was so pleased that he made me a present of his magnificent book); Bunsen's "God in History," Max Müller's "Chips from a German Workshop," and Mrs. Manning's "Ancient and Mediæval India." Each of these is a careful essay on one or other of the Oriental faiths referring to many other books on each subject. Beside these there are in the same volume two articles on "Unconscious Cerebration and Dreams," which excited some interest in their day; and seem to me (if I be not misled by vanity) to have forestalled a good deal which has been written of late years about the "subliminal" or "subjective" consciousness.

In 1875, Messrs. Ward, Lock & Tyler, for whose "New Quarterly Magazine" I had written two long articles on "Animals in Fable and Art," and the "Fauna of Fancy," asked my consent to republishing them in their "Country House Library." To this I gladly agreed, adding my article in the "Quarterly Review" on the "Consciousness of Dogs;" and that in the "Cornhill:" "Dogs whom I have met." The volume was prettily got up, and published under the name of "False Beasts and True."

(From the close of 1874, when I undertook the antivivisection crusade, my literary activity dwindled down rapidly to small proportions. In the course of eight

years I wrote enough magazine articles to fill one volume, published in 1882, and containing essays on
"Magnanimous Atheism;" "Pessimism and One of its
Professors," and a few other papers, of which the most
important — the "Peak in Darien" — gives its name
to the book. It is an argument (with many facts cited
in its support) for believing that the dying, as they are
passing the threshold, not seldom become aware of the
presence of beloved ones waiting for them in the new
state of existence which they are actually entering.

After this book I wrote little for some years, but in
1888 I was asked to contribute an article to the "Universal Review" on "The Scientific Spirit of the Age."
I gladly acceded, but the editor desired to cut down my
MS., so I published it as a book with a few other older
papers; notably one on the "Town Mouse and the
Country Mouse;" a half-humorous study of the *pros* and
cons of life in London, and life in a country-house.

After this, again, I published two editions of a little
compilation, the "Friend of Man and His Friends the
Poets;" a collection (with running commentary) of
poems of all ages and countries relating to dogs, which
were likely, I thought, to aid my poor, four-footed
friends' claims to sympathy and respect.

Of my remaining books, the "Duties of Women," and
"The Modern Rack," I shall speak in the chapters
which respectively concern my work for women, and
the anti-vivisection movement.

CHAPTER XVI.

JOURNALISM is, to my thinking, a delightful profession, full of interest, and promise of ever-extending usefulness. During the years in which I was a professional journalist, when I had an occasion to go into a bank or a lawyer's office, I always pitied the clerks for their dull, monotonous, ugly work, as compared with mine. If not carried on too long or continuously — so that the brain begins to *churn* leaders sleeping or walking (a dreadful state of things into which we *may* fall), — it is preëminently healthy, being so full of variety and calling for so many different mental faculties one after another. Promptitude, clear and quick judgment as to what is, and is not, expedient and decorous to say; a ready memory well stored with illustrations and unworn quotations, a bright and strong style ; and, if it can be attained, a playful (not saturnine) humor superadded — all these qualities and attainments are called for in writing for a daily newspaper ; and the practice of them cannot fail to sharpen their edge. To be in touch with the most striking events of the whole world, and enjoy the privilege of giving your opinion on them to 50,000 or 100,000 readers within a few hours, this struck me, when I first recognized that such was my business as a leader-writer, as something for which many prophets and preachers of old would have given a house full of silver and gold. And I was to be *paid* for accepting it! It is one thing to be a "*vox*

clamantis in deserto," and quite another to speak in
Fleet Street, and, without lifting up one's voice, to
reach all at once as many men as formed the popula-
tion of ancient Athens, not to say that of Jerusalem!
But I must not "magnify mine office" too fondly!

From the time of my second journey to Italy I
obtained employment, as I have mentioned, as correspondent to the "Daily News" with whose Italian
politics I was in sympathy. I also wrote all sorts of
miscellaneous papers and descriptions for the "Spectator," the "Reader," the "Inquirer," the "Academy,"
and the "Examiner." When in London I was engaged
on the staff of the short-lived "Day" (1867) ; and much
lamented its untimely eclipse, when my friend Mr.
Haweis unkindly "chaffed" me by mourning over
it : —

> "*Sweet* Day!
> How *cool !* how bright !"

I was paid, however, handsomely for all I had written
for it, and a few months later I received an invitation
from Mr. Arthur Arnold (since M. P. for Salford) to
join his staff on the newly-founded "Echo." It was a
great experiment on the part of the proprietors, Messrs.
Petter & Galpin, to start a half-penny paper. Such a
thing did not then exist in England, and the ridicule
it encountered, and boycotting from the news-agents
who could not make enough profit on it to satisfy
themselves, were very serious obstacles to success.
Nevertheless Mr. Arnold's great tact and ability
cleared the way, and before many months our circulation, I believe, was very large indeed. My share in
the undertaking was soon arranged after a few interviews and experiments. It was agreed that I should
go on three mornings every week at ten o'clock to the
office in Catherine Street, Strand, and there in a private
room for my own use only, write a leading article on
some social subject after arranging with the editor what

it should be. I am proud to say that for seven years
from that time till I retired I never once failed to
keep my engagement. Of course I took a few weeks'
holiday every year; but Mr. Arnold never expected his
contributor in vain. Sometimes it was hard work for
me; I had a cold or was otherwise ill, or the snow lay
thick and cabs from South Kensington were not to be
had. Nevertheless I made my way to my destination
punctually; and, when there, I wrote my leader, and
as many "Notes" as were allotted to me, and thus
proved, I hope, once for all, that a woman may be relied on as a journalist no less than a man. I do not
think, indeed, that very many masculine journalists
could make the same boast of regularity as I have
done. My first article appeared in the third number
of the "Echo," December 10th, 1868, and the last on,
or about, March, 1875. Of course at first I found it a
little difficult to write exactly what and how much was
wanted, neither more nor less; but practice made this
easier. I wrote, of course, on all manner of subjects,
politics excepted; but chose in preference those which
offered some ethical interest — or (on the other hand)
an opening for a little fun! The reader may see
specimens of both, e. g., the papers on the great "Divorce Case;" "Lent in Belgravia;" and on "Fat
People;" "Sweeping under the Mats," etc., in "Re-
echoes," a little book compiled from a selection of my
"Echo" articles which Tauchnitz reproduced in his
library. A few incidents in my experience in Catherine Street recur to me, and may be worth recording.

Terrible stories of misery and death were continuously cropping up in the reports of coroners' inquests,
and I found that if I took these reports as they were
published and wrote leading articles on them, we were
almost sure next day to receive several letters begging
the editor to forward money (enclosed) to the surviv-

ing relations. It became a duty for me to satisfy myself of the veracity of these stories before setting them
forth with claims for public sympathy ; and in this way
I came to see some of the sadder sides of poverty in
London.) (There was one case I distinctly recall of a
poor lady, daughter of a country rector, who was found
(after having been missed for several days, but not
sought for) lying dead, scarcely clothed, on the bare
floor of a room in a miserable lodging-house in Drury
Lane.) I went to the house and found it a filthy coffee-
house frequented by unwashed customers. The mistress, though likewise unwashed, was obviously what
is termed "respectable." She told me that her unhappy lodger was a woman of forty or fifty, perfectly
sober and well conducted in every way. She had been
a governess in very good families, but had remained
unemployed till her clothes grew shabby. She walked
all day long over London for many weeks, seeking any
kind of work or means of support, and selling by degrees every thing she possessed for food. At last she
returned to her wretched room in that house into
which it was a pain for any lady to enter, and having
begged a last cup of tea from her landlady, telling
her she could not pay for it, she locked her door, and
was heard of no more. Many days afterwards the
busy landlady noticed that she had not seen her
going in or out, and finding her door locked, called the
police to open it. There was hardly an atom of flesh
on the poor worn frame, scarcely clothes for decency,
no food, no coals in the grate. "*Death from starva-
tion*" was the only possible verdict. When the case
had been made public, relatives, obviously belonging to
a very good class of society, came hastily and took
away the corpse for burial in some family vault. The
sight, the sounds, the fetid smells of that sordid lodging-house as endured by that lonely, dying, starving
lady, will haunt me while I live.

Another incident (in January, 1869) had a happier conclusion. There was a case in the law reports one day of a woman named Susannah Palmer, who was sent to Newgate for stabbing her husband. The story was a piteous one as I verified it. Her husband was a savage who had continually beaten her; had turned her out of the house at night; brought in a bad woman in her place; and then had deserted her for months, leaving her to support herself and their children. After a time he would suddenly return, take the money she had earned out of her pocket (as he had then a legal right to do), sell any furniture she possessed; kick and beat her again; and then again desert her. One day she was cutting bread for the children when he struck her, and the knife in her hand cut him; whereupon he gave her in charge for "feloniously wounding;" and she was sent to jail. The common sergeant humanely observed as he passed sentence that "Newgate would be ten times better for her than the hell in which she was compelled to live." It was the old epitaph exemplified : —

> " Here lies the wife of Matthew Ford,
> Whose soul we hope is with the Lord ;
> But if for Hell she 's changed this life
> 'Tis better than being Mat. Ford's wife ! "

Having obtained through John Locke, the well-known Member for Southwark, who had married my cousin, a special permit from the Lord Mayor, I saw the poor, pale creature in Newgate and heard her long tale of wrong and misery. The good ordinary of the jail felt deeply with me for her ; and when I had seen the people who employed her as charwoman (barbers and shoemakers in Cowcross Street) and received the best character of her, I felt justified in appealing, in the "Echo," for help for her, and also in circulating a little pamphlet on her behalf. Eventually, when Mrs. Palmer left Newgate a few weeks later, it was to take possession, as *caretaker for the chaplain,* of nice, tidy rooms where she and her children could live in peace, and where her brutal husband could not follow her, since the place belonged legally to the chaplain.

When there was a dearth of interesting news on the mornings of my leader-writing it was my custom to send for a certain newspaper, the organ of the extreme Ritualistic party, and out of this I seldom failed to extract *pabulum* for a cheerful article! One day, just after the 29th of September, I found such a record of — folly — vestments, processions, thuribles, and what not that I proceeded with glee to write a leader on "Michaelmas Geese." Next day, to my intense amusement, there was a letter at the office addressed to the author of the article, in which one of the "Geese," whom I had particularly attacked and who naturally supposed me to be a man, invited me to come and dine with him, and "talk of these matters over a good glass of sherry and a cigar!" The worldly wisdom which induced the excellent clergyman to try and thus "silence my guns" by inducing me to share his salt; and his idea of the irresistible attractions of sherry and cigars to a "poor devil" (as he obviously supposed) of a contributor to a half-penny paper, made a delightful joke. I had the greatest mind in the world to accept the invitation without betraying my sex till I should arrive at his door in the fullest of my feminine finery, and claim his dinner; but I was prudent, and he never knew who was the midge who had assailed him.

The incident reminds me of another journalistic experience not connected with the "Echo," which throws some light on certain charges recently discussed about "commissions" given to newspaper writers who puff the goods of tradesmen under the guise of instructing the public in the latest fashions in dress, furniture, and *bric-à-brac.* It was the only case in which any bribe of the kind ever came to my door. Some *grandes dames,* anx-

ious for the health of work-girls, had opened a millinery
establishment in Clifford Street on purely philanthropic
lines, and begged me to write an appeal in the "Times"
for support for it. After visiting the beautiful, airy
workrooms and dormitories, I did this with a clear conscience (of course gratuitously) to oblige my friends on
the committee. Next day a smart brougham drove
to my door in Hereford Square, and an exquisitely
dressed lady got out of it, and sent in her card, "Madame D——." I was so grossly ignorant of fashionable
millinery, that I did not know that my visitor was then
at the very apex of that lofty commerce. She remonstrated on my injustice in praising the Clifford Street
establishment, when *her* girls were exactly as well
lodged and fed. Would I not come and see for myself,
and then write and say so equally publicly? I agreed
that this would be only fair, and fixed an hour for my
inspection; on which she gracefully thanked me and departed, murmuring as she disappeared that she would
be happy to present me with "*Une jolie toilette!*" Poor
woman! She had come to the only gentlewoman perhaps in London to whom a "toilette" by Madame
D—— offered no attractions at all, and to whom (even
if I would have accepted one) it would have been useless, seeing that I never wore anything but the simply-
made skirts and jackets of my maid's manufacture. Of
course I visited and justly praised her establishment,
as I had promised; and I suppose she long expected me
to come and claim her "*jolie toilette!*"

There was another story of which the memory is in
my mind closely associated with a dear young friend —
Miss Letitia Probyn, who helped me ardently in my
efforts, very shortly before her untimely death while
bathing at Hendaye near Arcachon. The case of a woman named Isabel Grant moved us deeply. The poor
creature, in a drunken struggle with her husband at supper, had cut him with the bread-knife in such manner

that he died next day. Her remorse was most genuine and extreme. She was sentenced to be hanged; and just at the same time an Irishman who had murdered his wife under circumstances of exceptional brutality, and who had from first to last gloried in his crime, was set free after a week's imprisonment! We got up a memorial for Isabel Grant, Miss Probyn's family interest enabling her to obtain many influential signatures; and we contrived that both the cases of exceptional severity to the repentant woman and that of lenity to the unrepentant man should be set forth in juxtaposition in a score of newspapers. In the end Isabel Grant obtained a commutation of her sentence.

In 1875 the proprietors of the "Echo" sold the paper to Baron Grant; and Mr. Arnold and I at once resigned our positions as editor and contributor. He had created the paper — I may say even more — had created first-class half-penny journalism altogether; and it was deeply regretted that his able and judicious guidance was lost to the "Echo." After an interval the paper was redeemed from the first purchaser's hands by that generous gentleman, Mr. Passmore Edwards, than whom it could have no better proprietor.

I wrote in all more than one thousand leading articles, and a vast number of Notes for the "Echo," during the seven years in which I worked upon its staff. The contributors who successively occupied the same columns of second leaders on my off-days were willing (as I believe Mr. Arnold desired) to adopt on the whole the general line of sentiment and principle which my articles maintained; and thus I had the comfort of thinking that, as regarded social ethics, my work had given in some measure the tone to the paper. It was *my pulpit,* with permission to make in it (what other pulpits lack so sadly!) such jokes as pleased me; and to put forward on hundreds of matters my views of what was right and honorable. We did not profess to be " written by

gentlemen for gentlemen." The saturnine jests, the
snarls, and the pessimisms of the clubs were not in our
way ; and we did not affect to be *blasés*, or to think the
whole world was going to the dogs. There were of
course subjects on which a Liberal like Mr. Arnold and
a Tory like myself differed widely ; and then I left them
untouched, for (I need scarcely say) I never wrote a line
in that or any other paper not in fullest accordance with
my own opinions and convictions, on any subject small
or great. The work, I think, was at all events wholesome and harmless. I hope that it also did, now and
then, a little good.

After the sudden and unexpected termination of my
connection with the " Echo " I accepted gladly an engagement, not requiring personal attendance, on the staff of
the " Standard," and wrote two or three leaders a week
for that newspaper for a considerable time. At last
the vivisection controversy came in the way, when I
resigned my post in consequence of the appearance of
a pro-vivisecting paragraph. The editor assured me
generally of his approval of my crusade, and I wrote a
few articles more, but the engagement finally dropped.
My time had indeed become too much absorbed by the
other work to carry on regular journalism with the
needful vigor.

It may interest women who are entering the profession in which I found such pleasure and profit, to know
that as regards "filthy lucre" I found it more remu-
nerative than writing for the best monthly or quarterly
periodicals. I did both at the same period; often sitting down to spend some hours of the afternoon over a
"Study of Eastern Religion," or some such subject,
when I had gone to the Strand and written my leader
and notes in the forenoon. Putting all together and
the profits of my books (which were small enough) I
made by my literary and journalistic work, at one time,
a fair income. This golden epoch ended, however,

when I threw myself into the anti-vivisection movement, after which date I do not think I have ever earned more than £100 a year, and for the last twelve years not £20. I suppose in my whole life I have earned nearly £5,000, rather more than my whole patrimony.) What my poor father would have felt had he known that his daughter eked out her subsistence by going down in all weathers to write articles for a halfpenny newspaper in the Strand, I cannot guess. (My brothers, happily, had no objection to my industry) and the eldest — who drew, as usual with elder sons in our class, more money every year from the family property than I received for life — kindly paid off my charges on the estate and added £100 a year to the proceeds, so that I was thenceforth, for my moderate wants, fairly well off, especially since I had a friend who shared all expenses of housekeeping with me.

In reviewing my whole literary and journalistic life as I have done in these two chapters, I perceive that I have been from first to last *an Essayist,* almost *pur et simple.* I have done very little in any other way than to try to put forward — either at large in a book, or in a magazine article, or, lastly, in a newspaper leader — which was always a miniature essay — an appeal for some object, an argument for some truth, a vindication of some principle, an exposure of what I conceived to be an absurdity, a wrong, a falsehood, or a cruelty. (At first I had exaggerated hopes of success in these endeavors. Books had been a great deal to me in my own solitary life, and I far over-estimated their practical power. When editors and publishers readily accepted my articles and books, and reviewers praised them, I fancied (though they never sold very freely) that I was really given the great privilege of moving many hearts. But by degrees as years went on I felt the sorrowful limitation of literary influence. Sometimes I was wild with disappointment and indignation when critics lauded the "style" of my books while they never so much as noticed the *purpose* for the sake of which I had labored to make them good and strong literature.

For my own part I have shunned review-writing; partly (as regarded newspaper criticism) for the rather sordid reason that it involves the double labor of reading and writing for the same pay per column, but generally, and in all cases, because I cannot say — as dear Fanny Kemble used to remark in a sepulchral voice (quite falsely), "*I am nothing if not critical.*" On the contrary, I am several other things, and very little critical; and the pain and deadly injury I have seen inflicted by a severe review is a form of cruelty for which I have no predilection. It is necessary, no doubt, in the literary community that there should be warders and executioners at the public command to birch juvenile offenders, and flog garrotters, and hang anarchists; but I never felt any vocation for those disagreeable offices. The few reviews I have ever written have been properly essays on given subjects, taking some book which I could honestly praise for a peg. As in the old Egyptian "Book of the Dead" the soul of the deceased protests, among his forty-two abjurations, "I have not been the cause of others' tears" — so, I hope, I may say, I have given no brother or sister of the pen the wound (and often the ruinous loss) of a damaging critique of his or her books. If my writings have given pain to any persons, it can only have been to men whose dead consciences it would be an act of mercy to awaken, and towards whom I feel not the smallest compunction. Briefly I conclude in this book (doubtless my last) a long and moderately successful literary life, with no serious regrets, but with much thankfulness and rejoicing for all the interest, the pleasure, and the warm and precious friendships which the profession of letters has brought to me ever since I entered it — just forty years ago — when William Longman accepted my "Intuitive Morals."

CHAPTER XVII.

WHEN we had settled down, as we did rapidly, into our pretty little house in South Kensington, we began soon to enjoy many social pleasures of a quiet kind. Into Society (with a big *S!*) we had no pretentions to enter, but we had many friends, very genuine and delightful ones, ere long; and a great many interesting acquaintances. Happily death has spared not a few of these until now, and, of course, of them I shall not write here ; but of some of those who have "gone over to the majority" I shall venture to record my recollections, interspersed in some cases with their letters. I may premise that we were much given to dining out, but not to attending late evening parties ; and that in our small way we gave little dinners now and then, and occasionally afternoon and evening parties — the former held sometimes in summer under the lime trees behind our house. I attribute my long retention of good health to my persistence in going to bed before eleven o'clock, and never accepting late invitations.

I hope I shall be acquitted of the presumption of pretending to offer, in the scrappy *souvenirs* I shall now put together, any important contribution to the memoirs of the future. At best, a woman's knowledge of the eminent men whom she only meets at dinner-parties, and perhaps in occasional quiet afternoon visits, is not to be compared to that of their associates in their clubs, in Parliament, and in all the work of the world. Nevertheless, as all of us human beings resemble diamonds in

having several distinct facets to our characters, and as
we always turn one of these to one person and another
to another, there is generally some fresh side to be seen
in a particularly brilliant gem. The relation, too, which
a good and kindly man (and such I am happy to say
were most of my acquaintances) bears to a woman who
is neither his mother, sister, daughter, wife nor potential
wife, but merely a reasonably intelligent listener and
companion of restful hours, is so different from that
which he holds to his masculine fellow workers — rivals,
allies, or enemies as they may be — that it can rarely
happen but that she sees him in quite a different light
from theirs. Englishmen are not eaten up with *Invidia*,
like Italians and Frenchmen, such as made D'Azeglio
say to me that it was a positive danger to a statesman to
win a battle, or gain a diplomatic triumph, so much envy
did it excite among his own party. In our country, men,
and still more emphatically, women, glory enthusiastically in the successes of their friends, if not of others.
But the masculine mind, so far as I have got to the
bottom of it (as George Eliot says, " it is always so superior — *what there is of it !* "), is not so quick in gather-
ing impressions of character as ours of the softer (and
therefore, I suppose, more wax-like) sex ; and when fifty
men have said their say on a great man, I should always
wish to hear *also*, what the women who knew him socially
had to add to their testimony. In short, dear Fanny
Kemble's "Old Woman's Gossip" seems to me admissi-
ble on the subject of the character and " little ways " of
everybody worthy of record.

It was certainly an advantage to us in London to be,
as we were, without any kind of ulterior aim or object
in meeting our friends and acquaintances, beyond the
pleasure of the hour. We never had anything in view
in the way of social ambition ; not even daughters to
bring out ! It was not *de l'Art pour l'Art*, but *la Société pour la Société*, and nothing beyond the amusement

of the particular day and the interest of the acquaint-
anceships we had the good fortune to make. We had
no rank or dignity of any kind to keep up. I think
hardly any of our friends and *habitués* even knew who
we were, from Burke's point of view! I was really
pleased once, after I had been living for years in London, to find at a large dinner-party, where at least half
the company were my acquaintances, that not one present suspected that I had any connection with Ireland
at all. Our host (a very prominent M. P. at the time),
having by chance elicited from me some information on
Irish affairs, asked me, " What do you know about Ireland ?" "Simply that the first thirty-six years of my
life were spent there," was my reply ; which drew forth
a general expression of surprise. The few who had
troubled themselves to think who I was, had taken it
for granted that I belonged to a family of the same
name, *minus* the final letter, in Oxfordshire. In a
country neighborhood the one prominent fact about me,
known and repeated to every one, would have been that
I was the daughter of Charles Cobbe of Newbridge. I
was proud to be accepted and, I hope, liked, on the
strength of my own talk and books, not on that of my
father's acres.

We did not (of course) live in London all the year
round, but came every summer to Wales to enable my
friend to look after her estate ; and I went every two or
three years to Ireland, and more frequently to the houses
of my two brothers in England — Maulden Rectory,
in Bedfordshire, and Easton Lyss, near Petersfield —
where they respectively lived, and where both they and
their wives were always ready to welcome me affection-
ately. I also paid occasional visits at two or three
country houses, notably Broadlands and Aston Clinton,
where I was most kindly invited by the beloved owners ;
and twice or three times we let our house for a term,
and went to live on one occasion in Cheyne Walk, and

another time at Byfleet. We always fell back, however,
on our dear little house in Hereford Square, till we let
it finally to our old friend Mrs. Kemble, and left London for good in the spring of 1884.

I think the first real acquaintances we made in London (whether through Mrs. Somerville or otherwise I
cannot recall) were Sir Charles and Lady Lyell, and
their brother and sister, Colonel and Mrs. Lyell. The
house, No. 73, Harley Street — in after years noticeable
by its bright blue door (so painted to catch Sir Charles's
fading eyesight on his return from his daily walks) —
became very dear to us, and I confess to a pang when it
was taken by Mr. and Mrs. Gladstone after the death of
our dear old friends. Like Lord Shaftesbury's house
in Grosvenor Square, pulled down after his death and
replaced by a brand new mansion in the latest London-
esque architecture, there was a "bad-dreaminess" about
both transformation scenes. The Lyells regularly
attended Mr. Martineau's chapel in Little Portland
Street, as we did; and ere long it became a habit for us
to adjourn after the service to Harley Street and spend
some of the afternoon with our friends, discussing the
large supply of mental food which our pastor never
failed to lay before us. Those were never-to-be-forgotten
Sundays.

Sir Charles Lyell realized to my mind the man of
science as he was of old; devout, and yet entirely free-
thinking in the true sense; filled with admiring, almost
adoring love for Nature, and also (all the more for
that enthusiasm) simple and fresh-hearted as a child.
When a good story had tickled him, he would come and
tell it to us with infinite relish. I recollect especially
his delight in an American boy (I think somehow
connected with our friend Mr. Herman Merivale), who,
being directed to say his prayers night and morning,
replied that he had no objection to do so at *night*, but
thought that "a boy who is worth anything can take

care of himself *by day.*"[1]   Another time we had been discussing evolution, and some of us had betrayed the impression that the doctrine (which he had then recently adopted) involved always the survival of the *best*, as well as of the "fittest."   Sir Charles left the room and went downstairs, but suddenly rushed back into the drawing-room, and said to me all in a breath, standing on the rug: " I'll explain it to you in one minute!   Suppose *you* had been living in Spain three hundred years ago, and had had a sister who was a perfectly commonplace person, and believed everything she was told.   Well! your sister would have been happily married and had a numerous progeny, and that would have been the survival of the fittest; but *you* would have been burnt at an *auto-da-fé*, and there would have been an end of you.   You would have been unsuited to your environment.   There! that's evolution!   Good-bye!"   On went his hat, and we heard the hall door close after him before we had done laughing.

Sir Charles's interest in his own particular science was eager as that of a boy.   One day I had a long conversation with him at his brother, Colonel Lyell's hospitable house, on the subject of the glacial period.   He told me that he was employing regular calculators at Greenwich to make out the results of the ice-cap and how it would affect land and sea; whether it would cause double tides, etc.   He said he had pointed out (what no one else had noticed) that the water to form this ice-cap did not come from another planet, but must have been deducted from the rest of the water on the globe.   Another day I met him at a very imposing private concert in Regent's Park.   The following is my

---

[1] Not quite so good a story as that of another American child who, having been naughty and punished, was sent up to her room by her mother and told to ask for forgiveness.   On returning downstairs the mother asked her whether she had done as she had directed.   "Oh, yes! Mamma," answered the child, " *and God said to me, 'Pray don't mention it, Miss Perkins!'* "

description of our conversation in a letter to my friend, Miss Elliot: —

"Sir Charles sat beside me yesterday at a great musical party at the D.'s, and I asked him, 'Did he like music?' He said, 'Yes! *for it allowed him to go on thinking his own thoughts.*' And so he evidently did, while they were singing Mendelssohn and Händel! At every interval he turned to me: 'Agassiz has made a discovery. I can't sleep for thinking of it. He finds traces of the glaciers in tropical America.' (Here intervened a sacred song.) 'Well, as I was saying, you know 230,000 years ago the eccentricity of the earth's orbit was at one of its maximum periods; and we were 11,000,000 miles further from the sun in winter, and the cold of those winters must have been intense; because heat varies, not according to direct ratio, but the squares of the distances.' 'Well,' said I, 'but then the summers were as much hotter?' (Sacred song.) 'No, the summers were n't! They could not have conquered the cold.' 'Then you think that the astronomical 230,000 years corresponded with the glacial period? Is that time enough for all the strata since?' (Händel.) 'I don't know. Perhaps we must go back to the still greater period of the eccentricity of the orbit three million years ago. Then we were fourteen millions of miles out of the circular path.' (Mendelssohn.) 'Good-bye, dear Sir Charles — I must be off.'

"Another day last week, he came and sat with me for two hours. I would not light candles, and we got very deep into talk. I was greatly comforted and instructed by all he said. I asked him how the modern attacks on the argument from Design in Nature, and Darwin's views, touched him religiously. He replied, 'Not at all.' He thought the proofs in Nature of the Divine Goodness quite triumphant; and that he watched with secret pleasure even skeptical men of science whenever they forget their theories, instinctively using phrases, all *implying* designing wisdom."

I remember on another occasion Sir Charles telling me with much glee of two eminent agnostic friends of ours who had been discussing some question for a long time, when one said to the other, "You are getting very *teleological!*" To which the friend responded, "I can't help it!"

At another of his much prized visits to me (April 19th, 1866) he spoke earnestly of the future life, and made this memorable remark of which I took a note: "The further I advance in science, the less the mere physical difficulties in believing in immortality disturb me. I have learned to think nothing too amazing to be within the order of Nature."

The great inequalities in the conditions of men and the sufferings of many seemed to be his strongest reasons for believing in another life. He added: "Aristotle says that every creature has its instincts given by its Creator, and each instinct leads to its good. Now the belief in immortality is an instinct tending to good."

After the death of his beloved wife — the truest "helpmeet" ever man possessed — he became even more absorbed in the problem of a future existence, and very frequently came and talked with me on the subject. The last time I had a real conversation with him was not long before his death, when we met one sweet autumn day by chance in Regent's Park, not far from the Zoölogical Gardens. We sat down under a tree and had a long discussion of the validity of religious faith. I think his argument culminated in this position: —

"The presumption is enormous that all our faculties, though liable to err, are true in the main, and point to real objects. The religious faculty in man is one of the strongest of all. It existed in the earliest ages, and instead of wearing out before advancing civilization, it grows stronger and stronger; and is, to-day, more developed among the highest races than ever it was before.

I think we may safely trust that it points to a great truth."

Here is another glimpse of him from a letter : —

"After service I went to Harley Street, Sir Charles, I thought, looking better than for a long time. He thinks the caves of Aurignac can never be used as evidence ; the witnesses were all tampered with from the first. He saw a skeleton found at Mentone fifteen feet deep, which he thinks of the same age as the Gibraltar caves. The legs were distinctly platycnemic, and there was also a curious process on the front of the shoulder — like the breast of a chicken. The skull was full-sized and good. I asked him how he accounted for the fact that with the best will in the world we could not find the *least* difference between the most ancient skulls and our own ? He said the theory had been suggested that all the first growth went to brain, so that very early men acquired large brains, as was necessary. This is not very Darwinian, is it ? "

It is the destiny of all books of science to be soon superseded and superannuated, while those of literature may live for all time. I suppose Sir Charles Lyell's " Principles of Geology " has undergone, or will undergo, this fate ere long ; but the magnanimity and candor which made him, in issuing the tenth edition of that book, abjure all his previous arguments against evolution and candidly own himself Darwin's convert, was an evidence of genuine loyalty to truth which I trust can never be quite forgotten. He was, as Professor Huxley called him, the " greatest Geologist of his day " — the man " who found Geology an infant science feebly contending for a few scattered truths, and left it a giant, grasping all the ages of the past." But to my memory he will always be something more than *an* eminent man of science. He was the type of what *such men ought to be ;* with the simplicity, humility, and gentleness which should be characteristic of the true student of Nature. Of the priestlike arrogance of some representatives of the modern scientific spirit he had not a taint. In one of his last letters to me, he said: —

"I am told that the same philosophy which is opposed to a belief in a future state undertakes to prove that every one of our acts and thoughts are the necessary result of antecedent events and conditions, and that there can be no such thing as free-will in man. I am quite content that both doctrines should stand on the same foundation; for, as I cannot help being convinced that I have the power of exerting free-will, however great a mystery the possibility of this may be, so the continuance of a spiritual life may be true, however inexplicable or incapable of proof.

"I am told by some that if any of our traditionary beliefs make us happier and lead us to estimate humanity more highly, we ought to be careful not to endeavor to establish any scientific truths which would lessen and lower our estimate of man's place in nature; in short, we should do nothing to disturb any man's faith, if it be a delusion which increases his happiness.

"But I hope and believe that the discovery and propagation of every truth, and the dispelling of every error tends to improve and better the condition of man, though the act of reforming old opinions causes so much pain and misery."

It will give me pleasure if these few reminiscences of my honored friend send fresh readers to his excellent and spirited biography, by his sister-in-law Mrs. Lyell, Lady Lyell's sister, who was also his brother Colonel Lyell's wife, the mother of Sir Leonard Lyell, M. P.

I saw a great deal of Dr. Colenso during the years he spent in England; I think about 1864-5. He lived near us in a small house in Sussex Place, Glo'ster Road (not Sussex Place, Onslow Square), where his large family of sons and daughters practised the piano below stairs and produced detonations with chemicals

above, while visitors called incessantly, interrupting
his arduous and anxious studies! He was in all senses
an iron-gray man.   Iron-gray hair, pale, strong face,
fine but somewhat rigid figure, a powerful, strong-
willed, resolute man, if ever there were one, and an
honest one also, if such there have been on earth.   His
friend, Sir George W. Cox, whom I may venture to call
mine also, has, in his admirable biography, printed the
three most important letters which the Bishop of
Natal wrote to me, and I can add nothing to Sir
George's just estimate of the character of this modern
Confessor.   I will give here, however, another letter I
received from him at the very beginning of our intercourse, when I had only met him once (at Dr. Carpenter's table); and also a record in a letter to a friend of
a *tête-à-tête* conversation with him, further on.   I have
always thought that he made a mistake in returning to
Natal, and that his true place would have been at the
head of a Christian-Theistic Church in London : —

23, SUSSEX PLACE, KENSINGTON,
February 6th, 1863.

MY DEAR MISS COBBE, — I thank you sincerely for
your letter, and for the volume which you have sent
me.   I have read the preface with the deepest interest
—and heartily respond to *every* word which you have
written in it.   A friend at the Cape had lent me a
German edition of De Wette, which I had consulted
carefully.   But, about a fortnight ago, a lady, till then
a stranger to me, sent me a copy of Parker's edition.
I value it most highly for the sake both of the author's
and editor's share in it.   But the criticism of the
present day goes, if I am not mistaken, considerably
beyond even De Wette's, in clearing up the question
of the age and authorship of the different parts of
the Pentateuch.   I shall carefully consider the tables
of Elohistic and Jehovistic portions, as given in De

Wette; but, in many important respects, my conclusions will be found to differ from his, and, as I think, upon certain grounds. De W. leant too much to the judgment of Stäbelin.

The above, however, is the only one of Th. Parker's works, which has yet come into my hands, till the arrival of your book this morning. When I repeat that every word of your preface went to my very heart — and that many of them drew the tears from my eyes and the prayer from my heart that God would grant me grace to be in any degree a follower of the noble brother whose life you have sketched, and whose feet have already trodden the path, which now lies open before me — you will believe that I shall not leave long the rest of the volume unread. But, whatever I may find there, your preface will give comfort and support to thousands, if only they can be brought to read it. Would it not be possible to have it printed separate, as a *cheap tract?* It would have the effect of recommending the book itself, and Parker's works, generally, to multitudes, who might otherwise not have them brought under their notice effectively. I think if largely circulated it might help materially the progress of the great work, in which I am now engaged.

You will allow me, I hope, to have the pleasure of renewing my acquaintance with you, by making a call upon you before long — and may I bring with me Mrs. Colenso, who will be very glad to see you?

Very truly yours,

Jo. Natal.

Please accept a copy of "Romans," which Macmillan will send you. The *spirit* of it will remain, I trust, abiding, though much of the *letter* must now be changed.

Writing of **Dr.** Colenso to a friend in February, 1865, I said : —

"I never felt for him so much as last night. We came to talk on what we felt at standing so much alone; and he said that when the extent of his discoveries burst on him, he felt as if he had received a paralyzing electric shock. A London clergyman wrote to him the other day to give him solemn warning that he had led one of his parishioners to drunkenness and destruction. Colenso answered him, that 'it was not *he* who led men to doubt of God and duty, but those teachers who made them rest their faith on God and Duty on a foundation of falsehood which every new wave of thought was sweeping away.' The clergyman seems to have been immensely dumbfounded by this reply."

Another most interesting man whom I met at Dr. Carpenter's table was Charles Kingsley.

One day, while I was still a miserable cripple, I went to dine in Regent's Park and came rather late into the drawing-room full of company, supported by what my maid called my "*best* crutches!" The servant did not know me, and announced "Miss Cobble." I corrected her loudly enough for the guests to hear, in that moment of pause: "No! Miss Hobble!" There was of course a laugh, and from the little crowd rushed forward to greet me with both hands extended, a tall, slender, stooping figure with that well-known face so full of feeling and tenderness — Charles Kingsley. "At *last*, Miss Cobbe, at *last* we meet," he said, and a moment later gave me his arm to dinner. This greeting touched me, for we had exchanged, as theological opponents, some tolerably sharp blows for years before, but his large, noble nature harbored no spark of resentment. We talked all dinner time and a good deal in the evening, and then he offered to escort me home to South Kensington — a proposal which I greedily accepted, but, somehow, when he found that I had a brougham, and was not going in miscellaneous vehicles (in my best evening toggery!) from one end of London to the other at night, he retracted, and could not be induced to come with me. We met, however, not unfrequently afterwards, and I always felt much attracted to him; as did, I may mention, my friend's little fox terrier, who, travelling one day with her mistress in the Underground, spied Kingsley entering the carriage, and incontinently leaving her usual safe retreat under the seat made straight to him, and without invitation, leaped on his knee and began gently kissing his face! The dog never did the same or anything like it to any one else in her life before or afterwards. Of course, my friend apologized to Mr. Kingsley, but he only said in his deep voice, "Dogs always do that to me,"—and coaxed the little beast kindly, till they left the train.

The last time I saw Canon Kingsley was one day late in the autumn some months before he died. Somebody whom, I thought, he would like to meet was coming to dine with me at short notice, and I went to Westminster in the hope of catching him and persuading him to come without losing time by sending notes. The evening was closing, and it was growing very dark in the cloisters, where I was seeking his door, when I saw a tall man, strangely bent, coming towards me, evidently seeing neither me nor anything else, and absorbed in some most painful thought. His whole attitude and countenance expressed grief amounting to despair. So terrible was it that I felt it an intrusion on a sacred privacy to have seen it; and would fain have hidden myself, but this was impossible where we were standing at the moment. When he saw me he woke out of his reverie with a start, pulled himself together, shook hands, and begged me to come into his house; which of course I did not do. He had an engagement which prevented him from meeting my guest (I think it must have been Keshub Chunder Sen), and

I took myself off as quickly as possible. I have often
wondered what dreadful thought was occupying his
mind when I caught sight of him that day in the
gloomy old cloisters of Westminster in the autumn twi-
light.

The quotation made a few pages back of Sir Charles
Lyell's observations on belief in Immortality reminds
me that I repeated them soon after he had made them,
to another great man whom it was my privilege to
know — John Stuart Mill. We were spending an afternoon with him and Miss Helen Taylor at Blackheath ; and a quiet conversation between Mr. Mill and
myself having reached this subject, I told him of what
Sir C. Lyell had said. In a moment the quick blood
suffused his cheeks and something very like tears were
in his eyes. The question, it was plain, touched his
very heart. This wonderful sensitiveness of a man
generally supposed to be "dry" and devoted to the
driest studies struck me, I think, more than anything
about him. His special characteristic was extreme delicacy of feeling; and this showed itself, singularly
enough, for a man advanced in life, in transparency of
skin, and changes of color and expression as rapid as
those in a mountain lake when the clouds shift over it.
When Watts painted his fine portrait of him, he failed
to notice this peculiarity of his thin and delicate skin,
and gave him the common thick, muddy complexion of
elderly Englishmen. The result is that the *ethos* of the
face is missing — just as in the case of the portrait of
Dr. Martineau he is represented with weak, sloping
shoulders and narrow chest. The look of power which
essentially belongs to him is not to be seen. I remarked
when I saw this picture first exhibited: "I should
never have 'sat under' *that* Dr. Martineau!" (Mill
and I, of course, met in deep sympathy on the woman
question) and he did me the honor to present me with a
copy of his "Subjection of Women" on its publication.

He tried to make me write and speak more on the subject of Women's Claims, and used jestingly to say that my laugh was worth — I forget how much ! — to the cause. I insert a letter from him showing the minute care he took about matters hardly worthy of his attention.

Avignon, February 23d, 1869.

Dear Miss Cobbe, — I have lately received a communication from the American publisher Putnam, requesting me to write for their magazine, and I understand that they would be very glad if you would write anything for them, more especially on the woman question, on which the magazine (a new one) has shown liberal tendencies from the first. The communications I have received have been through Mrs. Hooker, sister of Mrs. Stowe and Dr. Ward Beecher, and herself the author of two excellent articles in the magazine on the suffrage question, by which we had been much struck before we knew the authorship. I enclose Mrs. Hooker's last letter to me, and I send by post copies of Mrs. Hooker's articles and some old numbers of the magazine, the only ones we have here; and I shall be very happy if I should be the medium of inducing you to write on this question for the American public.

My daughter desires to be kindly remembered, and I am, Dear Miss Cobbe,

Very truly yours,
J. S. Mill.

P. S. — May I ask you to be so kind as to forward Mrs. Hooker's letter to Mrs. P. A. Taylor, as she will see by it that Mrs. Hooker has no objection to put her name to a reprint of her articles.

There never was a more unassuming philosopher than Mr. Mill, just as there never was a more unassuming poet than Mr Browning. All the world knows how

Mr. Mill strove to give to his wife the chief credit of his works; and, after her death, his attitude towards her daughter, who was indeed a daughter also to him, was beautiful to witness, and a fine exemplification of his own theories of the rightful position of women. He was, however, equally unpretentious as regarded men. Talking one day about the difficulty of doing mental work when disturbed by street music, and of poor Mr. Babbage's frenzy on the subject, Mr. Mill said it did not much interfere with him. I told him how intensely Mr. Spencer objected to disturbance. "Ah yes; of course! writing *Spencer's* works one must want quiet!" As if nothing of the kind were needed for such trivial books as his own "System of Logic," or "Political Economy"! He really was quite unconscious of the irony of his remark. I have been told that he would allow his cat to interfere sadly with his literary occupation when she preferred to lie on his table, or sometimes on his neck, — a trait like that of Newton and his "Diamond." This extreme gentleness is ever, surely, a note of the highest order of men.

Here are extracts from letters concerning Mr. Mill, which I wrote to Miss Elliot in August, 1869. I believe I had been to Brighton and met Mr. Mill there.

"We talked of many grave things, and in everything his love of right and his immense underlying faith impressed me more than I can describe. I asked him what he thought of coming changes, and he entirely agreed with me about their danger, but thought that the mischief they will entail must be but temporary. He thought the loss of reverence unspeakably deplorable, but an inevitable feature of an age of such rapid transition that the son does actually outrun the father. He added that he thought even the most skeptical of men generally had an *inner altar to the Unseen Perfection* while waiting for the true one to be revealed to them. In a word the 'dry old philosopher' showed

himself to me as an enthusiast in faith and love.) The
way in which he seemed to have thought out every
great question and to express his own so modestly and
simply, and yet in such clear-cut outlines, was most impressive. I felt (what one so seldom does!) the delightful sense of being in communication with a mind
deeper than one would reach the end of, even after a
lifetime of intercourse. I never felt the same, so
strongly, except towards Mr. Martineau; and though
the forms of *his* creed and philosophy are, I think, infinitely truer than those of Mill (not to speak of the
feelings one has for the man whose prayers one follows), I think it is more in form than in spirit that the
two men are distinguished. The one has only an 'inner,' the other has an outward 'altar;' but both *kneel*
at them."

A month or two earlier in the same year I wrote to
the same friend : —

"Last night I sat beside Mr. Mill at dinner and enjoyed
myself exceedingly. He is looking old and worn, and
the nervous twitchings of his face are painful to see,
but he is so thoroughly genial and gentlemanly, and
laughs so heartily at one's little jokes, and keeps up an
argument with so much play and good humor, that I
never enjoyed my dinner-neighborhood more. Mr. Fawcett was objurgating some M. P. for taking office, and
said : 'When I see *Tories* rejoice, I know it must be an
injury to the Liberal cause.' 'Do you never, then, feel
a qualm,' I said, 'all you Liberal gentlemen, when you
see the *priests* rejoice at what you have just done in
Ireland? Do you reflect whether *that* is likely to be
an injury to the Liberal cause?' The observation
somehow fell like a bomb (the entire company, as I
remember, were Radicals, our host being Mr. P. A. Taylor). For two minutes there was a dead silence. Then
Mrs. Taylor said : ('Ah, Miss Cobbe is a bitter Conservative!' 'Not a *bitter* one,' said Mr. Mill.) 'Miss

Cobbe is a Conservative. I am sorry for it; but Miss Cobbe is never bitter.'"

It has been a constant subject of regret to me that Mr. Mill's intention (communicated to me by Miss Taylor) of spending the ensuing summer holiday in Wales, on purpose to be near us, was frustrated by his illness and death. How much pleasure and instruction I should have derived from his near neighborhood there is no need to say.

A friend of Mr. Mill for whom I had great regard was Professor Cairnes. He underwent treatment at Aix-les-Bains at the same time as I; and we used to while away our long hours by interminable discussions, principally concerning ethics, a subject on which Mr. Cairnes took the Utilitarian side, and I, of course, that of the school of Independent Morality, (*i. e.,* of Morality based on other grounds than Utility). He was an ardent disciple of Mill, but his extreme candor caused him to admit frankly that the "mystic extension" of the idea of *Usefulness* into *Right* was unaccountable, or at least unaccounted for; and that when we had proved an act to be preëminently useful and likely to promote "the greatest happiness of the greatest number," there yet remained the question for each of us, "Why should *I* perform that useful action, if it cost *me* a moment's pain?" To find the answer (he admitted) we must fall back on an inward "categoric imperative," "*ought ;*" and having done so (I argued), we must thenceforth admit that the basis of Morality rests on something beside Utility. All these controversies are rather by-gone now, since we have been confronted with "hereditary sets of the brain." I think it was in these discussions with Professor Cairnes that I struck out what several friends (among others Lord Arthur Russell) considered an "unanswerable" argument against the Utilitarian philosophy; it ran thus : —

"Mr. Mill has nobly said, that if an Almighty Tyrant

were to order him to worship him and threaten to
send him to hell if he refused, then, sooner than worship that unjust God, '*to Hell would I go!*' Mr. Mill,
of course, desired every man to do what he himself
thought right; therefore it is conceivable that, in the
given contingency, we might behold the apostle of the
Utilitarian philosophy *conducting the whole human race
to eternal perdition,* for the sake of — shall we say the
'*greatest happiness of the greatest number?*'"

Professor Cairnes did great public service both to
England and America at the time of the war of seces-
sion by his wise and able writing on the subject. In a
small way I tried to help the same cause by joining Mrs.
P. A. Taylor's committee formed to promote and express English sympathy with the North; and wrote
several little pamphlets, "The Red Flag in John Bull's
Eyes;" "Rejoinder to Mrs. Stowe," etc. This common
interest increased, of course, my regard for Mr. Cairnes,
and it was with real sorrow I saw him slowly sink
under the terrible disease (a sort of general ossification
of the joints) of which he died. I have said he *sank*
under it, but assuredly it was only his piteously stiffened
body which did so, for I never saw a grander triumph
of mind over matter than was shown by the courage and
cheerfulness wherewith he bore as dreadful a fate as
that of any old martyr. I shall never forget the impression of *the nobility of the human Soul* rising over its
tenement of clay, which he made upon me, on the occasion of my last visit to him at Blackheath.

Another man, much of the character and calibre of
Professor Cairnes, whom I likewise had the privilege to
know well, was Professor Sheldon Amos. He also, alas!
died in the prime of life; to the loss and grief of the
friends of every generous movement.

The following is a memorandum of the first occasion
on which I met Mr. John Bright :—

"February 28th, 1866. Dined at Mr. S.'s, M. P. Sat

between Bright and Mr. Buxton. Bright so exquisitely *clean* and with such a sweet voice! His hands alone are coarse. Great discussion, in which Mr. B. completely took the lead; the other gentlemen present seeming to hang on his words as I never saw Englishmen do on those of one another. Talking of Ireland he said he would, if he ever had the power, force all the English companies and great English landlords to sell their estates there; the land to be cut up into small farms. I asked, did he believe in small farming in 1866, and in Celtic capitalists ready to purchase farms? He then told us how he picked up much information travelling through Ireland *on cars*, from the drivers (as if every Irish car-driver did not recognize him in a moment from Punch's caricatures!), and how, especially, he visited the only small farm he had heard of where the occupier was a freeholder; and how it was exceedingly prosperous. I asked where this was? He said 'in a place called the Barony of Forth.' Of course I explained that Forth and Bargy in Wexford have been for four hundred years isolated English (or rather Welsh) colonies, and afford no sort of sample of *Irish* farming. Bright's way of speaking was dogmatic, but full of genial fun and quiet little bits of wit. He spoke with great feeling of the wrongs and miseries of the poor, but seemed to enjoy in full the delusion that it only depended on rich people being ready to sacrifice themselves, to remove them all to-morrow.

"I ventured to ask him why he labored so hard to get votes for working carpenters and bricklayers, and never stirred a finger to ask them for women, who possessed already the property qualification. He said: 'Much was to be said for women,' but then went on maundering about our proper sphere, and 'would they go into Parliament?'"

Again another time I sat beside him (I know not at whose hospitable table), and he told me a most affecting story of a poor crippled woman in a miserable cottage near Llandudno, where he usually spent his holidays. He had got into the habit of visiting this poor creature, who could not stir from her bed, but lay there all day long alone, her husband being out at work as a laborer. Sometimes a neighbor would look in and give her food, but unless one did so she was entirely helpless. Her only comforter was her dog, a fine collie, who lay beside her on the floor, ran in and out, licked her poor useless hands, and showed his affection in a hundred ways. Bright grew fond of the dog, and the dog always welcomed him each year with gambols and joy. One summer he came to the cottage, and the hapless cripple lay on her pallet still, but the dog did not come out to him as usual, and his first question to the woman was: "Where is your collie?" The answer was that *her husband had drowned the dog* to save the expense of feeding it.

Bright's voice broke when he came to the end of this story, and we said very little more to each other during that dinner.

Another day I was speaking to Mr. Bright of the extraordinary *canard* which had appeared in the "Times" the day before announcing (quite falsely) that Lord Russell, then Premier, had resigned. "What on earth," I asked, "can have induced the 'Times' to publish such intelligence?" (As it happened, it inconvenienced Lord Russell very much.) "I will tell you," said Bright; "I am sure it is because Delane is angry that Lady Russell has not asked him to dinner. He expected to go to the Russells' as he did to the Palmerstons', and get his news at first hand!" A day or two later I met Lord Russell, and told him what Mr. Bright had said was the reason of the mischievous trick Mr. Delane had played him. Lord Russell chuckled a great deal and said, rubbing his hands in his characteristic way: "I believe it is! I do believe it is!"

My beautiful cousin, Laura, one of my father's wards, had married (from Newbridge in old days) Mr. John Locke, Q. C., who was for a long time M. P. for Southwark. Their house, 63, Eaton Place, was always most cordially opened to me, and beside Mr. Locke, who was generally brimful of political news, I met at their table many clever barristers and M. P.'s. Among the latter was Mr. Ayrton, against whom a virulent set was made by the scientific *clique*, in consequence of his endeavors, on behalf of the public, to open Kew Gardens earlier in the day. He was rather saturnine, but an incorruptible, unbending sort of man, for whom I felt respect. Another *habitué* was Mr. Warren, author of "Ten Thousand a Year." He was a little ugly fellow, but full of fire and fun, retorting right and left against the Liberals present. Sergeant Gazelee, a worn-looking man, with keen eyes, one day answered him fairly. There was an amusing discussion whether the Tories could match in ability the men of the opposite party? Warren brought up an array of clever Conservatives, but then pretended to throw up the sponge, exclaiming in a dolorous voice, "But then you Liberals have got — Whalley!"

Beside my cousin Mrs. Locke and her good and able husband, I had the pleasure for many years of constantly seeing in London her two younger sisters, Sophia and Eliza Cobbe, who were my father's favorite wards, and have been from their childhood, when they were always under my charge in their holidays, till now in our old age, almost like younger sisters to me. They were of course rarely absent from the Eaton Place festivities.

There was a considerable difference between dinner parties in the Sixties and those of thirty years later. They lasted longer at the earlier date; a greater number of dishes were served at each course, and much more wine was taken. I cannot but think that there must be a certain declension in the general vitality of our race of late years for, I think, few of us, young or old, would be inclined to share equally now in those banquets of long ago which always lasted two hours and sometimes three. There were scarcely any teetotalers, men or women, at the time I speak of, in the circles to which I belonged; and the butlers, who went round incessantly with half a dozen kinds of wine, and (after dinner) liqueurs, were not, as now, continually interrupted in their courses by "No wine, thank you! Have you Apollinaris or Seltzer?" I never saw any one the worse for the sherry and the milk-punch and the hock or chablis, and champagne and claret; but certainly there was generally a little more gaiety of a well-bred sort towards the end of the long meals. My cousins kept a particularly good cook and good cellar, and their guests — especially some who hailed from the City — certainly enjoyed at their table other "feasts" beside those of reason. And so I must confess did *I*, in those days of good appetite after a long day's literary work; and I sincerely pitied Dean Stanley, who had no sense of taste, and scarcely knew the flavor of anything which he put in his mouth. When the company was not quite up to his mark, the tedium of the dinners which he attended must have been dreadful to him; whereas, in my case, I could always — provided the *menu* was good — entertain myself satisfactorily with my plate and knife and fork. The same great surgeon who had treated my sprained ankle so unsuccessfully, told me with solemn warning when we were taking our house in Hereford Square, that, if I lived in South Kensington and went to dinner parties, I should be a regular victim to gout. As it happened I lived in South Kensington for just twenty years, and went out, I should think to some two thousand dinners, great and small, and I never had the gout at all, but, on the contrary, by my own guidance, got rid of the tendency before I left London. There has certainly been a perceptible diminution in the *animal spirits* of men and women in the last thirty years, if not of their vital powers.   Of course there was always, among well-bred people, a certain average of spirits in society, neither boisterous not yet depressed; and the better the company the softer the general "*susurro*" of the conversation.   I could have recognized blindfold certain drawing-rooms wherein a mixed congregation assembled, by the strident, high note which pervaded the crowded room.   But the ripple of gentle laughter in good company has decidedly fallen some notes since the Sixties.

I am led to these reflections by remembering among my cousin's guests that admirable man — Mr. Fawcett. He was always, not merely fairly cheerful, but more gay and apparently light-hearted than those around him who were possessed of their eyesight.   The last time I met him was at the house of Madame Bodichon in Blandford Square, and we three were all the company. One would have thought a blind statesman alone with two elderly women, would not have been much exhilarated; but he seemed actually bursting with boyish spirits; pouring out fun, and laughing with all his heart.   Certainly his devoted wife (in my humble opinion the ablest woman of this day), succeeded in cheering his darkened lot quite perfectly.

Mr. and Mrs. Fawcett were the third couple who in this century have afforded a study for Mr. Francis Galton of "Hereditary Genius."   The first were Shelley and his Mary (who again was the daughter of Godwin and Mary Wollastoncraft).   Their son, the late Sir Percy Shelley, was a very kindly and pleasant gentleman, with good taste for private theatricals, but not a genius.   The second were Robert and Elizabeth Barrett Browning.   They also have left a son, of whose gifts as a painter I do not presume to judge.   The third were Mr. Fawcett and Millicent Garrett, who, though not claiming the brilliant genius of the others, were each, as all the world knows, very highly endowed persons. *Their* daughter, Miss Philippa Garrett Fawcett, — the Senior Wrangler, *de jure*, — has at all events vindicated Mr. Galton's theories.

Many of us, in those days of the Sixties, were deeply interested in the efforts of women to enter the medical profession in spite of the bitter opposition which they encountered. Miss Elizabeth Garrett, Mrs. Fawcett's sister, occupied a particularly prominent place in our eyes, succeeding as she did in obtaining her medical degree in Paris, and afterwards a seat on the London School Board, which last was quite a new kind of elevation for women. While still occupying the foreground of our ambition for our sex, Miss Garrett resolved to make (what has proved, I believe, to be) a happy and well assorted marriage, which put an end, necessarily, to her further projects of public work. I sent her, with my cordial good wishes, the following verses : —

> The Woman's cause was rising fast
> When to the Surgeons' College past
> A maid who bore in fingers nice
> A banner with the new device,
>
> > Excelsior!

> " Try not to pass ! " the Dons exclaim,
> " M.D. shall grace no woman's name " —
> " Bosh ! " cried the maid, in accents free,
> " To France I'll go for my degree."
>
> > Excelsior !

> The School-Board seat came next in sight,
> " Beware the foes of woman's right ! "
> " Beware the awful husting's fight ! "
> Such was the moan of many a soul —
> A voice replied from top of poll —
>
> > Excelsior!

> In patients' homes she saw the light
> Of household fires beam warm and bright ;
> Lectures on Bones grew wondrous dry,
> But still she murmured with a sigh,
>
> > Excelsior !

" Oh, stay ! " — a lover cried — " Oh, rest
Thy much-learned head upon this breast;
Give up ambition !   Be my bride ! "
— Alas! no clarion voice replied,
                                        Excelsior !

At end of day, when all is done,
And woman's battles fought and won,
Honor will aye be paid to one
Who erst called foremost in the van,
                                        Excelsior !

But not for her that crown so bright,
Which hers had been, of surest right,
Had she still cried, — serene and blest —
" The Virgin throned by the West," [1]
                                        Excelsior !

Some years after this I brought from Rome as a
present for my much-valued friend and lady-doctor,
Mrs. Hoggan, M. D. (widow of Dr. George Hoggan), a
large photograph of the statue in the Vatican of *Minerva
Medica*.   Under it I wrote these lines : —

" *Minerva Medica !*   Shocking profanity !
How could these heathens their doctors vex,
Putting the cure of the ills of humanity
Into the hands of the ' weaker sex ? '
O Pallas sublime ! Would you come back revealing
Your glory immortal, our doctors should see —
Instead of proclaiming you Goddess of Healing,
They 'd prohibit your practice, refuse your degree ! "

The first dinner-party I ever attended in London,
before I went to live in town, was at Mr. Bagehot's
house.   I sat beside Mr. Richard Hutton, who has been
ever since my good friend, and opposite us there sat a
gentleman who at once attracted my attention.   He
had a strong dark face, a low forehead and hair parted
in the middle, the large loose mouth of an orator and a
manner quite unique ; as if he were gently looking
down on the follies of mortality from the superior

---

[1] See Spenser — The " West " District of London was the one which
elected Miss Garrett for the School Board.

altitudes of Olympus, or perhaps of Parnassus. "Do you know who that is sitting opposite to us?" said Mr. Hutton. I looked at him again, and replied: "I never saw him before, and I have never seen his picture, but I feel in my inner consciousness that it can only be Mr. Matthew Arnold;" and Mr. Arnold, of course, it was— with an air which made me think him (what he was not) an intellectual coxcomb. He wrote, about that time or soon afterwards, some dreadfully derisive things of my "Theism;" not on account, apparently, of its intrinsic demerits, but because of what he conceived to be its *upstart* character. We are all familiar with a certain tone of lofty superiority common to Roman Catholics and Anglicans in dealing with Dissenters of all classes; the tone, no doubt, in which the priests of On talked of Moses when he led the Israelitish schism in the wilderness. It comes naturally to everybody who stands serenely on "the old paths," and watches those who walk below, or strive to fray new ways through the jungle of poor human thoughts. But when Mr. Arnold had himself slipped off the old road so far as to have liquefied the Articles of the Apostles' Creed into a "Stream of Tendency;" and compared the doctrine of the Trinity to a story of "Three Lord Shaftesburys;" and reduced the Object of Worship to the lowest possible denomination as "a Power not ourselves which makes for righteousness;" he must, I think, have come to feel that it was scarcely his affair to treat other people's heresies as new-fangled, and lacking in the sanctities of tradition. As one after another of his brilliant essays appeared, and it became manifest that his own creed grew continually thinner, more exiguous, and less and less substantial, I was reminded of an old sporting story which my father told of a town-bred gentleman, the "Mr. Briggs" of those days, who for the first time shot a cock-pheasant, and after greatly admiring it laid it down on the grass. A keeper took up the bird and stroked it, pretending to wonder at its size, and presently shifted it aside and substituted a partridge, which he likewise stroked and admired, till he had an opportunity of again changing it for a snipe. At this crisis "Mr. Briggs" broke in furiously, bidding the keeper to stop stroking his bird: "Be hanged to you! If you go on like that, you'll rub it down to a wren!" The creed of many persons in these days seems to be undergoing the process of being patted and praised, while all the time it is being rubbed down to a wren!

But whatever hard things Mr. Arnold said of me, I liked and admired him, and he was always personally most kind to me. He had of all men I have ever known the truest insight — the true *Poet's* insight — into the feelings and characters of animals, especially of dogs. His poem, "Geist's Grave" is to me the most affecting description of the death of an animal in the range of literature. Indeed, the subject of Death itself, whether of beasts or of men, viewed from the same standpoint of hopelessness, has never, I think, been more tenderly touched. How deeply true to every heart is the thought expressed in the stanzas, which remind us that in all the vastness of the universe and of endless time there is not, and never will be, another being like the one who is dead! *That* being (some of us believe) may revive and live for ever, but *another* who will "restore its little self" will never be.

> . . . "Not the course
> Of all the centuries to come,
> And not the infinite resource
> Of Nature, with her countless sum
>
> "Of figures, with her fulness vast
> Of new creation evermore,
> Can ever quite repeat the past,
> Or just thy little self restore.

> "Stern law of every mortal lot!
> Which man, proud man, finds hard to bear
> And builds himself, I know not what
> Of second life, I know not where."

We knew dear *Geist*, I am glad to say. When Miss Lloyd and I came to live at Byfleet Mr. Arnold and his most charming wife — then living three miles off at Cobham — kindly permitted us to see a good deal of them, and we were deeply interested in poor Geist's last illness. He was a black dachshund, not a handsome dog, but possessed of something which in certain dogs and (those dogs only) seems to be the canine analogue of a human soul. As to Mr. Arnold's poem on his other dog, Kaiser, who is there that enjoys a gleam of humor and dog-love can fail to be enchanted with such a perfect picture of a dog — not a dog of the sentimental kind, but one —

> "Teeming with plans, alert and glad
> In work or play,
> Like sunshine went and came, and bade
> Live out the day!"

Does not every one feel how true is the likeness of a happy loving dog to sunshine in a house?

I met Mr. Arnold one day in William and Norgate's book-shop, and he inquired after my dog, and when I told him the poor beast had "gone where the good dogs go," he said, with real feeling, "And you have not replaced her? No! of course you could not." I asked his leave to give a copy of "Geist's Grave" for a collection of poems on animals, made for the purpose of humane propaganda, and he gave it very cordially. I was, however, deeply disappointed when he returned the following reply to my application for his signature to our first Memorial inviting the R. S. P. C. A. to undertake legislation for the restriction of vivisection. I do not clearly understand what he meant by disliking "the English way of employing for public ends private

Societies and Memorials to them."   The R. S. P. C. A.
is scarcely a "private society;" and, if it were so, I see
no harm in "employing it for public ends," instead of
leaving everything to Government to do; or to *leave
undone.*

Совнам, Surrey, January 8th, 1875.

DEAR MISS COBBE, — Your letter was directed to
Oxford, a place with which I have now no connection,
and it reaches me too late for signing your Memorial,
but I should in any case have declined signing it,
strongly as your cause speaks to my feelings; because,
first, I greatly dislike the English way of employing,
for public ends, private societies and Memorials to
them; secondly, the signatures you will profit by, in
this case, are not those of literary people, who will at
once be disposed of as a set of unpractical sentimental-
ists.   To yourself this objection does not apply, because
you are distinguished not in letters only, but also as a
lover and student of animals.   I hope if you read my
paper in the "Contemporary," you observe how I apolo-
gize for calling them the *lower* animals, and how thoroughly I admit that they *think and love.*

Sincerely yours,
MATTHEW ARNOLD.

In my first journey to Italy, on my way to Palestine,
I made acquaintance with R. W. Mackay, the author of
that enormously learned, but, perhaps, not very well
digested book, the "Progress of the Intellect."   I afterwards renewed acquaintance with him and his nice wife
in their house in Hamilton Terrace.   Mr. Mackay was
somewhat of an invalid and a nervous man, much absorbed in his studies.   I have heard it said that he was
the original of George Eliot's "Mr. Casaubon."   At all
events Mrs. Lewes had met him, and taken a strong
prejudice against him.   That prejudice I think was unjust.   He was a very honest and *real* student, and a

modest one, not a pretender like Mr. Casaubon. His books contain an amazing mass of knowledge (presented, perhaps, in rather a crude state), respecting all the great religious doctrines of the world. I had once felt that both his books and talk were hard and steel-cold, and that his religion, though dogmatically the same as mine, was all lodged in his intellect. One day, however, when he called on me and we took a drive and walk in the Park together, I learned to my surprise that he entirely felt with me that the one *direct* way of reaching truth about religion was prayer, and all the rest mere corroboration of what may so be learned. To have *come round* to this seemed to me a great evidence of intellectual sincerity.

I forget now what particular point we had been discussing when he wrote me the following curious bit of erudition : —

DEAR MISS COBBE, — Dixit Rabbi Simeon Ben Lakis — Nomina angelorum et mensium ascenderunt in domum Israelis ex Babylone.

This occurs in the treatise " Rosh Haschanah," which is part of the Mischna.

The Mischna (the earliest part of the Talmud) is said to have been completed in the third century, under the auspices of Rabbi Judah the Holy, and his disciples.

I send the above as promised. The professed aversion of the Jews for foreign customs seems strangely at variance with their practice, as seen, *e. g.*, in their names for the divisions of the heavenly hosts ; the words " Legion and Sistra " (castra) are evidently taken from the Roman army. Four Chief Spirits or Archangels are occasionally mentioned, as in " Pirke Eliezer " and " Henoch," cf. 48 : 1. Others make their number seven, as Tobit 12 : 5 ; Rev. 2 : 4-3, 1-4, 5. The angelic doings are partly copied from the usages of the Jewish Temple, hence the Jerusalem Targum

renders Exod. 14 : 24. "It happened in the morning
watch, the hour when the heavenly host sing praises
before God" — comp. Luke 2 : 13 — and the same reason
is applied by the Targumist for the sudden exit of the
angel in Gen. 32 : 26. One may perhaps, however, be
induced to ask whether (as in the case of Euthyphron
in the Platonic dialogue) a better cause for departure
might not be found in the inconvenience of remaining !

Though I have Haug's version of the Gathas, I am
far from able to decipher the grounds of difference between him and Spiegel. *Non nostrum est tantas com-
ponere lites.* A volume entitled "Erân," by Dr. Spiegel,
contains, among other Essays, one entitled "Avesta and
Veda," or the relation of Iran and India, and another,
"Avesta and Genesis," or the relation of Iran to the
Semites. Weber's "Morische Skizzen" also contains
interesting matter on similar subjects. We were speaking about the magical significance of names. See as to
this Origen against Celsus, 1–24; Diod. Sicul. 1–22;
Iamblicus de Myst. 2, 4, 5.

Socrates himself appears superstitiously apprehen-
sive about the use of divine names in the Philebus, 1, 2
and the Cratylus 400e. The suppression of it among
the Jews (for instance, in the Septuagint, where Κύριος
is substituted for Jehovah, and Sirach, Ch. 23, 9) express the same feeling.

We were talking of the original religion of Persia.
You, of course, recollect the passage on this subject in
the first book of Herodotus, Ch. 131, and Strabo 15, sec
13, p. 732 Casaub. The practice of prohibiting selfish
prayer mentioned in the next following chapter in
Herodotus, is remarkable.

I hope that in the above rigmarole a grain of useful
matter may be found. Mrs. Mackay is, I am glad to
say, better to-day.

      I remain, sincerely yours,   R. W. MACKAY.

20th February, 1865,
   41, HAMILTON TERRACE, N. W.

Another early acquaintance of mine in London was Lady Byron, the widow of the poet. I called on her one day, having received from her a kind note begging me to do so as she was unable to leave her house to come to me. She had been exceedingly kind in procuring for me valuable letters of introduction from Sir Moses Montefiore and others, which had been very useful to me in my long wanderings.

Lady Byron was short in stature and, when I saw her, deadly pale; but with a dignity which some of our friends called "royal," albeit without the smallest affectation or assumption. She talked to me eagerly about all manner of good works wherein she was interested; notably concerning Miss Carpenter's Reformatory, to which she had practically subscribed £1,000 by buying Red Lodge and making it over for such use. During the larger part of the time of my visit she stood on the rug with her back to the fire and the power and will revealed in her attitude and conversation were very impressive. I bore in mind all the odious things Byron had said of her : —

> "There was Miss Mill-pond, smooth as summer sea
> That usual paragon, an only daughter,
> Who seemed the cream of equanimity
> Till skimmed, and then there was some milk and water."

Also the sneers at her (very genuine) humor : —

> "Her wit, for she had wit, was Attic all;
> Her favorite science was the mathematical," etc., etc.

I thought that for a man to hold up such a woman as *this*, and that woman his wife, on the prongs of ridicule for public laughter was enough to make him detestable.

A lady whom I met long afterwards told me (I made a note of it November 13th, 1869) that she had been stopping at the time of Lady Byron's separation, at a very small seaside place in Norfolk. Lady Byron came there

on a visit to Mrs. Francis Cunningham, née Gurney, as
more retired than Kirkby Mallory. She had then been
separated about six weeks or two months. She was
(Mrs. B. said) singularly pleasing and healthful looking,
rather than pretty. She was grave and reticent rather
than depressed in spirits; and gave her friends to understand that there was something she could not
explain to them about her separation. Mrs. B. *heard
her say* that Lord Byron always slept with pistols
under his pillow, and on one occasion had threatened to
shoot her in the middle of the night. There was much
singing of duets going on in the two families, but Lady
Byron refused to take any part in it.

Miss Carpenter, who was entirely captivated by her,
received from her some charge amounting to literary
executorship; but after one or two furtive delvings into
the trunks full of papers (since, I believe, stored in
Hoare's bank), she gave up in despair. She told me
that the papers were in the most extraordinary confusion; letters both of the most trivial and of the most
serious and compromising kind, household accounts,
poems, and tradesmen's bills, were all mixed together in
hopeless disorder and dust. As is well known, Byron's
famous verses:

> " Fare thee well! and if for ever! "

were written on the back of a butcher's bill — *unpaid*
like most of the rest. Miss Carpenter vouched for this
fact.

Lady Byron was at one time greatly attracted by
Fanny Kemble. Among Mrs. Kemble's papers in my
possession are seven letters from Lady Byron to her.
Here is one of them worth presenting : —

DEAR MRS. KEMBLE, — The note you wrote to me
before you left Brighton made me revert to a train of
thought which had been for some time in my mind. I

alluded once to "your future." I submit to be considered a visionary, yet some of my decided visions have come to pass in the course of years; let me tell you my vision about *you* — that you are to be something *to the People;* that your strong sympathy with them (though you will not let them touch the hem of your garment) will bring your talents to bear upon their welfare; that the way is open to you, after your personal objects are fulfilled. My mind is so full of this, that though the time has not arrived for putting it in practice, I cannot help telling you of it. I am neither democratic nor aristocratic. I do not *see* those distinctions in looking at Humanity, but I feel most strongly that for every advantage we have received we are bound to offer something to those who do not possess it. Happy they who have gifts to place at the feet of their less favored fellow-Christians!

I cannot believe that a relation so truthful as yours and mine will be merely casual. Time will show. I might not have an opportunity of saying this in a visit. Yours most truly,

A. NOEL BYRON.

March 19th.

It is an unsolved mystery to me why such a woman did not definitely adopt one of either of two courses. The first (and far the best) would, of course, have been to bury her husband's misdeeds in absolute silence and oblivion, carefully destroying all papers relating to the tragedy of their joint lives. Or, if she had not strength for this, to write exactly what she thought ought to be known by posterity concerning him, and put her account in safe hands with all the needful *pièces justificatives* before she died. That she did not adopt either one course or the other must be a source of permanent regret to all who recognized her great merits and honored them as they deserved.

Among our neighbors in South Kensington, whom we were privileged to know, were many delightful people who are still, I am happy to say, living and taking active part in the world. Among them were Mr. Froude, Mr. and Mrs. W. E. H. Lecky, Mr. Leslie Stephen, Mrs. Brookfield, Mrs. Simpson, and Mrs. Richmond Ritchie. But of several others, alas! "the place that knew them knows them no more." Of these last were Mr. and Mrs. Herman Merivale, Sir Henry Maine, Mrs. Dicey, Lady Monteagle (who had written some of Wordsworth's poems to his dictation as his amanuensis), my dear old friend, Mrs. de Morgan.

Sir Henry Maine's interest in the claims of women and his strong statements on the subject, made me regard him with much gratitude. I asked him once a question about St. Paul's citizenship, to which he was good enough to write so full and interesting a reply that I quote it here *in extenso :*—

ATHENÆUM CLUB, PALL MALL, S. W, April 6th, 1874.

MY DEAR MISS COBBE, — There is no question that for a considerable time before the concession of the Roman citizenship to the whole empire, quite at all events, B. C. 89 or 90 — it could be obtained in various ways by individuals who possessed a lower franchise in virtue of their place of birth or who were even foreigners. The legal writer, Ulpian, mentions several of these modes of acquiring it; and Pliny more than once solicits the citizenship for protégés of his own. There is no authority for supposing that it could be directly purchased (at least *legally*), but it could be obtained by various processes which came to the same thing as paying directly, *e. g.,* building a ship of a certain burden to carry corn to Rome.

I suspect that St. Paul's ancestor obtained the citizenship by serving in some petty magistracy. The coins of Tarsus are said to show that its citizens in the reign of Augustus, enjoyed one or other of the lower Roman franchises; and this would facilitate the acquisition by individuals of the full Roman citizenship.

The Roman citizenship was necessarily hereditary. The children of the person who became a Roman citizen came at once under his *Patria Potestas* and each of them acquired the capacity for becoming some day a Roman *Paterfamilias.*

St. Paul, as a Roman citizen, lived under the Roman law of *Persons*, but he remained under the local law of *Property.* His allusions to the *Patria Potestas* and to the Roman law of wills and guardianship (which was like the *Patria Potestas*), are quite unmistakable, and more numerous than is commonly supposed. In the obscure passage, for example, about women having power over the head, "power" and "head" are technical terms from the Roman law.

Believe me, very sincerely yours,

H. S. MAINE.

George Borrow who, if he were not a gipsy by blood *ought* to have been one, was, for some years, our near neighbor in Hereford Square. My friend was amused by his quaint stories and his (real or sham) enthusiasm for Wales, and cultivated his acquaintance. I never liked him, thinking him more or less of a hypocrite. His missions, recorded in the "Bible in Spain," and his translations of the Scriptures into the out-of-the-way tongues, for which he had a gift, were by no means consonant with his real opinions concerning the veracity of the said Bible. Dr. Martineau once told me that he and Borrow had been schoolfellows at Norwich some sixty years before. Borrow had persuaded several of his other companions to rob their fathers' tills, and then the party set forth to join some smugglers on the coast. By degrees the truants all fell out of line and were picked up, tired and hungry along the road, and

brought back to Norwich school where condign chastisement awaited them. George Borrow it seems received his large share *horsed* on James Martineau's
back! The early connection between the two old men
as I knew them, was irresistibly comic to my mind.
Somehow when I asked Mr. Borrow once to come and
meet some friends at our house he accepted our invitation as usual, but, on finding that Dr. Martineau was to
be of the party, hastily withdrew his acceptance on a
transparent excuse; nor did he ever after attend our
little assemblies without first ascertaining that Dr.
Martineau would not be present!

I take the following from some old letters to my
friend referring to him:

"Mr. Borrow says his wife is very ill and anxious to
keep the peace with C. (a litigious neighbor). Poor
old B. was very sad at first, but I cheered him and sent
him off quite brisk last night. He talked all about the
Fathers again, arguing that their quotations went to
prove that it was *not* our gospels they had in their
hands. I knew most of it before, but it was admirably
done. I talked a little theology to him in a serious
way (finding him talk of his ' horrors ') and he abounded
in my sense of the non-existence of Hell, and of the
presence and action on the soul of *a* Spirit, rewarding
and punishing. He would not say ' God ;' but repeated
over and over that he spoke not from books but from
his own personal experience."

Some time later — after his wife's death : —

"Poor old Borrow is in a sad state. I hope he is
starting in a day or two for Scotland. I sent C. with a
note begging him to come and eat the Welsh mutton
you sent me to-day, and he sent back word, ' Yes.' Then,
an hour afterwards, he arrived, and in a most agitated
manner said he had come to say ' he would rather not.
He would not trouble any one with his sorrows.' I
made him sit down, and talked as gently to him as pos-

sible, saying: 'It won't be a trouble, Mr. Borrow; it will
be a pleasure to me.' But it was all of no use. He was
so cross, so *rude*, I had the greatest difficulty in talking
to him. I asked about his servant, and he said I could
not help him. I asked him about Bowring, and he
said: 'Don't speak of it.' [It was some dispute with
Sir John Bowring, who was an acquaintance of mine,
and with whom I offered to mediate.] I asked him
would he look at the photos of the Siamese, and he
said: 'Don't show them to me!' So, in despair, as he
sat silent, I told him I had been at a pleasant dinner-
party the night before, and had met Mr. L——, who
told me of certain curious books of mediæval history.
'Did he know them?' No, and he *dare said* Mr. L——
did not, either! Who was Mr. L——?' I described
that *obscure* individual [one of the foremost writers of
the day], and added that he was immensely liked by
everybody. Whereupon Borrow repeated at least twelve
times, 'Immensely liked! As if a man could be immensely liked!' quite insultingly. To make a diversion
(I was very patient with him as he was in trouble) I
said I had just come home from the Lyell's and had
heard—' . . . But there was no time to say what
I had heard! Mr. Borrow asked: 'Is that old Lyle I
met here once, the man who stands at the door (of some
den or other) and *bets?*' I explained who Sir Charles
was (of course he knew very well), but he went on and
and on, till I said gravely: 'I don't think you will
meet those sort of people here, Mr. Borrow. We don't
associate with blacklegs, exactly.' "

Here is an extract from another letter:

"Borrow also came, and I said something about the
imperfect education of women, and he said it was *right*
they should be ignorant, and that no man could endure
a clever wife. I laughed at him openly, and told him
some men knew better. What did he think of the
Brownings? 'Oh, he had heard the name; he did not

know anything of them. Since Scott, he read no modern writer; Scott *was greater than Homer!* What he liked were curious, old, erudite books about mediæval and northern things.' I said I knew little of such literature, and preferred the writers of our own age, but indeed I was no great student at all. Thereupon he evidently wanted to astonish me; and, talking of Ireland, said, 'Ah yes; a most curious, mixed race. First there were the Firbolgs — the old enchanters, who raised mists.' . . . 'Don't you think, Mr. Borrow,' I asked, 'it was the Tuatha-de-Danaan who did that? Keatinge expressly says that they conquered the Firbolgs by that means.' (Mr. B., somewhat out of countenance). 'Oh! Aye! Keatinge is *the* authority; a most extraordinary writer.' 'Well, I should call him the Geoffrey Monmouth of Ireland.' (Mr. B., changing the *venue*), 'I delight in Norse-stories; they are far grander than the Greek. There is the story of Olaf, the Saint of Norway. Can anything be grander? What a noble character!' 'But,' I said, 'what do you think of his putting all those poor Druids on the Skerry of Shrieks and leaving them to be drowned by the tide?' (Thereupon Mr. B., looked at me askant out of his gipsy eyes as if he thought me an example of the evils of female education!) 'Well! Well! I forgot about the Skerry of Shrieks. Then there is the story of Beowulf the Saxon going out to sea in his burning ship to die.' 'Oh, Mr. Borrow! that isn't a Saxon story at all. It is in the Heimskringla! It is told of Hakon of Norway.' Then, I asked him about the gipsies and their language, and if they were certainly Aryans. He didn't know (or pretended not to know) what Aryans were; and altogether displayed a miraculous mixture of odd knowledge and more odd ignorance. Whether the latter were real or assumed, I know not!"

With the leading men of science in the Sixties we had the honor of a good deal of intercourse. Through

Dr. W. B. Carpenter (who, as Miss Carpenter's brother, I had met often) and the two ever hospitable families of Lyell, we came to know many of them. Sir William Grove was also a particular friend of my friend Mrs. Grey. He and Lady Grove and their daughter, Mrs. Hall (Imogen), were all charming people, and we had many pleasant dinners with them. Professor Tyndall was, of course, one of the principal members of that scientific coterie, and in those days we saw a good deal of him. He was very friendly; as were also Mr. and Mrs. Francis Galton. Mr. Galton's speculations seemed always to me exceedingly original and interesting, and I delighted in reviewing them. The beginning of the antivivisection controversy, however, put an end to all these relations, so that since 1876, I have seen few of the circle. It is curious to recall how nearly we joined hands on some theological questions before this gulf of a great ethical difference opened before us. Some readers may recall a curious controversy raised by Professor Tyndall on the subject of the efficacy of prayer for *physical* benefits. Having read what he wrote on it, I sent him my own little book, "Dawning Lights," which vindicates the efficacy of prayer, for spiritual benefits only. The following was his reply, to which I will append another kindly note referring to a request I had proffered on behalf of Mrs. Somerville.

PROFESSOR TYNDALL TO F. P. C.
ROYAL INSTITUTION OF GREAT BRITAIN,
7th November, 1865.

MY DEAR MISS COBBE, — Our minds — that is yours and mine — sound the same note as regards the economy of nature. With clearness and precision you have stated the question. In fact, had I known that you had written upon the subject I might have copied your words and put my name to them.

I intend to *keep* your book, but I have desired my

publisher to send you a book of mine in exchange —
this is fair, is it not?

Your book so far as I have read it is full of strength.
Of course I could not have written it all. Your images
are too concrete and your personification of the mystery of mysteries too intense for me. But as long as
you are tolerant of others — which you are — the
shape into which you mould the power of your soul
must be determined by yourself alone.

Believe me, yours most truly,

JOHN TYNDALL.

ROYAL INSTITUTION OF GREAT BRITAIN,
21st June.

MY DEAR MISS COBBE, — I would do anything I
could for *your* sake and irrespectively of the interest of
your subject.

Had I Faraday's own letter, I could decipher at once
what he meant, for I was intimately acquainted with
his course of thought during the later years of his life.
It would however be running a great risk to attempt to
supply this hiatus without seeing his letter.

I should think it refers to the influence of *time* on
magnetic action. About the date referred to he was
speculating and trying to prove experimentally whether
magnetism required time to pass through space.

Always yours faithfully,

JOHN TYNDALL.

In a letter of mine to a friend written after meeting
Professor Tyndall at dinner at Edgbaston during the
Congress of the British Association in Birmingham,
after mentioning M. Vambéry and some others, I said:
"The one I liked best was Professor Tyndall, with
whom I had quite an 'awful' talk alone about the bearing of Science on Religion. He said in words like a
fine poem, that Knowledge seemed to him 'like an

instrument on which we went up, note after note, and
octave after octave; but at last there came a note which
our ears could not hear, and which was silent for us.
And at the other end of the scale there was another
silent note.' "

Many years after this, there appeared an article in
the "Pall Mall Gazette" which I felt sure was by Professor Tyndall, in which it was calmly stated that the
scientific intellect had settled the controversy between
Pantheism and Theism, and that the said scientific
intellect "permitted us to believe in an order of development," and would "allow the religious instincts and
the language of religion to gather round that idea;"
but that the notion of a "Great Director" can by no
means be suffered by the same scientific intellect.

I wrote a reply, begging to be informed *when* and
where the controversy between Pantheism and Theism
had been settled, as the statement, dropped so coolly in
a single paragraph, was, to say the least, startling; and
I concluded by saying, "We may be *driven* into the
howling wilderness of a Godless world by the fiery
words of these new Cherubim of Knowledge; but at
least we will not shrink away into it before their innuendoes!"

I have also lost in quitting this circle, the privilege of often meeting Mr. Herbert Spencer; though he
has never (to his honor be it remembered!) pronounced
a word in favor of painful experiments on animals.
With the great naturalist who has revolutionized
modern science I had rather frequent intercourse till
the same sad barrier of a great difference of moral
opinion arose between us. Mr. Charles Darwin's bro-
ther-in-law, Mr. Hensleigh Wedgwood, was, for a time
tenant here at Hengwrt; and afterwards took a house
named Caer-Deon in this neighborhood, where Mr. and
Mrs. Charles Darwin and their boys also spent part of
the summer. As it chanced, we also took a cottage

that summer close by Caer-Deon and naturally saw our
neighbors daily.   I had known Mr. Darwin previously,
in London, and had also met his most amiable brother,
Mr. Erasmus Darwin, at the house of my kind old friend
Mrs. Reid, the foundress of Bedford Square College.
The first thing we heard concerning the illustrious
arrivals was the report, that one of the sons had had
"*a fall off a Philosopher ;*" a word substituted by the
ingenious Welsh mind for "velocipede" (as bicycles
were then called) under an easily understood confusion
between the rider and the machine he rode !

Next, — the Welsh parson of the little church close
by, having fondly calculated that Mr. Darwin would
certainly hasten to attend his services, prepared for
him a sermon which should slay this scientific Goliath
and spread dismay through the ranks of the skeptical
host.   He told his congregation that there were in
these days persons, "puffed up by science, falsely-so-
called, and deluded by the pride of reason, who had
actually been so audacious as to question the story of
the six days' creation as detailed in Sacred Scripture.
But let them note how idle were these skeptical ques-
tionings!   Did they not see that the events recorded
happened before there was any man existing to record
them, and that, therefore, Moses *must* have learned
them from God himself, since there was no one else to
tell him ? "

Alas ! the philosopher, I fear, never went to be converted (as he surely must have been) by this ingenious
Welsh parson, and we were for a long time merry over
his logic.   Mr. Darwin was never in good health, I believe, after his Beagle experience of seasickness, and
he was glad to use a peaceful and beautiful old pony
of my friend's yclept Geraint, which she placed at his
disposal.   His gentleness to this beast and incessant
efforts to keep off the flies from his head, and his fondness for his dog Polly (concerning whose cleverness

and breeding he indulged in delusions which Matthew
Arnold's better dog-lore would have swiftly dissipated),
were very pleasing traits in his character.

In writing at this time to a friend I said : —

("I am glad you like Mill's book. Mr. Charles Darwin, with whom I am enchanted, is greatly excited
about it, but says that Mill could learn some things
from physical science; and that it is in the struggle
for existence and (especially) for the possession of women that men acquire their vigor and courage. Also
he intensely agrees with what I say in my review of
Mill about *inherited* qualities being more important
than *education*, on which alone Mill insists. All this
the philosopher told me yesterday, standing on a path
sixty feet above me and carrying on an animated dialogue from our respective standpoints!")

Mr. Darwin was walking on the footpath down from
Caer-Deon among the purple heather which clothes our
mountains so royally ; and impenetrable brambles lay
between him above and me on the road below ; so we
exchanged our remarks at the top of our voices, being
too eager to think of the absurdity of the situation, till
my friend coming along the road heard with amazement
words flying in the air which assuredly those "valleys
and rocks never heard" before, or since! When we
drive past that spot, as we often do now, we sigh as we
look at the "Philosopher's Path," and wish (Oh, *how*
one wishes!) that he could come back and tell us what
he has learned *since!*

(At this time Mr. Darwin was writing his "Descent
of Man," and he told me that he was going to introduce
some new view of the nature of the Moral Sense. I
said: "Of course you have studied Kant's 'Grundle-
gung der Sitten'?" No; he had not read Kant, and did
not care to do so. I ventured to urge him to study him,
and observed that one could hardly see one's way in
ethical speculation without some understanding of his

philosophy. My own knowledge of it was too imperfect to talk of it to him, but I could lend him a very good translation. He declined my book, but I nevertheless packed it up with the next parcel I sent him.

On returning the volume he wrote to me : —

"It was very good of you to send me *nolens volens* Kant, together with the other book. I have been extremely glad to look through the former. It has interested me much to see how differently two men may look at the same points. Though I fully feel how presumptuous it sounds to put myself even for a moment in the same bracket with Kant — the one man a great philosopher, looking exclusively into his own mind, the other a degraded wretch looking from the outside through apes and savages at the moral sense of mankind."

There was irony, and perhaps not a little pride in his reference to himself as a "degraded wretch looking through apes and savages at the moral sense of mankind!" (Between the two great schools of thinkers — those who study from the inside (of human consciousness), and those who study from the outside — there has always existed mutual animosity and contempt. For my own part, while fully admitting that the former needed to have their conclusions enlarged and tested by outside experience, I must always hold that they were on a truer line than the (exclusively) physico-scientific philosophers. Man's consciousness is not only *a* fact in the world but the *greatest* of facts ; and to overlook it and take our lessons from beasts and insects is to repeat the old jest of Hamlet with Hamlet omitted. A philosophy founded solely on the consciousness of man, *may*, and, very likely, will, be imperfect; and certainly it will be incomplete. But a philosophy which begins with inorganic matter and the lower animals, and only includes the outward facts of anthropology, regardless of human consciousness — *must* be worse than imperfect and incomplete.) It resembles a treatise on the solar system which should omit to notice the sun.

I mentioned to him in a letter, that we had found some seeds of Tropæolum, very carefully gathered from brilliant and multicolored varieties, all revert in a single year to plain scarlet. He replied: — "You and Miss Lloyd need not have your faith in inheritance shaken with respect to Tropæolum until you have prevented for six or seven generations any crossing between the varieties in the same garden. I have lately found the very shade of color is transmitted of a most fluctuating garden variety if the flowers are carefully self-fertilized during six or seven generations."

The "Descent of Man" of which Mr. Darwin was kind enough to give me a·copy before publication, inspired me with the deadliest alarm. His new theory therein set forth, respecting the nature and origin of conscience, seemed to me then, and still seems to me, of absolutely fatal import. I wrote the strongest answer to it in my power at once, and published it in the "Theological Review," April, 1871 (reprinted in my "Darwinism in Morals," 1872). Of course I sent my review to Down House. Here is a generous message which I received in reply: —

"Mr. Darwin is reading the 'Review' with the greatest interest and attention and feels so much the kind way you speak of him and the praise you give him, that it will make him bear your severity, when he reaches that part of the review."

Referring to an article of mine in the "Quarterly Review" (Oct., 1872) on the "Consciousness of Dogs," Mr. Darwin wrote to me, November 28th, 1872: —

"I have been greatly interested by your article in the 'Quarterly.' It seems to me the best analysis of the mind of an animal which I have ever read, and I agree with you on most points. I have been particularly glad to read what you say about the reasoning power of dogs, and about that rather vague matter, their self-consciousness. I dare say however that you would prefer criticism to admiration.

"I regret that you quote J. so often : I made inquiries about one case (which quite broke down) from a man who certainly ought to know Mr. J. well; and I was cautioned that he had not written in a scientific spirit. I regret also that you quote old writers. It may be very illiberal, but their statements go for nothing with me and I suspect with many others. It passes my powers of belief that dogs ever commit suicide. Assuming the statements to be true, I should think it more probable that they were distraught, and did not know what they were doing ; nor am I able to credit about fetishes.

"One of the most interesting subjects in your article seems to me to be about the moral sense. Since publishing the "Descent of Man" I have got to believe rather more than I did in dogs having what may be called a conscience. When an honorable dog has committed an undiscovered offence he certainly seems *ashamed* (and this is the term naturally and often used) rather than *afraid* to meet his master. My dog, the beloved and beautiful Polly, is at such times extremely affectionate towards me ; and this leads me to mention a little anecdote. When I was a very little boy, I had committed some offence, so that my conscience troubled me, and when I met my father, I lavished so much affection on him, that he at once asked me what I had done, and told me to confess. I was so utterly confounded at his suspecting anything, that I remember the scene clearly to the present day, and it seems to me that Polly's frame of mind on such occasions is much the same as was mine, for I was not then at all afraid of my father."

In a letter to a friend (November, 1869) I say : —

"We lunched with Mr. Charles Darwin at Mr. Erasmus D——'s house on Sunday. He told us that a

German man of science (I think Carl Vogt), the other
day gave a lecture, in which he treated the Mass as the
last relic of that *Cannibalism* which gradually took to
eating only the heart, or eyes of a man to acquire his
courage. Whereupon the whole audience rose and
cheered the lecturer enthusiastically! Mr. Darwin remarked how much more *decency* there was in speaking
on such subjects in England."

This pleasant intercourse with an illustrious man
was, like many other pleasant things, brought to a close
for me in 1875 by the beginning of the anti-vivisection
crusade. Mr. Darwin eventually became the centre of
an adoring *clique* of vivisectors who (as his biography
shows) plied him incessantly with encouragement to
uphold their practice, till the deplorable spectacle was
exhibited of a man who would not allow a fly to bite a
pony's neck, standing forth before all Europe (in his
celebrated letter to Professor Holmgren of Sweden) as
the advocate of vivisection.

We had many interesting foreign visitors in Hereford
Square. I have mentioned the two Parsee gentlemen
who came to thank me for having made (as they considered) a just estimate of their religion in my article,
"The Sacred Books of the Zoroastrians." The older of
them, Mr. Nowrozjee Furdoonjee, was President of the
Parsee Society of Bombay; but resided much in England, and had an astonishing knowledge of English and
American theological and philosophic literature. He
asked me one day to recommend him the best modern
books on ethics. My small library contained a good
many, but he not only knew every one I possessed, but
almost all others which I named as worthy of his attention. We talked very freely on religious matters and
with a good deal of sympathy. I pressed him one day
with the question, "Do you really believe in Ahri-
man?" "Of course I do!" "What! In a real per-

sonal Evil Being, who is as much a *person* as Ormusd?"
"Oh, no! I did not mean that! I believe in Evil existing in the world;"—and obviously in nothing more!

My chief Eastern visitors, however (and they were so
numerous that my artist-minded friend was wont to
call them my "Bronzes") were the Brahmos of Ben-
gal, and one or two of the same faith from Bombay.
There were very remarkable young men at that date,
members of the "Church of the One God;" nearly all
of them having risen from the gross idolatry in which
they had been educated into a purer Theistic faith, not
without encountering considerable family and social
persecution. Their leader, Keshub Chunder Sen, at
any other age of the world, would have taken his place
with such prophets as Nanuk (the founder of the Sikh
religion) and Gautama; or with the mediæval Saints
like St. Augustine and St. Patrick, who converted
nations. He was, I think, the most *devout* man with
whose mind I ever came in contact. When he left my
drawing-room after long conversations on the highest
themes — sometimes held alone together, sometimes
with the company of my dear friend William Henry
Channing — the impression left on me was one never to
be forgotten. I wrote of one such interview at the
time to my friend as follows (April 28, 1870) : —

"Keshub came and sat with me the other evening,
and I was profoundly impressed, not by his intellect
but by his goodness. He seems really to *live in God*,
and the single-mindedness of the man seemed to me
utterly un-English: much more like Christ! He said
some very profound things, and seemed to feel that the
joy of prayer was quite the greatest thing in life. He
said, 'I don't know anything about the future, but I
only know that when I pray I feel that my union with
God is eternal. In our faith the belief in God and in
Immortality are not two doctrines but one.' He also
said that we must believe in intercessory prayer, else

*the more we lived in Prayer the more selfish we should
grow.* He told me much of the *beginning* of his own
religious life, and, wonderful to say, his words would
have described that of my own! He said, indeed, that
he had often laid down my books when reading them in
India, and said to himself: 'How can this English
woman have felt all this just as I?'"

In his outward man Keshub Chunder Sen was the
ideal of a great teacher. He had a tall, manly figure,
always clothed in a long black robe of some light cloth
like a French *soutane*, a very handsome square face
with a powerful jaw; the complexion and eyes of a
southern Italian; and all the Eastern gentle dignity
of manner. He and his friend Mozoomdar and
several others of his party spoke English quite perfectly; making long addresses and delivering extem-
pore sermons in our language without error of any
kind, or a single betrayal of foreign accent. Keshub in
particular, was decidedly eloquent in English. I
gathered many influential men to meet him and they
were impressed by him as much as I was.

The career of this very remarkable man was cut short
a few years after his return from England by an early
death. I believe he had taken to ascetic practices, fast-
ing and watching; against which I had most urgently
warned him, seeing his tendency towards them. I had
argued with him that, not only were they totally foreign to the spirit of simple Theism, but dangerous to a
man who, living habitually in the highest realms of
human emotion, needed *all the more for that reason*
that the physical basis of his life should be absolutely
sound and strong, and not subject to the variabilities
and possible hallucinations attendant on abstinence.
My friendly counsels were of no avail. Keshub became
I believe, somewhat too near a "Yogi" (if I rightly
understand that word) and was almost worshipped by
his congregation of Brahmos. The marriage of his

daughter — who has since visited England — to the
Maharajah of Coosh Behar, involved very painful discussions about the legal age of the bride and the cere-
monies of a Hindoo marriage, which were insisted on
by the bridegroom's mother; and the last year or two
of Keshub's life were, I fear, darkened by the secessions
from his Church which followed an event otherwise
gratifying.

Oddly enough this Indian *Saint* was the only Eastern
it has ever been my chance to meet who could enjoy
a joke thoroughly, like one of ourselves. He came
to me in Hereford Square one day bursting with un-
controllable laughter at his own adventures. Lord
Lawrence, when Governor-General of India, had been
particularly friendly to him and had bidden him come
and see him when he should arrive in England. Keshub's friends had found a lodging for him in Regent's
Park, and having resolved to go and pay his respects
to Lord Lawrence at once, he sent for a four-wheeled
cab, and simply told the cabman to drive to that nobleman's house, fondly imagining that all London must
know it, as Calcutta knew Government House. The
cabman set off without the remotest idea where to go,
and after driving hither and thither about town for
three hours, set his fare down again at the door of his
lodgings; told him he could not find Lord Lawrence;
and charged him fourteen shillings! Poor Keshub
paid the scandalous charge and then referred to an old
letter to find Lord Lawrence's address, "Queen's Gate."
Oh, that was quite right! No doubt the late Governor-
General naturally lived close to the Queen! Drive to
Queen's Gate." The new cabman drove straight enough
to "Queen's Gate," but about one hundred and eighty-
five houses appeared in a row, and there was nothing to
indicate which of them belonged to Lord Lawrence;
not even a solitary sentinel walking before the door!
After knocking at many doors in vain, the cabman had

an inspiration! "We will try if the nearest butcher knows which house it is;" and so they turned into Gloucester Road, and the excellent butcher there did know which number in Queen's Gate belonged to Lord Lawrence, and Keshub was received and warmly welcomed. But that he should have to seek out a *butcher's shop* (in his Eastern eyes the most degraded of shops) to learn where he could find a man whom he had last seen as Viceroy of India, was, to his thinking, exquisitely ridiculous.

Ex-Governors-General and their wives must certainly find some difficulty in descending all at once so many steps from the altitude of the viceregal thrones of our great dependencies to the level of private citizens, scarcely to be noticed more than others in society, and dwelling in ordinary London houses unmarked by the "guard of honor" of even a single policeman!

At a later date I had other Oriental visitors, one a gentleman who had made a translation of the Bhagvat-Gita, and who brought his wife and children to England, and to my tea-table. The wife wore a lovely, delicate lilac robe wrapped about her in the most graceful folds, but the effect was somewhat marred by the vulgar English side-spring boots (very short in the leg), which the poor soul had found needful for use in London! The children sat opposite me at the tea-table, silently devouring my cakes and bon-bons; staring at me with their large black eyes, veritable *wells* of mistrust and hatred, such as only Eastern eyes can speak! I like dark *men* and *women* very well, but when the little ones are in question, I must confess that a child is scarcely a child to me unless it be a little Saxon, with golden hair and those innocent blue eyes which make one think of the forget-me-nots in a brook. Where is the heart which can help growing soft at sight of one of these little creatures toddling in the spring grass picking daisies and cowslips, or laughing with sheer ecstasy in the joy of existence? A dark child may be ten times as handsome, but it has no pretension, to my mind, to pull one's heart-strings in the same way as a blonde babykins.

A Hindoo lady, Ramabai, for whom I have deep respect, came to me before I left London, and impressed me most favorably. She, and a few other Hindoo women who are striving to secure education and freedom for their sisters, will be honored hereafter more than John Howard, for he strove only to mitigate the too severe punishment of *criminals* and delinquents; *they* are laboring to relieve the quite equally dreadful lot of millions of *innocent* women. An American missionary, Mr. Dall, long resident in India, told me that thousands of these unhappy beings *never put their feet to the earth* or go a step from the house of their husbands (to which they are carried from their father's Zenana at nine or ten years old) till they were borne away as corpses! All life for them has been one long imprisonment; its sole interest and concern the passions of the baser sort of love and jealousy! While writing these pages I have come across the following frightful testimony by the great traveller, Mrs. Bishop (*née* Isabella Bird), to the truth of the above observation concerning the dreadful condition of the women of India : —

"I have lived in Zenanas and harems, and have seen the daily life of the secluded women, and I can speak from bitter experience of what their lives are; the intellect dwarfed, so that the woman of twenty or thirty years of age is more like a child of eight intellectually, while all the worst passions of human nature are stimulated and developed in a fearful degree; jealousy, envy, murderous hate, intrigue, running to such an extent that in some countries I have hardly ever been in a woman's house or near a woman's tent without being asked for drugs with which to disfigure the favorite wife, to take away her life, or to take away the life of the favorite wife's infant son. This request has been made of me nearly two hundred times." (Quoted by Lady Henry Somerset in the "Woman's Signal," April 12th, 1894.)

I had the pleasure also of visits from several French and Belgian gentlemen who were good enough to call on me. Several were Protestant pastors of the "École Moderne;" M. Fontanés, M. Th. Bost, and M. Leblois being among them. I had long kept up a correspondence with M. Felix Pécaut, author of a beautiful book "Le Christ et la Conscience," of whom Dean Stanley told me that he (who knew him well) believed him to be "the most pious of living men." I never had the happiness to meet him, but seeing, some twenty years later, in a report by Mr. Matthew Arnold on French Training Schools, enthusiastic praise of M. Pécaut's school for female teachers, at Fontenaye-aux-Roses, near Paris, I sent it to my old friend, and we exchanged a mental handshake across time and space.

An illustrious neighbor of ours in South Kensington sometimes came to see me. Here is a lively complimentary letter from him : —

FROM M. LE SÉNATEUR VICTOR SCHŒLCHER TO MISS COBBE.

PARIS, 12, 1883.

DEAR, HONORED MISS POWER COBBE, — Je ne vous ai pas oublié, on ne vous oublie pas quand on a eu l'honneur et le plaisir de vous connaître. Moi je suis accablé d'ouvrage et je ne fais pas la moitié de ce que je voudrais faire. Je ne manque pas toutefois de lire votre "Zoöphile" Français qui aidera puissamment notre Ligue à combattre les abus de la vivisection. Tous ceux qui ont quelque sentiment d'humanité écouteront votre voix en faveur des pauvres animaux et vous aideront de toutes leur forces à les protéger contre un genre d'étude veritablement barbare. Quand à moi, l'activité, la persévérance et le talent que vous montrez dans votre œuvre de charité m'inspirent le plus vif et le plus respectueux intérêt.

Ne croyez pas ceux qui tentent de vous décourager en prétendant que votre journal est une substance trop aride pour attacher le lecteur Français. Je le sais ; il est convenu en Angleterre que les Français sont un peuple léger. Mais c'est là un vieux préjugé que ne gardent pas les Anglais instruits. Soyez bien assurée que vos efforts ne seront pas plus peine perdus dans mon noble pays que dans le vôtre. Notre Société Protectrice des Animaux a quarante ans d'existence.

A mon prochain voyage à Londres je m'empresserai d'aller vous faire visite pour retrouver le plaisir que j'ai goûté dans votre conversation et pour vous répéter, Dear Miss Power Cobbe, that I am yours most respectfully and faithfully,

V. Schœlcher.

"Permettez-moi de vous prier de me rappeler au souvenir de Madame la Doctoresse, et de M. le Dr. Hoggan."

It was M. Schœlcher who effected in 1848 the abolition of negro slavery in the French Colonies. He was a charming companion and a most excellent man. I interceded once with him to make interest with the proper authorities in France for the relaxation of the extremely severe penalties, which Louise Michel had incurred by one of her extravagances. To my surprise, I learned from him that I had gone to headquarters, since the matter would mainly rest in his hands. He was Vice-President — practically President — of the Department of Prisons in France. He repeated with indulgence, "Mais, Madame, elle est folle! elle est parfaitement folle, et très dangereuse." I quite agreed, but still thought she was well meaning, and that her sentence was excessive. He promised that when the first year of her imprisonment was over (with which, he said, they made it a rule never to interfere so as not to insult the judges) he would see what could be done to let her off by degrees. He observed, with more earnestness than I should have expected from one of his political school, how wrong, dangerous, and *wicked* it was to go about with a black flag at the head of a mob. Still he agreed with my view that the length of Louise Michel's sentence was unjustly great. Eventually the penalty was actually commuted; I conclude through the intervention of M. Schœlcher.

M. Schœlcher was the most attractive Frenchman I ever met. At the time I knew him, he was old and feeble and had a miserable cough; but he was most emphatically a gentleman, a tender, even soft-hearted man; and a brilliantly agreeable talker. He had made a magnificent collection of 9,000 engravings, and told me he was going to present it to the Beaux Arts in Paris. While sitting talking in my drawing-room his eye constantly turned to a particularly fine cast which I possessed of the Psyche of Praxiteles, made expressly for Harriet Hosmer and given by her to me in Rome. When he rose to leave me, he stood under the lovely creature and *worshipped* her as she deserves !

We had also many delightful American visitors, whose visits gave me so much pleasure and profit that I easily forgave one or two others who provoked Fanny Kemble's remark that "if the engineers would *lay on* Miss P. or Mr. H. the Alps would be bored through without any trouble !" Most of my American friendly visitors are, I rejoice to say, still living, so I will only name them with an expression of my great esteem for all and affection for several of them. Among them were Colonel Higginson, Mr. George Curtis, Mrs. Howe, Mrs. Livermore, Mr. and Mrs. Loring-Brace, Rev. J.

Freeman Clarke, Rev. W. Alger, Dr. O. W. Holmes, Mr. Peabody, Miss Harriet Hosmer, Mr. Hazard, Mrs. Lockwood, and my dearly beloved friends, W. H. Channing, Mrs. Apthorp, Mrs. Wister, Miss Schuyler and Miss Georgina Schuyler. Sometimes American ladies would come to me as perfect strangers with a letter from some mutual friend, and would take me by storm and after a couple of hours' conversation we parted as if we had known and loved each other for years. There is something to my mind unique in the attractiveness of American women, when they are, as usual, attractive; but they are like the famous little girl with the "curl in the middle of her forehead," —

> " When she was good, she was very, very good ;
> When she was bad, she was horrid ! "

The wholesome horror felt by us, Londoners, of out-staying our welcome when visiting acquaintances, and of trespassing too long at any hour, seems to be an unknown sentiment to some Americans, and also to some Australian ladies; and for my own part I fear that being bored is a kind of martyrdom which I can never endure in a Christian spirit, or without beginning to regard the man or woman who bores me with most uncharitable sentiments. My young Hindoo visitors drove me distracted till I discovered that they imagined a visit to me to be *an audience*, and that it was for me to *dismiss* them !

I met Longfellow during his last visit to England at the house of Mr. Wynne-Finch. His large, leonine head, surmounted at that date by a *nimbus* of white hair, was very striking indeed. I saw him standing a few moments alone, and ventured to introduce myself as a friend of his friends, the Apthorps, of Boston, and when I gave my name he took both my hands and pressed them with delightful cordiality. We talked for a good while, but I cannot recall any particular remark he may have made.

Mr. Wynne-Finch was stepfather of Alice L'Estrange, who, before her marriage with Laurence Oliphant was for a long time our most assiduous and affectionate visitor, having taken a young girl's *engouement* for us two elderly women. Never was there a more bewitching young creature, so sweetly affectionate, so clever and brilliant in every way. It was quite dazzling to see such youth and brightness flitting about us. An old letter of hers to my friend which I chance to have fallen on is alive still with her playfulness and tenderness. It begins thus: —

4, UPPER BROOK STREET,
London, October 3d, 1871.

Oh, yes! I know! It is n't so very long since I heard last, and *I am* in London, which I am enjoying, and am busy in a thousand little messy things which amuse me, and I was with Miss Cobbe on Tuesday which was bliss absolute, and above all I heard about you from her (beside all the talk on that forbidden subject, — it is *so* disagreeable of us, is n't it?). I felt that ingratitude for mercies received which characterizes our race so strong in me that I want a sight of your writing, as that is all I can get just now, etc., etc.

Alice was of an extremely skeptical turn of mind (which made her subsequent fanaticism the more inexplicable), and for months before she fell in with Mr. Oliphant in Paris I had been laboring with all my strength to lead her simply *to believe in God.* She did not see her way to such faith at all, though she was docile enough to read the many books I gave her, and to come with us and her stepfather to hear Dr. Martineau's sermons. She incessantly discussed theological questions, but always from the point of view of the evil in creation, and, as she used to say pathetically, of "the insufferableness of the suffering of others." She argued that the misery of the world was so great that a good God, if He could not relieve it, ought to hurl it

to destruction. In vain I argued that there is a higher
end of creation than Happiness to be wrought out
through trial and pain. She would never admit the
loftier conception of God's purposes as they appeared
to me, and was to all intents and purposes an Atheist
when she said good-bye to me, before a short trip to
Paris. She came back in a month or six weeks, not
merely a believer in the ordinary orthodox creed, but
inspired with the zeal of an *energumène* for the doctrines, very much over and above orthodoxy, of Mr.
Harris! Our gentle, caressing, modest young friend
was entirely transformed. She stood upright and
walked up and down our rooms, talking with vehe-
mence about Mr. Harris' doctrines, and the necessity
for adopting his views, obeying his guidance, and going
immediately to live on the shores of Lake Erie! The
transfiguration was, I suppose, *au fond*, one of the
many miracles of the little god with the bow and
arrows, and Mr. Oliphant was certainly not uncon-
cerned therein. But still there was no adequate explanation of this change, or of the boasting (difficult to
hear with patience from a clever and skeptical woman)
of the famous "method" of obtaining fresh supplies
of Divine spirit, by the process of holding one's breath
for some minutes — according to Mr. Harris' pneumato-
logy! The whole thing was infinitely distressing, even
revolting, to us; and we sympathized much with her
stepfather (my friend's old friend) who had loved her
like a father, and was driven wild by the insolent pretentions of Mr. Harris to stop the marriage, of which
all London had heard, unless his monstrous demands
were previously obeyed! At last Alice walked by herself one morning to her bank, and ordered her whole
fortune to be transferred to Mr. Harris; and this without the simplest settlement or security for her future
support! After this heroic proceeding, the Prophet of
Lake Erie graciously consented (in a way) to her mar-

riage; and England saw her and Mr. Oliphant no more for many years. What that very helpless and self-indulgent young creature must have gone through in her solitary cottage on Lake Erie, and subsequently in her poor little school in California, can scarcely be guessed. When she returned to England she wrote to us from Hunstanton Hall (her brother's house), offering to come and see us, but we felt that it would cause us more pain than pleasure to meet her again, and, in a kindly way, we declined the proposal. Since her sad death, and that of Mr. Oliphant, an American friend of mine, Dr. Leffingwell, travelling in Syria, wrote me a letter from her house at Haifa. He found her books still on the shelves where she had left them; and the first he took down was Parker's "Discourse of Religion," inscribed "From Frances Power Cobbe to Alice L'Estrange."

A less tragic *souvenir* of poor Alice occurs to me as I write. It is so good an illustration of the difference between English and French politeness that I must record it.

Alice was going over to Paris alone, and as I happened to know that a distinguished and very agreeable old French gentleman of my acquaintance was crossing by the same train, I wrote and begged him to look after her on the way. He replied in the kindest and most graceful manner as follows : —

CHÈRE MADEMOISELLE, — Vraiment vous me comblez de toutes les manières. Après l'aimable accueil que vous avez bien voulu me faire, vous songez encore à mes ennuis de voyage seul, et vous voulez bien me procurer la société la plus agréable. Agréez en tous mes remerciments, quoique je ne puisse m'empêcher de songer que s'il avait moins neigé sur la montagne (comme disent les Orientaux) vous seriez moins confiante. Je serai trop heureux de me mettre au service de votre amie.

Agréez, chère Mademoiselle, les hommages respectueux de votre

Dévoué serviteur,   BARON DE T.

1 Déc., 1871.

They met at Charing Cross, and no man could be more charming than M. le Baron de T. made himself in the train and on the boat. But on arrival at Boulogne it appeared that Alice's luggage had either gone astray or been stopped by the custom-house people ; and she was in a difficulty, the train for Paris being ready to start, and the French officials paying no attention to her entreaty that her trunks should be delivered and put into the van to take with her. Of course the appearance by her side of a French gentleman with the *Légion d'Honneur* in his buttonhole would have probably decided the case in her favor at once. But M. de T. had not the least idea of losing his train and getting into an imbroglio for the sake of a damsel in distress ; so, with many assurances that he was quite *désolé* to lose the enchanting pleasure of her society up to Paris, he got into his carriage and was quickly carried out of sight. Meanwhile a rather ordinary-looking Englishman who had noted Miss L'Estrange's awkward situation, went up to her and asked in a gruff fashion what was the matter. When he was informed, he let his train go off and ran hither and thither about the station, till at last the luggage was found and restored to its owner. Then, when Alice strove naturally to thank him, he simply raised his hat, said it was of " no consequence," and disappeared to trouble her no more.

" Which, therefore, was neighbor to him that fell among thieves ? "

CHAPTER XVIII.

I MUST not write here any personal sketch however slight of my revered friend Dr. Martineau, since he is still — God be thanked for it! — living, and writing as profoundly and vigorously as ever, in his venerable age of eighty-nine. But the weekly sermons which I had the privilege of hearing from his lips for many years, down to 1872, beside several courses of his lectures on the Gospels and on Ethical Philosophy which I attended, formed so very important, I might say vital, a part of my "Life" in London, that I cannot omit some account of them in my story.

Little Portland Street Chapel is a building of very moderate dimensions, with no pretensions whatever to ecclesiastical finery; whether of architecture, or upholstery, or art of any kind. But it was, I always thought, a fitting, simple place for serious people to meet to *think in ;* not to gaze round them in curiosity or admiration, or to be intoxicated with colors, lights, incense, and music; as would seem to be the intention of the administrators of a neighboring fane! Our services, I suppose, would have been pronounced cold, bare, and dull by an *habitué* of a Ritualistic or Romanist church; but for my own part I should prefer even to be "cold" (which we were *not*) rather than allow my religious feelings to be excited through the gratification of my æsthetic sense.

On this matter, however, each one must speak and choose for himself. For me I was perfectly satisfied

with my seat in the gallery in that simple chapel, where
I could well hear the noblest sermons and see the
preacher of whom they always seemed a part; his
" *Word* " in the old sense; not (like many other men's
sermons) things quite apart from the speaker, as we
know him in his home and in the street. Of all the
men with whom I have ever been acquainted the one
who most impressed me with the sense — shall I call
it of congruity or homogeneity? — of being, in short,
the same all through, was he to whom I listened on those
happy Sundays.

They were very varied sermons which Dr. Martineau
preached. The general effect, I used to think, was not
that of receiving lessons from a teacher, but of being
invited to accompany a guide on a mountain walk.
From the upper regions of thought where he led us, we
were able — nay, compelled — to look down on our
daily cares and duties from a loftier point of view; and
thence to return to them with fresh feelings and resolutions. Sometimes these ascents were very steep and
difficult; and I have ventured to tell him that the richness of his metaphors and similes, beautiful and original
as they always were, made it harder to climb after him,
and that we sometimes wanted him to hold out to us a
shepherd's crook, rather than a *jewelled crozier!* But
the exercise, if laborious, was to the last degree men-
tally healthful, and morally strengthening. There was
a great variety, also, in these wonderful sermons. To
hear one of them only, a listener would come away
deeming the preacher *par éminence* a profound and most
discriminating critic. To hear another, he would consider him a philosopher, occupied entirely with the
vastest problems of science and theology. Again
another would leave the impression of a poet, as great
in his prose as the author of " In Memoriam " in verse.
And lastly and above all, there was always the man
filled with devout feeling, who by his very presence

and voice communicated reverence and the sense of the nearness of an all-seeing God.

I could write many pages concerning these Sunday experiences ; but I shall do better, I think, if I give my readers, who have never heard them, some small samples of what I carried away from time to time of them, as noted down in letters to my friend. Here are a few of them : —

" Mr. Martineau preached of aiming at perfection. At the end he drew a picture of a soul which has made such struggles but has failed. Then he supposed what must be the feeling of such a soul entering on the future life, its regrets ; and then inquired what influence being lifted above the things of sense, the nearness to God and holiness would have on it ? Would it then arise ? *Yes !* and the Father would say, 'This my son was dead and is alive again ; he was lost and is found for evermore.' I cannot tell you how beautiful it was, how true in the sense of those deepest intuitions which I hold to be certainly true *because* they bear with them the sense of being absolutely *highest,* the echo of a higher harmony than belongs to our poor minds. He seemed, for a moment, to be talking in the old conventional way about repentance *when too late ;* and then burst out in faith and hope, so far transcending all such ideas that one felt it came from another source."

" Mr. Martineau gave us a magnificent sermon on Sunday. I was in great luck not to miss it. One point was this. Our moral judgments are always founded on what we suppose to be the *inward motive* of the actor, not on the mere external act itself, which may be mischievous or beneficent in the highest degree, without, properly speaking, affecting our purely *ethical* judgment — *e. g.,* an unintentional homicide. Now if (as our opponents affirm) our moral sense came to us *ab extra,* merely as the current opinion which society has attached to injurious or beneficial actions, then we should *not* thus

decide our judgment by the *internal*, but by the external
and visible part of the act, by which alone society is
hurt or benefited. The fact that our moral judgment
regards *internal* things exclusively is evidence that it
springs from an *internal* source; and that we judge another, because we are compelled to judge ourselves in
the same way."

Here is a note I took after hearing another sermon : —

"'If we confess our sins, He is faithful and just to
forgive us our sins and to cleanse us from all unright-
eousness.'

"There are two ways of looking at sin common in
our time. One is to proclaim it so infinitely black that
God *cannot* forgive it except by a method of atonement
itself the height of injustice. The other is to treat it as
so venial that God may be counted on as certain to pass
it over at the first moment of regret; and all the threats
of conscience may be looked on as those of a nurse to
a refractory child; threats which are never to be executed. The first of these views seems to honor God
most, but really dishonors Him, by representing Him
as governing the world on a principle abhorrent to reason and justice. The second can never commend itself
save to the most shallow minds who make religion a
thing of words, and treat sin and repentance as trivial
things, instead of the most awful. How shall we solve
the mystery? It is equally unjust for God to treat the
guilty as if they were innocent, and the penitent as if
they were impenitent. Each fact has to be taken into
account, and the most important practical consequences
follow from the view we take of the matter. First, we
must never lose hold of the truth that, as Cause and
Effect are never severed in the natural world, and the
whole order of nature would fall to ruin were God ever
to interfere with them, so, likewise, guilt and pain are,

in His Providence, indissolubly linked; and the order of the moral world would be destroyed were they to be divided. But beside the realm of Law, in which the Divine penalties are unalterable, there is the free world of Spirit wherein our repentance avails. When we can say to God, 'Put me to grief, I have deserved it. Only restore me Thy love,' the great woe is gone. We shall be the weaker evermore for our fall, but we shall be restored."

The following remarks were in a letter to Miss Elliot : —

"January, 1867.

"I wish I could write a *résumé* of a sermon which Mr. Martineau preached last Sunday. Just think how many sermons some people would make of this one sentence of his text (speaking of the longing for rest): 'If duty become laborious, do it more fervently. If love become a source of care and pain, love more nobly and more tenderly. If doubts disturb and torture, face them with more earnest thought and deeper study!'

"This was not a *peroration*, but just one phrase of a discourse full of other such things.

"It seems to me that the spontaneous response of our inner souls to such ideas is just the same proof of their truth as the shock we feel in our nerves when a lecturer has delivered a current of electricity proves *his* lesson to be true."

"January, 1867.

"While you were enjoying your cathedral, I was enjoying Little Portland Street Chapel, having bravely tramped through miles of snow on the way, and been rewarded. Mr. Martineau said we were always taunted with only having a *negative* creed, and were often foolish enough to deny it. But all reformation is a negation of error and return to the three pure articles of faith — God, Duty, Immortality. . . . The distinction was admirably drawn between *extent of creed* and *intensity of faith*."

On February 5th, 1871, Mr. Martineau preached : —

" Philosophers might and do say that all religion is only a projection of man himself on nature, lending to nature his own feelings, brightened by a supreme love or shadowed by infinite displeasure. Does this disprove religion ? Is there no reliance to be placed on the faculties which connect us with the infinite ? We have two sets of faculties : our senses, which reveal the outer world ; and a deeper series, giving us poetry, love, religion. Should we say that these last are more false than the others ? They are true *all round*. In fact, these are truest. Imagination is true. Affection is true. Do men say that affection is blind ? No ! It is the only thing which truly sees. Love alone really perceives. The cynic draws over the world a roof of dark and narrow thoughts and suspicions, and then complains of the close, unhealthy air. Memory, again, is more than mere Recollection. It has the true artist-power of seizing the points which determine the character and reconstructing the image without details. Suppose there be a God. By what faculties could we know Him save by those which now tell us of Him. And why should they deceive us ? "

Alas ! the exercise of preaching every Sunday became too great for Dr. Martineau to encounter after 1872, and, by his physician's orders, those noble sermons came to an end.

Beside Dr. Martineau, I had the privilege of friendship with three eminent Unitarian ministers, now, alas ! all departed — Rev. Charles Beard, of Liverpool, for a long time editor of the " Theological Review ; " the venerable and beloved John James Tayler ; and Rev. William Henry Channing, to whom I was gratefully attached, both on account of religious sympathies, and of his ardent adoption of our anti-vivisection cause, which he told me he had at first regarded as somewhat of a " fad " of mine, but came to recognize as a moral

crusade of deep significance. Among living friends of
the same body, I am happy to number Rev. Philip
Wicksteed, the successor of Dr. Martineau in Portland
Street, and the exceedingly able President of University
Hall, Gordon Square — an institution in the founda-
tion of which I gladly took part on the invitation of
Mrs. Humphrey Ward.

A man in whose books I had felt great interest in my
old studies at Newbridge, and whose intercourse was a
real pleasure to me in London, was Mr. W. R. Greg. I
intensely respected the courage which moved him, in
those early days of the Fifties, to publish such a book
as the "Creed of Christendom." He was then a young
man, entering public life with the natural ambitions
which his great abilities justified, and the avowal of
such exorbitant heresies (nothing short of pure Theism)
as the book contained was enough at that date to spoil
any man's career. He was a layman, too, and man of
the world. " *Que Diable allait-il faire*, writing on theology at all ? " That book remains to this day a most valuable manual of arguments and evidences against the
" Creed of Christendom," set forth in a grave and reverent spirit and in a clear and manly style. His " Enigmas
of Life " had, I believe, a larger literary success. The
world had moved much nearer to his standpoint ; and
the " Enigmas " concern the most interesting subjects.
We had a little friendly controversy over one passage
in the essay, " Elsewhere." Mr. Greg had laid it down
that, hereafter, Love must retreat from the discovery of
the sinfulness of the beloved ; and that both saint and
sinner will accept as inevitable an eternal separation
(" Enigmas," first edition, p. 263.) To this I demurred
strenuously in my " Hopes of the Human Race " (pp.
132–6). I said, "The poor self-condemned soul whom
Mr. Greg images as turning away in an agony of shame
and hopelessness from the virtuous friend he loved on
earth, and loves still at an immeasurable distance —

such a soul is not outside the pale of love, divine or
human. Nay, is he not — even assuming his guilt to
be black as night — only in a similar relation to the
purest of created souls, which that purest soul holds to
the All-Holy One above? If God can love *us*, is it not
the acme of moral presumption to think of a human
soul being too pure to love any sinner, so long as in him
there remains any vestige of affection? The whole problem is unreal and impossible. In the first place, there
is a potential moral equality between all souls capable
of equal love, and the one can never reach a height
whence it may justly despise the other. And, in the
second place, the higher the virtuous soul may have risen
in the spiritual world, the more it must have acquired
the god-like Insight which beholds the good under the
evil, and not less the god-like Love which embraces the
repentant prodigal."

In the next edition of his "Enigmas" (the 7th),
after the issue of my book, Mr. Greg wrote a most generous recantation of his former view. He said: —

"The force of these objections to my delineation
cannot be gainsaid, and ought not to have been over-
looked. No doubt a soul that can so love and so feel its
separation from the objects of its love cannot be wholly
lost. It must still retain elements of recovery and re-
demption, and qualities to win and to merit answering
affection. The lovingness of a nature — its capacity
for strong and deep attachment — must constitute, there
as here, the most hopeful characteristic out of which to
elicit and foster all other good. No doubt, again, if the
sinful continue to love in spite of their sinfulness, the
blessed will not cease to love in consequence of their
blessedness."

Later on he asks : —

"How can the blessed enjoy anything to be called
happiness if the bad are writhing in hopeless an-
guish?" "Obviously only in one way. By *ceasing*

to love, that is, by renouncing the best and purest part of their nature. . . . Or, to put it in still bolder language, '*How — given a hell of torment and despair for millions of his friends and fellow men — can the good enjoy Heaven* except *by becoming bad*, and without being miraculously changed for the worse ? ' "

The following flattering letters are unluckily all which I have kept of Mr. Greg's writing : —

PARK LODGE, WIMBLEDON COMMON, S. W., February 19th.

MY DEAR MISS COBBE, — I have been solacing myself this morning, after a month of harrowing toil, with your paper in the last "Theological," and I want to tell you how much it has gratified me.

I don't mean your appreciative cordiality towards myself, nor your criticisms on a portion of my speculations, which, however (though I fancy you have rather misread me), I will refer to again and try to profit by. I dare say you are mainly right, the more so as I see Mr. Thom in the same number remonstrates in an identical tone.

That your paper is, I think, not only beautiful in thought and much of it original, but singularly full of rich suggestions, and one of the most real *contributions* to a further conception of a possible future that I have met with for long. It is real *thought* — not like most of mine, mere sentiment and imagination.

I don't know if you are still in town, or have begun the villegiatura you spoke of when I last saw you, but I daresay this note will be forwarded.

When did No. 1 appear ?

I particularly like your remark about self-*reprobation*, p. 456, and from 463 onward. By the way, do you know Isaac Taylor's "Physical Theory of Another Life ? " It is very curious and interesting.

Yours faithfully,

W. R. GREG.

I have just finished an introduction (about 100 pp.) to a new edition of "The Creed of Christendom," which will be published in the autumn, and it contains some thoughts very analogous to yours.

PARK LODGE, WIMBLEDON COMMON, S. W., August 6th.

MY DEAR MISS COBBE, — I have read your "Town and Country Mouse" with much pleasure. I should have enjoyed your paper still more if I had not felt that it was suggested by your intention to cut London, and the desire to put as good a face upon that regrettable design as you could. However, you have stated the case with remarkable fairness. I, who am a passionate lover of nature, who have never lived in town, and should pine away if I attempted it, still feel in the decline of years the increasing necessity of creeping *towards* the world rather than retiring from it. I feel, as one grows old, the want of external stimulus to stave off stagnation. The vividness of youthful thought is needed, I think, to support solitude.

I retired to Westmoreland for fifteen years in the middle of life when I was much worn, and it did me good; but I was glad to come back to active life, and I think my present location — Wimbledon Common for a cottage, within five miles of London, and coming in five days a week — is perfection.

I dare say you may be right; but all your friends will miss you much — I not the least.

Yours faithfully,
W. R. GREG.

Mr. Greg's allusion to my "Town and Country Mouse" reminds me of a letter which was sent me by some unknown reader on the publication of that article. It repeats a famous story worth recording as told thus by an ear-witness who, though anonymous, is obviously worthy of credit.

Will Miss Cobbe kindly pardon the liberty taken by a reader of her delightful " Town and Country Mouse " in venturing to substitute the true version of Sir George Lewis' too famous dictum ?

In the *hearing of the writer* he was asked (by one of his subordinates in the Government) as they were getting into the train, returning to town : —

" Well ! How do you like life in Herefordshire ? "

" Ah ! It would be very tolerable, if it were not for *the amusements,*" was his reply.

Miss Cobbe has high authority for the mis-quotation : for the " Times " invariably commits it ; and the present writer has again and again intended to correct it, and failed to execute the intention.

If they *are* pleasures, they are *pleasures ;* and the paradox is absurd, instead of amusing ; but the oppressive stupidity of many of the " *amusements* " (to the author of " Influence of Authority," etc. !) may well call up in the mind the sort of amiable cynicism, which was a feature of his own character.

On arriving late and unexpectedly at home for a fortnight's *Rest,* he found his own study occupied by two young ladies (sisters) as a *bedroom* — it being the night of Lady Theresa's ball ! With his exquisite good nature he simply set about finding some other roost ; and all the complaint he ever made was *that ;* which has become perhaps *not* too famous !

At the time of the Franco-Prussian war, as will be remembered by every one living at the time in London, the cleavage between the sympathizers with the two contending countries was almost as sharp as it had previously been during the American War between the partisans of the North and of the South. Dean Stanley was one of our friends who took warmly the side of the Germans, and I naturally sent him a letter I had received from a Frenchman whom we both respected, remonstrating rather bitterly against the attitude of England. The Dean, in returning M. P.'s letter, wrote as follows : — [1]

DEANERY, March 25th, 1871.

DEAR MISS COBBE, — Although you kindly excuse me from doing so, I cannot but express, and almost, wish that you could convey to M. P., the melancholy interest with which we have read his letter. Interesting of course it is, but to us — I know not whether to you — it is deeply sad to see a man like M. P. so thoroughly blind to the true situation of his country. Not a word of repentance for the aggressive and unjust war! not a word of acknowledgment that, had the French, as they wished, invaded Germany, they would have entered Berlin and seized the Rhenish provinces without remorse or compunction! — not a spark of appreciation of the moral superiority by which the Germans achieved their successes! I do not doubt that excesses may have been committed by the German troops; but I feel sure that they have been exceeded by those of the French, and would have been yet more had the French entered Germany.

And how very superfluous to attack us for having done just the same as in 1848! Our sad crime was not to have prevented the war by remonstrating with the French Emperor and people in July, 1870, and of *that* poor P. takes no account! Alas! for France!

Yours sincerely,

A. P. STANLEY.

The following is a rather important note as recording the Dean's sentiments as regarded Cardinal Newman.

[1] Most of the following letters were lent by me to Mr. Walrond when he was preparing the biography of Dean Stanley, and in returning them he said that he had kept copies of them, and meant to include them in his book. The present editor not having used them, I feel myself at liberty to print them here.

I cannot recall what was the paper which I had sent him to which he alludes. I think I had spoken to him of my friendship with Francis Newman, and of the information given me by the latter that he could never remember his brother putting his hand to a single cause of benevolence or moral reform. I had asked him to solicit his support with that of Cardinal Manning (already obtained) to the cause for which I was then beginning to work — on behalf of animals.

January 15th, 1875.

MY DEAR MISS COBBE, — I return this with many thanks. I think you must have sent it to me, partly as a rebuke for having so nearly sailed in the same boat of ignorance and inhumanity with Dr. Newman.

I have just finished, with a mixture of weariness and nausea, his letter to the Duke of Norfolk. Even the fierce innuendoes and deadly thrusts at Manning cannot reconcile me to such a mass of cobwebs and evasions. When the sum of the theological teaching of the two brothers is weighed, will not " the *Soul* " of Francis be found to counterbalance, as a contribution to true, solid, catholic (even in any sense of the word) Christianity, all the writings of John Henry?

I have sent my paper on Vestments to the " Contemporary."   Yours sincerely,

A. P. STANLEY.

Read it in the light of his old letter to B. Ullathorne, published in (illegible).

The paper on Vestments, to which Dean Stanley alludes, had interested and amused me much when he read it at Sion College, and I had urged him to send it to one of the Reviews. Here is a report of that evening's proceedings which I sent next day to my friend Miss Elliot.

January 14th, 1875.

I do so much wish you had been with us last night at Sion College.   Dean Stanley was more delightful than ever.   He read a splendid paper, full of learning, wit, and sense on " Ecclesiastical Vestments."   In the course of it he said, referring to the position of the altar, etc., that on this subject he had nothing to add to the remarks of his friend, the Dean of Bristol, " whose authority on all matters connected with English ecclesiastical history was universally admitted to be the best."   After the reading of his paper, which lasted an hour and a quarter, that odious Dr. L——— got up, and in his mincing brogue attacked Dean Stanley very rudely.   Then they called on Martineau, and he made a charming speech, beginning by saying *he* had nothing to do with vestments, having received no ordination, and might for his part repeat the poem, " Nothing to Wear!"   Then he went on to say that if the Church were ever to regain the Nonconformists, it would certainly *not* be by proceeding in the sacerdotal direction.   He was much cheered.   Rev. H. White made, I thought, one of the best speeches of the evening.   Altogether, it was exceedingly amusing.

On the occasion of the interment of Sir Charles Lyell in Westminster Abbey, I sent the Dean, by his request, some hints respecting Sir Charles's views and character, and received the following reply : —

February 25th, 1875.

MY DEAR MISS COBBE, — Your letter is invaluable to me.   Long as was my acquaintance with Sir Charles Lyell, and kind as he was to me, I never knew him intimately, and therefore most of what you tell me was new. The last time he spoke to me was in urging me with the greatest earnestness to ask Colenso to preach.   Can you tell me one small point ?   Had he a turn for music ?

I must refer back to the last funeral (when I could not preach) of Sir Sterndale Bennett, and it would be a convenience for me to know this, *Yes* or *No.*

You will come (if you come to the sermon) and any friends — *thro' the Deanery* at 2.45 on Sunday.

Yours sincerely,

A. P. STANLEY.

Some time after this I sent him one of my theological articles on the Life after Death. He acknowledged it thus kindly : —

DEANERY, November 2d.

DEAR MISS COBBE, — Many thanks. Your writing on this subject is to me more nearly to the truth — at least more nearly to my hopes and desires — than almost any others which are now floating around us.

Yours sincerely,

A. P. STANLEY.

This next letter again referred to one of my books — and to Cardinal Newman : —

October 12th, 1876.

MY DEAR MISS COBBE, — Many thanks for your book. You will see by my letter last night that I had already made good progress in it ; as borrowed from the library. I shall much value it.

Do not trouble yourself about Newman's letter. I am much more anxious that the public should see it than that I should. I am amazed at the impression made upon me by the "Characteristics" of Newman. Most of the selections I had read before ; but the net result is of a farrago of fanciful, disingenuous nonentities ; all except the personal reminiscences.

Yours truly, A. P. STANLEY.

One day I had been calling on him at the Deanery, and said to him, after describing my office in Victoria

Street and our frequent committee meetings there:
"Now, Mr. Dean, *do* you think it right and as it ought
to be, that *I* should sit at that table as Honorable
Secretary with Lord Shaftesbury on my right, and
Cardinal Manning on my left — and that *you* should
not sit opposite to complete the "Reunion of Christendom?" He laughed heartily, agreed he certainly
ought to be there, and promised to come. But time
failed, and only his honored name graced our lists.

The following is the last letter I have preserved of
Dean Stanley's writing. It is needless to say how
much pleasure it gave me : —

October 16th, 1876.

DEAR MISS COBBE, — I have just finished re-reading
with real admiration and consolation your "Hopes of
the Human Race." May I ask these questions : 1. Is
it in, or coming into, a second edition ? If the latter,
is it too much to suggest that the note on p. 3 could, if
not omitted, be modified ? I appreciate the motive for
its insertion, but it makes the lending and recommending of the book difficult. 2. Who is "one of the
greatest men of science" — p. 20 ? 3. Where is there
an authentic appearance of the Pope's reply to Odo
Russell — p. 107 ? Yours sincerely,

A. P. STANLEY.

I afterwards learned from Dean Stanley, one day
when I was visiting him at the Deanery after his wife's
death, that he had read these essays to Lady Augusta
in the last weeks of her life, finding them, as he told
me, the most satisfactory treatment of the subject he
had met; and that after her death he read them
over again. He gave me with much feeling a sad
photograph of her as a dying woman, after telling me
this. Mr. Motley, the historian of the Netherlands,
having also lost his wife not long afterwards, spoke
to Dean Stanley of his desire for some book on the sub-

ject which would meet his doubts, and Dean Stanley
gave him this one of mine.

Dean Stanley, it is needless to say, was the most
welcome of guests in every house which he entered.
There was something in his *high-mindedness*, I can use
no other term, his sense of the glory of England, his
love of his church (on extremely Erastian principles!)
as the National Religion, his unfailing courtesy, his
unaffected enjoyment of drollery and gossip, and his
almost youthful excitement about each important subject which cropped up, which made him delightful to
every one in turn. There was no man in London I
think whom it gave me such pleasure to meet "in the
sixties and seventies" as the "Great Dean;" and he
was uniformly most kind to me. The last occasion, I
think, on which I saw him in full spirits was at a house
where the pleasantest people were constantly to be
found — that of Mr. and Mrs. Simpson, in Cornwall
Gardens. Renan and his wife were there, and I was
so favored as to be seated next to Renan; Dean Stanley being on the other side of our tactful hostess. The
Dean had been showing Renan over the Abbey in the
morning, and they were both in the gayest mood, but I
remember Dean Stanley speaking to Renan with inde-
scribable and concentrated indignation of the avowal
Mr. Gladstone had recently made that the Clerkenwell
explosion had caused him to determine on the disestab-
lishment of the Irish Church.

I have found an old letter to my friend describing
this dinner: —

"I had a most amusing evening yesterday. Kind
Mrs. Simpson made me sit beside Renan; and Dean
Stanley was across the corner, so we made, with nice Mrs.
W. R. G. and Mr. M., a very jolly little party at our end
of the table. The Dean began with grace, rather *sotto
voce*, with a blink at Renan, who kept on never minding.
His (Renan's) looks are even worse than his picture

leads one to expect. His face is exactly like a *hog*, so
stupendously broad across the ears and jowl! But he
is very gentlemanly in manner, very winning, and full
of fun and *finesse*. We had to talk French with him,
but the Dean's French was so much worse than mine
that I felt quite at ease, and rattled away about the
'Triduos' at Florence (to appease the wrath of Heaven
on account of his 'Vie de Jésus'), and had some private
jokes with him about his malice in calling the Publi-
cans of the Gospels 'douaniers,' and the ass a 'baudet!'
He said he did it on purpose; and that when he was
last in Italy, numbers of poor people came to him and
asked him for the lucky number for the lotteries, because they thought he was *so near the Devil* he must
know! I gave him your message about the Hengwrt
MSS., and he apologized for having written about the
'mesquines' considerations which had caused them to
be locked up [to wit, that several leaves of the 'Red
Book of Hergest' had been stolen by too enthusiastic
Welsh scholars!], and solemnly vowed to alter the passage in the next edition, and thanked you for the promise of obtaining leave for him to see them.

"I also talked to M. Renan of his essay on the
'Poésie de la Race Celtique,' and made him laugh at
his own assertion that Irishmen had such a longing for
'the Infinite' that when they could not attain to it
otherwise they sought it through a strong liquor '*qui
s'appelle le Whiskey.*'"

Sir Mountstuart Grand-Duff's delightful volume on
Renan has opened to my mind many fresh reasons for
admiring the great French scholar, whose works I had
falsely imagined I had known pretty well before reading it. But when all is said, the impression he has left
on me (and I should think on most other people) is one
of disappointment and short-falling.

M. Renan has written of himself the well-known and
often laughed-at boast: "*Seul dans mon siècle j'ai pu*

comprendre Jésus Christ et St. François d'Assise!" I do not know about his comprehension of St. Francis, though I should think it a very great *tour de force* for the brilliant French academician and critic to throw himself into *that* typical mediæval mind! But as regarded the former Person I should say that of all the tens of thousands who have studied and written about him during these last nineteen centuries, Renan was in some respects the *least* able to "comprehend" him. The man who could describe the story of the Prodigal as a *"délicieuse parabole"* is as far out of Christ's latitude as the pole from the equator. One abhors æsthetics when things too sacred to be measured by their standard are commended in their name. Renan seems to me to have been for practical purposes a Pantheist without a glimmer of that sense of moral and personal relation to God which was the supreme characteristic of Christ. When he translates Christ's pity for the Magdalenes as jealousy *"pour la gloire de son Père dans ces belles créatures;"* and introduces the term *"femmes d'une vie équivoque"* as a rendering for "sinners," he strikes a note so false that no praise lavished afterwards can restore harmony.

The late Lord Houghton was one of the men of note whom I met occasionally at the houses of friends. I had known him in Italy and he was always kind to me and invited me to his Christmas parties at Frystone, which were said to be delightful, but to which I did not go. For a poet he had an extraordinarily rough exterior and blunt manner. One day we had a regular set-to argument lasting a long time. He attacked the order of things with the usual pessimist observations on all the evil in the world, and implied that I had no reasonable right to my faith. I answered as best I could, with some earnestness, and he finally concluded the discussion by remarking with concentrated contempt: "You might almost as well be a Christian!" Next day I

went to Westminster Abbey and was sitting in the
Dean's pew, when, to my amusement, Lord Houghton
came in just below, with a party of ladies, and took
a seat exactly opposite me. He behaved of course
with edifying propriety, but I could not help reflecting with a smile on our argument of the night before,
and wondering how many members of that and similar
congregations who were naturally counted by outsiders
as faithful supporters of the orthodox creed, were as
little so, *au fond*, as either Lord Houghton or I.

With Carlyle, though I saw him very frequently, I
never interchanged more than a few *banale* words of
civility. When his biography appeared, I was (as I
frankly told the illustrious biographer) exceedingly
glad that I had never given him the chance of attaching one of his pungent epigrams to my poor person. I
had been introduced to him by a lady at whose house
he happened to call one afternoon when I was sitting
with her, and where he showed himself (as it seems to
me the roughest men invariably do in the society of
amiable Countesses), — extremely *apprivoisé*. Also I
continually met him out walking with one or other of
his great historian friends, who were also mine, but I
avoided trespassing on their good nature ; or addressing
him when he walked up and down alone daily before
our door in Cheyne Walk — till one day, when he had
been very ill, I ventured to express my satisfaction in
seeing him out of doors again. He then answered me
kindly. I never shared the admiration felt for him by
so many able men who knew him personally, and therefore had means which I did not possess of estimating
him aright. (To me his books and himself represented
an anomalous sort of human Fruit. The original stock
was a hard and thorny Scotch peasant-character, with
a splendid intellect superadded. The graft was not
wholly successful. A flavor of the old acrid sloe was
always perceptible in the plum.)

The following letter was received by Dr. Hoggan in reply to a letter to Mr. Carlyle concerning vivisection:

KESTON LODGE, BECKENHAM,
28th August, 1875.

DEAR SIR,—Mr. Carlyle has received your letter, and has read it carefully. He bids me say that ever since he was a boy, when he read the account of Majendie's atrocities, he has never thought of the practice of vivisecting animals but with horror. I may mention that I have heard him speak of it in the strongest terms of disgust long before there was any speech about public agitation on the subject. He believes that the reports about the good results said to be obtained from the practice of vivisection to be immensely exaggerated; with the exception of certain experiments by Harvey and certain others by Sir Charles Bell, he is not aware of any conspicuous good that has resulted from it. But even supposing the good results to be much greater than Mr. Carlyle believes they are, and apart too from the shocking pain inflicted on the helpless animals operated upon, he would still think the practice so brutalizing to the operators that he would earnestly wish the law on the subject to be altered, so as to make vivisection even in institutions like that with which you are connected a most rare occurrence, and when practised by private individuals an indictable offence.

You are not sure that the operators on living animals "can be counted on your fingers." Mr. Carlyle with an equal share of certainty believes vivisection and other kindred experiments on living animals to be much more largely practised, and that they are by no means uncommonly undertaken by doctors' apprentices and "other miserable persons."

You are mistaken if you look upon the "Times" as a mirror of virtue; on this very subject when it at first began to be publicly discussed last winter, it printed a

letter from . . . which your letter itself would prove
to be altogether composed of falsehoods.

With Mr. Carlyle's compliments and good wishes,

      I remain, dear sir,

          Yours truly,

            MARY CARLYLE AITKEN.

Mr. Carlyle supported our Anti-vivisection Society
from the outset, for which I was very grateful to him;
but having promised to join our first important deputation to the Home Office, to urge the Government to
bring in a Bill in accordance with the recommendations
of the Royal Commission, he failed at the last moment
to put in an appearance, having learned that Cardinal
Manning was to be also present. I was told that he
said he would not appear in public with the Cardinal,
who was, he thought, " the chief emissary of Beelzebub
in England!" When this was repeated to me, my
remark was: " Infidels *is riz!* Time was when Cardinals would not appear in public with infidels ! "

Nothing has surprised me more in reading the memoirs and letters of Mr. and Mrs. Carlyle than the
small interest either of them seems to have felt in the
great subjects which formed the lifework of their many
illustrious visitors. While humbler folk who touched
the same circles were vehemently attracted, or else
repelled, by the political, philosophical, and theological
theories and labors of such men as Mazzini, Mill, Colenso, Jowett, Martineau, and Darwin, and every conversation and almost every letter contained new facts, or animated discussions regarding them, the Carlyles received
visits from these great men continually, with (it would
seem) little or no interest in their aims or views one
way or the other, in approval or disapproval ; and wrote
and talked much more seriously about the delinquencies
of their own maidservants, and the great and never to
be sufficiently appealed against cock and hen nuisance.

I had known Cardinal Manning in Rome about 1861 or 1863 when he was "Monsignor Manning," and went a little into English society, resplendent in a beautiful violet robe. He was very busy in those days making converts among English young ladies, and one with whom we were acquainted, the daughter of a celebrated authoress, fell into his net. He had, at all times, a gentle way of ridiculing English doings and prejudices which was no doubt telling. One of the stories he told me was of an Italian sacristan asking him "what was the 'Red Prayer Book' which all the English tourists carried about and read so devoutly in the churches" (of course Murray's "Hand-books").[1]

A few years afterwards, when he had returned to England as Archbishop of Westminster, I met him pretty frequently at Miss Stanley's house in Grosvenor Crescent. He there attacked me cheerfully one evening: "Miss Cobbe, I have found out something against you. I have discovered that Voltaire was part owner of a slave-ship!"

"I beg you to believe," said I, "that I have no responsibility whatever respecting Voltaire! But I would ask your Grace, whether it be not true that Las Casas, the saintly Dominican, *founded* negro slavery in America?" A Church of England friend coming up and laughing, I discharged a second barrel: "And was not the Protestant saint, Newton of Olney — much worse than all — the *Captain* of a Slave-ship?"[2]

One evening at this pleasant house I was standing on

---

[1] We had many good stories floating about in Rome at that time and he was always ready to enjoy them, but one, I think, told me by the painter Penry Williams, would not have tickled him as it did us heretics. The Pope, it seems, offered one of his Cardinals (whose reputation was far from immaculate) a pinch of snuff. The Cardinal replied more facetiously than respectfully, "*Non ho questo vizio, Santo Padre.*" Pius IX. observed quietly, snapping his snuffbox, "*Se vizio fosse, l' avreste*" (If it had been a vice you would have had it)!

[2] Curiously enough, I have had occasion to repeat this remark this spring (1894) in a controversy in the columns of the *Catholic Times.*

the rug in one of the rooms talking to Mr. Matthew Arnold and two or three other acquaintances of the same set. The Archbishop on entering shook hands with each of us, and we were all talking in the usual easy, sub-humorous, London way when a tall military-looking man, a Major G., came in, and seeing Manning, walked straight up to him, went down on one knee and kissed his ring! A bomb falling amongst us would scarcely have been more startling; and Manning, Englishman as he was to the backbone under his fine Roman feathers, was obviously disconcerted, though dignified as ever.

In a letter to a friend dated Feb. 19th, 1867, I find I said : —

"I had an amusing conversation with Archbishop Manning the other night at Miss Stanley's. He was most good-humored, coming up to me as I was talking to Sir C. Trevelyan about Rome, and saying, 'I am glad you think of going to Rome next winter, Miss Cobbe. It proves you expect the Pope to be firmly established there still.' We had rather a long talk about Passaglia who he says *has* recanted (a fact I heard strongly contradicted later). Mr. J. (now Sir H. J.!) came behind him in the midst of our talk and almost pitched the Archbishop on me, with such a push as I never saw given in a drawing-room! The Dean and Lady Augusta came in later, and she asked eagerly : 'Where was Manning ?' having never seen him. He had gone away, so I told her of the enthusiastic meeting which had afforded a spectacle to us all an hour before, between him and Archdeacon Denison. It was quite a scene of ecclesiastical reconciliation ; a ' Re-union of Christendom !' (They had been told each that the other was in the adjoining room, and Archdeacon Denison literally rushed with both hands outspread to meet the Cardinal, whom he had not seen since his conversion.) "

In later years I received at least half a dozen notes from time to time from His Eminence asking for details of our anti-vivisection work, and exhibiting his anxiety to master the facts on which he proposed to speak at our meetings. Here are some of these notes : —

ARCHBISHOP'S HOUSE, WESTMINSTER, S. W., 2.
June 12th, 1882.

DEAR MISS COBBE, — I should be much obliged if you would send me some recent facts or utterances of the Mantegazza kind, for the meeting at Lord Shaftesbury's. I have for a long time lost all reckoning from overwork, and need to be posted up.

Believe me, always faithfully yours,
HENRY E., CARDINAL ARCHBISHOP.

CARDINAL MANNING TO MISS F. P. C.

EASTERN ROAD, BRIGHTON.

DEAR MISS COBBE, — I can assure you that my slowness in answering your letter has not arisen from any diminution of care on vivisection. I was never better able to understand it, for I have been for nearly three weeks in pain day and night from neuralgia in the right arm, which makes writing difficult.

I have not seen Mr. Holt's bill, and I do not know what it aims at.

Before I can say anything, I wish to be fully informed. The bill of last year does not content me.

But we must take care not to weaken what we have gained. I hope to stay here over Sunday, and should be much obliged if you could desire some one to send me a copy of Mr. Holt's bill.

Has sufficient organized effort been made to enforce Mr. Cross's act?

Believe me, always yours very truly,
HENRY E., CARDINAL ARCHBISHOP.

DEAR MISS COBBE, — I will attend the meeting of the 26th unless hindered by some unforeseen necessity, but I must ask you to send me a brief. I am so driven by work that for some time I have fallen behind your proceedings. Send me one or two points marked and I will read them up.

My mind is more than ever fixed on this subject.

Believe me, yours faithfully,

HENRY E., CARDINAL ARCHBISHOP.

MY DEAR MISS COBBE, — For the last three weeks I have been kept to the house by one of my yearly colds; but if possible I will be present at the meeting of the society. If I should be unable to be there I will write a letter.

I clearly see that the proposed Physiological and Pathological Institute would be centre and sanction of ever advancing vivisection.

I hope you are recovering health and strength by your rest in the country.

Believe me, always faithfully yours,

HENRY E., CARDINAL ARCHBISHOP.

MY DEAR MISS COBBE, — My last days have been so full that I have not been able to write. I thank you for your letter, and for the contents of it. The highest counsel is always the safest and best, cost us what it may. We may take the cost as the test of its rectitude.

I hope you will go on writing against this inflation of vain glory calling itself science.

Believe me, always very truly yours,

HENRY E., CARDINAL ARCHBISHOP.

At no less than seven of our annual meetings (at one of which he presided) did Cardinal Manning make speeches. All these I have myself reprinted in an ornamental pamphlet to be obtained at 20, Victoria Street. The reasons for his adoption of our anti-vivisection cause were, I am sure, mainly moral and humane; but I think an incident which occurred in Rome not long before our campaign began may have impressed on his mind a regret that the Catholic Church had hitherto done nothing on behalf of the lower animals, and a desire to take part himself in a humane crusade and so rectify its position before the Protestant world.

Pope Pio IX. had been addressed by the English in Rome through Lord Ampthill (then Mr. Odo Russell, our representative there) with a request for permission to found a Society for Prevention of Cruelty to Animals in Rome; where (as all the world knows) it was almost as deplorably needed as at Naples. After a considerable delay, the formal reply through the proper office was sent to Mr. Russell *refusing* the (indispensable) permission. The document conveying this refusal expressly stated that "a society for such a purpose could not be sanctioned in Rome. Man owed duties to his fellow men; but he owed no duties to the lower animals; therefore, though such societies might exist in Protestant countries they could not be allowed to be established in Rome.

The late Lord Arthur Russell, coming back from Italy to England just after this event, told me of it with great detail, and assured me that he had seen the Papal document in his brother's possession; and that if I chose to publish the matter in England, he would guarantee the truth of the story at any time. I *did* very much choose to publish it, thinking it was a thing which ought to be proclaimed on the housetops; and I repeated it in seven or eight different publications, ranging from the "Quarterly Review" to the "Echo."

Soon after this, if I remember rightly, began the anti-
vivisection movement, and almost immediately when
the Society for Protection of Animals from Vivisection
(afterwards called the Victoria Street Society) was
founded, by Dr. Hoggan and myself, Cardinal Manning
gave us his name and active support. He took part in
our first deputation to the Home Office, and spoke at
our first meeting, which was held on the 10th June,
1876, at the Westminster Palace Hotel. On that occasion, when it came to the Cardinal's turn to speak, he
began at once to say that "much misapprehension existed as to the attitude of his Church on the subject of
duty to animals." [As he said this, with his usual
clear, calm, deliberate enunciation, he looked me
straight in the face and I looked at him!] He proceeded to say: "It was true that man owed no duty
directly to the brutes, but he owed it to God, whose
creatures they are, to treat them mercifully."

This was, I considered, a very good way of reconcil-
ing adhesion to the Pope's doctrine with humane principles; and I greatly rejoiced that such a *mezzo-termine*
could be put forward on authority. Of course in my
private opinion the Cardinal's ethics were theoretically
untenable, seeing that if it were possible to conceive of
such a thing as a creature made by a man (as people in
the thirteenth century believed that Arnaldus de Villa-
Nova had made a living man), or even such a thing as
a creature made by the Devil, that most wretched being would still have a right to be spared pain if *he were
sensitive to pain;* and would assuredly be a proper object of measureless compassion. That a dog or horse is
a creature of God; that its love and service to us come
of God's gracious provisions for us; that the animal is
unoffending to its Creator, while we are suppliants for
forgiveness for our offences; all these are true and tender reasons for *additional* kindness and care for these
our dumb fellow-creatures. But they are not (as the

Cardinal's argument would seem to imply) the *only* reasons for showing mercy towards them.

Nevertheless it was a great step — I may say an historical event — that a principle practically including universal humanity to the lower animals should have been enunciated publicly and formally by a "Prince of the Church" of Rome. That Cardinal Manning was not only the first great Roman prelate to lay down any such principle, but that he far outran many of his contemporaries and co-religionists in so doing, has become painfully manifest this year (1894) from the numerous letters from priests which have appeared in the "Tablet" and "Catholic Times," bearing a very different complexion. Cardinal Manning repeated almost *verbatim* the same explanation of his own standpoint in his speech on March 9th, 1887, when he occupied the chair at our annual meeting. He said: —

"It is perfectly true that obligations and duties are between moral persons, and therefore the lower animals are not susceptible of those moral obligations which we owe to one another; but we owe a seven-fold obligation to the Creator of those animals. Our obligation and moral duty is to Him who made them, and, if we wish to know the limit and the broad outline of our obligation, I say at once it is His Nature and His perfections; and, among those perfections, one is most profoundly that of eternal mercy. (Hear, hear.) And, therefore, although a poor mule or a poor horse is not indeed a moral person, yet the Lord and Maker of that mule and that horse is the highest law-giver, and His Nature is a law to Himself. And, in giving a dominion over His creatures to man, He gave them subject to the condition that they should be used in conformity to His own perfections, which is His own law, and, therefore, our law."

On the first occasion a generous Roman Catholic nobleman present gave me £20 to have the Cardinal's speech translated into Italian and widely circulated in Italy.

I have good reason to believe that when Cardinal Manning went to Rome after the election of Leo XIII. he spoke earnestly to His Holiness on the subject of cruelty to animals generally in Italy, and especially concerning vivisection, and that he understood the Pope to agree with him and sanction his attitude. I learned this from a private source, but His Eminence referred to it quite unmistakably in his speech at Lord Shaftesbury's house on the 21st June, 1882, as follows : —

"I am somewhat concerned to say it, but I know that an impression has been made that those whom I represent look, if not with approbation, at least with great indulgence, at the practice of vivisection. I grieve to say that abroad there are a great many (whom I beg to say I do not represent) who do favor the practice; but this I do protest, that there is not a religious instinct in nature, nor a religion of nature, nor is there a word in revelation, either in the Old Testament or the New Testament, nor is there to be found in the great theology which I do represent, no, nor in any Act of the Church of which I am a member, no, nor in the lives and utterances of any one of those great servants of that Church who stand as examples, nor is there an authoritative utterance anywhere to be found in favor of vivisection. There may be the chatter, the prating, and the talk of those who know nothing about it. And I know what I have stated to be the fact, for some years ago I took a step known to our excellent secretary, and brought the subject under the notice and authority where alone I could bring it. And those before whom it was laid soon proved to have been profoundly ignorant of the outlines of the alphabet even of vivisection. They believed entirely that the practice of surgery and the science of anatomy owed everything to the discoveries of vivisectors. They were filled to the full with every false impression, but when the facts were made known to them, they experienced a revulsion of feeling."

Cardinal Manning also (as I happen likewise to know) made a great effort about 1878 or 1879, to induce the then General of the Franciscans to support the anti-vivisection movement *for love of St. Francis,* and his tenderness to animals. In this attempt, however, Cardinal Manning must have been entirely unsuccessful, as no modern Franciscan that ever I have heard of has stirred a finger on behalf of animals anywhere, or given his name to any society for protecting them either from vulgar or from scientific cruelty. Knowing this, I confess to feeling some impatience when the name of St. Francis and his amiable fondness for birds and beasts is perpetually flaunted whenever the lack of common humanity to animals visible in Catholic countries happens to be mentioned. It is a very small matter that a saint, six hundred years ago, sang with nightingales and fed wolves, if the monks of his own order and the priests of the Church which has canonized him never warn their flocks that to torment God's creatures is even a venial sin, and, when forced to notice barbarous cruelties to a brute, invariably reply, "*Non è Cristiano,*" as if all claims to compassion were dismissed by that consideration !

The answer of the General of the Franciscans to Cardinal Manning's touching appeal was, "that he had consulted his doctor and that his doctor assured him that *no such thing as vivisection was ever practised in Italy !* "

I was kindly permitted to call at Archbishop's House and see Cardinal Manning several times ; and I find the following little record of one of my first visits in a letter to my friend, written the same, or next day : —

"I had a very interesting interview with the Cardinal. I was shown into a vast, dreary dining-room quite monastic in its whitey-brown walls, poverty-stricken furniture, crucifix, and pictures of half a dozen Bishops who did not exhibit the 'Beauty of Holiness.' The Cardinal received me most kindly, and said he was so glad to see me, and that he was much better in health after a long illness. He is not much changed. It was droll to sit talking *tête-à-tête* with a man with a pink *octagon* on his venerable head, and various little scraps of scarlet showing here and there to remind one that '*Grattez*' the English gentleman and you will find the Roman Cardinal! He told me, really with effusion, that his heart was in our work; and he promised to go to the meeting to-morrow. . . . I told him we all wished *him* to take the chair. He said it would be much better for a layman like Lord Coleridge to do so. I said, 'I don't think you know the place you hold in English (I paused and added *avec intention*) *Protestant* estimation!' He laughed very good-humoredly and said: 'I think I do, very well.'"

At the meeting on the following day when he *did* take the chair, I had opportunities as honorable secretary, of which I did not fail to avail myself, of a little quiet conversation with His Eminence before the proceedings. (I spoke of the moral results of Darwinism on the character and remarked how paralyzing was the idea that Conscience was merely an hereditary instinct fixed in the brain by the interests of the tribe, and in no sense the voice of God in the heart or His law graven on the "fleshly tablets." He abounded in my sense, and augured immeasurable evils from the general adoption of such a philosophy. I asked him what was the Catholic doctrine of the origin of Souls. He answered, promptly and emphatically: "Oh, that each one is a distinct creation of God."

The last day on which His Eminence attended a

committee meeting in Victoria Street I had a little
conversation with him as usual, after business was
over; and reminded him that on every occasion when
he had previously attended, we had had our beloved
President, Lord Shaftesbury, present. "Shall I tell
Your Eminence," I asked, "what Mrs. F." (now Lady
B.) "told me Lord Shaftesbury said to her shortly before he died, about our committees here ? He said that
'if our society had done nothing else but bring you and
him together, and make you sit and work at the same
table for the same object, it would have been well
worth while to have founded it!'" "*Did* Lord Shaftesbury say that ?" said the Cardinal, with a moisture in
his eyes. "*Did* he say that ? I *loved* Lord Shaftesbury !"

And *these*, I reflected, were the men whom narrow
bigots of both creeds looked on as the very chiefs of
opposing camps and bitter enemies! The one rejoiced
at an *excuse* for meeting the other in friendly coöperation! The other said as his last word: "I *loved*
him !"

I was greatly touched by this little scene, and going
straight from it to the house of the friend who had
told me of Lord Shaftesbury's remark, I naturally
described it to her and to Mr. Lowell, who was taking
tea with us. "Ah, yes!" Lady B. said, "I remember it well, and I could show you the very tree in the
park where we were sitting when Lord Shaftesbury
made that remark. But " (she added) "why did you
not tell the Cardinal that he included *you?* What Lord
Shaftesbury said was that 'the society had brought the
Cardinal and you and himself to work together.'" Mr.
Lowell was interested in all this, and the evidence it
afforded of the width of mind of the great philanthropist, so often supposed to be " a narrow Evangelical."

Alas! he also has "gone over to the majority." I
met him often and liked him (as every one did)

extremely. Though in so many ways different, he had some of Mr. Gladstone's peculiar power of making every conversation wherein he took part interesting; of turning it off dusty roads into pleasant paths. He had not in the smallest degree that tiresome habit of *giving information* instead of *conveying impressions*, which makes some worthy people so unspeakably fatiguing as companions. I had once the privilege of sitting between him and Lord Tennyson when they carried on an animated conversation, and I could see how much the great poet was delighted with the lesser one, who was also a large-hearted statesman; a silver link between two great nations.

I shall account it one of the chief honors which have fallen to my lot that Tennyson asked leave, through his son, to pay me a visit. Needless to say I accepted the offer with gratitude and fortunately I was at home, in our little house in Cheyne Walk, when he called on me. He sat for a long time over my fire, and talked of poetry; of the share melodious words ought to have in it; of the hatefulness of scientific cruelty, against which he was going to write again; and of the new and dangerous phases of thought then apparent. Much that he said on the latter subject was, I think, crystallized in his " Locksley Hall Sixty Years Later." After he had risen to go and I had followed him to the stairs, I returned to my room and said from my heart, " *Thank God!* " The great poem which had been so much to me for half a lifetime was not spoiled; the Man and the Poet were one. Nothing that I had now seen and heard of him in the flesh jarred with what I had known of him in the spirit.

After this first visit I had the pleasure of meeting Lord Tennyson several times and of making Lady Tennyson's charming acquaintance; the present Lord Tennyson being exceedingly kind and friendly to me in welcoming me to their house. On one occasion when I met Lord Tennyson at the house of a mutual friend, he told me (with an innocent surprise which I could not but find diverting) that a certain great professor had been positively angry and rude to him about his lines " In the Children's Hospital " concerning those who "carve the living hound ! " I tried to explain to him the fury of the whole *clique* at the discovery that the consciences of the rest of mankind had considerably outstepped theirs in the matter of humanity, and that while they fancied themselves (in his words) "the heirs of all the ages, in the foremost files of time," it was really in the Dark Ages, as regarded humane sentiment — or at least one or two centuries past — in which they lingered; practising the art of torture on beasts, as men did on men in the sixteenth century. I also tried to explain to him that his ideal of a vivisector with red face and coarse hands was quite wrong, and as false as the representation of Lady Macbeth as a tall and masculine woman. Lady Macbeth *must* have been small, thin, and concentrated, not a big, bony, conscientious Scotch woman; and vivisectors (some of them at all events) are polished and handsome gentlemen, with peculiarly delicate fingers (for drawing out nerves, etc., as Cyon describes).

Lord Tennyson from the very first beginning of our anti-vivisection movement, in 1874, to the hour of his death, never once failed to append his name to every successive memorial and petition — and they were many — which I, and my successors, sent to him; and he accepted and held our honorable membership and afterwards the Vice-Presidency of our society from first to last.

The last time I saw Lord Tennyson was one day in London after I had taken luncheon at his house. When I rose to leave the table, and he shook hands with me at the door as we were parting, as we supposed, for that season, he said to me : " Good-bye,

Miss Cobbe — fight the good fight. Go on! Fight the good fight." I saw him no more; but I shall do his bidding, please God, to the end.

I shall insert here two letters which I received from Lord Tennyson which, though trifling in themselves, I prize as testimonies of his sympathy and good will. I am fortunately able to add to them two papers of some real interest — the contemporary estimate of Tennyson's first poems by his friends the Kembles; and the announcement of the death of Arthur Hallam by his friend John Mitchell Kemble to Fanny Kemble. They have come into my possession with a vast mass of family and other papers given me by Mrs. Kemble several years ago, and belong to a series of letters, marvellously long and closely written, by John Kemble, during and after his romantic expedition to Spain along with the future Archbishop Trench and the other young enthusiasts of 1830. The way in which John Mitchell Kemble speaks of his friend Alfred Tennyson's poems is satisfactory, but much more so is the beautiful testimony he renders to the character of Hallam. It is touching, and uplifting, too, to read the rather singular words "of a holier heart," applied to the subject of "In Memoriam," by his young companion.

FARRINGFORD, FRESHWATER, ISLE OF WIGHT,
June 4th, 1880.

DEAR MISS COBBE, — I have subscribed my name, and I hope that it may be of some use to your cause.

My wife is grateful to you for remembrance of her, and

I am, ever yours, A. TENNYSON.

ALDWORTH, HASLEMERE, SURREY,
January, 9th, 1882.

MY DEAR MISS COBBE, — I thank you for your essay, which I found very interesting, though perhaps

somewhat too vehement to serve your purpose. Have
you seen that terrible book by a Swiss (reviewed in
the "Spectator"), "Ayez Pitié"? Pray pardon my
not answering you before. I am so harried with letters
and poems from all parts of the world, that my friends
often have to wait for an answer.

Yours ever,   A. Tennyson.

Farringford, Freshwater, Isle of Wight,
June 12th, 1882.

Dear Miss Cobbe,—I am sorry to say that I shall
not be in London the 21st, so that I cannot be present
at your meeting. Many thanks for asking me. My
father has been suffering from a bad attack of gout,
and does not feel inclined to *write* more about vivisection. You have, as you know, his warmest good
wishes in all your great struggle. When are we to see
you again? Can you not pay us a visit at Haslemere
this summer?

With our kindest regards,
Yours very sincerely,
Hallam Tennyson.

Extract from letter from John M. Kemble to Fanny
Kemble. No date. In packet of 1830-1833 : —

"I am very glad that you like Tennyson's poems;
if you had any poetry in you, you could not help it; for
the general system of criticism and the notion that a
poet is to be appreciated by everybody, if he be a poet,
are mighty fallacies. It was only the high priest who
was privileged to enter the holy of holies; and so it
is with that other holy of holies, no less sacred and
replete with divinity, a great poet's mind: therein no
vulgar foot may tread. To meet this objection, it is
often said that all men appreciate, etc., etc., Shakespeare and Milton, etc. To this I answer by a direct
denial. Not one man in a hundred thousand cares

three straws for Milton; and though from being a
dramatic poet Shakespeare must be better understood
I believe I may say that not one in a hundred thousand
feels all that is to be felt in him. There is no man
who has done so much as Tennyson to express poetical
feeling by *sound*; Titian has done as much with colors.
Indeed, I believe no poet to have lived since Milton,
so perfect in his form, except Goethe. In this matter,
Shelley and Keats and Byron, even Wordsworth, have
been found wanting. Coleridge expresses the greatest
admiration for Charles Tennyson's sonnets; we have
sent him Alfred's poems, which, I am sure, will delight
him."

Extract from letter from John Mitchell Kemble to
Fanny Kemble : —

"It is with feelings of inexpressible pain that I
announce to you the death of poor Arthur Hallam, who
expired suddenly from an attack of apoplexy at Vienna,
on the 15th of last month. Though this was always
feared by us as likely to occur, the shock has been a bitter one to bear; and most of all so to the Tennysons,
whose sister Emily he was to have married. I have
not yet had the courage to write to Alfred. This is a
loss which will most assuredly be felt by this age, for
if ever man was born for great things he was. Never
was a more powerful intellect joined to a purer and
holier heart; and the whole illuminated with the rich-
est imagination, the most sparkling yet the kindest wit.
One cannot lament for him that he is gone to a far better life, but we weep over his coffin and wonder that we
cannot be consoled. The Roman epitaph on two young
children : *Sibimet ipsis dolorem abstulerunt, suis reli-
quere* (from themselves they took away pain, to their
friends they left it!) is always present to my mind, and
somehow the miserable feeling of loneliness comes over
one even though one knows that the dead are happier
than the living. His poor father was with him only.

They had been travelling together in Hungary and were on their return to England; but there had been nothing whatever to announce the fatal termination of their journey; indeed, bating fatigue, Arthur had been unusually well. Our other friends, though all mourning for him as if he had been our brother, are well."

In my chapter on Italy I have written some pages concerning Mr. and Mrs. Browning, and printed two or three kind letters from him to me. It is a great privilege, I now feel, to have known even in such slight measure these two great poets. But what an unspeakable blessing and honor it has been for England all through the Victorian Age to have for her representatives and teachers in the high realm of poetry two such men as Tennyson and Browning: men of immaculate honor, blameless and beautiful lives and lofty and pure inspiration! Not one word which either has ever published need be blotted out by any recording angel, and, widely different as they were, their high doctrine was the same. The one tells us that "good" will be "the final goal of ill; " the other that —

> "God 's in His Heaven !
> All 's right with the world! ' "

I have had also the good fortune to find other English poets ready to sympathize with me on the subject of vivisection. Sir Henry Taylor wrote many letters to me upon it and called my attention to his own lines which go so deep into the philosophy of the question, and which I have since quoted so often : —

> "Pain in man
> Bears the high mission of the flail and fan,
> In brutes 't is purely piteous."

Here is one of his notes to me : —

THE ROOST, BOURNEMOUTH, November 25th, 1875.

DEAR MISS COBBE, — I return your papers that they may not be wasted. I wish you all the success you

deserve, which is all you can desire. But I can do
nothing. My hands are full here, and my pockets are
empty.

Two months ago I succeeded in forming a local
Society for the Prevention of Cruelty in this place.

We have ordered prosecutions every week since, and
have obtained convictions in every case. And these
local operations are all that I can undertake or assist.

Believe me, yours sincerely,
HENRY TAYLOR.

He was also actively interested in an effort to improve the method of slaughtering cattle by using a
mask with a fixed hole in the centre, through which a
long nail may be easily driven, straight through the
exact suture of the skull to the brain, causing instant
death. Sir Henry specially approved the masks for
this purpose, made, I believe, under his own direction
at Bournemouth, by Mr. Mendon, a saddler at Lans-
downe.

Mr. Lewis Morris has also written some beautiful
and striking poems touching on the subject of scientific
cruelty, and I have reason to hope that a younger man,
whom many of us look upon as the poet of the future in
England, Mr. William Watson, is entirely on the same
side. In short, if the *Priests* of science are against us,
the *Prophets* of humanity, the poets, are with us in
this controversy, almost to a man.

It will be seen that we had politicians, historians,
and thinkers of various parties among our friends in
London ; but there were no novelists except that very
agreeable woman Miss Jewsbury and the two Misses
Betham Edwards. Mr. Anthony Trollope I knew but
slightly. I had also some acquaintance with a very
popular novelist, then a young man, who was introduced
in the full flush of his success to Mr. Carlyle, whereon
the "Sage of Chelsea" greeted him with the *encouraging*

question, " Well, Mr. ——, when do you intend to *begin to do something sairious ?* "

With Mr. Wilkie Collins I exchanged several friendly letters concerning some information he wanted for one of his books. The following letter from him exhibits the " sairious " spirit, at all events (as Mr. Carlyle might admit), in which he set about spinning the elaborate web of his exciting tales.

90, GLOUCESTER PLACE, PORTMAN SQUARE, W.,
23d June, 1882.

DEAR MADAM, — I most sincerely thank you for your kind letter and for the pamphlets which preceded it. The " Address " seems to me to possess the very rare merit of forcible statement combined with a moderation of judgment which sets a valuable example, not only to our enemies, but to some of our friends. As to the " Portrait," I feel such a strong universal interest in it that I must not venture on criticism. You have given me exactly what I most wanted for the purpose that I have in view — and you have spared me time and trouble in the best and kindest of ways. If I require further help, you shall see that I am gratefully sensible of the help that has been already given.

I am writing to a very large public both at home and abroad ; and it is quite needless (when I am writing to *you*) to dwell on the importance of producing the right impression by means which keep clear of terrifying and revolting the ordinary reader. I shall leave the detestable cruelties of the laboratory to be merely inferred, and, in tracing the moral influence of those cruelties on the nature of the man who practises them, and the result as to his social relations with the persons about him, I shall be careful to present him to the reader as a man *not* infinitely wicked and cruel, and to show the efforts made by his better instincts to resist the inevitable hardening of the heart, the fatal

stupefying of all the finer sensibilities, produced by the
deliberately merciless occupations of his life. If I can
succeed in making him, in some degree, an object of
compassion as well as of horror, my experience of readers of fiction tells me that the right effect will be produced by the right means.

Believe me, very truly yours,
WILKIE COLLINS.

Of another order of acquaintances was that excellent
man Mr. James Spedding; also Mr. Babbage (in whose
horror of street music I devoutly sympathized); and
Mr. James Fergusson the architect, in whose books and
ideas generally I found great interest. He avowed
to me his opinion that the ancient Jews were never
builders of stone edifices, and that all the relics of stone
buildings in Palestine were the work either of Tyrians
or of the Idumean Herod, or of other non-Jewish rulers.
His conversation was always most instructive to me,
and I rejoiced when I had the opportunity of writing a
long review (for Fraser I think) of his "Tree and
Serpent Worship"; with which he was so well pleased
that he made me a present of the magnificent volume,
of which I believe only a hundred copies were printed.
Mr. Fergusson taught me to see that the whole civilization of a country has depended historically on the
stones with which it happens naturally to be furnished.
If these stones be large and hard and durable like
those of Egypt, we find grand, everlasting monuments
and statues made of them. If they be delicate and
beautiful like Pentelic marble, we have the Parthenon.
If they be plain limestone or freestone as in our northern climes, richness of form and detail take the place of
greater simplicity, and we have the great cathedrals of
England, France and Germany. Where there is no
good stone, only brick, we may have fine mansions, but
not great temples, and where there is neither clay for

bricks, nor good stone for building, the natives can erect no durable edifices, and consequently have no places to be adorned with statues and paintings and all the arts which go with them. I do not know whether I do justice to Mr. Fergusson in giving this *résumé* of his lesson, but it is my recollection of it, and to my thinking worth recording.

One of the friends of whom we saw most in London was Sir William Boxall, whose exquisite artistic taste was specially congenial to my friend, and his varied conversation and love of his poor, dear old dog "Garry" to me. After Lord Coleridge's charming obituary of him nothing need be added in the way of tribute to his character and gifts, or to the refined feeling which inspired him always. I may add, however (what the Lord Chief Justice naturally would not say on his own account), namely, that Boxall, in his latter years of weakness and almost constant confinement to the house, frequently told us when we went to visit him how Lord Coleridge had found time from all his labors to come frequently to sit with him and cheer him; and after a whole day spent in the hot law courts would dine on his old friend's chops, and spend the evening in his dingy rooms in Welbeck Street. Here is a letter from Sir William which I happen to have preserved. It refers to an article I had written in the "Echo" on the death of Landseer: —

My DEAR MISS COBBE, — Your sympathetic notice of my old friend Landseer and his friends has delighted me — a grain of such feeling is worth a newspaper load of worn-out criticism. I thank you very sincerely for it.

I should have called upon you, but I have been shut up with the cold which threatened me when I last saw you.

Yours very sincerely, W. BOXALL.

October 6th, 1879.

There is no hope of my getting to Dolgelly. It will be a great escape for Miss Lloyd, for I am utterly worn out.

I find that the most common opinion about Lord Shaftesbury is that he was an excellent and most disinterested man, who did a vast amount of good in his time among the poor, and in the factories and on behalf of the climbing-boy sweeps, but that he was somewhat narrow-minded; and dry, if not stern in character. Perhaps some would add that his extreme Evangelicalism had in it a tinge of Calvinistic bigotry. I shared very much such ideas about him till one day in 1875, when I had gone to Stanhope Street to consult Lord and Lady Mount-Temple, my unfailing helpers and advisers, about some matter connected with Lord Henniker's bill then before Parliament — for the restriction of vivisection. After explaining my difficulty, Lady Mount-Temple said, " We must consult Lord Shaftesbury about this matter. Come with me now to his house." I yielded to my kind friend, but not without hesitation, fearing that Lord Shaftesbury would, in the first place, be too much absorbed in his great philanthropic undertakings to spare attention to the wrongs of the brutes; and, in the second, that his religious views were too strict to allow him to coöperate with such a heretic as I, even if (as I was assured) he would tolerate my intrusion. How widely astray from the truth I was as regarded his sentiments in both ways, the sequel proved. He had already, it appeared, taken great interest in the anti-vivisection controversy then beginning, and entered into it with all the warmth of his heart; not as something *taking him off* from service to mankind, but *as a part of his philanthropy.* He always emphatically endorsed my view : that, if we could save vivisectors from persisting in the sin of cruelty, we should be doing them a moral service greater than to save them from becoming pickpockets or drunkards. He also felt what I may call passionate pity for the tortured brutes. He loved dogs, and always had a large beautiful collie lying under his writing-table; and was full of tenderness to his daughters' Siamese cat, and spoke of all animals with intimate knowledge and sympathy. As to my heresies, though he knew of them from the first, they never interfered with his kindness and consideration for me, which were such as I can never remember without emotion.

I shall speak in its place in another chapter of the share he took as leader and champion of our party in all the subsequent events connected with the anti-vivisection agitation. I wish here only to give (if it may be possible for me) some small idea to the reader of what that good man really was, and to remove some of the absurd misconceptions current concerning him. For example. He was no bigot as to Sabbatarian observances. I told him once that I belonged to the Society for Opening Museums on Sundays. He said : "I think you are mistaken — the working men do not wish it. See! I have here the result of a large inquiry among their Trades Unions and clubs. Nearly all of them deprecate the change. But I am on this point not at all of the same opinion as most of my friends. I have told them (and they have often been a little shocked at it) that I think if a lawyer has a brief for a case on Monday and has had no time to study it on Saturday, he is quite justified in reading it up on Sunday after church."

Neither did he share the very common bigotry of teetotalism. He said to me, "The teetotalers have added an Eleventh Commandment, and think more of it than of all the rest." Again, when (as is well known) Lord Palmerston left the choice of Bishops for many years practically in his hands (I believe that seven owed their sees to him) and he, of course, selected Evangelical

clergymen who would uphold what he considered to be
vital religious truth, he was yet able to concur heartily in the appointment of Arthur Stanley to the
Deanery of Westminster. He told me that Lord Palmerston had written to him before inviting Dr. Stanley, and said that he would not do it if he (Lord
Shaftesbury) disapproved; and that he had answered
that he was well aware that Dr. Stanley's theological
views differed widely from his own, but that he was an
admirable man and a gentleman, with special suitability
for this post and a claim to some such high office; and
that he cordially approved Lord Palmerston's choice.
I do not suppose that Dean Stanley ever knew of this
possible *veto* in Lord Shaftesbury's hands, but he entertained the profoundest respect for him, and expressed
it in the little poem which he wrote about him (of
which Lord Shaftesbury gave me an MS. copy), which
appears in Dean Stanley's biography. He compares
the aged philanthropist to " a great rock's shadow in a
weary land."

It was a charge against Howard and some other great
philanthropists that while exhibiting the enthusiasm
of humanity on the *largest* scale they failed to show it
on a small one, and were scantily kind to those immediately around them. Nothing could be less true of
Lord Shaftesbury. While the direction of a score of
great charitable undertakings rested on him, and his
study was flooded with reports, bills before Parliament,
and letters by the hundred, he would remember to
perform all sorts of little kindnesses to individuals
having no special claim on him; and never by any
chance did he omit an act of courtesy. No more perfectly high-bred gentleman ever graced the old school;
and no young man, I may add, ever had a fresher or
warmer heart. Indeed, I know not where I should
look among old or young for such ready and full response of feeling to each call for pity, for sympathy.

for indignation, and, I may add, for the enjoyment of humor, the least gleam of which caught his eye in a moment. He was always particularly tickled with the absurdities involved in the doctrine of Apostolic Succession, and whenever a clergyman or a bishop did anything he much disapproved, he was sure to stigmatize it from that point of view. One day he was giving me a rather long account of some Deputation which had waited on him and endeavored to bully him. As he described the scene : " There they stood in a crowd in the room, and I said to them : 'Gentlemen! I'll see you.'" . . . (Good Heavens! I thought. *Where* did he say he would see them ?) — "I'll see you *at the bottom of the Red Sea* before I'll do it !" The revulsion was so ludicrous and the allusion to the " Red Sea " instead of "another place " so characteristic, that I broke into a peal of laughter which, when explained, made him also laugh heartily. Another day I remember his great amusement at a story not reported, I believe, in the "Times," but told me by an M. P. who was present in the House when Sir P. O. had outdone Sir Boyle Roche. He spoke of " the ingratitude of the Irish to Mr. Gladstone *who had broken down the bridges which divided them from England !* "

A lady whose reputation was less unblemished than might have been wished, and of whom I fought very shy in consequence, went to call on him about some business. When I saw him next he told me of her visit, and said, "When she left my study, I said to myself : 'There goes a *dashing Cyprian !* '" One needed to go back a century to recall this droll old phrase. More than once he repeated, chuckling with amusement, the speech of an old beggar woman to whom he had refused alms, and who called after him, "You withered specimen of bygone philanthropy!" On another occasion when he was in the chair at a small meeting, one of the speakers persisted in expressing

over and over again his conviction that the venerable
Chairman could not be expected to live long. Lord
Shaftesbury turned aside to me and said *sotto voce*,
"I declare he's telling me I'm going to die immediately! There he is saying it again! Was there
ever such a man?" Nobody was more awake than he
to the "dodges" of interested people trying to make
capital out of his religious party. A most ridiculous
instance of this he described to me with great glee. At
the time of the excitement (now long forgotten) about
the Madiai family, Barnum actually called upon him
(Lord Shaftesbury) and entreated him to allow of the
Madiai being taken over to be *exhibited* in New York!
"It would be such an affecting sight," said Barnum, "to
see *real* Christian Martyrs!"

As an instance of his thoughtfulness, I may mention
that having one day just received a ticket for the
private view of the Academy he offered it to me and
I accepted it gladly, observing that since the recent
death of Boxall I feared we should not have one given
to us, and that my friend would be pleased to use it.
"Oh, I am so glad!" said Lord Shaftesbury; and from
that day every year till he died he never once failed to
send her, addressed by himself, his tickets for each of
the two annual exhibitions. When one thinks of how
men who do not do in a year as much as he did in a
week would have scoffed at the idea of taking such
trouble, one may estimate the good nature which
prompted this over-worked man to remember such a
trifle unfailingly.

The most touching interview I ever had with him
was one of the last, in his study in Grosvenor Square,
not long before his death. Our conversation had
fallen on the woes and wrongs of seduced girls and
ruined women; and he told me many facts which he
had learned by personal investigation and visits to
dreadful haunts in London. He described all he saw

and heard with a compassion for the victims and yet a horror of vice and impurity, which somehow made me think of Christ and the woman taken in adultery. After a few moments' silence, during which we were both rather overcome, he said, "When I feel age creeping on me, and know I must soon die, I hope it is not wrong to say it, but I *cannot bear to leave the world with all the misery in it.*" No words can describe how this simple expression revealed to me the man in his inmost spirit. He had long passed the stage of moral effort which does good *as a duty,* and had ascended to that wherein even the enjoyment of Heaven itself (which of course his creed taught him to expect immediately after death) had less attractions for him than the labor of mitigating the sorrows of earth.

I possess 280 letters and notes from Lord Shaftesbury written to me during the ten years which elapsed from 1875, when I first saw him, till his last illness in 1885. Many of them are merely brief notes, giving me information or advice about my work as honorable secretary of the Victoria Street Society, of which he was President. But many are long and interesting letters. The editor of his excellent biography probably did not know I possessed these letters, nor did I know he was preparing Lord Shaftesbury's life or I should have placed them at his disposal. I can only here quote a few as characteristic, or otherwise specially interesting to me.

CASTLE WEMYSS, WEMYSS BAY, N. B.,
September 3d, 1878.

DEAR MISS COBBE, — Your letter is very cheering. We were right to make the experiment. We were right to test the man and the law: Cross, and his administration of it. Both have failed us, and we are bound in duty, I think, to leap over all limitations, and go in for the total abolition of this vile and cruel form of Idolatry; for idolatory it is, and, like all idolatry, brutal, degrading, and deceptive. . . .

May God prosper us! These ill-used and tortured animals are as much His Creatures as we are, and to say the truth, I had, in some instances, rather be the animal tortured than the man who tortured it. I should believe myself to have higher hopes and a happier future.

Yours truly,   SHAFTESBURY.

July 10th, 1879.

DEAR MISS COBBE, — I have sent your letter to Judas of X ——. I find no fault in it, but that of too much courtesy to one so lost to every consideration of feeling and truth.

Did you know him, as I know him, you would find it difficult to restrain your pen and your tongue. . . .

.   .   .   .

Some good will come out of the discussion.

I have unmistakable evidence that many were deeply impressed, but adhesion to political leaders is a higher law with most politicians than obedience to the law of truth.

What do you think now of the doctrine of " Apostolic Succession"?

Would St. Peter, St. Paul, and St. John have made such a speech as that of my Lord of P—— ?

Yours truly,   SHAFTESBURY.

CASTLE WEMYSS, WEMYSS BAY, N. B.,
September 16th, 1879.

DEAR MISS COBBE, — You do that Bishop too much honor. He is not worth notice.

It is frightful to see that the open champions of vivisection are not Bradlaugh and Mrs. B., but Bishops, " Fathers in God," and "Pastors" of the people!

We shall soon have Bradlaugh and his company

claiming the Apostolic Succession ; and, if that succession be founded on truth, mercy, and love, with as good a right as Dr. G., Dr. M. or D.D. anything else.

Your letter has crushed (if such a hard substance can be crushed) his Lordship of C. . . .

Yours truly,   SHAFTESBURY.

The next letter is in acknowledgment of the following verses which I had sent to him on his eightieth birthday. They were repeated by the late Chamberlain of the City of London, and Benjamin Scott, in his oration on the presentation of freedom of the city to Lord Shaftesbury. I print the letter (though all too kind in its expression about my poor verses), on account of the deeply interesting review of his own life which it contains : —

A BIRTHDAY ADDRESS

TO ANTHONY ASHLEY COOPER, 7TH EARL OF SHAFTESBURY, K. G.
APRIL 28TH, 1881.

> For eighty years ! Many will count them over,
> But none save He who knoweth all may guess
> What those long years have held of high endeavor,
> Of world-wide blessing and of blessedness.
>
> For eighty years the champion of the right
> Of hapless child neglected and forlorn;
> Of maniac dungeon'd in his double night;
> Of woman overtasked and labor-worn;
>
> Of homeless boy in streets with peril rife;
> Of workman sickening in his airless den;
> Of Indian parching for the streams of life;
> Of Negro slave in bonds of cruel men;
>
> O Friend of all the friendless 'neath the sun,
> Whose hand hath wiped away a thousand tears,
> Whose fervent lips and clear strong brain have done
> God's holy service, lo! these eighty years, —
>
> How meet it seems thy grand and vigorous age
> Should find beyond man's race fresh pangs to spare,

And for the wrong'd and tortured brutes engage
　　In yet fresh labors and ungrudging care!

O tarry long amongst us! Live, we pray,
　　Hasten not yet to hear thy Lord's "Well done!"
Let this world still seem better while it may
　　Contain one soul like thine amid its throng.

Whilst thou art here our inmost hearts confess,
　　Truth spake the kingly Seer of old who said —
"Found in the way of God and righteousness,
　　A crown of glory is the hoary head."

LORD SHAFTESBURY TO MISS F. P. C.

24, GROSVENOR SQUARE, W., April 14th, 1880.

DEAR MISS COBBE, — Had I not known your handwriting, I should never have guessed either that you
were the writer of the verses or that I was the subject
of them.

Had I judged them simply by their ability and force,
I might have ascribed them to the true author; but it
required the envelope and the ominous word "eighty,"
to justify me in applying them to myself.

They both touched and gratified me, but I will tell
you the origin of my public career, which you have been
so kind as to commend. It arose while I was a boy at
Harrow School, about, I should think, fourteen years of
age — an event occurred (the details of which I may
give you some other day) which brought painfully before me the scorn and neglect manifested towards the
poor and helpless. I was deeply affected; but, for
many years afterwards, I acted only on feeling and sentiment. As I advanced in life, all this grew up to a
sense of duty; and I was convinced that God had called
me to devote whatever advantages He might have bestowed upon me, to the cause of the weak, the helpless,
both man and beast, and those who had none to help
them.

I entered Parliament in 1826, and I commenced operations in 1828, with an effort to ameliorate the conditions of lunatics, and then I passed on in a succession of attempts to grapple with other evils, and such has been my trade for more than half a century.

Do not think for a moment that I claim any merit. If there be any doctrine that I dislike and fear more than another it is the "Doctrine of Works." Whatever I have done has been given to me; what I have done I was enabled to do; and all happy results (if any there be) must be credited, not to the servant, but to the great Master who led and sustained him.

My course, however, has raised up for me many enemies, and very few friends, but among those friends I hope that you may be numbered.

Yours truly,   SHAFTESBURY.

I sent him another little *souvenir* two years later : —

TO LORD SHAFTESBURY ON HIS 82D BIRTHDAY.

WITH A CHINA TABLET.

THE Lord of Rome, historians say,
Lamented he had "lost a day,"
When no good deed was done.
Scarce one such day, methinks, appears
In the long record of the years
Of England's worthier son.

If on this tablet's surface light
His hourly tolls should Shaftesbury write
All may be soon effaced :
But in our grateful memories graven
And in the registers of Heaven
They will not be erased.

LONDON, April 28th, 1883.

The next letter refers to my lectures on the "Duties of Women" which I had just delivered.

24, GROSVENOR SQUARE, W., May 14th, 1880.

DEAR MISS COBBE, — . . . I admire your lectures. But do you not try to make "the sex" a little too pugnacious? And why do you give "truth" to the men, and deny it to the women?

If you mean by "truth" abstinence from fibs, I think that the females are as good as the males. But if you mean steadiness of friendship, adherence to principles, conscientiously not superficially entertained, and sincerity in a good cause, why, the women are far superior.

Yours truly,   SHAFTESBURY.

24, GROSVENOR SQUARE, W., May 21st, 1880.

DEAR MISS COBBE, — . . . Your lecture on vivisection was admirable — we must be "mealy mouthed" no longer.

Shall you and I have a conversation on your lectures and the " Duties of Women"? We shall not, I believe, have much difference of opinion; perhaps none. I approve them heartily, but there are one or two expressions which, though intelligible to myself, would be greatly misconstrued by a certain portion of Englishmen.

I could give you instances by the hundred of the wonderful success that, by a merciful Providence, has followed with our ragged children, male and female.[1] In fact, though after long intervals we have lost sight of a good many, we have very few cases, indeed, of the failure of our hopes and efforts.

In thirty years we took off the streets of London, and sent to service or provided with means of honest livelihood, more than two hundred and twenty thousand "waifs and strays."

Yours truly,   SHAFTESBURY.

July 23d, 1880.

DEAR MISS COBBE, — I have had a very friendly letter from Gladstone; but on reference to him for permission to publish it, he seems unwilling to assent.

[1] I had talked to him of our Ragged School at Bristol.

Our testimony, thank God, is cumulative for good. We may hope, and we must pray, for better things.

I send you Gladstone's letter. Pray return it to me, and take care that it does not appear in print.[1]

I am glad that you liked the "dinner." It was, I think, a success in showing civility to foreign friends.

Yours truly,   SHAFTESBURY.

Lord Shaftesbury made the following remarks about the future state of animals, in a very sympathizing reply to a letter I had written to him in which I mentioned to him that my dog had died : —

September 29th, 1883.

I have ever believed in a happy future for animals; I cannot say or conjecture how or where; but sure I am that the love, so manifested, by dogs especially, is an emanation from the Divine essence, and, as such, it can, or rather it *will*, never be extinguished.[2]

24, GROSVENOR SQUARE, W., May 14th, 1885.

MY DEAR MISS COBBE, — You must not suppose that because I did not answer your letter at the moment, I am indifferent to you or your correspondence.

Far from it, but when I have little to do, being almost confined to the house, I have much to write, and to get through my work I must frequently be relieved by a recumbent posture.

Nevertheless, by God's mercy, I am certainly better;

---

[1] When our bill was debated in Parliament in 1883, Mr. Gladstone left us, totally unaided, to the mercies (not tender) of Sir William Harcourt, who interrupted Mr. George Russell's speech in support of our bill by the remark that the demonstrations to students, to which he referred, were forbidden by the vivisection act. *Sixteen* certificates granting permission for the performance of such experiments in demonstration to students passed through his own office that year !

[2] This opinion of the great *philanthropist* deserves to be remembered with those of the many thinkers who have reached the same conclusion from other sides.

FRANCES POWER COBBE.

and I think that were we blessed with some warm, genial weather I should recover more rapidly.

Bryan [1] is a good man, he is able, diligent, zealous, and has an excellent judgment. I have not been able to attend his committee, but his reports to me show attention and good sense.

I have left, as perhaps you have seen, the Lunacy Commission. It was at the close of fifty-six years of service that I did so. I dare say that you have had time to read my letter of resignation in the "Times" of the 8th.

I am very glad that Miss Lloyd is determined to print those lines. They are very beautiful; and you must be sure to send a copy to Miss Marsh. She admires them as much as I do.

The thought of Calvary [2] is the strength that has governed all the sentiments and actions of my manhood and later life; and you can well believe that I greatly rejoice to find that one, whom I prize so highly, has kindred sympathies. . . .

May God prosper you.

Yours truly,   SHAFTESBURY.

The most remarkable woman I have known, not excepting Mrs. Somerville (described in my chapter on

[1] The General Secretary then, and I am happy to say still, of the Victoria Street Society.

[2] The lines to which Lord Shaftesbury refers — "Rest in the Lord" (since included in many collections) — begin with the words: —

> " God draws a cloud over each gleaming morn.
>   Wouldst thou ask, why?
>   It is because all noblest things are born
>   In agony.
>
>   Only upon some Cross of pain or woe
>   God's Son may lie.
>   Each soul redeemed from self and sin must know
>   Its Calvary."

Lord Shaftesbury entirely understood the point of view from which I regarded that sacred spot.

Italy), Elizabeth Barrett Browning, and Mrs. Beecher Stowe, was, beyond any doubt or question, my dear friend Fanny Kemble. I have told of the droll circumstances of our first meeting at Newbridge in the early Fifties. From that time till her death in 1892, her brilliant, iridescent genius, her wit, her spirit, her tenderness, the immense "go" and momentum of her whole nature, were sources of endless pleasure to me. When I was lame, I used to feel that for days after talking with her I could almost dispense with my crutches, so much did she, literally, lift me up!

Mrs. Kemble paid us several visits here in Wales, and was perhaps even more delightful in our quiet country quarters than in London. She would sit out for many hours at a time in our beautiful old garden, which she said was to her "an idyll," and talk of all things in heaven and earth; touching in turn every note in the gamut of emotion from sorrowful to joyous. One summer she came to us early, and thus sat daily under a great cherry tree "in the midst of the garden," which was at the time a mass of odorous and snowy blossoms. Alas! the blossoms have returned and are blooming as I write — but the friend sleeps under the sod in Kensal Green.

Mr. Henry James's obituary article and Mr. Bentley's generous-hearted letter concerning her in the "Times" — in rebuke of the mean and grudging notice of her which that paper had published — seem to me to have been by far the most truthful sketches which appeared of the "grand old lioness," as Mr. Thackeray called her. Everybody could admire, and most people a little feared her; but it needed to come very close to her and brush past her formidable thorns of irony and sarcasm to know and *love* her, as she most truly deserved to be loved.

There is always something startling and perhaps the reverse of attractive to those of us who have been brought up in the usual English way to *repress* our emotions, in women who have been trained reversely by histrionic life to give all possible outwardness and vividness of expression to those same emotions. It is only when we get below both the extreme demonstrativeness on one hand, and the conventional reserve and self-restraint on the other, and meet on common ground of deep sympathies, that real friendship is established; a friendship which in my case was at once an honor and a delight.

Mrs. Kemble in her generous affection made a present to me of the MSS. of her Memoirs, which subsequently I induced her to take back, and publish herself, as her "Old Woman's Gossip," her "Records of a Girlhood" and "Records of Later Life." Besides these, which, as I have said, I returned to her one after another, she gave me, and I still possess, an immense packet of her own old letters to her beloved H. S. (Harriet St. Leger) and others; and the materials of five large and thick volumes of autograph letters addressed to her, extending over more than fifty years. They include whole correspondences with W. Donne, Edward Fitzgerald, Henry Gréville, Mrs. Jameson, John Mitchell Kemble, George Combe, and several others; and besides these there are either one or half a dozen letters from almost every man and woman of eminence in England in her time. Mr. Bentley has very liberally purchased from me for publication about one hundred letters from Edward Fitzgerald to Mrs. Kemble. The rest of Mrs. Kemble's correspondence I have, as I have mentioned, bound together in five volumes, and I do not intend to publish them. Had any of Mrs. Kemble's "Records" remained inedited at the time of her death I should have undertaken (as she no doubt intended me to do) the task of writing her biography. The work was, however, so fully done by herself in her long series of volumes that there was neither need nor room for more. I am happy to add, in conclusion, that in the arrangements I have made regarding my dear old friend's literary remains, I have the consent and approval of her daughters.

I knew Mrs. Gaskell a little, but not enough to harmonize in my mind the woman I saw in the flesh with the books I liked so well as "Mary Barton" and "Libbie Marsh's Three Eras." Of Mrs. Stowe's delightful conversation on the terrace of our villa on Bellosguardo I have written my recollections, and recorded the glimpses I had of Mrs. Browning. I have also described Harriet Hosmer and Rosa Bonheur; our sculptor and painter friends, and Mary Carpenter, my leader and fellow-worker at Bristol. I must not speak here of the affection and admiration I entertained for my dear, living friend Anna Swanwick, the translator of Æschylus and Faust; and for Louisa Lee Schuyler, the woman who led the organization of relief in the great war; and (as if that were not enough for one life, as was Miss Nightingale's noble work at Scutari!) founded and carried to its present marvellous extent of power and usefulness the State Charities Aid Association of New York. Again, I have known in England Mme. Bodichon (who furnished Girton with its first thousand pounds); Mrs. Josephine Butler; Mrs. Webster the classic poetess; and Mrs. Emily Pfeiffer, another poetess and very beautiful woman, at whose house I once witnessed an interesting scene — a large party of ladies and gentlemen dressed in the attire of Athenians of the Periclean age. Miss Swanwick and I, who were alone permitted to attend in English costume, were immensely impressed by the *ennobling* effect of the classic dress, not only for young and graceful people but for those who were quite the reverse.

I never saw Harriet Martineau; but was so desirous of doing it that I intended to make a journey to Ambleside for the purpose, and with that view begged our mutual friend, the late Mrs. Hensleigh Wedgwood, to ask leave to introduce me to her. It was an unfortunate moment, and I only received the following kind message : —

"I need not say how happy I should have been to become acquainted with Miss Cobbe; but the time is past and I am only fit for old friends who can excuse my shortcomings. I have lost ground so much of late that the case is clear. I must give up all hopes of so great a pleasure. Will you say this to her, and ask her to receive my kind and thankful regards I venture to send on the grounds of our common friendships ?"

Of my living, beloved, and honored friends, Mrs. William Grey, Lady Mount-Temple, Miss Shirreff, Mrs. Fawcett, Miss Caroline Stephen, Miss Julia Wedgwood, Miss Florence D. Hill, and Miss Augusta Spottiswoode, I must not here speak. I have had the pleasure also of meeting that very fine woman-worker, Miss Octavia Hill.

George Eliot I did not know, nor, as I have just said, did I ever meet Harriet Martineau. But with those two great exceptions I think (I may boast of having come into contact with nearly all the more gifted English women of the Victorian era; and thus when I speak, as I shall do in the next chapter, of my efforts to put the claims of my sex fairly before the world, I may boast of writing with practical personal knowledge of what women are, and can be, both as to character and ability.)

The decade which began in 1880 brought me many sorrows. The first was the death of my second brother, Thomas Cobbe, of Easton Lyss. I loved him much for his own sweet and affectionate nature; and much, too, for the love of our mother which he shared especially with me. I was also warmly attached to his beautiful and good Scotch wife, who survived him only a few years; and to his dear children, who were my pets in infancy and have been almost like my own daughters ever since. My brother ought to have been a very successful and brilliant barrister, but his life was broken by the faults of others, and when in advanced years he wrote, with immense patience and research, a really valuable "History of the Norman Kings" (thought to be so by such competent judges as Mr. William Longman, and the Historical Society of Normandy, which asked leave to translate it), the book was practically *killed* by a cruel and most unfair review which attributed to him mistakes which he had not made, and refused to publish his refutation of the charge. If this review were written (as we could not but surmise) by an eminent historian, now dead, whose own book my brother had, very unwisely, ignored, I can only say it was a malicious and spiteful deed. My brother's ambition was not strong enough to carry him over such a disappointment, and he never attempted to write again for the press, but spent his later years in the solitary study of his favorite old chronicles and his Shakespeare. A little later my eldest brother also died, leaving no children. I must be thankful at my age that the youngest, the Rector of Maulden, though five years older than I, still survives in health and vigor, rejoicing in his happy home and family of affectionate daughters. I trust yet to welcome him into the brotherhood of the pen when his great monograph on "Luton Church, Historical and Descriptive," sees the light this year.

I lost also in this same decade my earliest friend, Harriet St. Leger; and a younger, very dear one, Emily Shaen. Mrs. Shaen and her admirable husband had been much drawn to me by religious sympathies; and I regarded her with more heartfelt respect, I might say reverence, than I can well express. She endured twenty years of seclusion and suffering with the spirit at once of a saint and of a philosopher. Had her health enabled her to take her natural place in the world, I have always felt assured she would have been recognized as one of the ablest as well as one of the best women of the day, and more than the equal of her two gifted sisters, Catharine and Susanna Winkworth. The friendship between us was of the closest kind. I often said that I *went to church* to her sick-room. In her last days, when utterly crushed by incessant suffering and by the death of her beloved husband and her favorite son, she bore in whispers to me (she could scarcely speak for mortal weakness) this testimony to our common faith: "I sent for you, — to tell you, — *I am more sure than ever that God is Good.*"

(All these deaths and the heart-wearing anti-vivisection work combined with my own increasing years to make my life in London less and less a source of enjoyment and more of strain than I could bear. In 1884 Miss Lloyd, with my entire concurrence, let our dear little house in Hereford Square to our friend Mrs. Kemble, and we left London altogether and came to live in Wales.)

CHAPTER XIX.

THE CLAIMS OF WOMEN.

(It was not till I was actively engaged in the work of Mary Carpenter at Bristol, and had begun to desire earnestly various changes of law relating to young criminals and paupers, that I became an advocate of "Woman's Rights.") It was good old Rev. Samuel J. May, of Syracuse, New York, who, when paying us a visit, pressed on my attention the question: "*Why should you not have a vote?* Why should not women be enabled to influence the making of the laws in which they have as great an interest as men ?"

My experience probably explains largely the indifference of thousands of women, not deficient in intelligence, in England and America to the possession of political rights. They have much anxiety to fulfil their home duties, and the notion of undertaking others, requiring (as they fully understand) conscientious enquiry and reflection, rather alarms than attracts them. But the time comes to every woman worth her salt to take ardent interest in some question which touches legislation. Then she begins to ask herself, as Mr. May asked me: "Why should the fact of being a woman close to me the use of the plain, direct means of helping to achieve some large public good or stopping some evil ?" The timid, the indolent, the conventional will here retreat, and try to believe that it concerns men only to right the wrongs of the world in some more effectual way than by single-handed personal efforts in special cases. Others again — and of their number was I —

become deeply impressed with the need of woman's
voice in public affairs, and thenceforth attach themselves to the "woman's cause" more or less earnestly.
For my own part I confess I have been chiefly moved
by reflection on the sufferings and wrongs borne by women, in great measure owing to the *déconsidération* they
endure consequent on their political and civil disabili-
ties.   Whilst I and other happily circumstanced women
have had no immediate wrongs of our own to gall us,
we should still have been very poor creatures had we
not felt bitterly those of our less fortunate sisters, the
robbed and trampled wives, the mothers whose children
were torn from them at the bidding of a dead or living
father, the daughters kept in ignorance and poverty
while their brothers were educated in costly schools
and fitted for honorable professions.   Such wrongs as
these have inspired me with the persistent resolution to
do everything in my power to protect the property, the
persons, and the parental rights of women.

I do not think that this resolve has any necessary
connection with theories concerning the equality of the
sexes; and I am sure that a great deal of our force has
been wasted on fruitless discussions such as : "Why has
there never been a female Shakespeare?"   A Celt claiming equal representation with a Saxon, *or any representation at all*, might just as fairly be challenged to
explain why there has never been a Celtic Shakespeare
or a Celtic Tennyson.   My own opinion is, that women
en masse are by no means the intellectual equals of men
en masse; and whether this inequality arises from irre-
mediable causes or from alterable circumstances of education and heredity is not worth debating.   If the nation
had established an intellectual test for political equality,
and admission to the franchise were confined to persons
passing a given standard, well and good.   Then, no
doubt, there would be (as things now stand) fifty per
cent. of men who would win votes, and perhaps only

thirty per cent. of women. So much may be freely
admitted. But then that thirty per cent. of females
would obtain political rights; and those who failed
would be debarred by a natural and real, not an arbi-
trary, inferiority. Such a state of things would not
present such ludicrous injustice as that which obtains
— for example — in a parish not a hundred miles from
my present abode. There is in the village in question
a man universally known therein as "The *Idiot;*" a
poor slouching, squinting fellow, who yet rents a house
and can do rough field work, though he can scarcely
speak intelligibly. *He* has a vote, of course. The
owner of his house and of half the parish, who holds
also the advowson of the living, is a lady who has travelled widely, understands three or four languages, and
studies the political news of Europe daily in the columns of the "Times." That lady, equally of course,
has *no* vote, no power whatever to keep the representation of her county out of the hands of the demagogues
naturally admired by the Idiot and his compeers. Under the regulations which create inequalities of this
kind is it not rather absurd to insist perpetually (as is
the practice of our opponents) on the *intellectual* inferiority of women — as if it were really in question ?
(I hold, however, that whatever be our real mental
rank)— to be tested thoroughly only in future generations, under changed conditions of training and heredity
—(we women are the *equivalents*, though not the *equals*,
of men.) (And to refuse a share in the law-making of a
nation to the most law-abiding half of it; to exclude on
all largest questions the votes of the most conscientious,
temperate, religious, and (above all) most merciful and
tender-hearted moiety, is a mistake which cannot fail,
and *has* not failed, to entail great evil and loss.)
(I wrote, as I have mentioned in Chapter XV., a great
many articles (chiefly in Fraser and Macmillan) on
women's concerns about the years 1861, 2, 3: "What

shall we do with our Old Maids?" "Female Charity,
Lay and Monastic;" "Women in Italy in 1862;" "The
Education of Women;" "Social Science Congresses and
Women's Part in Them;" and, later, "The Fitness of
Women for the Ministry of Religion." These made
me known to many women who were fighting in the
woman's cause: Miss Bessie Parkes (now Madame
Belloc), Madame Bodichon, Mrs. Grey, Miss Shirreff,
Mrs. Peter Taylor, Miss Becker, and others; and when
committees were formed for promoting woman suffrage, I was invited to join them. I did so; and frequently attended the meetings, though not regularly.)
We had several Members of Parliament and other gentlemen (notably Mr. Frederick Hill, brother of my old
friend Recorder Hill and of Sir Rowland) who generally helped our deliberations; and many able women,
among others Mrs. Augusta Webster, the poetess, and
Lady Anna Gore Langton, an exceedingly sensible
woman, who also held drawing-room suffrage meetings
(at which I spoke) in her house. We had for secretary
Miss Lydia Becker: a woman of singular political
ability, for whom I had a sincere respect. Her pre-
mature death has been an incalculable loss to the
women of England. She gave me the impression of
one of those ill-fated people whose outward persons do
not represent their inward selves. I am sure she had
a large element of softness and sensitiveness in her
nature, unsuspected by most of those with whom she
labored. She was a most courageous and straightfor-
ward woman, with a single eye to the great political
work which she had undertaken, and which I think no
one has understood so well as she.

After Miss Becker's lamented death the great schism
between Unionists and Home Rulers extended far
enough to split even our committee (which was
avowedly of no party) into two bodies. I naturally
followed my fellow-Unionist, Mrs. Fawcett, when she

re-organized the moiety of the society and established
an office for it in College Street, Westminster. Believing her to be quite the ablest woman economist and pol-
itician in England, I entertain the hope that she may
at last carry a woman suffrage bill and live to see
qualified single women recording their votes at Parliamentary elections. When that time arrives every one
will scoff at the objections which have so long closed
the "right of way" to us of the "weaker sex."

(Beside the committee of the Society for Woman
Suffrage I also joined for a time the committee which
— long afterwards — effected the splendid achievement
of procuring the passage of the "Married Women's
Property Act;" the greatest step gained up to the
present time for women in England. I can claim no
part of that real honor, which is due in greatest measure to Mrs. Jacob Bright.)

(The question of granting university degrees to women was opened as far back as 1862. In that year I
read in the Guildhall in London at the social science
congress a paper, pleading for the privilege. Dean
Milman, who occupied the chair, was very kind in
praising my crude address, and enjoyed the little jokes
wherewith it was sprinkled; but next morning every
daily paper in London laughed at my demand, and for
a week or two I was the butt of universal ridicule.
Nevertheless, just seventeen years afterwards I was
invited to join a deputation headed by Lady Stanley of
Alderley, to thank Lord Granville for having (as President of London University) conceded those degrees to
women, precisely as I had demanded! I took occasion
at the close of the pleasant interview to present him
with one of the very few remaining copies of my original and much ridiculed appeal.)

From this time I wrote and spoke not unfrequently
on behalf of women's political and civil claims. One
article of mine in Fraser, 1868, was reprinted more

than once. ⎛It was headed " Criminals, Idiots, Women,
and Minors;" and enquired "whether the classifica-
tion should be counted sound." I hope that the discussion it involved on the laws relating to the property
of married women was of some service in helping on
the great measure of justice afterwards granted. ⎞

Another paper of mine, circulated by the "London
National Society for Women's Suffrage," for which I
wrote it, was entitled " Our Policy." It was, in effect,
an address to women concerning the best way to secure
the suffrage. I began this pamphlet by the following
remarks : —

" There is an instructive story, told by Herodotus, of
an African nation which went to war with the South
Wind. The wind had greatly annoyed these Psyllians
by drying up their cisterns, so they organized a campaign and set off to attack the enemy at headquarters
— somewhere, I presume, about the Sahara. The army
was admirably equipped with all the military engines
of those days : swords and spears, darts and javelins,
battering rams and catapults. It happened that the
South Wind did not, however, suffer much from these
weapons, but got up one fine morning and blew ! The
sands of the desert have lain for a great many ages
over those unfortunate Psyllians ; and, as Herodotus
placidly concludes the story, 'The Nasamones possess
the territory of those who thus perished.'

" It seems to me that we women, who have been
fighting for the suffrage with logical arguments — syl-
logisms, analogies, demonstrations, and reductions-to-
the-absurd of our antagonists' position, in short, all the
weapons of ratiocinative warfare — have been behaving
very much like those poor Psyllians, who imagined that
darts and swords and catapults would avail against
the Simoom. The obvious fact is that it is *Sentiment*
we have to contend against, not Reason ; Feeling and
Prepossession, not intellectual Conviction. Had logic

been the only obstacle in our way, we should long ago
have been polling our votes for Parliamentary as well
as for Municipal and School Board elections. To those
who hold that property is the thing intended to be represented by the Constitution of England, we have
shown that we possess such property. To those who
say that tax-paying and representation should go together, we have pointed to the tax-gatherers' papers,
which, alas! lie on our hall-tables wholly irrespective
of the touching fact that we belong to the 'protected
sex.' Where intelligence, education, and freedom
from crime are considered enough to confer rights of
citizenship, we have remarked that we are quite ready
to challenge rivalry in such particulars with those illit-
erates for whose exercise of political functions our
Senate has taken such exemplary care. Finally, to the
ever-recurring charge that we cannot fight, and therefore ought not to vote, we have replied that the logic of
the exclusion will be manifest when all the men too
weak, too short, or too old for the military standard be
likewise disfranchised, and when the actual soldiers of
our army are accorded the suffrage.

"But it is sentiment, not logic, against which we
have to struggle; and we shall best do so, I think, by
endeavoring to understand and make full allowance for
it; and then by steady working, shoulder to shoulder,
so as to conquer, or rather *win* it over to our side."

In 1876, May 13th, I made a rather long and elaborate speech on the subject of women's suffrage in a
meeting in St. George's Hall, at which Mr. Russell
Gurney, the Recorder of London, took the chair. John
Bright had spoken against our bill in the House, and
though I had not intended to speak at our meeting I
was spurred by indignation to reply to him. In this
address I spoke chiefly of the wrongs of mothers whose
children are taken from them at the will of a living or
dead father. I ended by saying : —

"I advocate woman suffrage as the natural and needful constitutional means of protection for the rights of the weaker half of the nation. I do this as a woman pleading for women. But I do it also, and none the less confidently, as a citizen, and for the sake of the whole community, because it is my conviction that such a measure is no less expedient for men than just for women; and that it will redound in coming years ever more and more to the happiness, the virtue, and the honor of our country."

Several years after this I wrote a letter which was printed in the (American) "Woman's Tribune," May 1st, 1884. It expresses so exactly what I feel still on the subject that I shall redeem it if possible from oblivion. The following are the passages for which I should like to ask the reader's attention: —

"If I may presume to offer an old woman's counsel to the younger workers in our cause, it would be that they should adopt the point of view — that it is before all things our *duty* to obtain the franchise. If we undertake the work in this spirit, and with the object of using the power it confers, whenever we gain it, for the promotion of justice and mercy and the kingdom of God upon earth, we shall carry on all our agitation in a corresponding manner, firmly and bravely, and also calmly and with generous good temper. And when our opponents come to understand that this is the motive underlying our efforts, they, on their part, will cease to feel bitterly and scornfully toward us, even when they think we are altogether mistaken.

"That people MAY conscientiously consider that we are mistaken in asking for woman suffrage is another point which it surely behoves us to carry in mind.

"We naturally think almost exclusively of many advantages which would follow to our sex and to both sexes from the entrance of woman into political life. But that there are some 'lions in the way,' and rather formidable lions, too, ought not to be forgotten.

" For myself, I would far rather that women should remain without political rights to the end of time than that they should lose those qualities which we comprise in the word ' womanliness ; ' and I think nearly every one of the leaders of our party in America and in England agrees with me in this feeling.

"The idea that the possession of political rights will destroy ' womanliness,' absurd as it may seem to us, is very deeply rooted in the minds of men; and when they oppose our demands, it is only just to give them credit for doing so on grounds which we should recognize as valid, *if their premises were true.* It is not so much that our opponents (at least the better part of them) despise women, as that they really prize what women *now are* in the home and in society so highly that they cannot bear to risk losing it by any serious change in their condition. These fears are futile and faithless, but there is nothing in them to affront us To remove them, we must not use violent words, for every such violent word confirms their fears; but, on the contrary, show the world that while the revolutions wrought by men have been full of bitterness and rancor and stormy passions, if not of bloodshed, we women will at least strive to accomplish our great emancipation calmly and by persuasion and reason.")

I was honored about this time by several friendly advances from American ladies and gentlemen interested like myself in woman's advancement. The astronomer, Professor Maria Mitchell, wrote me a charming letter, which I exceedingly regret should have been lost, as I felt particular interest in her great achievements. I had the pleasure of receiving Mrs. Julia Ward Howe in Hereford Square, and also Mrs. Livermore, whose speech at one of our suffrage meetings realized my highest ideal of a woman's public address. Her noble face and figure like that of a Roman matron, her sweet manners and playful humor without a scintilla of bitterness

in it — as if she were a mother remonstrating with a
foolish schoolboy son — were all delightful to me.

Colonel T. W. Higginson, who has been so good a
friend and adviser to women, also came to see me, and
gave me some bright hours of conversation on his wonderful experiences in the war, during which he com-
manded a colored regiment, which fought valiantly
under his leadership. Finally I had the privilege of
being elected a member of the famous "Sorosis" Club of
New York, and of receiving the following very pleasant
letter conveying the gift of a pretty gold and enamel
brooch, the badge of the sisterhood : —

DEAR MADAM, — The ladies of "Sorosis" — the Woman's Club of New York — beg your acceptance of
the accompanying pin, the insignia of their organization, which they send by the hand of their foreign correspondent, Mrs. Laura Curtis Bullard.

Trifling as is this testimonial in itself, they feel
that if you knew the genuine appreciation of you and
your work that goes with it — the gratitude with which
each one regards you as a faithful worker for women —
you would not consider it unworthy your acceptance.
With best wishes for your continued health, which in
your case means continued usefulness,

I am, dear madam,

With great respect and esteem,

Your obedient servant,

CELIA BURLEIGH,

Cor. Sec. Sorosis.

37 HUNTINGDON STREET, BROOKLYN, NEW YORK,
        June 21, 1869.

The part of my work for women, however, to which
I look back with most satisfaction was that in which I
labored to obtain protection for unhappy wives, beaten,
mangled, mutilated, or trampled on by brutal husbands.

(One day in 1878 I was by chance reading a newspaper in which a whole series of frightful cases of this kind were recorded, here and there, among the ordinary news of the time. I got up out of my armchair, half dazed, and said to myself: "I will never rest till I have tried what I can do to stop this.")

I thought anxiously what was the sort of remedy I ought to endeavor to put forward. A Parliamentary Blue Book had been printed in 1875 entitled: "Reports on the State of the Law relating to Brutal Assaults," and the following is a summary of the results. (There was a large consensus of opinion that the law as it now stands is insufficient for its purpose.) Lord Chief Justice Cockburn, Mr. Justice Lush, Mr. Justice Mellor, Chief Baron Kelly, Barons Bramwell, Pigott, and Pollock, all expressed the same judgment (pp. 7–19). The following gave their opinion in favor of flogging offenders in cases of brutal assaults. Lord Chief Justice Cockburn, Mr. Justices Blackburn, Mellor, Lush, Quain, Archibald, Brett, Grove, Chief Baron Kelly, Barons Bramwell, Pigott, Pollock, Charles, and Amphlett. Only Lord Coleridge and Lord Denman hesitated, and Mr. Justice Keating opposed flogging. Of Chairmen of Quarter Sessions sixty-four (out of sixty-eight, whose answers were sent to the Home Office), and the Recorders of forty-one towns, were in favor of flogging. After all this testimony of the opinions of experts (collected of course at the public expense), *three years* elapsed during which absolutely nothing was done to make any practical use of it! During the interval, scores of bills, *interesting to the represented sex*, passed through Parliament; but *this* question on which the lives of women literally hung was never mooted! Something like five thousand women, judging by the published judicial statistics, were in those years "brutally assaulted;" *i. e.,* not merely struck, but maimed, blinded, burned, trampled on by strong men in heavy shoes, and in many cases

murdered outright; and thousands of children were
brought up to witness scenes which (as Colonel Leigh
said) "infernalize a whole generation." Where lay the
fault? Scarcely with the government, or even with Parliament, but with the simple fact that, (under our present
constitution, women, having no votes, can only exception-
ally and through favor bring pressure to bear to force
attention even to the most crying of injustices under
which they suffer.) The Home Office *must* attend first
to the claims of those who can bring pressure to bear
on it; and Members of Parliament *must* bring in the
measures pressed by their constituents; and thus the
unrepresented *must* go to the wall.

The cases of cruelty of which I obtained statistics,
furnished to me mainly by the kindness of Miss A.
Shore, almost surpassed belief. It appeared that about
1,500 cases of aggravated (over and above ordinary)
assaults on wives took place every year in England; on
an average about four a day. Many of them were of
truly incredible savagery; and the victims were, in the
vast majority of cases, not drunken viragos (who usually escape violence or give as good as they receive),
but poor, pale, shrinking creatures who strove to earn
bread for their children and to keep together their
miserable homes; and whose very tears and pallor were
reproaches which provoked the *heteropathy* and cruelty
of their tyrants.

After much reflection I came to the conclusion that
in spite of all the authority in favor of flogging the
delinquents it was *not* expedient on the women's behalf that they should be so punished, since after they
had undergone such chastisement, however well merited,
the ruffians would inevitably return more brutalized
and infuriated than ever; and again have their wives
at their mercy. (The only thing really effective, I considered, was to give the wife the power of separating
herself and her children from her tyrant.) Of course in

the upper ranks, where people could afford to pay for
a suit in the Divorce Court, the law had for some years
opened to the assaulted wife this door of escape. But
among the working classes, where the assaults were ten-
fold as numerous and twenty times more cruel, no legal
means whatever existed of escaping from the husband
returning after punishment to beat and torture his wife
again. / I thought the thing to be desired was the extension of the privilege of rich women to their poorer
sisters, to be effected by an act of Parliament which
should give a wife whose husband had been convicted
of an aggravated assault on her, the power to obtain a
separation order under summary jurisdiction.)

(Mr. Alfred Hill, J. P., of Birmingham, son of my old
friend Recorder Hill, most kindly interested himself in
my project, and drafted a bill to be presented to Parliament embodying my wishes. Meanwhile, I set
about writing an article setting forth the extent of the
evil, the failure of the measures hitherto taken in various acts of Parliament, and, finally, the remedy I
proposed.) This article my friend Mr. Percy Bunting
was good enough to publish in the "Contemporary Review" in the spring of 1878. I also wrote an article in
"Truth on Wife Torture," afterwards reprinted.
Meanwhile, I had obtained the most cordial assistance
from Mr. Frederick Pennington and Mr. Hopwood, both
of whom were then in Parliament, and it was agreed
that I should beg Mr. Russell Gurney to take charge of
the bill which these gentlemen would support. I went
accordingly, armed with the draft bill, to the Recorder's house in Kensington Palace Gardens, and, as I
anxiously desired to find him at home, I ventured to
call as early as 10.30. Mr. Gurney read the draft bill
carefully, and entirely approved it. "Then," I said,
"you will take charge of it, I earnestly hope?" "No,"
said Mr. Gurney, "I cannot do that; I am too old and
overworked to undertake all the watching and labor

which may be necessary; but I will put my name on
the back of it with pleasure."

I knew, of course, that his name would give the
measure great importance and also help me to find some
other M. P. to take charge of it, so I could not but
thank him gratefully. At that moment of our interview, his charming wife entered the room leading a
little boy, I believe his nephew. Naturally I apologized to Mrs. Gurney for my presence at that unholy
hour of the morning; and said, " I came to Mr. Gurney
in my anxiety, as the friend of women." Mr. Gurney, hearing me, put his hands on the little lad's
shoulder and said to him, " Do you hear that, my boy ?
I hope that when you are an old man, as I am, some
lady like Miss Cobbe may call you *the friend of
women !* "

At last the bill, embodying precisely the purport of
that drawn up for me by Mr. Hill and subsequently
published in the "Contemporary Review," was read a
first time, the names of Mr. Herschel (now Lord Herschel) and Sir Henry Holland (afterwards Lord Knuts-
ford) being on the back of it. Every arrangement was
made for the second reading; and for avoiding the opposition which we expected to meet from a party which
seems always to think that by *calling* certain unions
"holy" a Church can sanctify that which has become
a bond of savage cruelty on one side, and soul degrading slavery on the other. Just at this crisis, Lord
Penzance, who was bringing a bill into the House of
Lords to remedy some defects concerning the costs of
the intervention of the Queen's Proctor in matrimonial
causes, introduced into it a clause dealing with the case
of the assaulted wives, and giving them precisely the
benefit contemplated in our bill and in my article;
namely, that of separation orders to be granted by the
same magistrates who have convicted the husband of
aggravated assaults upon them. That Lord Penzance

had seen our bill, then before the Lower House (it was ordered to be printed February 14th), and had had his attention called to the subject, either by it or by my article in the "Contemporary Review," I have taken as probable, but have no exact knowledge. I went at once to call on him and thank him from my heart for undertaking to do this great service of mercy to women; and also to pray him to consider certain points about the custody of the children of such assaulted wives. Lord Penzance received me with the utmost kindness and likewise gave favorable consideration to a letter or two which I ventured to address to him. It is needless to say that his advocacy of the measure carried it through the House of Lords without opposition. I believe that in speaking for it he said that if any noble Lord needed proof of the grievous want of such protection for wives they would find it in my article, which he held in his hand.

There was still, we feared, an ordeal to go through in the House of Commons; but the fates and hours were propitious, and the bill, coming in late one night as already passed by the House of Lords, and with Lord Penzance's great name on it, escaped opposition and was accepted without debate. (By the 27th of May, 1878, it had become the law of the land, and has since taken its place as chapter 19, of the 41st Vict., "An Act to amend the Matrimonial Causes Acts." The following are the clauses which concern the assaulted Wives : —

"4. If a husband shall be convicted summarily or otherwise of an aggravated assault within the meaning of the statute twenty-fourth and twenty-fifth Victoria, chapter one hundred, section forty-three, upon his wife, the Court or magistrate before whom he shall be so convicted may, if satisfied that the future safety of the wife is in peril, order that the wife shall be no longer bound to cohabit with her husband; and such order shall have the force and effect in all respects of a) decree of judicial separation on the ground of cruelty; and such order may further provide, —

"1. That the husband shall pay to his wife such weekly sum as the Court or magistrate may consider to be in accordance with his means, and with any means which the wife may have for her support, and the payment of any sum of money so ordered shall be enforceable and enforced against the husband in the same manner as the payment of money is enforced under an order of affiliation; and the Court or magistrate by whom any such order for payment of money shall be made shall have power from time to time to vary the same on the application of either the husband or the wife, upon proof that the means of the husband or wife have been altered in amount since the original order or any subsequent order varying it shall have been made.

"2. That the legal custody of any children of the marriage under the age of ten years shall, in the discretion of the Court or magistrate, be given to the wife."

At first the magistrates were very chary of granting the separation orders. One London police magistrate had said that the House of Commons would never put such power in the hands of one of the body, and he was, I suppose, proportionately startled when just six weeks later it actually lay in his own. (By degrees, however, the practice of granting the orders on proper occasions became common, and appears now to be almost a matter of course.) I hope that at least a hundred poor souls each year thus obtain release from their tormentors, and probably the deterrent effect of witnessing such manumission of ill-treated slaves may have still more largely served to protect women from the violence of brutal husbands.

Six years after the act had passed in 1884, I received a letter from a very energetic and prominent woman-worker with whom I had slight acquaintance, in

which the following passages occur. I quote them here
(though with some hesitation on the score of vanity)
for they have comforted me much and deeply, and will
do so to my life's end.

" On Wednesday last I was two hours with a widow
——— of O———, near W———; one of those persons who
make a country, so good, brave, loving, and hardworking!
For thirty-three long years she lived with a fiend of a
husband, and suffered furious blows, kicks, and attacks
with ropes, hot water, and crockery; was hurled down
cellar steps, etc., starved and insulted. All the time,
up early and at work managing a large shop and super-
intending thirty-five girls. . . .

" I wish you could have been there to hear her tell
me that 'the law was altered now,' and how her niece
had got a separation for brutal treatment; and (best of
all) 'her two bairns' (children). As for the 8s. a week
ordered — the wife never 'bothers after that.' 'The
Lord has stopped that villain's ways, and she wants no
more.' I could not help crying, as I looked at the exquisitely clean person and home, the determined face,
and thought of the diabolical horrors this good, clever
woman had gone through. I told her how you had got
the law altered — and she kept saying, 'She's a lady —
she's a lady. Bring her to O———, Missis! and we'll
percession her down t' street!' . . .

" You have love and gratitude from our hearts, I
assure you; we live wider lives and better for your
presence. I have ventured to write freely on a subject
some would find wearisome, but your heart is big and
will sympathize; and I am always longing for you to
know the active result of your achieved work. This:
that poor battered, bruised women are relieved — are
safer — and bless you, and so do I, from a full heart.

> " I am, dear Miss Cobbe,
> " Yours faithfully,
> " A. S."

If I could hear before I die that I had been able to
do as much for tortured brutes, I should say, "*Nunc
Dimittis*," and wish no more.

Some time after this (I have kept no copy or record
of date) I delivered a lecture, which was a good deal
noticed at the time, on the "Little Health of Ladies."
It was an exposure of the evils resulting to families
from the state of semi-invalidism in which so many
women live, usually gently lapped therein by interested
advisers. I exhorted women to do, as a duty to God and
man, everything possible to avoid falling into this
wretched condition, with the self-indulgence and neglect
of home and social duties leading to it or consequent
on it. I did not then know as much as I subsequently
learned of the inner history of a great deal of this
misery, or I might have added to my warning some
remarkable denunciations by honorable doctors of the
practices of their colleagues.[1]

A singular incident followed the publication of this
address in one of the magazines.

---

[1] Here is what Dr. Russell Reynolds, F. R. S., said in 1881 in an address
to the Medical Society of University College : "There is meddling and
muddling of a most disreputable sort, and the patients" (he is speaking
of women) "grow sick of it, and give it all up and get well ; or they go
from bad to worse." . . . "Physicians have coined names for trifling mal-
adies, if they have not invented them, and have set fashions of disease.
They have treated or maltreated their patients by endless examinations,
applications, and the like, and this sometimes for months, sometimes for
years, and then, when by some accident the patient has been removed
from their care, she has become quite well and there has been no more
need for caustic," etc., etc.

And here is what Dr. Clifford Allbut said in the Gulstonian lecture for
1884 at the Royal College of Physicians. After admitting that women
feel more pain than men, he mentioned the "*morbid claims*," the "*mental
abasement*," into which fall "the flock of women who lie under the wand
of the Gynæcologist" (specialist of women's diseases) ; "the women who
are *caged up in London back drawing-rooms*, and visited almost daily ;
their brave and active spirits broken under a *false* (! !) *belief in the presence of a secret and over-mastering local malady ;* and the best years of
their lives honored only by a distressful victory over pain." (Italics
mine.) — *Medical Press*, March 19th, 1884.

There was a lady, whose husband was a wealthy manufacturer in the North of England, who came to London once or twice a year, and for several years called on me, having much sympathy with my various interests. She appeared to be a confirmed invalid, crawling with great difficulty out of her carriage into our dining-room, and lying on a sofa during her visits. One day I was told she had come, and I was hastening to receive her downstairs, when a tall, elegant woman, whom I scarcely recognized, walked firmly and lightly into my drawing-room, and greeted me cordially with laughter in her eyes at my astonishment.

"So glad to see you so well!" I exclaimed, "but what has happened to you ?"

"It is *you* who have effected the cure!" she answered.

"Good gracious! How ?"

"Why, I read your 'Little Health of Ladies,' and I resolved to set my doctor at naught and go about like other people. And you see how well I am! There was really nothing the matter with me but want of exercise !"

I saw her several times afterward in good health ; and once she brought me a beautiful gold bracelet with clasp of diamonds set in black enamel, which she had had made for me, and which she forced me to accept as a token of her gratitude. I am fond of wearing it still.

Another incident strongly confirmed my belief in the source of much of the evil and misery arising from the little health of ladies. Travelling one day from Brighton I fell into conversation with a nice-looking, well-bred woman, the only other occupant of the railway carriage. Speaking of the salubrity of Brighton, she said, "I am sure I have reason enough to bless it. I was for fourteen years a miserable invalid on my sofa in London ; my doctor telling me I must never go out

or move. At last I said to my husband, 'It is better to
die than to go on thus;' and, in defiance of our doctor,
he brought me away to Brighton, and there I soon grew,
as you see, quite strong; and — and — I must tell you,
I have a little baby, and my husband is so happy!"

(That clever gynæcologist lost, I daresay, a hundred,
or perhaps two hundred, a year by the escape of his
patient from his assiduous visitations; but the lady
gained health and happiness; her husband his wife's
companionship; and both of them a child! How much
of the miseries and ill-health, and, in many cases, death
of women (of the poorer classes especially) lies at the
door of medical practitioners and operators, too fond by
half of the knife, is known to those who have read the
recent articles and correspondence respecting the women's hospitals and "Human Vivisection" therein in
the "Daily Chronicle" (May, 1891) and in the " Homœ-
opathic World " for June.)

(Quite apart from the doctors, however, a great deal
of the sickliness of women is undoubtedly due to
wretched fashions of tight-lacing, and wearing long and
heavy skirts, and tight thin boots, which render free
exercise of their limbs impossible. Nothing makes
me really despair of my sex, except looking at
fashion-plates; or seeing (what is much worse still,
being wicked, as well as foolish) the adornments so
many women use of dead birds, stuck on their empty
heads and heartless breasts. These things are a
disgrace to women, for which I have often felt
they *deserve* to be despised and swept aside by men
as soulless creatures unworthy of freedom. But alas!
it is precisely the women who adopt these idiotic fashions in dress, and wear (abominable cruelty!) egrets
as ornaments, who are *not* despised but admired by
men, who reserve their indifference and contempt for
their homely and sensible sisters. Men in these respects are as silly as the fish in the river caught by a

gaudy artificial fly on a hook, or enticed into a net by a scrap of scarlet cloth, and a glittering morsel of brass. I often wonder whether women are generally as little capable of forming a discriminating judgment of men.

(Lastly, there is a cause of female ill-health which always impresses me with profoundest pity, and which has never, I think, been fairly brought to the front as the origin of a large part of feminine feebleness. I mean the common want, among women who earn their livelihood, of sufficiently brain-nourishing and stimulating food.) Let any man, the strongest in the land in body and mind, subsist for one week on tea without milk, and bread and butter, and at the end of that time he will, I venture to predict, have lost half his superiority. His nervous excitability and cheerfulness may remain, or even be enhanced, but the faculty of largely grasping and strongly dealing with the subjects presented to him, and of doing thorough and complete work, nay even the *desire* of such perfection and finish, will have abated; and the fatal *slovenliness* of women's work will probably have begun to show itself. The physical conditions under which the human spirit can alone (in this life) carry out its purpose and attain its maximum of vigor are more or less lacking to half the women even in our country; and almost completely wanting to the poor prisoners of the Zenanas of India and the cripples of China. Exercise in the open air, wholesome and sufficient food, plenty of sleep at night — every one of these *sine qua non* elements of real health of mind, as well as of body, are out of reach of one woman out of every two; yet we remark, curiously, on the inferiority of their work! It is a vicious circle in which they are caught. They take lower wages because they can live more cheaply than men; and they necessarily live on those low wages too poorly to do anything but poor work; and again their wages are paltry because their work is so poor!

I confess, however, that — on the other hand — the spectacle of feminine feebleness and futility when (as continually happens) it is exhibited without the smallest excuse from inadequate food supply is indescribably irritating, nay, to me, humiliating and exasperating. Watch (for example of what I mean by "feminine futility") a woman asked to open a just-arrived box, or a bottle of champagne or of soda-water. She has been given a cold-chisel for opening the box, and a hammer; but they are invariably "astray" when required, or she does not think it worth while to fetch them from up or downstairs, so she kneels down before the box and begins by fumbling with her fingers at the knots in the cord. After five minutes' efforts and broken nails she gives this up in despair, and "thinks she must cut it." But how? She never by any chance has a knife in her pocket; so she first tries her scissors, which she *does* keep there, but which, being always quite blunt, fail to sever the rope; and then she fetches a dinner-knife, and gives one cut — when the feminine passion for economy suggests to her that she can save the rest of the cord by pushing it (with immense effort) an inch or two along the box, first at one side and then at the other. Then she hopes by breaking open the top of the box at one end only, to get out the contents without dealing further with the recalcitrant rope; and she endeavors to pull it open where the nails seem least firm. Alas! those nails will never yield to her weak hands; so her scissors are in requisition again, and being inserted and used as a wedge, immediately break off at the points, and are hastily withdrawn with an exclamation of agonizing regret for the blunt, but precious, instrument. Something must be thrust in, however, to pry open the box. The cold-chisel and hammer having been at last sought, but sought in vain, the kitchen cleaver, covered with the fat of the last joint it has cut, is brought into play; or, happy thought! she knows where her master keeps a fine sharp chisel, and this is pushed in — of course against a nail which breaks the edge and makes it useless for ever. The poker serves sufficiently well as a hammer to knock in the chisel, or the cleaver, and to bang up the protruding lid of the box; and at last one plank of the top is loosened, and she tears it off triumphantly, with a cry of rejoicing: "There! Now we shall get at everything in the box!" The goods, however, stubbornly refuse to be extricated through the hole on any terms; and eventually all the planks have to be successively broken up, and the long cared-for cord (for the preservation of which so much trouble has been undergone) is cut into little pieces of a foot or two in length, each attached to a hopelessly entangled knot, while the box itself is entirely wrecked.

The case of the soda-water or champagne bottle is worse again; so much so that experience warns the wise to forbear from calling for effervescent drinks where parlor-maids prevail. The preliminary ineffectual attempt to loosen the wires with the fingers (the proper pliers being, of course, missing); the resort to a steel carving-fork to open them, and, in default of the steel fork, to a silver one, which is of course bent immediately; the endeavor to cut the hempen cord with the bread knife with the result of blunting that tool against the wire; the struggle to cause the cork to fly by wobbling it with the right hand, while clasping the neck of the bottle till it and the contents are hot in the left; then (on the failure of this bold attempt) the cutting off the head of the cork with a carving knife, and at the same time a small slice of the operator's hand, which, of course, bleeds profusely; the consequent hasty transference of the bottle and the job to a second attendant; the hurried search of the same in the side-table drawer for the corkscrew; her rush to the kitchen to fetch that instrument where it has been

nefariously borrowed and where the point of the screw
has been broken off; the difficult (and crooked) insertion of the broken screw into the cork; the repeated
frantic tugs at the bottle, held tight between the knees,
finally the climax, when the cork bursts out and the
champagne along with it, up in the reddening face and
over the white muslin apron of the poor, anxious
woman, who hurries nervously to wipe it off, and then
pours the small quantity of liquor which remains bubbling over the glasses, till the tablecloth is swamped —
such in brief is feminine futility, as exhibited in the
drawing of corks!　Luckily it is possible to find parlor-
maids who know how to use, and will keep at hand,
both cold-chisels and corkscrews.　But they are exceptions.　The normal woman, in the presence of a nailed-
down box or a champagne bottle, behaves as I have
depicted from careful study; and the irritation she pro-
duces in me is past words, especially if a man be waiting for his beverage and observing the spectacle of the
helplessness of my sex.　If "man" be "a tool-making
animal," I am afraid that "woman" is a "tool-break-
ing" one.　I think every girl, as well as every boy,
ought to be given a month's training in a carpenter's
shop to teach her how to strike a nail straight; what
is the difference between the proper insertion and extrac-
tion of nails and of screws; why chisels should not be
employed as screw-drivers; how far preferable for making holes are gimlets to hairpins or the points of scissors; and, finally, the general superiority of glue over
paste or gum for sticking wooden furniture when broken
by her besom of destruction!

My dear friend Emily Shaen wrote an excellent tract
which I should like to see republished, urging that it is
absurd to go on talking of the house being the proper
sphere of a woman, while we neglect to teach her the
very rudiments of a *Hausfrau's* duties, and leave her to
find them all out, at her husband's expense, when she

marries. The nature of gas and of gasometers, and
how *not* to cause explosions nor be cheated in the bill;
the arrangements of water-works in houses, pipes,
drains, cisterns, ball-cocks and all the rest, for hot and
cold water; the choice of properly morticed, not merely
glued, furniture; what constitutes a good kitchen
range, and how coal should be economized in it; how
to choose fresh meat, etc., such should be her lessons.
To this might be usefully added an inkling of the laws
relating to masters and servants, debts, bills, etc., etc., and
of the elementary arrangements of banking and invest-
ing money. It was once discovered at my school that a
very clever young lady, who could speak four languages
and play two instruments well, *could not read the clock!*
I think there are many grown-up women, well-educated
according to the ordinary standard of their class, whose
ignorance concerning the simplest matters of household
duty is not a whit less absurd.

In 1881 I prepared and delivered to an audience
of about 150 ladies, in the Westminster Palace Hotel,
a course of six lectures on the " Duties of Women."
My dear friend Miss Anna Swanwick took the chair
for me on these occasions, and performed her part with
such tact and geniality as to give me every advantage.
My auditors were very attentive and sympathetic, and
altogether the task was made very pleasant to me. I
repeated the course again at Clifton the same year,
Mrs. Beddoe, the wife of Dr. John Beddoe the anthro-
pologist, who was then living at that place, most obli-
gingly lending me her large drawing-rooms.

These lectures when printed went through three editions in England and, I think, eight in America, the
last being brought out by Miss Willard, who adopted
the little book as the first of a series on women's concerns, published by her vast and wonderful organization, the W. C. T. U.

My object in giving these lectures was to impress

women as strongly as might be in my power with the unspeakable importance of adding to our claims for just *Rights* of all kinds, the adoption of the highest standard of *Duty ;* and the strict preservation amongst us of all womanly virtues, while adding to them those others to the growth of which our conditions have hitherto been unfavorable — namely, Truth and Courage. I desired also to discuss the new views current amongst us respecting filial and conjugal "obedience ; " the proper attitude to be held towards (unrepentant) vice, and many other topics. Finally I wished to place the efforts to obtain political freedom on what I deem to be their proper ground. I ask : —

"What ought we to do at present, as concerns all public work wherein it is possible for us to obtain a share ?

"The question seems to answer itself in its mere statement. We are bound to do all we can to promote the virtue and happiness of our fellowmen and women, and *therefore* we must accept and seize every instrument of power, every vote, every influence which we can obtain, to enable us to promote virtue and happiness.

" . . . Why are we not to wish and strive to be allowed to place our hands on that vast machinery whereby, in a constitutional realm, the great work of the world is carried on, and which achieves by its enormous power ten-fold either the good or the harm which any individual can reach ; which may be turned to good or turned to harm according to the hands which touch it ? [In almost every case it is only by legislation that the roots of great evils can be reached at all, and that the social diseases of pauperism, vice and crime can be brought within hope of cure.\

"You will judge from these remarks the ground on which, as a matter of duty, I place the demand for woman's political emancipation. I think we are bound to seek it, in the first place, as a means — a very great means — of fulfilling our social duty, of contributing to the virtue and happiness of mankind, and advancing the Kingdom of God.   There are many other reasons, viewed from the point of expediency; but this is the view from that of duty.   We know too well that men who possess political rights do not always, or often, regard them in this fashion; but this is no reason why we should not do so.   We also know that the individual power of one vote at any election seems rarely to effect any appreciable difference; but this also need not trouble us, for, little or great, if we can obtain any influence at all we ought to seek for it, and the multiplication of the votes of women bent on securing conscientious candidates would soon make it not only appreciable but weighty.   Nay, further, the direct influence of a vote is but a small part of the power which the possession of the political franchise confers. Its indirect influence is far more important.   In a government like ours, where the basis of representation is so immensely extensive the whole business of legislation is carried on by pressure — the pressure of each represented class and party to get its grievances redressed, to make its interests prevail. . . .   It is one of the sore grievances of women that, not possessing representation, the measures which concern them are for ever postponed to the bills promoted by the represented classes (*e. g.*, the married woman's property bill, was, if I mistake not, six times set down for reading in one session in vain, the House being counted out on every occasion).

"Thus, in asking for the Parliamentary franchise, we are asking, as I understand it, for the power to influence legislation generally; and in every other kind of franchise, municipal, parochial, or otherwise, for similar power to bring our sense of justice and righteousness to bear on public affairs. . . .

"What is this, after all, my friends, but *public spirit;* in one shape called patriotism, in another philanthropy; the extension of our sympathies beyond the narrow bounds of our homes, and disinterested enthusiasm for every good and sacred cause? As I said at first, all the world has recognized from the earliest times how good and noble and wholesome a thing it is for men to have their breasts filled with such public spirit; and we look upon them when they exhibit it as glorified thereby. Do you think it is not equally an ennobling thing for a *woman's* soul to be likewise filled with these large and generous and unselfish emotions?"

I draw the lectures to a conclusion thus: —

"None of us, I am sure, realize how blessed a thing we might make of our lives if we would but give ourselves, heart and soul, to fulfil *all* the obligations, personal, social, and religious, which rest upon us; to gain the strength —

> ' To think, to feel, to do, only the holy Right,
> To yield no step in the awful race, no blow in the fearful fight,'

to live, in purity and truth and courage, a life of love to God and to man; striving to make every spot where we dwell, every region to which our influence can extend, God's kingdom, where His will shall be done on earth as it is done in heaven."

Some time after the delivery of these addresses, when the Primrose League was in full activity, I wrote at the request of the committee of the Women's Suffrage Association a circular-letter to the "Dames" (of whom I am one), begging them to endeavor to make the granting of votes to women a "plank" in their platform. I received many friendly letters in reply — but the men who influenced the league, apparently finding that they could make the Dames do their political work for them *without votes,* discouraged all movement in the desired direction, and I do not suppose that anything was gained by my attempt.

My last effort on behalf of women was to read a paper on "Women's Duty to Women" at the Conference of women workers held at Birmingham in November, 1890. This address was received with such exceeding kindness and sympathy by my audience that the little event has left very tender recollections which I am glad to carry with me.

I will record here two paragraphs which I should like to leave as my last appeal on behalf of my sex.

"It may be an open question whether any individual woman suffers more severely in body or mind than any individual man. There are some who say that all our passions matched with theirs —

'Are as moonlight unto sunlight, and as water unto wine,'

a sentiment which, I am happy to tell you, Lord Tennyson has angrily disclaimed as his own, declaring that he only 'put it into the mouth of an impatient fool.' But that our *whole sex together* suffers more physical pain, more want, more grief, than the other is not, I think, open to doubt. Even if we put aside the poor Chinese women maimed from infancy, the Hindoo women against whose cruel wrongs their noble countryman, Malabari, has just been pleading so eloquently in London — if we put these and all the other prisoners of Eastern harems, and miserable wives of African and Australian savages out of question, and think only of the comparatively free and happy women of Christendom, how much more *liable to suffering,* if not always actually condemned to suffer, is the life of women! 'To be weak is to be miserable,' and we *are* weak; always comparatively to our companions and weak often, absolutely, and in reference to the wants we must supply, the duties we must perform. Now, it seems to me that just in proportion as any one is possessed of strength of

mind or of body, or of wealth or influence, so far it behoves him, or her, to turn with sympathy and tender
helpfulness to the weakest and most forlorn of God's
creatures, whether it be man or woman or child, or even
brute.   The weight of the claim is in exact ratio of the
feebleness and helplessness and misery of the claimant.

.   .   .   .

"Thus, then, I would sum up the counsels which I
am presuming to offer to you.   You will all remember
the famous line of Terence, at which the old Roman
audience rose in a tumult of applause : 'I am a *Man* —
nothing human is alien to me.'   I would have each of
you add to this in an emphatic way: '*Mulier sum.*
Nihil muliere a me alienum puto.' 'I am a *woman*.
Nothing concerning the interests of women is alien to
me.'   Take the sorrows, the wants, the dangers (above
all the dangers) of our sisters closely to heart, and,
without ceasing to interest yourself in charities having
men and boys for their objects, recognize that your
earlier care should be for the weakest, the poorest, those
whose dangers are worst of all — for (after all) ruin
can only drive a *man* to the workhouse; it may drive a
woman to perdition! Think of all the weak, the helpless, the wronged women and little children, and the
harmless brutes; and save and shield them as best you
can; even as the mother-bird will shelter and fight for
her little helpless fledgelings.   This is the natural field
of feminine courage.   Then, when you have found your
work, whatever it be, give yourself to it with all your
heart, and make the resolution in God's sight never to
go to your rest leaving a stone unturned which may
help your aims.   Half-and-half charity does very little
good to the objects; and is a miserable, slovenly affair
for the workers.   And when the end comes and the
night closes in, the long, last night of earth, when no
man can work any more in this world, your milk-and-
water, half-hearted charities will bring no memories of

comfort to you. They are not so many 'good works' which you can place on the credit side of your account, in the mean, commercial spirit taught by some of the churches. Nay, rather they are only solemn evidences that you *knew your duty*, knew you *might* do good, and did it not, or did it half-heartedly! What a thought for those last days when we know ourselves to be going home to God, God — whom at bottom after all, we have loved and shall love for ever — that we *might* have served Him here, *might* have blessed his creatures, *might* have done His will on earth as it is done in Heaven, but we have let the glorious chance slip by us for ever."

CHAPTER XX.

THE CLAIMS OF BRUTES.

READERS who have reached this twentieth chapter of my Life will smile (as I have often done of late years) at the ascription to me in sundry not very friendly publications, of exclusive sympathy for animals and total indifference to human interests.) I have seen myself frequently described as a woman "who would sacrifice any number of men, women, and children, sooner than that a few rabbits should be inconvenienced." Many good people apparently suppose me to represent a personal survival of Totemism in England; and to worship dogs and cats, while ready to consign the human race generally to destruction.

The foregoing pages, describing my life in old days in Ireland and the years which I spent afterwards working in the slums in Bristol, ought, I think, to suffice to dissipate this fancy picture. As a matter of fact, (it has only been of late years and since their wrongs have appealed alike to my feelings of pity and to my moral sense, that I have come to bestow any peculiar attention on animals) or have been concerned with them more than is common with the daughters of country squires to whom dogs, horses, and cattle are familiar subjects of interest from childhood. I have indeed always felt much affection for dogs; that is to say, for those who exhibit the true dog-character — which is far from being the case of every canine creature! Their eagerness, their joyousness, their transparent little wiles, their caressing and devoted affection, are to me more winning, even I may say, more really and intensely *human* (in the sense in which a child is human), than the artificial, cold, and selfish characters one meets too often in the guise of ladies and gentle-men. It is not the four legs, nor the silky or shaggy coat of the dog which should prevent us from discern-ing his inner nature of thought and love; limited thought, it is true; but quite unlimited love. That he is dumb is to me only another claim (as it would be in a human child) on my consideration. But be-cause I love good dogs, and, in their measure also, good horses and cats and birds (I had once a dear and lovely white pea-hen), I am not therefore a morbid Zoöphilist I should be very sorry indeed to say or think like Byron when my dog dies, that I "had but one true friend, and here he lies!" I have — thank God ! — known many men and women, who have all a dog's merits of honesty and single-hearted devotion *plus* the virtues which can only flourish on the high level of humanity ; and to them I give a friendship which the best of dogs cannot share.

That there are some Timons in the world whose hearts, embittered by human ingratitude, have turned with relief to the faithful love of a dog, I am very well aware. Surely the fact makes one appeal the more on behalf of the creatures who thus by their humble devo-tion heal the wounds of disappointed or betrayed affec-tion ; and who come to cheer the lonely, the unloved, the dull-witted, the blind, the poverty-stricken whom the world forsakes. I think Lamartine was right to treat this love of the dog for man as a special provi-sion of Divine mercy, and to marvel —

"Par quelle pitié pour nos cœurs Il vous donne
Pour aimer celui qui n'aime plus personne !"

Not a few deep thanksgivings, I believe, have gone up to the Maker of man and brute for the silent sympathy — expressed perhaps in no nobler way than by the gentle licking of a passive hand — which has yet saved a human heart from the sense of utter abandonment.

But *I* have no such sorrowful or embittering experience of human affection. I do not say, "The more I know of men the more I love dogs;" but, "The more I know of dogs the more I love *them*," without any invidious comparisons with men, women, or children. As regards the children, indeed, I have been always fond of those which came in my way; and if the Tenth Commandment had gone on to forbid coveting one's neighbor's "*child*," I am not sure that I should not have had to plead guilty to breaking it many times.

In my old home I possessed a dear Pomeranian dog of whom I was very fond, who, being lame, used constantly to ensconce herself (though forbidden by my father) in my mother's carriage under the seat, and never showed her little pointed nose till the britzska had got so far from home that she knew no one would put her down on the road. Then she would peer out and lie against my mother's dress and be fondled. Later on I had the companionship of another beautiful, mouse-colored Pomeranian, brought as a puppy from Switzerland. In my hardworking life in Bristol in the schools and workhouse she followed me and ingratiated herself everywhere, and my solitary evenings were much the happier for dear Hajjin's company. Many years afterwards she was laid under the sod of our garden in Hereford Square. Another dog of the same breed whom I sent away at one year old to live in the country was returned to me *eight years* afterwards, old and diseased. The poor beast recognized me after a few moments' eager examination, and uttered an actual scream of joy when I called her by name; exhibiting every token of tender affection for me ever afterwards. When one reflects what eight years signify in the life of a dog — almost equivalent to the distance between sixteen and sixty in a human being — some measure is afforded by this incident of the durability of a dog's attachment. Happily, kind Dr. Hoggan cured poor Dee of her malady, and she and I enjoyed five happy years of companionship ere she died here in Hengwrt. I have dedicated my "Friend of Man" to her memory.

Among my smaller literary tasks in London I wrote an article for which Mr. Leslie Stephen (then editing the "Cornhill Magazine" in which it appeared) was kind enough to express particular liking. It was called "Dogs Whom I Have Met;" and gave an account of many canine individualities of my acquaintance. I also wrote an article in the "Quarterly Review" on the "Consciousness of Dogs" of which I have given above (p. 127) Mr. Darwin's favorable opinion. Both of these papers are reprinted in my "False Beasts and True." Such has been the sum total, I may say, of my personal concern with animals before and apart from my endeavors to deliver them from their scientific tormentors.

(It was, as I have stated, the abominable wrongs endured by animals which first aroused, and has permanently maintained, my special interest in them. My great-grandfather had an office in the yard at Newbridge for his magisterial work, and over his own seat he caused to be inscribed the text: "*Deliver him that is oppressed from the hand of the adversary.*" I know not whether it were a juvenile impression, but I have felt all my life an irresistible impulse to rush in wherever any one is "oppressed" and try to "deliver" him, her, or *it*, as the case may be, from the "adversary"! In the case of beasts, their helplessness and speechlessness appeal, I think, to every spark of generosity in one's heart ; and the command, "Open thy mouth for the dumb," seems the very echo of our consciences. Everything in us, manly or womanly (and the best in us all is *both*), answers it back.

When I was a little child, living in a house where

hunting, coursing, shooting, and fishing were carried on by all the men and boys, I took such field-sports as part of the order of things, and learned with delight from my father to fish in our ponds on my own account. Somehow it came to pass that when, at sixteen, my mind went through that strange process which Evangelicals call "conversion," among the first things which my freshly-awakened moral sense pointed out was — that I must give up fishing! I reflected that the poor fishes were happy in their way in their proper element; that we did not in the least need, or indeed often use, them for food; and that I must no longer take pleasure in giving pain to any creature of God.) It was a little effort to me to relinquish this amusement in my very quiet, uneventful life; but, as the good Quakers say, it was "borne in on me" that I had to do it, and from that time I have never held a rod or line (though I have been out in boats where large quantities of fish were caught on the Atlantic coast), and I freely admit that angling scarcely comes under the head of cruelty at all, and is perfectly right and justifiable when the fish are wanted for food and are killed quickly. I used to stand sometimes, after I had ceased to fish, over one of the ponds in our park and watch the bright creatures dart hither and thither, and say in my heart a little thanksgiving on their behalf instead of trying to catch them.

Fifty years after this incident, I read in John Woolman's (the Quaker Saint's) "Journal," chapter xi., this remark : —

"I believe, where the love of God is verily perfected and the true spirit of government watchfully attended, a tenderness towards all creatures made subject to us will be experienced, and a care felt in us that we do not lessen that sweetness of life in the animal creation which the great Creator intends for them under our government."

To me, as I have said, it was almost the *first*, and not an *advanced*, much less "perfected," religious impulse, which led me to begin to recognize the claims of the lower animals on our compassion. (Of course, I disliked then, and always, hunting, coursing, and shooting; but as a woman I was not expected to join in such pursuits, and I did not take on myself to blame those who followed them. I do not now allow of any comparison between the cruelty of such *field-sports* and the deliberate *chamber-sport* of vivisection.)

I shall now relate as succinctly as possible the history of the anti-vivisection movement, so far as I have had to do with it. Of course an immense amount of work for the same end has been carried on all these twenty years by other Zoöphilists with whom I have had no immediate connection, or perhaps cognizance of their labors, but without whose assistance the society which I helped to found certainly could not have made as much way as it has done.(I only presume here to tell the story of the Victoria Street Society, and the occurrences which led to its formation.)

In the year 1863 there appeared in several English newspapers complaints of the cruelties practised in the veterinary schools at Alfort near Paris. The students were taught there, as in most other continental veterinary schools, to perform operations on *living* animals, and so to acquire (at the cost, of course, of untold suffering to the victims) the same manipulative skill which English students gain equally well by practising on dead carcases. Living horses were supplied to the Alfort students on which, at the time I speak of, they performed sixty operations apiece, including every one in common use, and many of which were purely academic, being never employed in actual practice because the horse after enduring them becomes necessarily useless. These operations lasted eight hours, and the aspect of the mangled creatures, hoofless, eyeless, burned, gashed, eviscerated, skinned, mutilated in every conceivable way, appalled the visitors, who reported the facts, while it afforded, they said, a subject of merriment to the horde of students. The English Society for Prevention of Cruelty to Animals laudably exerted itself to stop these atrocities, and appealed to the Emperor to interfere; not, perhaps, very hopefully, since, as I have heard, Napoleon III. was in the habit of attending these hideous spectacles in his own imperial person on the Thursdays on which they took place. This circumstance, taken in connection with the Empress' patronage of bull-fights, has made Sedan seem to me an event on which the animal world, at all events, has to be congratulated.

Some years later Mr. James Cowie took over to France an appeal, signed by 500 English veterinarians, entreating their French colleagues to adopt the English practice of using only dead carcases for the exercises of students. Through this and other good offices it is understood that the number and severity of the operations performed at Alfort, and elsewhere in France, have been greatly reduced. Unhappily the same sort of vivisection for the acquirement of skill is going on more or less barbarously in veterinary schools all over the continent.

(On reading of these cruelties I wrote an article, "The Rights of Man and the Claims of Brutes," which I hoped might help to direct public attention to them. In this paper I endeavored to work out as best I could the ethical problem (which I at once perceived to be beset with difficulties) of a definition of the limits of human rights over animals. My article was published by Mr. Froude in "Fraser's Magazine" for November, 1863, and was subsequently reprinted in my "Studies, Ethical and Social." It was, so far as I know, the first effort made to deal with the moral questions involved in the torture of animals, either for the sake of scientific and therapeutic research or for the acquirement of manipulative skill) In the thirty years which have elapsed since I wrote it I have seen reason to raise considerably the "claims" which I then urged on behalf of the brutes, but I observe that new recruits to our anti-vivisection party usually begin exactly where I stood at that time, and announce their ideas to me as their mature conclusions.

The same month of November, 1863, in which my article (written some weeks before, while I was ill and lame at Aix-les-Bains) appeared in Fraser, I was living near Florence, and was startled by hearing of similar cruelties practised at the *Specola,* where Professor Schiff had his laboratory. My friend Miss Blagden and I were holding our usual weekly reception in Villa Brichieri on Bellosguardo, and we learned that many of our guests had been shocked by the rumors which had reached them. In particular, the American physician who had accompanied Theodore Parker to Florence and attended him in his last days — Dr. Appleton, of Harvard University — told us that he himself had gone over Professor Schiff's laboratory, and had seen dogs, pigeons, and other animals in a frightfully mangled and suffering state. A Tuscan officer had seen a cat so tortured that he forced Schiff to kill it. Some fifty or sixty letters had been (or were afterwards) lodged at the Mairie from neighbors complaining of the disturbance caused by the cries and moans of the victims in the *Specola.* After much conversation I asked what could be done to check these systematic cruelties, which no Tuscan law could then touch in any way. It was suggested that a memorial should be addressed to Professor Schiff himself, urging him to spare his victims as much as possible. This memorial I drafted at once, and it was translated into Italian and sent round Florence for signatures. Mrs. Somerville

placed her name at the head of it; and through her
earnest exertions and those of her daughters and of
several other friends, the list of supporters soon became
very weighty.   Among the English signatures was that
of Walter Savage Landor (who added some words so
violent that I was obliged to suppress them!); and
among the Italians almost the whole historic aristocracy
of old Florence — Corsis and Corsinis, and Aldobran-
dinis and Strozzis, and a hundred more, the reading of
whose names recalled Medicean times.   In all, there
were 783 signatories.   Very few of them were of the
mezzo-ceto class, and *none* belonged to the (Red) repub-
lican party.   Schiff was himself a "Red," and, as such,
he might apparently commit any cruelty he thought
fit, inasmuch as he and the other vivisectors (we were
told by a lady prominent in that party) were seeking
"the religion of the future" — in the brains and entrails
of the tortured beasts!   The same lady expressed to
me her wish that "every animal in creation should be
immolated, if only to discover a single fact of science."
Another English woman (also married to a foreigner)
wrote to the "Daily News" to praise Schiff for "actively
pursuing vivisection."

The memorial, as often happens, did no *direct* good;
Professor Schiff tossing it aside, and politely qualifying
the signatories (in the "Nazione" newspaper) as "*un tas
de Marquis.*"   But it certainly caused the subject to be
much discussed, and doubtless prepared the way for the
complaints and lawsuits concerning the "nuisances" of
the moaning dogs, which eventually made Florence an
unpleasant abode for Professor Schiff.   He retreated
thence to Geneva in 1877.   The Florentine *Società Prottettrice degli Animali* was founded by Countess Baldelli
in 1873, and has led the agitation there against vivisection ever since.

Meanwhile on the presentation of the memorial, Professor Schiff wrote a letter in the "Nazione" (the chief

newspaper of Florence) denying the facts mentioned in the letter of the official correspondent of the "Daily News," and challenging the said correspondent to come forward and make good the statement. I instantly wrote a letter saying that I was the "Daily News'" correspondent in Florence; that the letter complained of was mine; and that for verification of my assertions therein I appended a full and signed statement by Dr. Appleton of what he had himself witnessed in the *Specola*.

It was rather difficult for me then to believe that this letter of mine (in Italian of course), duly signed and authenticated with name, date, and place, was refused publication in the paper wherein I had been challenged to come forward! On learning this amazing fact, I requested Dr. Appleton to go down again to Florence and ask the editor of the "Nazione" to publish my letter if in no other way, at least *as a paid advertisement*. The answer made by the editor to Dr. Appleton was that it might be inserted, but only among the advertisements in certain columns of the paper where no decent reader would look for it. N. B. — The "Nazione" replenished its exchequer by the help of that class of notices which are declined by every reputable English newspaper. After this Dr. Appleton went in despair to Professor Schiff himself, and told him he was bound in honor (seeing he had made the challenge to us) to compel the editor to print our answer. The learned and scientific gentleman shrugged his shoulders and laughed in the face of the American who could imagine him to be so simple!

I left Florence soon after this first brush with the demon of vivisection, but retained (as will easily be understood) very strong feelings on the subject.

At a meeting of the British Association in Liverpool in 1870 a committee was appointed to consider the subject of "Physiological Experimentation," and their report was published in the "Medical Times and Gazette," February 25th, 1871, and in "British Association Reports," 1871, p. 144. It consists of the following four rules or recommendations on the subject of vivisection : —

"(I.) No experiment which can be performed under the influence of an anæsthetic ought to be done without it. (II.) No painful experiment is justifiable for the mere purpose of illustrating a law or fact already demonstrated; in other words, experimentation without the employment of anæsthetics is not a fitting exhibition for teaching purposes. (III.) Whenever, for the investigation of new truth, it is necessary to make a painful experiment, every effort should be made to ensure success, in order that the sufferings inflicted may not be wasted. For this reason, no painful experiment ought to be performed by an unskilled person, with insufficient instruments and assistants, or in places not suitable to the purpose; that is to say, anywhere except in physiological and pathological laboratories, under proper regulations. (IV.) In the scientific preparation for veterinary practice, operations ought not to be performed upon living animals for the mere purpose of obtaining greater operative dexterity."

These four rules were countersigned by M. A. Lawson, G. M. Humphry (now Sir George Humphry), J. H. Balfour, Arthur Gamgee, William Flower, J. Burdon-Sanderson, and George Rolleston. Of course we, who attended that celebrated Liverpool meeting of the British Association and had heard the President laud Dr. Brown-Séquard enthusiastically, greatly rejoiced at this humane ukase of autocratic Science.

But as time passed we were surprised to find that nothing was done to enforce these rules in any way or at any place; and that the particular practice which they most distinctly condemn, namely, the use of vivisections as illustrations of recognized facts, was flourishing more than ever without let or hindrance. The prospectuses of University College for 1874–5, of Guy's Hospital Medical School, 1874–5, of St. Thomas's Hospital of Westminster Hospital Medical School, etc., all mentioned among their attractions: " Demonstrations on living animals; " "Gentlemen will themselves perform the experiments; " etc., and quite as if nothing whatever had been said against them.

But worse remained. One of the signatories of the above rules (or as perhaps we may more properly call them, these "*pious opinions*"*!*), the most eminent of English physiologists, Professor Burdon-Sanderson himself, edited and brought out in 1873, the "Handbook of the Physiological Laboratory," to which he, Dr. Lauder-Brunton, Dr. Klein, and Dr. Foster were joint contributors. This celebrated work is a manual of exercises in vivisection, intended (as the preface says) "for beginners in physiological work." The following are observations on this book furnished to the Royal Commission by Mr. Colam, and printed in Appendix iv., p. 379, of their Report and Minutes of Evidence: —

"That the object of the editor and his coadjutors was to induce young persons to perform experiments on their own account and without adequate surveillance is manifest throughout the work by the supply of elementary knowledge and elaborate data. Not only are the names and quantities of necessary chemicals given, but the most careful description is provided in letter-press and plates of implements for holding animals during their struggles, so that a novice may learn at home without a teacher. Besides, the editor's preface states that the book is 'intended for beginners,' and that 'difficult and complicated' experiments consequently have been omitted; and that of Dr. Foster allures the student by assurances of inexpensive as well as easy manipulation. . . . Very seldom indeed is the student told to anæsthetize, and then only during an operation. It cannot be alleged that 'beginners' know when to narcotize, and when not; but if they do then the few directions to use chloral, etc., are unnecessary. No doubt should have been left on this point in a handbook designed 'for beginners.' Besides, where will students find cautions against the infliction of unnecessary pain and wanton experimentation? On the contrary, the student is encouraged to repeat the torture 'any number of times.' These facts are significant."

In the " Minutes of Evidence " of the Royal Commission we find that the late Professor Rolleston, of Oxford, being under examination, was asked by Mr. Hutton : " Then I understand that your opinion about the 'Handbook' is, that it is a dangerous book to society, and that it has warranted to some extent the feeling of anxiety in the public which its publication has created ? " Professor Rolleston : " *I am sorry to have to say that I do think it is so* " (1351). In his own examination Professor Burdon-Sanderson admitted that the use of anæsthetics whenever possible "ought to have been stated much more distinctly at the beginning of his book " (2265), and agreed to Lord Cardwell's suggestion, " Then I may assume that in any future communication with ' beginners ' *greater pains will be taken to make them distinctly understand how animals may be saved from suffering than has been taken in this book ?* " " Yes," said Dr. B.-S., " I am quite willing to say that " (2266).

Esoteric vivisection, it will be observed, as revealed in handbooks for "beginners," is a very different thing from esoteric vivisection, described for the benefit of the outside public as if regulated by the four rules above quoted !

The following year, 1874, certain experiments were performed before a medical congress at Norwich. They consisted in the injection of alcohol and of absinthe into the veins of dogs ; and were done by M.

Magnan, an eminent French physiologist, who has in recent years described sympathy for animals as a special form of insanity. Mr. Colam, on behalf of the R. S. P. C. A., very properly instituted a prosecution against M. Magnan, under the act 12 and 13 Vict., c. 92; and brought Sir William Fergusson and Dr. Tufnell (the President of the Irish College of Surgeons) to swear that his experiments were useless. M. Magnan withdrew speedily to his own country, or a conviction would certainly have been obtained against him. But it was not merely on proof of the *infliction of torture* that Mr. Colam's Society relied to obtain such conviction, but on the high scientific authority which they were able to bring to prove that the torture was *scientifically useless.* Failing such testimony, which would generally be unattainable, it was recognized that the application of the act in question (Martin's act amended) to *scientific* cruelties, which it had not been framed to meet, would always be beset with difficulties. It became thenceforth apparent to the friends of animals that some new legislation calculated to reach offenders pleading scientific purpose for barbarous experiments was urgently needed; and the existence of the "Handbook," with minute directions for performing hundreds of operations, many of them of extreme severity, proved that the danger was not remote or theoretical; but already present and at our doors.

A few weeks after this trial at Norwich had taken place, and had justly gained great applause for Mr. Colam and the R. S. P. C. A., Mrs. Luther Holden, wife of the eminent surgeon, then Senior Surgeon of St. Bartholomew's Hospital, called on me in Hereford Square to talk over the matter and take counsel as to what could be done to strengthen the law in the desired direction. The great and wealthy R. S. P. C. A. was obviously the body with which it properly lay to promote the needed legislation; and it only seemed

necessary to give the committee of that society proof
that public opinion would strongly support them in
calling for it, to induce them to bring a suitable bill
into Parliament backed by their abundant influence.   I
agreed to draft a memorial to the committee of the R.
S. P. C. A. praying it to undertake this task; after
learning from Mr. Colam that such an appeal would be
altogether welcome; and I may add that I received
cordial assistance from him in arranging for its presentation.

It was a difficult task for me to draw up that memorial, but, such as it was, it acted as a spark to tinder,
showing how much latent feeling existed on the subject.   Many ladies and gentlemen, notably the Countess of Camperdown, the Countess of Portsmouth (now
the Dowager Countess), General Colin Mackenzie, Colonel Wood (now Sir Evelyn), and others, exerted themselves most earnestly to obtain influential signatures in
their circles, and distributed in all directions copies of
the memorial and of two pamphlets I wrote to accompany it, — "Reasons for Interference" and "Need
of a Bill."   With their help in the course of about six
weeks (without advertisements or paid agency of any
kind) we obtained six hundred signatures; every one
of which represented a man or woman of some social
importance.   The first to sign it was my neighbor and
friend, Rev. Gerald Blunt, rector of Chelsea.   After
him came Mr. Carlyle, Tennyson, Browning, Mr. Lecky,
Sir Arthur Helps, Sir W. Fergusson, John Bright, Mr.
Jowett, the Archbishop of York (Dr. Thomson), Sir
Edwin Arnold, the Primate of Ireland (Marcus Beres-
ford), Cardinal Manning (then Archbishop of Westminster), the Duke and Duchess of Northumberland, John
Ruskin, James Martineau, the Duke of Rutland, the
Duke of Wellington, Lord Coleridge, Lord Selborne,
Sir Fitzroy Kelly, the Bishops of Winchester, Exeter,
Salisbury, Manchester, Bath and Wells, Hereford, St.

Asaph, and Derry, Lord Russell, and many other peers and M. P.'s, and no less than seventy-eight medical men, several of whom were eminent in the profession.

I shall insert here a few of the replies, favorable and otherwise, which I received to my invitations to sign the memorial.

Bishopthorpe, York, December 28, 1874.

The Archbishop of York presents his compliments to Miss Cobbe and begs to enclose the memorial signed by him.

"Exception to suggestion third," on the prohibition of publishing, which he thinks unworkable, and therefore (illegible) to the memorial. If, however, it is too late to alter it he will not stand out even on that point.

He thinks the practices in question detestable. The Norwich case was a disgrace to the country.

The Archbishop thanks Miss Cobbe for inviting him to sign.

A. B. Beresford-Hope to Miss F. P. C.

Bedgebury Park, Cranbrook,
January 26th, 1875.

Dear Madam, — Lady Mildred and myself trust that it is not too late to enclose to you the accompanying signatures to the memorial against vivisection, although the day fixed for its return has unfortunately been allowed to elapse. We can assure you of our very hearty sympathy in the cause; the delay has wholly come of oversight.

In regard to the details of the suggestions, I must be allowed to express my doubt as to the feasibility of the third suggestion. Its stringency would I fear defeat its own object. I sympathize too much with the question in itself to decline signing on account of this proposal, but I must request to be considered as a dissentient on that head.

Believe me, dear madam, yours very faithfully,

A. B. Beresford-Hope.

B. JOWETT TO MISS F. P. C.

DEAR MISS COBBE, — I have much pleasure in signing the paper which you kindly sent me.

Yours very sincerely,　　　B. JOWETT.

January 15th, Oxford.

5, GORDON STREET, LONDON, W. C.,
January 5th, 1875.

MY DEAR MISS COBBE, — I should have been very sorry not to join in the protest against this hideous offence, and am truly obliged to you for furnishing me with the opportunity. The simultaneous loss, from the morals of our "advanced" scientific men, of all reverent sentiment toward beings *above* them and toward beings *below*, is a curious and instructive phenomenon, highly significant of the process which their nature is undergoing at both ends.

With truest wishes for many a happy and beneficent year,

Ever faithfully yours,
JAMES MARTINEAU.

MANCHESTER, December 26th, 1874.

The Bishop of Manchester [Dr. Fraser] presents his compliments to Miss Cobbe, and thanks her for giving him the opportunity of appending his name to this memorial, which has his most hearty concurrence.

PALACE, SALISBURY, 11th January, 1875.

The Bishop of Salisbury's compliments to Miss Cobbe. He cannot withhold his signature to her paper after reading the reasons which she has kindly sent him.

ADDINGTON PARK, CROYDON,
January 2d, 1875.

MADAM, — I have received your letter of the 31st ult. on the subject of the memorial to the Society for

Prevention of Cruelty to Animals with regard to vivi-section.

I hardly think I should be right, considering my imperfect acquaintance with the subject, in adding my name thereto at present.

> Believe me to be yours faithfully,
> A. C. CANTUAR.
> (Archbishop Tait.)

DEANERY, CARLISLE, January 20th, 1885.

DEAR MADAM, — If I had a hundred signatures you should have them all !

My heart has long burned with indignation against these murderers and torturers of innocent animals.

Was it for *this* that the great God made man the lord of the creation ?

It is incredible hypocrisy and folly to pretend that such wholesale torture is necessary to enlighten these stupid doctors !

It seems to me peculiarly ungrateful in man to break forth in this wholesale *animal inquisition* when Providence has so recently revealed to us several new natural powers whereby human suffering is so much diminished.

But I must restrain my feelings, and *you* must pardon me. I did not know that this good work was begun.

Only get some thoroughgoing and able friend of the animal world to tell the tale to a British House of Parliament, and these philosophic torturers will be stayed in their detestable course.

> Yours, E. CLOSE.
> (Dean of Carlisle.)

27, CORNWALL GARDENS, S. W.,
December 30th, 1874.

MY DEAR MISS COBBE, — I have an impression that the subject of vivisection is to be brought before the Senate of the University of London, which consists

574 FRANCES POWER COBBE.

mainly of great physicians and surgeons, but of which I am a member. Hence I think I hardly ought to sign the paper you have sent me.

This you see is an official answer, but I am glad to be able to make it, for the truth is I have neither thought nor enquired sufficiently about vivisection to be ready with a clear opinion.

Even if the utmost be proved against the vivisectors, I am inclined to think that they ought to be dealt with as guilty of a *new* offence, and not of an old one. I do not at all like the notion of bringing old laws such as Martin's act against cruelty to animals to bear on a class of cases never contemplated at the time of their enactment. It has a certain resemblance to enforcing the old law of blasphemy against persons who discuss Christianity in the modern philosophical spirit. Perhaps I am the more sensitive on this point since a friend elaborately demonstrated to me that I was liable to prosecution for what seemed to me a very innocent passage in a book of mine!

Believe me very truly yours,

H. S. MAINE.

(Sir Henry Sumner Maine.)

16, GEORGE STREET, HANOVER SQUARE, W.,
19th December, 1874.

DEAR MISS COBBE, — I have affixed my name with much satisfaction to this memorial, and I presume that you intend that men should be in largest number on the list.

Yours faithfully,   W. FERGUSSON.

(Sir William Fergusson, F. R. S.,

Serjeant-Surgeon to the Queen.)

This memorial having a certain importance in the history of our movement, I quote the principal paragraphs here : —

" The practice of vivisection has received of recent years enormous extension. Instead of an occasional experiment, made by a man of high scientific attainment, to determine some important problem of physiology or to test the feasibility of a new surgical operation, it has now become the every-day exercise of hundreds of physiologists and young students of physiology throughout Europe and America. In the latter country, lecturers in most of the schools employ living animals instead of dead for ordinary illustrations, and in Italy one physiologist alone has for some years past experimented on more than eight hundred dogs annually. A recent correspondence in the "Spectator" shows that many English physiologists contemplate the indefinite multiplication of such vivisections ; some (as Dr. Pye-Smith) defending them as illustrations of lectures, and some (as Mr. Ray-Lankester) frankly avowing that one experiment must lead to another *ad infinitum.* Every real or supposed discovery of one physiologist immediately causes the repetition of his experiments by scores of students. The most numerous and important of these researches being connected with the nervous system, the use of complete anæsthetics is practically prohibited. Even when employed during an operation, the effect of the anæsthetic of course shortly ceases, and, for the completion of the experiment, the animal is left to suffer the pain of the laceration to which it has been subjected. Another class of experiments consists in superinducing some special disease ; such as alcoholism (tried by M. Magnan on dogs at Norwich), and the peculiar malady arising from eating diseased pork (*Trichiniasis*) superinduced on a number of rabbits in Germany by Dr. Virchow. How far public opinion is becoming deadened to these practices is proved by the frequent recurrence in the newspapers of paragraphs simply alluding to them as matters of scientific interest involving no moral question whatever. One such

recently appeared in a highly respectable review, detail-
ing a French physiologist's efforts, first to drench the
veins of dogs with alcohol, and then to produce spontaneous combustion. Such experiments as these, it is
needless to remark, cannot be justified as endeavors to
mitigate the sufferings of humanity, and are rather to
be characterized as gratifications of the 'dilettantism
of discovery.'

"The recent trial at Norwich has established the fact
that, in a public medical congress, and sanctioned by a
majority of the members, an experiment was tried
which has since been formally pronounced by two of
the most eminent surgeons in the kingdom to have
been 'cruel and unnecessary.' We have, therefore, too
much reason to fear that in laboratories less exposed to
public view, and among inconsiderate young students,
very much greater abuses take place which call for
repression.

"It is urgently urged by your memorialists that the
great and influential Royal Society for the Prevention
of Cruelty to Animals may see fit to undertake the task
(which appears strictly to fall within its province) of
placing suitable restrictions on this rapidly increasing
evil. The vast benefit to the cause of humanity which
the society has in the past half-century effected would,
in our humble estimation, remain altogether one-sided
and incomplete; if, while brutal carters and ignorant
costermongers are brought to punishment for maltreat-
ing the animals under their charge, learned and refined
gentlemen should be left unquestioned to inflict far
more exquisite pain upon still more sensitive creatures;
as if the mere allegation of a scientific purpose removed
them above all legal or moral responsibility.

"We therefore beg respectfully to urge on the committee the immediate adoption of such measures as may
approve themselves to their judgment as most suitable
to promote the end in view, namely, the restriction of

vivisection; and we trust that it may not be left to others, who possess neither the wealth nor organization of the Royal Society for the Prevention of Cruelty to Animals, to make such efforts in the same direction as might prove to be in their power."

It was arranged that the memorial should be presented in Jermyn Street in a formal manner on the 25th January, 1875, by a deputation introduced by my cousin's husband, Mr. John Locke, M. P., Q. C., and consisting of Sir Frederick Elliot, Lord Jocelyn Percy, General G. Lawrence, Mr. R. H. Hutton, Mr. Leslie Stephen, Dr. Walker, Colonel Wood (now Sir Evelyn), and several ladies.

Prince Lucien Bonaparte, who always warmly befriended the cause, took the chair at first, and was succeeded by Lord Harrowby, President of the R. S. P. C. A., supported by Lady Burdett-Coutts, Lord Mount-Temple (then Mr. Cowper Temple), and others.

After some friendly discussion it was agreed that the committee of the R. S. P. C. A. would give the subject their most zealous attention; and a sub-committee to deal with the matter was accordingly appointed immediately afterwards.

When I drove home to Hereford Square from Jermyn Street that day, I rejoiced to think that I had accomplished a step towards obtaining the protection of the law for the victims of science; and I fully believed that I was free to return to my own literary pursuits and to the journalism which then occupied most of my time. A few days later I was requested to attend (for the occasion only) the first meeting of the sub-committee for vivisection of the R. S. P. C. A. On entering the room my spirits sank, for I saw round the table a number of worthy gentlemen, mostly elderly, but not one of the more distinguished members of their committee or (I think) a single Peer or Member of Parliament. In short, they were not the men to take the lead in such a movement and make a bold stand against the claims of science. After a few minutes the chairman himself asked me : "Whether *I* could not undertake to get a bill into Parliament for the object we desired?" As if all my labor with the memorial had not been spent to make *them* do this very thing! It was obviously felt by others present that this suggestion was out of place, and I soon retired, leaving the sub-committee to send Mr. Colam round to make enquiries among the physiologists, a mission which might, perhaps, be represented as a friendly request to be told frankly "whether they were really cruel." I understood, later, that he was shown a painless vivisection on a cat and offered a glass of sherry; and there (so far as I know or ever heard) the labors of that sub-committee ended. Mr. Colam afterwards took immense pains to collect evidence from the published works of vivisectors of the extent and severity of their operations, and this very valuable mass of materials was presented by him some months later to the Royal Commission, and is published in the Blue Book as an appendix to their minutes.

I was, of course, miserably disappointed at this stage of affairs, but on the 2d February, 1875, there appeared in the "Morning Post" the celebrated letter from Dr. George Hoggan, in which (without naming Claude Bernard) he described what he had himself witnessed in his laboratory when recently working there for several months. This letter was absolutely invaluable to our cause, giving, as it did, reality and firsthand testimony to all we had asserted from books and reports. In the course of it Dr. Hoggan said : —

"I venture to record a little of my own experience in the matter, part of which was gained as an assistant in the laboratory of one of the greatest living experimental physiologists. In that laboratory we sacrificed daily from one to three dogs, besides rabbits and other animals, and after four months' experience I am of opinion

that not one of those experiments on animals was justified or necessary. The idea of the good of humanity
was simply out of the question, and would be laughed
at, the great aim being to keep up with, or get ahead
of, one's contemporaries in science, even at the price of
an incalculable amount of torture needlessly and iniqui-
tously inflicted on the poor animals. During three
campaigns I have witnessed many harsh sights, but I
think the saddest sight I ever witnessed was when the
dogs were brought up from the cellar to the laboratory
for sacrifice. Instead of appearing pleased with the
change from darkness to light, they seemed seized with
horror as soon as they smelt the air of the place, divin-
ing, apparently, their approaching fate. They would
make friendly advances to each of the three or four
persons present, and as far as eyes, ears, and tail could
make a mute appeal for mercy eloquent, they tried it in
vain.

" Were the feelings of the experimental physiologists
not blunted, they could not long continue the practice
of vivisection. They are always ready to repudiate any
implied want of tender feeling, but I must say that
they seldom show much pity ; on the contrary, in practice they frequently show the reverse. Hundreds of
times I have seen, when an animal writhed with pain
and thereby deranged the tissues, during a delicate dissection, instead of being soothed it would receive a
slap and an angry order to be quiet and behave itself.
At other times, when an animal had endured great pain
for hours without struggling or giving more than an
occasional low whine, instead of letting the poor mangled wretch loose to crawl painfully about the place in
reserve for another day's torture, it would receive pity
so far that it would be said to have behaved well
enough to merit death ; and, as a reward, would be
killed at once by breaking up the medulla with a needle,
or 'pithing,' as this operation is called. I have often

heard the professor say, when one side of an animal had been so mangled and the tissues so obscured by clotted blood that it was difficult to find the part searched for, 'Why don't you begin on the other side ?' or, 'Why don't you take another dog ? What is the use of being so economical ?' One of the most revolting features in the laboratory was the custom of giving an animal, on which the professor had completed his experiment, and which had still some life left, to the assistants to practice the finding of arteries, nerves, etc., in the living animal, or for performing what are called fundamental experiments upon it — in other words, repeating those which are recommended in the laboratory handbooks. I am inclined to look upon anæsthetics as the greatest curse to vivisectible animals. They alter too much the normal conditions of life to give accurate results, and they are therefore little depended upon. They, indeed, prove far more efficacious in lulling public feeling towards the vivisectors than pain in the vivisected."

I had met Dr. Hoggan one day just before this occurrence at Mme. Bodichon's house, but I had no idea that he would, or could, bear such valuable testimony ; and I have never ceased to feel that in thus nobly coming forward to offer it spontaneously, he struck the greatest blow on our side in the whole battle. Of course I expressed to him all the gratitude I felt, and we thenceforth took counsel frequently as to the policy to be pursued in opposing vivisection.

It soon became evident that if a bill were to be presented to Parliament that session it must be promoted by some parties other than the committee of the R. S. P. C. A. Indeed in the following December "The Animal World," in a leading article, avowed that "the Royal Society (P. C. A.) is not so entirely unanimous as to desire the passing of any special legislative enactment on this subject" (vivisection). Feeling convinced that some such obstacle was in the way I turned to my friends to see if it might be possible to push on a bill independently, and with the most kind help of Sir William Hart Dyke (the Conservative whip) it was arranged that a bill for "Regulating the Practice of Vivisection" should be introduced with the sanction of Government into the House of Lords by Lord Henniker (Lord Hartismere). It is impossible to describe all the anxiety I endured during the interval up to the 4th May, when this bill was actually presented. Lord Henniker was exceedingly good about it and took much pains with the draft prepared at first by Sir Frederick Elliot, and afterwards completed for Lord Henniker by Mr. Fitzgerald. Lord Coleridge also took great interest in it, and gave most valuable advice, and Mr. Lowe (who afterwards bitterly opposed the almost identical measure of Lord Cross in the Commons) was willing to give this earlier Bill much consideration. I met him one day at luncheon at Airlie Lodge, where were also Lord Henniker, Lady Minto, Lord Airlie, and others interested, and the bill was gone over clause by clause till adjusted to Mr. Lowe's counsels.

Lord Henniker introduced the bill thus drafted for "Regulating the Practice of Vivisection" into the House of Lords on the 4th May, 1875; but on the 12th May, to our great surprise another bill to prevent abuse in experiments on animals was introduced into the House of Commons by Dr. (now Lord) Playfair. On the appearance of this latter bill, which was understood to be promoted by the physiologists themselves — notably by Dr. Burdon-Sanderson, and by Mr. Charles Darwin — the Government, which had sanctioned Lord Henniker's bill, thought it necessary to issue a Royal Commission of Enquiry into the subject before any legislation should be proceeded with. This was done accordingly on the 22d June, and both bills were then withdrawn.

The student of this old chapter of the history of the
anti-vivisection crusade will find both of the above-
named bills (and also the ineffective sketch of what
might have been the bill of the R. S. P. C. A.) in the
appendix to the "Report of the Royal Commission,"
pp. 336-8. Mr. Charles Darwin, in a letter to the
"Times," April 18th, 1881, said that he "took an
active part in trying to get a bill passed such as would
have removed all just cause of complaint, and at the
same time have left the physiologists free to pursue
their researches — a *"bill very different from that
which has since been passed."* As Mr. Darwin's biographer, while reprinting this letter, has not quoted my
challenge to him in the "Times" of the 23d to point
out *"in what respect the former bill is very different
from the act of* 1876," I think it well to cite here the
lucid definition of that difference as delineated in the
"Spectator" of May 15th, doubtless by the editor, Mr.
Hutton.

The Vivisection-Restriction Bills.

On Wednesday afternoon last, Dr. Lyon Playfair
laid on the table of the House of Commons a bill for
the restriction of vivisection, which has been drawn
up by physiologists, no doubt in part, in the interest of
physiological science, but also in part, no doubt, in the
interest of humanity. The contents of this bill are
the best answer which it is possible to give to the
ignorant attack made in a daily contemporary on
Tuesday on Lord Henniker's bill, introduced into the
House of Lords last week. The two bills differ in
principle only on one important point. Both of them
clearly have been maturely considered by men of
science as well as by humanitarians. Both of them
assume the great and increasing character of the evil
which has to be dealt with. Both of them approach
that evil in the same manner, by insisting that scientific

experiments which are painful to animals shall be
tried only on the avowed responsibility of men of the
highest education, whose right to try them may be
withdrawn if it be abused. Both of them aim at com-
pelling the physiologists who are permitted to try such
experiments at all to use anæsthetics throughout the
experiment, whenever the use of anæsthetics is not
fatal to the investigation itself. . . . The bills differ,
however, on a most important point. It is certain that
all the contempt showered on Lord Henniker's bill by
the ignorant assailants of the humanitarian party
might equally have been showered on Dr. Lyon Playfair's. But Lord Henniker's bill contemplates making
physiological and pathological experiments on living
animals, even under complete anæsthesia, illegal, except under the same responsibility and on the same
conditions as those experiments which are not, and
cannot be, conducted under complete anæsthesia —
while Dr. Lyon Playfair leaves all experiments conducted under anæsthetics — and will practically, though
not theoretically, leave, we fear, those which only
profess to be so conducted (a very different thing) —
as utterly without restriction as they now are. Indeed,
it attempts no sort of limitation upon them. If a
whole hecatomb of guinea-pigs, or even dogs, were
known to be imported, and their carcasses exported
daily from the private house of any man who declared
that he *always used anæsthetics*, Dr. Playfair's bill
provides, we believe, no sort of machinery by which
the truth of his assertion could be even tested. . . . It
is, however, no small matter to have obtained this clear
admission on scientific authority that the victimization
of animals in the interest of science is an evil of a
growing and serious kind which needs legislative interference, and calls for at least the threat of serious
penalties. . . .

In short, the bill promoted by the physiologists and Mr. Darwin was, like the resolutions of the Liverpool British Association, a "pious opinion" or *Brutum fulmen.* Nothing more.

The Royal Commission on Vivisection was issued, as I have said, on the 22d June, 1875, and the "Report" was dated January 8th, 1876. The intervening months were filled with anxiety. I heard constantly all that went on at the commission, and my hopes and fears rose and fell week by week. Of the constitution of the commission much might be said. Writing of it in the "British Friend," May, 1876, the late Mr. J. B. Firth, M. P., Q. C., remarked: —

" If it were possible for a Royal Commission to be appointed to enquire into the practice of Thuggee, I should have very little confidence in their report if one-third of the commissioners were prominent practisers of the art. On the same principle the constitution of this commission is open to the observation that it included two notorious advocates of vivisection, Dr. Erichsen and Professor Huxley, both of whom had to 'explain' their writings and practices in connection with it, in the course of the enquiry."

Certain it is, as I heard at the time, and as any one may verify by looking over the "Minutes of Evidence," these two able gentlemen acted, not as judges on the bench examining evidence dispassionately, but as exceedingly vigorous and keen-eyed counsel for the physiologists. On the humanitarian side there was but a single pronounced opponent of vivisection — Mr. R. H. Hutton — who nobly sacrificed his time for half a year to doing all that was in the power of a single member of the commission, and he a layman, to elicit the truth concerning the alleged cruelty of the practice. At the end, after receiving a mass of evidence in answer to 3,764 questions from fifty-three witnesses, the commission reported distinctly *in favor of legislative interference.* They say: —

"Even if the weight of authority on the side of legislative interference had been less considerable, we should have thought ourselves called upon to recommend it by the reason of the thing. It is manifest that the practice is, from its very nature, liable to great abuse, and that since it is impossible for society to entertain the idea of putting an end to it, it ought to be subjected to due regulation and control. . . . It is not to be doubted that inhumanity may be found in persons of very high position as physiologists. . . . Beside the cases in which inhumanity exists, we are satisfied that there are others in which carelessness and indifference prevail to an extent sufficient to form a ground for legislative interference."

Yet in the face of these and other weighty sentences to the same purpose, it has been persistently asserted that the Royal Commission *exonerated* English physiologists from all charge of cruelty! In Mr. Darwin's celebrated letter to Professor Holmgren, of Upsala, published in the "Times," April, 1881, he said: "The investigation of the matter by a Royal Commission proved that the accusations made against our English physiologists *were false.*" Commenting on this letter the "Spectator," April 23d, 1881 (doubtless Mr. Hutton himself), observed: —

"The Royal Commission did not report this. They came to no such conclusion, and though that may be Mr. Darwin's own inference from what they did say, it is only his inference, not theirs. In our opinion it was proved that very great cruelty had been practised, with hardly any appreciable results, by more than one British physiologist."

Nor must it be left out of sight in estimating the disingenuousness of the advocates of vivisection, that the above quoted sentences from the report of the commission were countersigned by those representatives of science, Professor Huxley and Mr. Erichsen; as were, of course, also the subsequent paragraphs, formally recommending a measure almost identical with Lord Carnarvon's bill.   In spite of this the vivisecting clique has not ceased to assert that English physiologists were exculpated, and to protest against the measure which we introduced in strict accordance with that recommendation. a measure which was even still further mitigated (as regarded freedom to the vivisectors), under the pressure of their deputation to the Home Office, till it became the present *quasi* ineffectual act.

While the Royal Commission was still sitting in the autumn, and when it had become obvious that much would remain to be done before any effectual check could be placed on vivisection, (Dr. Hoggan suggested to me that we should form a society to carry on the work.   I abhorred societies, and knew only too well the huge additional labor of working the machinery of one, over and above my direct help to the object in view.   I had hitherto worked independently and freely, taking always the advice of the eminent men who were so good as to counsel me at every step.   But I felt that this plan could not suffice much longer, and that the authority of a formally constituted society was needed to make headway against an evil which daily revealed itself as more formidable.   Accordingly I agreed with Dr. Hoggan that we should do well to form such a society, he and I being the honorary secretaries, *provided* we could obtain the countenances of some men of eminence to form the nucleus.   "I will write," I said, "to Lord Shaftesbury and to the Archbishop of York. If they will give me their names, we can conjure with them.   If *not*, I will not undertake to form a society.")

I wrote that night to those two eminent persons.   I received next day from Lord Shaftesbury a telegram, which he must have dispatched *instantly* on receiving my letter, which answered "Yes."   Next day the post brought from him the letter which I shall here print. The next post brought also the letter from Archbishop Thomson. Thus the society consisted for two days of Lord Shaftesbury, the Archbishop, Dr. Hoggan, and myself!

LORD SHAFTESBURY TO MISS F. P. C.

ST. GILES'S HOUSE, CRANBOURNE, SALISBURY,
November 17th, 1875.

DEAR MISS COBBE, — It is needful, I am sure, to found a society, in order to have unity and persistency of action.

I judge, by the terms of the circular, that the object of the society will be restriction and not prohibition.

Possibly, this end is as much as you will be able to attain. Prohibition, I doubt not, would be evaded; but restriction will, I am certain, be exceeded.

Not but that a little is better than nothing.

But you will find many who will think with much show of reason, that, by surrendering the principle, you have surrendered the great argument.

Faithfully yours,

SHAFTESBURY.

BISHOPTHORPE, YORK,
November 16th, 1875.

DEAR MISS COBBE, — I am quite ready to join the society for restricting vivisection. I agree with you; total prohibition would be impossible.

I am yours very truly,

W. EBOR.

(With these names to "conjure with," as I have said, we found it easy to enroll a goodly company in the ranks of our new society.) Cardinal Manning was one of the first to join us. (On the 2d December, 1875, the first committee meeting was held) in the house of Dr. and Mrs. Hoggan, 13, Granville Place, Portman Square,

Mr. Stansfeld taking the chair. Mrs. Wedgwood, wife
of Mr. Hensleigh Wedgwood and mother of my friend
Miss Julia Wedgwood, was present at that first meeting,
and (so long as her health permitted) at those which
followed — a worthy example of "heredity," since her
father and mother, Sir James and Lady Mackintosh,
had been among the principal supporters of Richard
Martin, and founders of the R. S. P. C. A.   At the third
meeting of the committee, on February 18th, 1876,
Lord Shaftesbury took the chair, for the first time, and
again he took it on the occasion of a memorable meeting on the first of March, but vacated it on the arrival
of Archbishop Thomson, who proved to be an admirably
efficient chairman.   We had a serious job that day;
that of discussing the "Statement" of our position and
objects.   I had drafted this Statement in preparation, as
well as compiled from the "Minutes of Evidence," a
series of extracts exhibiting the extension and abuses of
vivisection; and also evidence regarding anæsthetics
and regarding foreign physiologists.   These appendices
were all accepted and appear in the pamphlet; but my
Statement was most minutely debated, clause for clause,
and at last adopted, not without several modifications.
After summarizing the report of the Royal Commission
which "has been in some respects seriously misconstrued" (I might add, persistently misconstrued ever
since) and also Mr. Hutton's independent report, in
which he desired that the "household animals" should
be exempted from vivisection, the committee carefully
criticise this report and express their confident hope
that "a bill may be introduced immediately by Government to carry out the recommendations of the commission."   They observe, in conclusion, that they find
"a just summary of their sentiments in Mr. Hutton's
expression of his view: —

"'The measure will not at all satisfy my own con-
ceptions of the needs of the case, unless it result in

putting an end to all experiments involving not merely torture *but anything at all approaching thereto.*' "

Such was our attitude at that memorable date when we commenced the regular steady work which has now gone on for just eighteen years. On the second or third of March I took possession of the offices where so large a part of my life was henceforth to be spent. When my kind colleagues had left me and I locked the outer door of the offices and knew myself to be alone, I resolved very seriously to devote myself, so long as might be needful, to this work of trying to save God's poor creatures from their intolerable doom ; and I resolved "never to go to bed at night leaving a stone unturned which might help to stop vivisection." I believe I have kept that resolution. I commend it to other workers.

It may interest the reader to know who were the persons then actually aiding and supporting our movement.

There was — first and most important — my colleague and friend Dr. George Hoggan, who labored incessantly (and wholly gratuitously) for the cause. His wife, Dr. Frances Hoggan, who I am thankful to say still survives, was also a most useful member of the Committee.

The other members of the executive were : Sir Frederick Elliot, K. C. M. G., who had long been Permanent Secretary at the Colonial Office ; Major-General Colin Mackenzie, a noble old hero of the Afghan wars and the mutiny ; Mr. Leslie Stephen ; Mrs. Hensleigh Wedgwood ; Dr. Vaughan (the late Master of the Temple); the Countess of Portsmouth ; the Countess of Camperdown ; my friend Miss Lloyd ; my cousin, Mr. Locke, M. P., Q. C. ; Mr. William Shaen ; Colonel (now Sir Evelyn) Wood ; and Mr. Edward de Fonblanque. The latter gentleman was one of the most useful members of the committee, whose retirement three years later after our adoption of a more advanced policy I have never ceased to regret.

Beside these members of the committee we had then as Vice-Presidents, the Archbishop of York, the Marquis of Bute, Cardinal Manning, Lord Portsmouth, Mr. Cowper-Temple (afterwards Lord Mount-Temple), Right Honorable James Stansfeld, Lord Shaftesbury, the Bishop of Gloucester and Bristol (Dr. Ellicott), the Bishop of Manchester (Dr. Fraser), Lord Chief Justice Coleridge, and the Lord Chief Baron, Sir Fitzroy Kelly.

Dr. Hoggan had invited Mr. Spurgeon to join our society, but received from him the following reply : —

REV. C. H. SPURGEON TO DR. HOGGAN.

NIGHTINGALE LANE, CLAPHAM,
December 24th.

DEAR SIR, — I do not like to become an officer of a society for I have no time to attend to the duties of such an office, and it strikes me as a false system which is now so general, which allows names to appear on committees and requires no service from the individuals.

In all efforts to spare animals from needless pain I wish you the utmost success. There are cases in which they *must* suffer, as we also must, but not one pang ought to be endured by them from which we can screen them.

Yours heartily,   C. H. SPURGEON.

I shall aid your effort in my own way.

Mr. Spurgeon wrote on one occasion a letter to Lord Shaftesbury to be read from the chair at a meeting; but, much as we wished to use it, the extreme strength of the *expletives* was considered to transgress the borders of expediency !

We invited Professor Rolleston to give us his support. The following was his reply : —

OXFORD, November 28th, 1875.

DEAR MISS COBBE, — I would have answered your letter before had I been able to make up my mind to do as you ask. This, however, I think I should not, in the interests of the line of legislation which I advocate, do well to do. I believe I speak with greater weight from keeping an independent position. And as I have a great desire to throw away none of the advantages which that position gives me, I am obliged to decline your invitation. Allow me to say that I am much gratified by your writing to ask me to do what I decline to do out of considerations of expediency.

It is also a great pleasure to me to think that what I said at Bristol has met with your approbation. The bearing of parts at the end or towards the end of that address upon the future of vivisection was, I hope, tolerably obvious.

I am yours very truly,
GEORGE ROLLESTON.

(The newly-formed society had been clumsily named by Dr. Hoggan: "The Society for Protection of Animals liable to Vivisection," and its aim was "to obtain the greatest possible protection for animals liable to vivisection.") I was obliged to yield to my colleague as regarded this awkward title which exactly defined the position he desired to take up; but it was a constant source of worry and loss to us. As soon as possible, however, after we had taken our offices in Victoria Street, I called our Society, unofficially and for popular use, simply "The Victoria Street Society.")

These offices are large and handsome, and so conveniently situated that the society has retained them ever since. They are on the first floor of a house—

formerly numbered "1," now numbered "20" — in
Victoria Street, ten or eleven doors up the street from
the Broad Sanctuary and the Westminster Palace Hotel; and with Westminster Abbey and the Towers of
the Houses of Parliament in view from the street door.
The offices contain an ante-room (now piled with our
papers), a large airy room with two windows for the
clerks, a secretary's private room, and a spacious and
lightsome committee-room with three windows. Out
of this last another room was accessible, which at one
time was taken for my especial use. I put up book-
shelves, pictures, curtains, and various little feminine
relaxations, and thus covered, as far as might be, the
frightful character of our work, so that friends should
find our office no painful place to visit.

We did not let the grass grow under our feet after
we had settled down in these offices. On the 20th of
March there went out from them to the neighboring
Home Office a deputation to Mr. (now Lord) Cross to
urge the Government to bring in a bill in accordance
with the recommendations of the Royal Commission.
The deputation was headed by Lord Shaftesbury, and
included the Earl of Minto, Cardinal Manning, Mr.
Froude, Mr. Mundella, Sir Frederick Elliot, Colonel
Evelyn Wood, and Mr. Cowper-Temple. Mr. Carlyle
was to have joined the deputation, but held back
sooner than accompany the Cardinal.

Chief Baron Kelly wrote us the following cordial expressions of regret for non-attendance : —

WESTERN CIRCUIT, WINCHESTER.
4th March, 1876.

The Lord Chief Baron presents his compliments to
Miss Cobbe, and very greatly regrets that, being engaged at the assize on the Western Circuit until nearly
the middle of April, he will be unable to accompany
the deputation to Mr. Cross on the subject of vivisection, to which, however, he earnestly wishes success.

We had invited Canon Liddon, who was a subscriber to our funds from the first, to join this deputation, but received from him the following reply : —

AMEN COURT, 6th March, 1876.

MY DEAR MISS COBBE, — I should be sincerely glad to be able to obey your kind wishes in the matter of the proposed deputation, if I could. But I am unable to be in London again between to-morrow and April 1st, and this I fear will make it impossible.

I shall be sincerely glad to hear that the deputation succeeds in persuading the Home Secretary to make legislation on the report of the Vivisection Commission a government question. Mr. Hutton appeared to me to resist the —— criticisms of the "Times" on the report very admirably !

Thanking you for your note,
I am, my dear Miss Cobbe,
Yours very truly,
M. C. LIDDON.

A few weeks afterwards when I invited him to attend a meeting he wrote again a letter, to the last sentence of which I desire to call attention as embodying the opinion of this eminent man on the *human* moral interest involved in our crusade.

CHRIST CHURCH, OXFORD, May 22d, 1876.

MY DEAR MISS COBBE, — I sincerely wish that I could obey your summons. But, as a professor here, I have public duties on Thursday, the first of June, which I cannot decline or transfer to other hands.

I think I told you I was a useless person for these good purposes ; and so, you see, it is.

Still you are very well off in the way of speakers, and will not miss such a person as I. Heartily do I hope that the meeting may reward the trouble you have taken about it by strengthening Lord Carnarvon's hands. The cause you have at heart is of *even greater importance to human character than to the physical comfort of those of our fellow creatures who are most immediately concerned.*

I am, my dear Miss Cobbe,

Yours very truly,
C. Liddon.

The deputation of March 20th to the Home Office was most favorably received, and our society was invited to submit to Government suggestions respecting the provisions of the intended bill. These suggestions were framed at a committee held at our office on the thirtieth of March, and they were adopted by Government after being approved by its official advisers, and presented by Lord Carnarvon in the House of Lords. The second reading took place on the twenty-second of May. On that occasion Lord Coleridge made a most judicious speech in defence of the bill, and Lord Shaftesbury the long and beautiful one reprinted in our pamphlet, "In Memoriam." The next morning all the newspapers came out with leading articles in praise of the bill. It is hard now to realize that, previous to undergoing the medical pressure which has twisted the minds — (or at least the *pens*) — of three-fourths of the press, even the great paper which has been our relentless opponent for seventeen years was then our cordial supporter. Everything at that time looked fair for us. The bill, as we had drafted it, did, practically, fulfil Mr. Hutton's aspiration. No experiment whatever under any circumstances was permitted on a dog, cat, horse, ass, or mule; nor any on any other animal except under conditions of complete anæsthesia from beginning to end. The bill included licenses, but no certificates dispensing with the above provisions. Our hopes of carrying this bill seemed amply justified by

the reception it received from the House of Lords and
the press ; and from a great conference of the R. S. P.
C. A. and its branches held on the twenty-third of May.
We held our first general meeting at Westminster
Palace Hotel on the first of June and resolutions in
support of the bill were passed enthusiastically ; Lord
Shaftesbury presiding, and the Marquis of Bute, Lord
Glasgow, Cardinal Manning, and others speaking with
great spirit. It only needed, to all appearance, that the
bill should be pushed through its final stage in the
Lords and sent down to the House of Commons to
secure its passage intact that same session.

At this most critical moment, and through the whole
month of June, Lord Carnarvon, in whose hands the
bill lay, was drawn away from London and occupied by
the illness and death of Lady Carnarvon. No words
can tell the anxiety and alarm this occasioned us, when
we learned that a large section of the medical profession, which had so far seemed quiescent if not approv-
ing, had been roused by their chief wire-puller into a
state of exasperation at the supposed " insult " of pro-
posing to submit them to legal control in experimenting
on living animals (as they were already subjected to it,
by the Anatomy act, in dissecting dead bodies). These
doctors, to the number of three thousand, signed a
memorial to the Home Secretary, calling on him to
modify the bill so as practically to reverse its character,
and make it a measure, no longer protecting vivisected
animals from torture, but vivisectors from prosecution
under Martin's act. This memorial was presented on
the tenth of July by a deputation, variously estimated
at three hundred and at eight hundred doctors, who, in
either case, were sufficiently numerous to overflow the
purlieus of the Home Office and to overawe Mr. Cross.
On the tenth of August the bill, essentially altered in
submission to the medical memorialists, was brought
by Mr. Cross into the House of Commons, and was read

a second time. On the 15th August, 1876, it received the royal assent and became the act 39–40 Vict., c. 77, commonly called the " Vivisection Act."

The world has never seemed to me quite the same since that dreadful time. My hopes had been raised so high to be dashed so low as even to make me fear that I had done harm instead of good, and brought fresh danger to the hapless brutes for whose sake, as I realized more and more their agonies, I would have gladly died. I was baffled in an aim nearer to my heart than any other had ever been, and for which I had strained every nerve for many months; and of all the hundreds of people who had seemed to sympathize and had signed our memorials and petitions, there were none to say: " *This shall not be !* " Justice and mercy seemed to have gone from the earth.

We left London — the session and the summer being over — and came as usual to Wales; but our enjoyment of the beauty of this lovely land had in great measure vanished. Even after twenty years my friend and I look back to our joyous summers before that miserable one, and say, " Ah! *that* was when we knew very little of vivisection."

In my despair I wrote several letters of bitter reproach to the friends in Parliament who had allowed our bill to be so mutilated that the " British Medical Journal " crowed over it, as affording full liberty to " science ; " and I also wrote to several newspapers saying that after this failure to obtain a reasonable restrictive bill, I, for one, should labor henceforth to obtain total prohibition. In reply to my letter (I fear a very petulant one) Lord Shaftesbury wrote me this full and important explanation which I commend to the careful reading of such of our friends as desire now to rescind the act of 1876.

CASTLE WEMYSS, WEMYSS BAY, N. B.,
August 16th, 1876.

DEAR MISS COBBE, — Until we shall have seen the act in print we cannot form a just estimate of the force of the amendments. Some few, so I see by the papers, were introduced in committee, after my last interview with Mr. Cross; but of their character I know nothing. I am disposed, however, to believe that he would not have admitted anything of real importance.

Mr. Cross's difficulties were very great at all times; but they increased much as the session was drawing to a close. The want of time, the extreme pressure of business, the active malignity of the scientific men, and the indifference of his colleagues, left the Secretary of State in a very weak and embarrassing position.

Your letter, which I have just received, asks whether "the bill cannot be turned out in the House of Lords." The reply is that, whether advisable or unadvisable, it cannot now be done, for the Parliament is prorogued.

In the bill as submitted to me, just before the second reading at a final interview with Mr. Cross, Mr. Holt and Lord Cardwell being present, some changes were made which I by no means approved. But the question then, was simply, "The bill as propounded, or no bill," for Mr. Cross stoutly maintained that, without the alterations suggested, he had no hope of carrying anything at all. I reverted, therefore, to my first opinion, stated at the very commencement of my coöperation with your committee, that it was of great importance, nay indispensable, to obtain a bill, however imperfect, which should condemn the practice, put a limit on the exercise of it, and give us a foundation on which to build amendments hereafter as evidence and opportunity shall be offered to us.

The bill is of that character. I apprehended that if there were no bill then, there would be none at any time. No private member, I believed, and I still believe, could undertake such a measure with even a shadow of hope; and there was more than doubt, whether a Secretary of State would again entangle himself with so bitter and so wearisome a question in the face of all science, and the antipathies of most of his colleagues. Public sympathy would have declined, and would not have easily been aroused a second time. The public sympathy, at its best, was only noisy, and not effective; and this assertion is proved by the few signatures to petitions compared with the professed feeling; and by the extreme difficulty to raise any funds in proportion to the exigency of the case.

The evidence, too, given to the Commission, which was, after all, our main reliance, would have grown stale; and the physiologists would have taken good care that, for some time at least, nothing should transpire to take its place.

We have gained an enactment that experiments shall be performed by none but licensed persons, thereby excluding, should the act be well enforced, the host of young students and their bed-chamber practices.

We have gained an enactment that all experiments shall be performed under the influence of anæsthetics;[1] and, thirdly, the greatest enactment of all, that the Secretary of State is responsible for the due execution of all these provisions in Parliament, and in this Office, instead of the College of Physicians, or some such unreachable and intangible body, as many Secretaries of State, except Mr. Cross, would have evasively appointed.

This provision, under the Statutes, so unexpected and valuable, could have been suggested to Parliament by a Secretary of State only, and I feel sure that no Secretary of State in any "Liberal" administration would listen to the proposal; and I very much doubt

---

[1] The certificate (A) dispensing with anæsthetics was doubtless inserted after Lord Shaftesbury saw the bill.

whether Mr. Cross himself, had his present bill been rejected, would have, in the case of a new bill, repeated his offer of making it a measure for which the cabinet has to answer.

I have seen your letter to the " Echo " and the " Daily News." You are quite justified in your determination to agitate the country on the subject of vivisection, and obtain, if it be possible, the total abolition of it. Such an issue may be within reach, and it is only by experience that we can ascertain how far such a blessed consummation is practicable. You will have a good deal of sympathy with your efforts, and from no one more than from myself.

Yours truly,   SHAFTESBURY.

When we all returned to town in October, the committee placed on the minutes a letter from me, saying that I could only retain the office of Honorary Secretary if the society should adopt the principle of total prohibition. A circular was sent out calling for votes on the point, and by the 22d November, 1876, the resolution was carried, "That the society would watch the existing act with a view to the enforcement of its restrictions and its extension to the total prohibition of painful experiments on animals."

In February, 1877, the committee, to my satisfaction, unanimously agreed to support Mr. Holt's bill for total prohibition ; and in aid thereof exhibited on the hoardings of London, 1,700 handbills and 300 posters, which were enlarged reproductions of the illustrations of vivisection from the physiological handbooks. These posters certainly were more effective than as many thousands of speeches and pamphlets ; and the indignation of the scientific party sufficiently proved that such was the case. On the 27th April we held our second annual meeting in support of Mr. Holt's bill, and had for speakers Lord Shaftesbury, the good Bishop of

Winchester, Dr. Harold - Browne (now, alas ! dead),
Lord Mount-Temple, Professor Sheldon Amos, Cardinal
Manning, and Prince Lucien Bonaparte. The last remarkable man and erudite scholar (who most closely
resembled his uncle in person, if we could imagine Napoleon I. commanding only armies *of books!*) was, from
first to last, a warm friend of our cause. After this
meeting we elected him Vice-President, and here is his
letter of acknowledgment : —

PRINCE LUCIEN BONAPARTE TO MISS F. P. C.

6, NORFOLK TERRACE, BAYSWATER,
4th May, 1877.

MY DEAR MISS COBBE, — I feel highly honored at
being nominated one of the Vice-Presidents of the Society for Protection of Animals liable to vivisection,
and ask you to return the committee my best thanks.

I am a great admirer of a society which, like yours,
opposes so strongly the abominable practice of vivisection, because for my own part, I consider it, even in
its mildest form, as a shame to science, a dishonor to
modern civilization, and (what I think more important)
a great offence against the law of God.

Believe me, my dear Miss Cobbe,

Yours very sincerely,

L. BONAPARTE.

Here are some further letters concerned with that
meeting or written to me soon afterwards : —

CHRIST CHURCH, OXFORD,
March 26th, 1877.

MY DEAR MISS COBBE, — I beg to thank you sincerely for your kind letter.

So far as I can see there is, I fear, little chance of
my being at liberty to take part in the proceedings on
the twenty-seventh of April.

However, with the names which you announce, you

will be more than able to dispense with any assistance that I could lend to the common object. You will, I trust, be able to strengthen Mr. Holt's hands. If what I have heard of his measure is at all accurate, it seems to be at once moderate and efficient.

I was much struck by an observation which you were, I think, said to have made the other day at Bristol, to the effect that as matters now stand everything depends upon the discretion, or rather, upon the moral sympathies of the Home Secretary. Mr. Cross, I believe, would always do well in all such matters. But it does not do to reckon with the Roman Empire, as if it were always to be governed by a Marcus Aurelius.

I am, my dear Miss Cobbe,

Yours very truly,

M. C. LIDDON.

HOUSE OF COMMONS,
26th March.

DEAR MISS COBBE, — I am sorry I cannot undertake to speak at your meeting on the twenty-seventh of April. I am not sure that I shall be in London on that day, but request you to send me any notice of the meeting.

My time and strength are somewhat overtaxed owing to an inability, and I may add indisposition, to say No when I think I may be useful. I am, however, I can assure you, in sympathy with you in your attempt to put down torture in every form.

I am yours very sincerely,

S. MORLEY.

(Samuel Morley, M. P.)

MY DEAR MISS COBBE, — I will come in at some stage of your proceedings. I am bound first to convocation — and am engaged at Kingston before five.

What I should like would be to thank Lord Shaftesbury; but this must depend on the time that I come, and *that* must depend on the exigencies of convocation.

Yours truly,   A. P. STANLEY.
(The Dean of Westminster.)

April 25th, 1877.

MY DEAR MISS COBBE, — I am very sorry that through absence from home my answer to your note has been delayed. I shall not be able to take part in your meeting on the 27th, for I am not in a state of health to take part in any public meeting; but if I am at all able I should like much to attend it and hear for myself the views of the speakers. I have not expressed publicly any opinion on the question of vivisection, being anxious at first to await the determination of the commission, and then to see how the restrictions were likely to work.

I confess that my own mind is leaning very strongly to the conclusion that there is no safe, right course other than entire prohibition. The more I think of it, the more I dread the brutality which in spite of the influence of the best men will inevitably be developed in our young experimenters, in these days of almost fanatical devotion to scientific research. It seems to me to more than counterbalance the physical advantages to our sick that may grow out of the practice of vivisection.

And I am very skeptical about these physical advantages. I doubt whether the secrets of nature can be successfully discovered by torture, any more than the secrets of hearts. We have abandoned the one endeavor, finding the results to be by no means worth the cost. I am persuaded that we shall soon, for the same reason, have to abandon the other.

I am not able, as I say, to take part in a meeting, but as soon as I am able I intend to preach on the subject, and if you can forward to me any information which will be useful I shall be much obliged to you.   Believe me

Ever, my dear Miss Cobbe,

Yours very faithfully,   J. Baldwin Brown.

(Rev. J. B. Brown.)

By this time there were two other anti-vivisection societies in London, beside Mr. Jesse's society at Macclesfield, all working for total prohibition; and though of course we had various small difficulties and rivalries in the course of time, yet practically we all helped each other and the cause.   Eventually the International Society, of which Mr. and Mrs. Adlam were the spirited leaders, coalesced with ours and added to our committee several of its most valuable members including our present much respected chairman, Mr. Ernest Bell. The London Anti-vivisection Society, though I expended all my blandishments on it, has never consented to amalgamation, but has done a great work of its own for which we have all reason to hold it in honor.

(The revolt against the cruelties of science spread also about this time to the continent.) Baron Weber read his "Torture Chamber of Science" in Dresden, and created thereby a great sensation, followed by the formation of the German League, of which he is President, and the foundation of its organ, the "Thier-und-Menschen-Freund," edited by Dr. Paul Förster, now a member of the Reichstag.   Other anti-vivisection societies were founded then or in subsequent years in Hanover, in Berlin, and in Stockholm.   In Copenhagen those devoted friends of animals, M. and Mme. Lembcké, had long contended vigorously against the local vivisector, Panum.   In Italy the Florence "Società Prottettrice," of which our Queen is Patroness and Countess Baldelli the indefatigable Honorary Secretary, has steadily worked against vivisection from its foundation; and so has the Torinese Society of which Dr.

Riboli is President and Countess Biandrate Morelli the leading member. In Riga there has also been a persevering movement against vivisection by the excellent society of which the "Anwalt der Thiere" is the (first-class) organ, and Madame V. Schilling the presiding spirit.

(In short, by the end of the decade, though we had been so cruelly defeated, we were conscious that our movement had extended and had become to all appearance one of those permanent agitations, which, once begun, go on till the abuses which aroused them are abolished.) In America the movement only took definite shape in February, 1883, when, under the auspices of the indefatigable Mrs. White, the American Anti-vivisection Society was founded at Philadelphia; to be followed up by its most flourishing Illinois branch, carried on with immense spirit by Mrs. Fairchild Allen. Mrs. Lovell of Bryn Mawr has further secured the most important support for the cause in the great W. C. T. U., founded by Miss Willard, and numbering 100,000 members.

On the second of May, Mr. Holt's bill for total prohibition was debated in the House of Commons, and on a division there were 83 votes in its favor and 222 against it.

At last the committee of the Victoria Street Society formally adopted the thoroughgoing policy; and at a meeting, August 7th, 1878, resolved "to appeal henceforth to public opinion in favor of the total prohibition of vivisection." We then changed our title to that of the "Society for Protection of Animals from vivisection." Dr. Hoggan and his wife, Mrs. Hoggan, M. D., and also Mr. de Fonblanque retired from the committee with cordial goodwill on both sides, and the Archbishop of York withdrew from the Vice-Presidency. But, besides these losses, I do not believe that we had any others, and there was soon a large batch of fresh recruits of new members who had long resented our previous half-hearted policy — as they considered it to have been.

For my own part I had accepted from the outset the assurance I received on all hands that a bill for the total prohibition of vivisection had not the remotest chance of passing through Parliament in the present state of public opinion; but that a bill might be framed, which, proceeding only on the grounds of restriction, might effectually and thoroughly exclude *" not only torture but anything at all approaching thereto ;"* and that such a bill had every chance of becoming law. To promote such a bill had been my single aim and hope, and when it had been prepared and presented and received so favorably it really appeared as if we were on the right and reasonable tack ; much as we hated any concession whatever to the demands of the vivisectors.

But when we found that the compromise which we proposed had failed, and that our bill providing the *minimum* of protection for animals at all acceptable by their friends was twisted into a bill protecting their tormentors, we were driven to raise our demands to the total prohibition of the practice, and to determine to work upon that basis for any number of years till public opinion be ripe for our measure.

This was one aspect of our position ; but there was another. (We had in truth gone into this crusade almost as our forefathers had set off for the Holy Land, with scarcely any knowledge of the power which we were invading. We knew that dreadful cruelties had been done ; but we fondly imagined they were abuses which were *separable* from the *practice* of experimenting on living animals. We accepted blindly the representation of vivisection by its advocates as a rare resource of baffled surgeons and physicians, intent on some discovery for the immediate benefit of humanity

or the solution of some pressing and important physiological problem; and we thought that with due and
well-considered restrictions and safeguards on these
occasional experiments, we might effectually shut out
cruelty. By slow, very slow degrees, we learned that
nothing was much further from the truth than these
fancy pictures of ideal vivisection, and that real vivisection is *not* the occasional and regretfully adopted
resource of a few, but the *daily employment* (Carl Vogt
called it his "daily bread") of hundreds of men and
students, devoted to it as completely and professionally
as butchers to cutting up carcases.) Finally we found
that to extend protection by any conceivable act of
Parliament to animals once delivered to the physiologists in their laboratories was chimerical. Vivisection
we recognized at last to be a *method of research* which
may be either sanctioned or prohibited as a method,
but which cannot be restricted efficiently by rules
founded on humane considerations wholly irrelevant to
the scientific enquiry.

(On the moral side, also, we became profoundly impressed with the truth of the principle to which Canon
Liddon refers in the letter I have quoted, viz., that the
anti-vivisection cause is "of even greater importance
to human character than to the physical comfort of our
fellow creatures who are most immediately concerned."
As I wrote of it, about this time, in "Bernard's Martyrs": —

("We stand face to face with a *new vice*, new, at least
in its vast modern development and the passion wherewith it is pursued — the vice of scientific cruelty.) It
is not the old vice of cruelty for cruelty's sake. It
is not the careless brutal cruelty of the half-savage
drunken drover, the low ruffian who skins living cats
for gain, or of the classic Roman or modern Spaniard,
watching the sports of the arena with fierce delight in
the sight of blood and death. The new vice is nothing

of this kind. . . . It is not like most other human vices, hot and thoughtless. The man possessed by it is calm, cool, deliberate; perfectly cognizant of what he is doing; understanding, as indeed no other man understands, the full meaning and extent of the waves and spasms of agony he deliberately creates. It does not seize the ignorant or hunger-driven or brutalized classes; but the cultivated, the well-fed, the well-dressed, the civilized, and (it is said) the otherwise kindly-disposed and genial men of science, forming part of the most intellectual circles in Europe. Sometimes it would appear as we read of these horrors — the baking alive of dogs, the slow dissecting out of quivering nerves, and so on — that it would be a relief to picture the doer of such deeds as some unhappy, half-witted wretch, hideous and filthy in mien or stupefied by drink, so that the full responsibility of a rational and educated human being should not belong to him, and that we might say of him, 'He scarcely understands what he does.' But, alas! this new vice has no such palliations; and is exhibited not by such unhappy outcasts, but by some of the very foremost men of our time; men who would think scornfully of being asked to share the butcher's honest trade; men addicted to high speculation on all the mysteries of the universe; men who hope to found the Religion of the Future, and to leave the impress of their minds upon their age, and upon generations yet to be born."

Regarding the matter from this point of view — as our leaders, the most eminent philanthropists of their generation, Lord Shaftesbury, Lord Mount-Temple, Samuel Morley, and Cardinal Manning, emphatically did — the reasons for calling for the total prohibition of vivisection rather than for its restriction became actually clearer in our eyes on the side of the human moral interests than on that of the physical interests of the poor brutes. We felt that so long as the practice should be sanctioned at all, so long the vice of scientific cruelty would spring up in the fresh minds of students, and be kept alive everywhere. It was therefore absolutely needful to reach the germ of the disease, and not merely to endeavor to allay the worst symptoms and outbreaks. It is the *passion itself* which needs to be sternly suppressed; and this can only be done by stopping altogether the practice which is its outcome, and on which it feeds and grows.

(But (say our opponents), "Are you prepared to relinquish all the benefits which this practice brings to humanity at large ? "

Our answer to them, of course, is, that we question the reality of those benefits altogether, but that, placing them at their highest estimation, they are of no appreciable weight compared to the certain moral injury done to the community by the sanction of cruelty.) The discovery of the *Elixir Vitæ* itself would be too dearly purchased if the hearts of men were to be rendered one degree more callous and selfish than they are now. And that the practice of vivisection by a body of men at the intellectual summit of our social system, whose influence must dribble down through every stratum of society, would infallibly tend to increase such callousness, there can exist no reasonable doubt. For my own part, though believing that little or nothing worth mentioning has been discovered for the healing art through vivisection, and that Dr. Leffingwell is right in saying that "if agony could be measured in money, no mining company in the world would sanction prospecting in such barren regions," I yet deprecate the emphasis which many of our friends have laid on this argument against vivisection. We have gone off our rightful ground of the simple moral issues of the question, and have seemed to admit (what very few of us would deliberately do) that *if* some important discovery *had been* made by vivisection our case against

it would be lost or weakened. I have been so anxious
to warn our friends against this, as I think, very grave
mistake in tactics, that I circulated some time ago a
little "Parable" which I may as well summarize here : —

"A party of Filibusters once proposed to ravage a
neighboring island, inhabited by poor and humble people who had always been faithful servants and friends
of our country, and had in no way deserved ill-treat-
ment. Some friends of justice protested that the Filibusters ought to be prohibited from carrying on their
expedition, but unluckily they did not simply arraign
the moral lawfulness of the project, but went on to discuss the *inexpediency* of the invasion, arguing that the
island was very poor and barren, and would not repay
the cost of conquest. Here the Filibusters saw their
advantage and broke in : 'No such thing ! *We* are the
only people who know anything about the island, and
we assure you it is full of mines of gold and silver.'
'Bosh !' replied the just men ; 'we defy you to show
us a single nugget.' On this there was a good deal of
shuffling of feet among the Filibusters, and they exhibited some glittering fragments as gold, but being tested
these proved to be worthless, and again other fragments
which they produced were traced to quite another part
of the district, far away from the island. Still it became
evident that the Filibusters would go on interminably
bringing up specimens, and some day might possibly
produce one the value of which could not be well dis-
puted. Moreover the Filibusters (who, like other pi-
rates, were addicted to telling fearful yarns) had the
great advantage of talking all along of things they had
studied and seen, whereas the men of the party of justice were imperfectly informed about the resources of
the island, having never gone thither, and thus they
were easily placed at a disadvantage and made to appear foolish. It is true that the Filibusters had set
them on the wrong track by clamoring for the invasion

on the avowed ground of the spoil they should gather
for the nation, and they had only tried to nullify the
effect of such appeals to general selfishness by showing
that there was really no spoil to be had; and that the
invasion was a blunder as well as a crime. But in
bandying such appeals to expediency they had put
themselves in the wrong box because *to discuss the
value of the spoil was,* by implication, *to admit that, if it
only were rich, it might possibly be justifiable to go and
seize it!*"

I have made this long explanation of our policy, because I am painfully aware that among practical people
and men of the world, accustomed to compromise on
public questions, our adoption of the demand for total
prohibition has placed us at a great disadvantage as
" irreconcilables; " and our movement has appeared as
the " fad " of enthusiasts and fanatics. For the reasons
I have given above I think it will appear that while
compromise offered any hope of protecting our poor
clients from the very worst cruelties, we tried it frankly
and in earnest; first in Lord Henniker's and secondly
in Lord Carnarvon's bill. When this last effort failed
we were left no choice but either to abandon our dumb
friends to their fate, or demand for them the removal
of the source of their danger.

It will not be necessary for me to recount further
with as much detail the history of the Victoria Street
Society, of which I continued to act as honorary secretary till I finally left London in 1884. Abundance of
other friends of animals, active and energetic, were in
the field, and our movement, in spite of a score of
checks and defeats, continued to spread and deepen.
Campbell's familiar line often occurred to me (with a
variation) : —

> " The cause of *Mercy* once begun,
> Though often lost is always won ! "

On July 15, 1879, Lord Truro brought into the House of Lords a bill for the prohibition of vivisection. It was not promoted by us, and was in many respects unfortunately managed, but our society, of course, supported it. Lord Shaftesbury made in defence of it one of his longest speeches. I was in the House of Lords at the time, and thought that there could never be a much more affecting sight than that of the noble old man, who had pleaded so often in that "gilded chamber" for men, women, and children, standing there at last in his venerable age, urging with all his simple eloquence the claims of dumb animals to mercy. Against him rose and spoke Lord Aberdare, actually (as he took pains to explain) *as President* of the Society for Prevention of Cruelty to Animals! The Bishop of Peterborough, Dr. Magee, afterwards Archbishop of York, also made then his unhappy speech about the rabbits and the surgical operation; (with which the inventor of that operation, Dr. Clay, said they had "no more to do than the Pope of Rome"). Only sixteen Peers voted for the bill, ninety-seven against it.

On the 16th March, 1880, Mr. Holt's bill for total prohibition was down for second reading in the House of Commons, but was stopped by notice of dissolution. From that time our friend, Sir Eardley Wilmot, took charge of a similar bill promoted by our society. Notice of it was given by Mr. Firth on the 3d February, 1881. The second reading was postponed, first to July 13th, next to July 27th, and then that day was taken by government. In October of that year (1881) Mr. R. T. Reid took charge of our bill, on the resignation of Sir Eardley Wilmot. The second reading was postponed on June 28th, 1882, and not till the 4th of April, 1883, after all these heartbreaking postponements and failures, there was at last a debate. Mr. Reid and Mr. George Russell spoke admirably in favor of the bill, but they were talked out without a division by a whole series of advocates of vivisection, of whom Sir William Harcourt, Mr. Cartwright, and Lord Playfair were most eminent. This was the last occasion on which we have been able to obtain a debate in either House. Mr. Reid brought in his bill again in 1884, but could obtain no day for a second reading.

One touching incident of these earlier years I must not omit. Our Honorable Correspondent at the Hague, Madame van Manen-Thesingh, had written me several letters exhibiting remarkable good sense as well as ardent feeling. One day I received a short note from her telling me that she was dying; and begging me to send over some trustworthy agent at once to the Hague, if (as she feared) I could not go to her myself. I telegraphed that I would be with her next day, and accordingly sailed that night to Flushing. When I reached her house M. van Manen received me very kindly; but as a man half bewildered with grief. His wife's disease was cancer of the tongue, and she could no longer speak. She was waiting for me in her drawing-room. It may be imagined how affecting was our half-speechless interview. After a time M. van Manen at a sign from his wife unlocked a bureau and took out a large packet of papers. These he placed before her on the table and then left the room. Of course I understood this proceeding was intended to satisfy me that it was with her husband's entire consent that Madame van Manen gave these papers to me. There were a great many of them, Dutch, Russian, and American securities of one sort or another, and she marked them off one by one on a list which she had prepared. Then she wrote down that she gave me all these, and also some laces and jewellery, to further the anti-vivisection cause in whatever way I thought best; reserving a donation for the London Anti-vivisection Society. A few efforts to convey my gratitude and sympathy were all I could make. The dear, noble woman stood calm and brave in the immediate prospect of death in its most painful form, and all her anxiety seemed to be that the poor brutes should be effectually aided by her gifts. I left her sorrowfully, and carried her parcel in my travelling bag, first to Amsterdam for a day or two, and then to London, where having summoned our finance committee I placed it in their hands. The contents (duly estimated and sold through the Army and Navy Society) realized (over and above the legacy to the London Society) about £1,350. With this sum we started the "Zoöphilist."

The "Zoöphilist" thus founded (May 2, 1881), under the editorship of Mr. Adams, then our Secretary, has of course been of enormous value to our cause. A new series began on the 1st January, 1883, which I edited till my resignation of the honorary secretary-ship June, 1884. I also started and edited a French journal of the same size and character, "Le Zoöphile," from November 1st, 1883, to April, 1884, when the undertaking was abandoned, French readers having obviously found the paper too dry for their taste. Some of them also remonstrated with me against the occasional references in it to religious considerations, and I was frankly counselled by a very influential French gentleman to *cease altogether to mention God* — a piece of advice which I distinctly declined to take! The late celebrated Mlle. Deraismes sent me a beautiful article for "Le Zoöphile," of which I should have gladly availed myself if she would have allowed me the editorial privilege of dropping about half a page of aggressive atheism; but this after a pretty sharp correspondence she refused peremptorily to do. Altogether I was evidently out of touch both with my French staff and French readers.

Beside these two periodicals our society from the first issued an almost incredible multitude of pamphlets and leaflets. I should be afraid to make any calculation

of the number of them and of the thousands of copies
sent into circulation.   My own share must have ex-
ceeded four hundred.   Beside these and those of our
successive secretaries (some extremely able) we printed
valuable pamphlets, sermons, and speeches by Lord
Shaftesbury, Cardinal Manning, the Lord Chief Justice,
the Dean of Llandaff, Professor Ruskin, Bishop Barry,
Mr. R. T. Reid, Honorable B. Coleridge, Lady Paget,
Canon Wilberforce, Mr. Mark Thornhill, Mr. Leslie
Stephen, the Bishop of Oxford (Dr. Mackarness), Rev.
F. O. Morris, Dr. Arnold, George Macdonald, Mr.
Ernest Bell, Baron Weber, and (above all for scientific
importance) Mr. Lawson Tait, Dr. Bell Taylor, Dr.
Berdoe, and Dr. Clarke.

Some of my own anti-vivisection pamphlets were
collected a few years ago and published by Messrs.
Sonnenschein in a volume (crown 8vo., pp. 272) entitled
the "Modern Rack."   Several very useful books of reference were compiled by our Secretary, Mr. Bryan, and
published by the society; notably the "Vivisectors'
Directory," the "English Vivisectors' Directory," and
"Anti-vivisection Evidences." Of the "Nine Circles,"
compiled for me and printed (first edition) at my
expense, I shall speak presently.

I must here be allowed to say that the spirited letters, pamphlets, and articles by our medical allies, Dr.
Berdoe, Dr. Clarke, Dr. Bowie, and Dr. Arnold, above
all Dr. Berdoe's contributions to our scientific literature, have been of immeasurable value to our cause.
The day of Dr. Berdoe's accession to our party at one
of our annual meetings must ever be remembered by
me with gratitude.   His ability, courage, and disinter-
estedness have been far beyond any praise I can give
them.   Mr. Mark Thornhill also (a distinguished
Indian civil servant, author of "The Indian Mutiny,"
etc.), has done us invaluable service by his calm, lucid,
and most convincing writings, notably "The Case

against Vivisection," and "Experiments on Hospital Patients." Mr. Pirkis, R. N., has been for many years, not only by his steady attendance at the committee but by his unwearied exertions in preparing and disseminating anti-Pasteur literature, one of the chief benefactors of the society.

Among our undertakings on behalf of the victims of science was the prosecution of Professor Ferrier at Bow Street on the 17th November, 1881, on the strength of certain reports in the two leading medical journals. We had ascertained that he had no license for vivisection, and yet we read as follows in a report of the proceedings at the International Medical Congress of 1881 : —

"The members were shown two of the monkeys, a portion of whose cortex had been removed by Professor Ferrier." — "British Medical Journal," 20th August, 1881.

" The interest attaching to the discussion was greatly enhanced by the fact that Professor Ferrier was willing to exhibit two monkeys which he had operated upon some months previously." . . .

" In startling contrast to the dog were two monkeys exhibited by Professor Ferrier. One of them had been operated upon in the middle of January, the left motor area having been destroyed." — "Lancet," October 8th, 1881.

When the reporters who had sent in their reports to the two journals were produced the following ludicrous examination took place in court : —

Dr. Charles Smart Roy (the reporter for the " British Medical Journal") was asked : —

Q. Did Professor Ferrier offer to exhibit two of the monkeys upon which he had so operated ?

A. At the congress, no.

Q. Did he subsequently ?

A. No; he showed certain of the members of the congress two monkeys at King's College.

Q. What two monkeys ?

A. Two monkeys upon which an operation had been performed.

Q. By whom ?

A. By Professor Yeo (! !).

The editor of the "Lancet," Dr. Wakeley, was next examined.

Dr. Wakeley, sworn, examined by Mr. Waddy :—

Q. Are you the editor of the "Lancet ?"

A. I am.

Q. Can you tell me who it was furnished this report ?

A. I have the permission of the gentleman to give his name, Professor Gamgee, of Owen's College, Manchester.

Mr. Waddy : What I should ask is that one might have an opportunity of calling Professor Gamgee.

Mr. Gully (Counsel for the defendant) : We have communicated with Professor Gamgee, and I know very well he will say precisely what was said by Dr. Roy. — Report of Trial, November 17th, 1881.

The position of the anti-vivisectionists on the occasion was, it must be confessed, like that of the simple countryman in the fair. "You lay your money that Professor Ferrier is under that cup ?" "Yes, certainly ! I saw both Professor Roy and Professor Gamgee put him there about five minutes ago." "Here then, see ! Hay Presto ! Hocus-pocus ! There is only Professor Yeo !"

The group of vivisectors and their allies, Dr. Michael Foster, Dr. Burdon-Sanderson, Dr. Ernest Hart, Professor Ferrier, Dr. Roy, and many more who filled the court, all evinced the utmost hilarity at the success of the device whereby (as a matter of necessity, the anti-vivisection case collapsed.

At last, in the Philosophical Transactions of the Royal Society for 1884, the truth came to light. In the prefatory note to a record of experiments by David Ferrier and Gerald F. Yeo, M. D., occurs the statement : —

"The facts recorded in this paper are partly the results of a research made conjointly by Drs. Ferrier and Yeo, aided by a grant from the British Medical Association, and partly of a research made by Dr. Ferrier alone, aided by a grant from the Royal Society."

The conjoint experiments are distinguished by an asterisk ; and among them we find those of the two monkeys which formed the subject of the trial. Thus it stands confessed — actually in the Transactions of the Royal Society — that Professor Ferrier *had* the leading share (his name always appears first) in the experiments ; and that, conjointly with Professor Yeo, he received a grant from the British Medical Association for performing the same !

If after this experience we have ceased to hope much from proceedings in courts of justice against our antagonists, it will not be thought surprising. The society has been frequently twitted with the failure of this prosecution, "for which" our opponents say we "had not a tittle of evidence." Elaborate reports in the two leading medical journals do not, it appears, afford even "a tittle of evidence !"[1]

Among other modes in which we endeavored to push forward our cause have been special appeals to win over particular churches or other bodies to adopt our prin-

[1] Mr. Cartwright, speaking in the House of Commons, April 4th, 1883, in reply to Mr. R. T. Reid, said: "The honorable member should have said something about the prosecution of Dr. Ferrier for having evaded the act. He does not do that. He has wisely given the go-by to it, for that prosecution lamentably failed, altogether broke down. The charge brought against Dr. Ferrier was that he operated without license and infringed the law by doing those things to which the honorable and learned member referred; but the charge was not supported by one tittle of evidence."

ciples. Enormous numbers of circulars have been addressed in this manner by our society to the clergy of the Church of England, and it is believed that at least 4,000 are on our side in the controversy; more than 2,000 had signed our memorial several years ago.

Another appeal was addressed by me personally to the Society of Friends through the clerks of the monthly and quarterly meetings in England and Ireland.

It has proved eminently successful, and has led to the formation of a powerful "Friends' Anti-vivisection Society," which lately issued an appeal to other members of their body signed by 2,000 Friends, many of them being among the most eminent in England. This has again formed the ground of a fresh appeal on an immense scale in Pennsylvania. Another recent appeal to the Congregationalists has, I hear, been very well received. On one occasion a special petition to the House of Lords was signed by every Unitarian minister in London. It was presented by the Archbishop of York, who also presented a memorial (for restriction) in 1876 signed by all the heads of colleges in Oxford.

Another appeal which I ventured to make (printed as a large pamphlet) to "the Humane Jews of England," entreating them to remonstrate with the forty German Jews who are the worst vivisectors in Europe, was, unfortunately, a deplorable failure. Four of my own private friends, Jewesses, all expressed their sympathy warmly, and sent handsome contributions to our funds; but *not one* other Jew or Jewess, high or low, rallied to us, albeit I presented pamphlets to nearly 200 recommended to me as specially well disposed. I shall never be tempted to address the "*Humane*" Jews of England again!

One other circular I may mention as more successful. I sent to 700 head school masters the following letter.

with which were enclosed the pamphlets mentioned therein : —

HENGWRT, DOLGELLY,
September, 1880.

DEAR SIR, — Permit me respectfully to ask your perusal of the accompanying little paper on "Physiology as a Branch of Education." I have written it under a strong sense of the necessity which at present exists for some similar caution.

The leaflet describing a "Specimen of Modern Physiological Instruction" refers to a scene in Paris which could not be precisely paralleled in an English school, so far as concerns the actual torture of the animals used for exhibition, since the vivisection act of 1876 provided that anæsthetics must be used in all cases of vivisection for illustration of lectures.

It is, however, to be seriously questioned whether even painless (and therefore not *shocking*) operations on living animals, performed before boys and girls, by the enthusiastic English admirers of Claude Bernard and Paul Bert, may not excite in the minds of the young witnesses a curiosity unmingled with pity, such as may subsequently prompt them to become the most merciless experimenters; or, at least, advocates and apologists of scientific cruelty.

Trusting, sir, that you will pardon the trespass of this letter,

I am sincerely yours,

FRANCES POWER COBBE.

Twelve of these head-masters, including some of the most eminent, *e. g.*, Mr. Welldon, of Harrow, Dr. Haig, of the Charterhouse, and the lamented Mr. Thring, of Uppingham, wrote me most interesting letters in reply expressing approval of my views. I shall here insert that of Mr. Thring as in many respects noteworthy.

Rev. Edward Thring to Miss F. P. C.

PITLOCHRY, PERTHSHIRE, N. B.,
September 6th, 1889.

MY DEAR MADAM, — I received your little pamphlet
on physiology, but I hardly know what you expect me
to do. My writings on education sufficiently show
how strongly I feel on the subject of a literary education; or rather how confident I am in the judgment that
there can be no worthy education which is not based on
the study of the highest thoughts of the highest men,
in the best shape.

As for science (most of it falsely so called), if a few
leading minds are excepted, it simply amounts, to the
average dull worker, to no more than a kind of upper
shop-work, weighing out, and labelling, and learning
alphabetical formulæ: a superior grocery-assistant's
work; and has not a single element of higher mental
training in it. Not to mention that it leaves out all
knowledge of man and life, and *therefore* is eminently
fitted to train men for life and its struggles! Physiology, in its worser sense, adds to this a brutalizing of
the average practitioner, or rather a devilish combina-
tion of intellect-worship and cruelty at the expense of
feeling and character. For my part, if it were true that
vivisection had wonderfully relieved bodily disease for
men, if it were at the cost of lost spirits, then I should
say, Let the body perish! And it *is* at the cost of lost
spirits! I do not say that under no circumstances
should an experiment take place, but I do say that
under no circumstance should an experiment take place
for teaching purposes. You will see how decided my
judgment is on this matter. I send you three addresses
on education which, in smaller space than my books,
will illustrate the positive side of my experience and
beliefs.

Yours faithfully,   EDWARD THRING.

Our committee was, in all the years in which I had
to do with it, the most harmonious and friendly of which
I have ever heard. Lord Shaftesbury, who presided
forty-nine times, and never once failed us when he was
expected, was, of course, as all the world knows, a first-
rate chairman, getting through an immense amount of
business, while allowing every member his, or her, legitimate rights of speech and voting. He never showed
himself (I have been told) anywhere more genial and
zealous than with us. Lord Mount-Temple attended
very frequently, and Lady Mount-Temple from first
to last has been one of our warmest and wisest friends.
General Colin Mackenzie, a devout and noble old soldier, spoke little, but what he did say was always
straight to the mark, and the affectionate respect we all
felt for him made his presence delightful. Lady Portsmouth (now the Dowager Countess) attended in those
days very regularly, and Lady Camperdown has given
us her unwearied help from that time to this. I have
spoken of the very valuable services of Mr. E. de Fonblanque. In later years my friend Rev. William Henry
Channing was a great support to me. The Cardinal
was, perhaps, a little reserved, but always carefully
kind and courteous, and whatever he said bore great
weight. Lord Bute's advice was very valuable and full
of good sense. Mr. Shaen's legal knowledge served us
often. In brief, each member was useful. There
never were any parties or cabals in the committee. It
was my business as Hon. Secretary (especially after
my colleague, Dr. Hoggan, retired) to lay proposals
for action before the committee. They were sometimes rejected and often completely modified; but we
all felt that the one thing we desired was simply to find
the best way of forwarding our cause, and we were
thankful for the guidance of the wise and experienced
men who were our leaders. In short, the feelings which
inspired us round that long oak office-table were not ill

befitting our work; and now that so many of those who sat there beside me in the earlier years have passed from earth, I find myself pondering whether they have met " *Elsewhere ;* " where, ere long, I may join them. They must form a blessed company in any world. May my place be with *them*, please God! rather than with the votaries of science, in the " secular to be."

In later years the *personnel* of the committee has of course been largely renewed. Lady Mount-Temple, Lady Camperdown, and Mrs. Frank Morrison almost alone remain from the earlier body. Miss Marston also, who originally founded the "London Anti-vivisection Society," has been for many years one of the firmest and wisest friends of the Victoria Street Society also. I have spoken above of all that we owe to Captain Pirkis's unfailing help at the committee, even while residing far out of town; and of the zeal wherewith he and his gifted wife founded the first of our branches, and have labored in circulating our literature. Miss Monro, Miss Rees, Miss Bryant, and Mrs. Arthur Arnold have never wearied through many years in patiently and vigorously aiding our work. Of our excellent chairman Mr. Ernest Bell's services to the anti-vivisection cause it is needless for me to speak, as they must be recognized gratefully by the whole party throughout England.

We have had several successive secretaries who sometimes took the work much off my hands, sometimes left it to fall very heavily on me and Miss Lloyd. On one occasion, we two, having also lost the clerk, did the entire work of the office for many weeks, inclusive of writing, editing, folding, addressing, and actually *posting* an issue of the " Zoöphilist!" But my toils and many of my anxieties ended when I was fortunate enough to obtain the services, as Secretary, of Mr. Benjamin Bryan, who had long shown his genuine interest in the cause as editor of a Northern newspaper; and after a year or two of work in concert with him I felt free to leave the whole burden on his shoulders, and tendered my resignation. The constant presence on the committee of my long-tried and most valued allies, Mr. Ernest Bell, Captain Pirkis, and Miss Marston, left me entirely at rest respecting the course of our future policy in the straight direction of prohibition.

The last event which I need record is a disagreeable incident which occurred in the autumn of 1892. I had been seriously ill with acute sciatica, and had been only partially relieved by a large subcutaneous dose of morphia given me by my country doctor. In this state, with my head still swimming and scarcely able to sit at a table, I found myself involved in the most acrimonious newspaper controversy which I ever remember to have seen in any respectable journal. It will be best that another pen than mine should tell the story; so I will quote the calm and lucid statement of the author of the excellent pamphlet, " Vivisection at the Folkestone Church Congress " (p. 6).

After a *résumé* of the notorious debate at Folkestone the writer says : —

"The main point of attack in Mr. Victor Horsley's paper was a book called the ' Nine Circles ' which had been published some months before, and contained reports of different classes of cruel experiments on animals, both in England and on the continent. To this book Miss Cobbe had given the sanction of her name, but she was not personally responsible for any of the quotations, having entrusted the compilation of the book to friends living in London, and who had access to the journals and papers in which the experiments were recorded. Mr. Horsley's indignation was roused because in a certain number of cases — 22 out of the 170 narratives of different classes of experiments, many of them involving a *series*, and the use of large numbers of animals in each — the mention of the use of morphia or chloroform was omitted. Miss Cobbe, in a letter to the 'Times' of October 11th, while acknowledging that the compilers were bound to quote the fact if stated, expressed her conviction that such statements are misleading, because insensibility is not and cannot be complete during the whole period of the experiment. Dr. Berdoe also wrote in several papers defending Miss Cobbe against Mr. Horsley's imputations of fraud and intent to deceive, etc., and explaining that the compilers of the book were alone responsible for the omissions. He added, however, a further explanation that, as it was often the painful results, and not the operations which caused them, that it was desired to illustrate, and as these results lasted sometimes for many days or weeks or months and to maintain insensibility during that period was impossible, the omissions were not so important after all." . . .

. . . "The assailant, however, returned to the charge and in a more violent style than before. His letter to the 'Times' of October 17th was a tirade against Miss Cobbe, worthy, as the 'Spectator' remarked, only of the fifteenth century, in which the words 'false' and 'lie' were freely used. It was a letter of so libellous a character that it is a matter for wonder that it obtained publication. Miss Cobbe very naturally and properly at once retired from a controversy conducted, as she expressed it in a letter to the 'Times,' 'outside of all my experience of civilized journalism.' She concluded with these words : 'I need scarcely say that I maintain the veracity of every word of the letter which you did me the honor to publish of the fifteenth inst., as well as the *bona fides* of all I have spoken or written on this or other subjects during my threescore years and ten.'"

After a week or two I went to Bath to recruit my health after the attack of sciatica; and the first newspaper I took up at the York Hotel contained a still

more violent attack on me than those which had preceded it. On reading it I walked into the telegraph
office next door, wired for rooms at my favorite South
Kensington Hotel and went up to town with my maid,
presenting myself at once to our committee, which happened to be sitting and arranging for the impending
meeting in St. James's Hall. "Shall I attend," said I,
"and speak, or not? I will do exactly what you wish."
The committee were unanimously of opinion that I
should go to the meeting and take part in the proceedings, and I have ever since rejoiced that I did so. It was
on the evening of October 27th. My ever kind friend
Canon Basil Wilberforce took the chair, Colonel Lockwood, Bishop Barry, Dr. Berdoe, Mr. Bell, and Captain Pirkis were on the platform supporting me, but
above all Mr. George W. E. Russell (then Under Secretary of State for India) made a speech on my behalf for
which I shall feel grateful to him so long as I live.
We had but slight acquaintance previously, and I shall
always feel that it was a most generous and chivalrous
action on his part to stand forth in so public a manner
as my champion on such an occasion. The audience
was more than sympathetic. There was a storm of
genuine feeling when I rose to make my explanation,
and I found it, for once, hard to command my voice.
This is what I said, as reported in the "Zoöphilist,"
November 1st, 1892 : —

"Now to come to the story of the 'Nine Circles,'
which I will tell as quickly as possible. When I gave
up the honorary secretaryship of the Victoria Street Society six years ago, I retired to live among the mountains in Wales; and the chief thing which remained for
me to do was to publish as many pamphlets and papers as seemed likely to help the cause. I have just
got here my printer's list of the papers which I have
printed in those six years. I have made up the totals,
and I find that the number in the six years of books,

pamphlets, and leaflets has been 320 — that is about one
a week — and that 271,350 copies of them were printed;
173 papers having been written by myself. (Cheers.)
Some of these were adopted by the society and honored
by coming out under its auspices; and others I issued
quite independently. Amongst those which I issued
'on my own hook,' I am happy to say, was this book
called the 'Nine Circles.' Therefore our dear and honored society is not responsible for that book. I am
alone responsible; it was printed at my expense, and
Messrs. Sonnenschein published it for me. Therefore,
I am the only person concerned with it, and the society
has nothing to do with it. I am thankful to hear that
the revised edition will come out under the auspices of
the society. My only privilege will be to pay for it,
and that I shall most thankfully do, in order to wipe
out the wrong I have done as concerns the present edition. When the present book was got up, I sketched a
plan of it and asked a lady often employed by us who
was living in London, and is a good German scholar, to
make extracts for me. She knows a great deal about
the subject; she also knows German (which I do not do
sufficiently for the purpose), and she was living in London while I was two hundred miles away. Therefore I
asked her to make the extracts of which this book is
compiled, and it was afterwards revised — as Dr. Berdoe
has told us — by him. The book came out; and it appears now that there are some mistakes in it. My
assistant had left out certain things which ought to
have been stated. I took it for granted — I was quite
wrong to do so — that all my directions had been carried
out, and I made myself responsible for the book.
Therefore, whatever error there is in the matter is mine,
and I beg that that will be quite understood. (Cheers.)
But what is all this tremendous storm which has been
raised, and this pulling of the house down about these
mistakes ? Do they wish us to understand that there

are no such things as painful experiments in England? Apparently that is what they are trying to make us think — that there never has been anything of the kind; that they are perfectly incapable of putting any animal to pain. Do they really mean that? Is that what they wish us to understand? If they do *not* mean that, I do not know what it is they mean. It seems to me that they are raising this tremendous storm very much as if the old slave-holders were to have danced a war-dance round Mrs. Stowe and scalped her for having said that Legree had flogged Uncle Tom with a thousand lashes, when really there were only nine hundred and ninety-nine. (Laughter.) That seems to me to be the case in a nutshell."— "Zoöphilist," November 1st, 1892.

I had the gratification to receive soon after the following most kind address and expression of confidence from the leading members of the Victoria Street Society: —

ADDRESS.

To Miss FRANCES POWER COBBE: —

We, the undersigned, being supporters of the Victoria Street Society, and others interested in the movement against vivisection, wish to express the strong feeling of indignation with which we have seen your integrity called in question by men who seem unable to conceive of the pure unselfish devotion of high intellectual gifts to the service of God's humbler creatures.

It is impossible for those who know anything of the early history of this movement to forget the great personal sacrifice at which you undertook to make it the chief work of your life.

It is equally impossible for us who have watched its progress, to say how highly we have esteemed the indomitable courage and forcible eloquence with which you have exposed the evils inseparable from experiments on living animals.

Further, we wish to record our firm conviction that you have, throughout, recognized the wisdom, and the duty of founding your attack on vivisection upon the truth, and nothing but the truth, so far as you have been able to arrive at it.

We wish, in conclusion, to assure you not only of our special sympathy with you at a time when you have been subjected to a personal attack of an unusually coarse and violent character, but also of our determination to give still more earnest support to the cause to which you have, at so great a cost, devoted yourself : —

Strafford
  (*Earl of Strafford*).
Coleridge
  (*Lord Chief Justice*).
Worcester
  (*Marquis of Worcester*).
Haddington
  (*Earl of Haddington*).
Arthur, Bath and Wells
  (*Bishop of Bath and Wells*).
J., Manchester
  (*Bishop of Manchester*).
W. Walsham, Wakefield
  (*Bishop of Wakefield*).
H. B., Coventry
  (*Bishop of Coventry*).
John Mitchinson (*Bishop*).
F. Cramer-Roberts
  (*Bishop*).
Edward G. Bagshawe
  (*R. C. Bishop of Nottingham*).
Sidmouth
  (*Viscount Sidmouth*).

Pollington
  (*Viscount Pollington*).
Colville of Culross
  (*Lord Colville of Culross*).
Cardross (*Lord Cardross*).
H. Abinger (*Lady Abinger*).
Robartes (*Lord Robartes*).
Leigh (*Lord Leigh*).
C. Buchan (*Dowager Countess of Buchan*).
Harriet de Clifford
  (*Dowager Lady de Clifford*).
F. Camperdown
  (*Countess of Camperdown*).
Kinnaird (*Lord Kinnaird*).
Alma Kinnaird
  (*Lady Kinnaird*).
Clementine Mitford (*Lady Clementine Mitford*).
Eveline Portsmouth
  (*Dowager Countess of Portsmouth*).

H. Kemball (*Lady Kemball*).

J. Brotherton (*Lady Brotherton*).

Evelyn Ashley (*Hon. Evelyn Ashley*).

Bernard Coleridge (*Hon. B. Coleridge, M. P.*).

Geraldine Coleridge (*Hon. Mrs. S. Coleridge*).

Stephen Coleridge (*Hon. Stephen Coleridge*).

George Duckett (*Sir George Duckett, Bt.*).

Henry A. Hoare (*Sir Henry Hoare, Bt.*).

George F. Shaw, LL. D.

Samuel Smith, M. P.

Theodore Fry, M. P.

George W. E. Russell, M. P.

Jacob Bright, M. P.

Th. Burt, M. P.

Julius Barras (Colonel).

Richard H. Hutton.

R. Payne Smith, LL. D.

H. Wilson White, D. D.

Edward Whately (*Archdeacon Whately*).

George W. Cox (*Rev. Sir George Cox, Bt.*).

R. M. Grier (*Prebendary Grier*).

Eleanor Vere C. Boyle (*Hon. Mrs. R. C. Boyle*).

E. G. Deane Morgan (*Hon. Mrs. Deane Morgan*).

Georgina Mount-Temple (*Lady Mount-Temple*).

Alex. Bowie, M. D., C. M.

John H. Clarke, M. D.

Henry Downes, M. D.

Henry M. Duncalfe.

William Adamson, D. D.

William Adlam.

Amelia E. Arnold.

Ernest Bell.

Rhoda Broughton.

Olive S. Bryant.

W. K. Burford.

A. Gallenga and Mrs. Gallenga.

Maria G. Grey.

Emily A. E. Shirreff.

Frances Holden.

Eleanor Mary James.

Francis Griffith Jones.

E. J. Kennedy.

Edith Leycester.

W. S. Lilly.

Mary Charlotte Lloyd.

Ann Marston.

Mary J. Martin.

S. S. Munro.

Frank Morrison.

Harriet Morrison.

Josiah Oldfield.

Rose Pender.

Fred. Pennington.

Herbert Philips.

Fred. E. Pirkis and Mrs. Pirkis.

R. Ll. Price.

Evelyn Price.

R. M. Price.

Charles Bell Taylor, M. D.   Lester Reed.
Edward Berdoe, M. R. C. S.   Ellen Eleum Rees.
J. Herbert Satchell.   Mark Thornhill, J. P.

In conclusion, and as a consolation for all annoyance
and trouble, I have the satisfaction of knowing that
our anti-vivisection cause is recruiting new friends
every day, and registering new branch societies almost
every month.   When I began to attack scientific
cruelty there was no society in existence to oppose it.
There are now (1894) no less than fifty-seven such
societies in Europe and America.

Many of these, which have been founded by us or
have voluntarily affiliated themselves to the Victoria
Street Society, I proudly count as my *grandchildren* —
the offspring of my own society !   To know that they
are flourishing and multiplying is to me a source of
unmeasured satisfaction.   I cannot here record all
these hopeful ramifications of our work, but must
mention a few most interesting to me.

There is one very strong branch in Manchester for
the existence of which and its most able direction we
are principally indebted to my friends Mr. and Mrs.
Herbert Philips, Mr. and Mrs. W. T. Arnold, and Mr.
Sugden.   It has long kept an office of its own (9,
Albert Square, Manchester), with an efficient Secretary,
and is doing splendid work in the centre of England.
There is another strong branch in Bristol which has
likewise an office of its own (20, Triangle, Bristol) and
a devoted Secretary, and also an excellent Lecturer,
Mr. T. A. Williams.   The venerable Chairman, Rev.
David Wright, the Hon. Secretary, Mrs. Roscoe, and
the Misses Marriot, carry on its work with never
flagging energy ; and have several sub-branches through
the West of England.   The Irish Branch, founded and
worked almost single-handed by the Hon. Secretary,
Mrs. Tisdall, of Dulargy, has had great difficulties

to encounter, but, nevertheless, has extended year by year, and regularly subsidizes the parent society as do the branches of East Kent, Macclesfield, Torquay, Windsor and Leeds.

The Macclesfield Branch, founded by my friends Miss Booth and Miss Brocklehurst, has held excellent meetings every year, and is at all times full of vigor. The Torquay Society, of which Mrs. Loraine is Hon. Secretary (in close alliance with the Newton Abbot S. P. C. A. and its Hon. Secretary, Captain Quintanilha), has been very successful and likewise generous to the parent society. Branches have also been formed and are fully organized at Dulwich and Derby, Exeter, East Kent, Hawkshead, North Devon, Nottingham, Oxford, Sheffield, York, Windsor, etc.—in all twenty.

The Scottish Anti-vivisection Society is a large and important society affiliated to ours. Beside all these local branches there exist the church "Anti-vivisection League;" the Society for "United Prayer against Vivisection," with 4,415 members, including fourteen English Bishops; the "Friends' Anti-vivisection League;" the recently founded "Working Men's Anti-vivisection League," and a new "Independent Anti-vivisection League." Two or three years ago we sent up a memorial to Mr. Matthews (then Home Secretary) with 41,315 signatures. We could undoubtedly double that number now. Such is the present state of hopefulness of our cause of mercy in England.

Looking back on this long struggle of twenty years, in which so much of my happiness and the happiness of others dearer than myself has been engulfed, I can see that, starting from the apparently small and subordinate question of scientific cruelty, the controversy has been growing and widening till the whole department of ethics dealing with man's relation to the lower animals has gradually been included in it. That this department is an obscure one, and that neither the Christian churches nor yet philosophic moralists have hitherto paid it sufficient attention, is now admitted. That it is time that it should be carefully studied and worked out, is also clear.

Sometimes I have thought (as by a law of our being we seem driven to do whenever our hearts are deeply concerned) that a Divine guidance may have presided over all the heart-breaking delays and disappointments of this weary movement; and that it has not been allowed to terminate, as it would certainly have done, had we carried our bill of 1876 in its original form through Parliament. *Then* our society would have dissolved at once; and, after a time, perhaps, the act, however well designed, would have become more or less a dead letter; and the hydra-heads of vivisection would have reared themselves once more. But, as it has actually happened, the delay and failure of our earlier efforts, and our consequent persistence in them, have fixed attention on this culminating sin against the lower animals, and through it on all other sins against them. A great revision of opinion on the subject is undoubtedly taking place; and while some (especially Roman Catholic) Zoöphilists have diligently sought in decrees and manuals and treatises of casuistry for some authority defining cruelty to animals to be a sin, the poverty of the results of all such investigations, and of the anxious collation of Biblical texts by Protestants, is gradually revealing the fact that, in this whole department of human duty, we must look to the God-enlightened consciences of *living* men rather than to the *dicta* of departed saints, or casuists, whose attention was directed exclusively to the relations of human beings with each other and with God, and who obviously never contemplated those which we hold to the brutes with adequate seriousness, — if at all. Of course we are here met, just as the first anti-slavery apostles were met, and as the advocates of every fresh development of morality will be met for many a day to come, by the fundamental fallacy of the Christian churches (in that respect resembling Islam) that there is a finality in Divine teaching, and that they have been for two thousand years in possession of the last word of God to man. Protestants are certainly not bound in any way to occupy such a position, or to assume that a final revise has ever been issued or ever will be issued by Divine authority of a *Whole Duty of Man.* Rather are they called on piously and gratefully to look for fresh light to come down, age after age, from the Father of Lights; or (if they please rather so to consider it) further development of the Christian spirit to be manifested as men learn better to incarnate it in their minds and lives. As for Theists like myself, it is natural for us, and in accordance with all our opinions, to believe that such a movement as is now taking place over the civilized world on behalf of dumb animals is a fresh Divine impulse of mercy, stirring in thousands of human hearts, and deserving of reverent cherishing and thankful acceptance.

It is my supreme hope that when, with God's help, our Anti-vivisection controversy ends in years to come, long after I have passed away, mankind will have attained *through it* a recognition of our duties towards the lower animals far in advance of that which we now commonly hold. If the beautiful dream of the later Isaiah can never be perfectly realized on this planet, and none may ever find that thrice "Holy Mountain" whereon they "shall not hurt nor destroy," — yet at least the time will come when no man worthy of the name will take *pleasure* in killing; and he who would torture an animal will be looked upon as (in the truest sense) "*inhuman ;*" unworthy of the friendship of man or love of woman. The long-oppressed and suffering

brutes will then be spared many a pang and their innocent lives made far happier; while the hearts of men
will grow more tender to their own kind by cultivating
pity and tenderness to the beasts and birds.   The earth
will at last cease to be "full of violence and cruel
habitations."

CHAPTER XXI.

MY HOME IN WALES.

In April, 1884, my friend and I quitted London, having permanently let our house in South Kensington to Mrs. Kemble. The strain of London life had become too great for me, and advancing years and narrowed income together counselled retreat in good time. I continued then and ever since, of course, to work for the anti-vivisection cause; but I resigned my honorary secretaryship, June 26th, 1884, and left the entire charge of the office and of editing the "Zoöphilist" to Mr. Bryan.[1]

A few months later I was disturbed to hear that the Hon. Stephen Coleridge (Lord Coleridge's second son), who had always been particularly kind and considerate towards me, had started a fund to form a farewell testimonial to me from my fellow-workers. Mr. Coleridge addressed our leading members and friends in the following letter: —

12, OVINGTON GARDENS, S. W.,
August, 1884.

SIR OR MADAM, — At the general meeting of the Victoria Street and International Societies for the Total Abolition of Vivisection, on the 26th June, Miss Frances Power Cobbe, for reasons set forth in the annual report, gave in her resignation of the post of Honorary Secretary, and it was accepted with deep reluctance.

---

[1] Many persons have supposed that I am still concerned with the management of that journal; but, except as an occasional contributor, such is not the case. The credit of the editorship for the last ten years (which I consider to be great) rests entirely with Mr. Bryan.

The executive committee, meeting shortly afterwards, unanimously passed a resolution to the effect that the occasion ought not to be passed over by the society unrecognized, and a list of subscribers to a testimonial for Miss Cobbe has been opened. The object of this letter is to acquaint you of these facts and to afford you the opportunity of adding your name to the list should you desire to do so.

Year after year from the foundation of the societies and before, Miss Cobbe has fought against the practice of the torture of animals, with constant earnestness, conspicuous power, and enthusiasm born of a noble cause.

That testimonials are too plentiful it may perhaps be urged with truth; but many of us who deprecate the practice of vivisection feel that such a life as this, of honor and devotion, were it to stand unrecognized and unacknowledged, would mark us as entirely ungrateful.

I remain your faithful servant,

STEPHEN COLERIDGE.

(Honorary Secretary and Treasurer to the fund.)

In a short space of time, I was told, a thousand pounds was collected; and it was kindly and thoughtfully expended in buying me an annuity of a hundred pounds a year. The amount of labor and trouble which all these arrangements must have cost Mr. Stephen Coleridge must have been very great indeed, and only most genuine kindness of heart and regard for me could have induced him to undertake them. I was very much startled when I heard of this gift and very unwilling to accept it, as in some degree taking away the pleasurable sense I had had of working all along gratuitously for the poor beasts, and of having sacrificed for some years nearly all my literary earnings to devote myself to their cause. My objections were overruled by friendly insistence, and Lord Shaftesbury presented the Testimonial to me in the following letter : —

24, Grosvenor-Square, W., February 26th, 1885.

My Dear Miss Cobbe, — The committee of the Anti-vivisection Society, and other contributors, have assigned to me the agreeable duty of requesting you to do them the kindness and the honor to accept the accompanying testimonial.

It expresses, I can assure you, their deep and real sense of the vast services you have rendered to the world, by the devotion of your time, your talents, and indefatigable zeal, to the assertion of principles which, though primarily brought into action for the benefit and protection of the inferior orders of the creation, are of paramount importance to the honor and security of the whole human race.

We heartily pray that you may enjoy all health and happiness in your retirement, which, we trust, will be but temporary. We shall frequently ask the aid of your counsels, and live in hope of your speedy return to active exertion in the career in which you have labored so vigorously, and which you so sincerely love. Believe me to be very truly yours,

SHAFTESBURY.

I acknowledged Lord Shaftesbury's letter as follows:

Hengwrt, Dolgelly, N. Wales, February 27th.

Dear Lord Shaftesbury, — I find it very difficult to express to you the feelings with which I have just read your letter, and received the noble gift which accompanied it. You and all the good friends and fellow-workers who have thus done me honor and kindness will have added much to the material comfort and enjoyment of such years as may remain to me; but you have done still more for me by filling my heart with the happy sense of being cared for.

That you should estimate such work as I have been able to do so highly as your letter expresses, while it far surpasses anything I can myself think I have accomplished, yet makes me very proud and very thankful to God.

Whatever has been done by me in the way of raising up opposition to scientific cruelty has been attained only because I had the inestimable advantage of being supported and guided by you from first to last, and aided step by step by the unwearied sympathy and co-operation of my dear and generous fellow-laborers.

These words are very inadequate to convey my thanks to you for this gift and all your past goodness towards me, and those which I would fain offer through you to the committee and all the subscribers to this splendid testimonial ; especially to the Honorary Secretary, who has undertaken the great trouble which the collection of it must have involved. I can but repeat, I thank you and them with my whole heart.

> Most sincerely, dear Lord Shaftesbury, and
> > Gratefully yours,
> > > FRANCES POWER COBBE.

This addition to my little income made up for certain losses which I had incurred, and raised it to about its original moderate level, enabling me to share the expenses of our Welsh cottage. I was, however, of course, a poor woman, and not in a position to help my friend to live (as we both earnestly desired to do) in her larger house in Hengwrt. We made an effort to arrange it so, loving the place and enjoying the beauty of the woods and gardens exceedingly. But we knew it could not be our permanent home ; and a suitable tenant having come on the field, offering to take it for a term of years which would naturally reach beyond our lives, we felt that the end of our possession was drawing near. I was very sorrowful for my own sake, and still more for that of my friend, who had always had a peculiar attachment to the place. I reflected painfully that if I had been only a little better off, she might not have been obliged to relinquish her proper home.

All this was occupying me much. It was a Thursday morning, and the gentleman who proposed to become the tenant of Hengwrt was to come on Monday to make a definite offer which, once accepted, would have been held to bind my friend.

I went downstairs into the old oak hall in the morning and opened the post-bag. Among the large packet of letters which usually awaits me there was one from a solicitor in Liverpool. I knew that my kind old friend Mrs. Yates had died the week before, and I had been informed that she had left me her residuary legatee; but I imagined her to be in narrow circumstances, and that a few hundreds would be the uttermost of my possible inheritance; not sufficient, at all events, to effect appreciably my available income. I opened the solicitor's letter very coolly and found myself to be, so far as all my wants and wishes extend, a rich woman.

The story of this legacy is a very touching one. I never saw or heard of Mrs. Yates till a few years before her death, and when she was already very aged. She began by sending large and generous donations of £50 and £80 at a time to our society. Later, she came up from Liverpool to London when I was managing affairs without a secretary, and, finding me at the office, she gave me a still larger donation, actually in bank-notes. She was an Unitarian, or rather a Theist like myself; and having taken very warm interest in my books, she seemed to be drawn to me by a double sympathy, both on account of religious sympathies and those we shared on behalf of the vivisected animals. Of course I explained to her the details of my work, and she took the warmest interest in it. After I resigned my office of Honorary Secretary, she seemed to prefer to give her principal contributions personally to me to expend for the cause according to my judgment, and twice she sent me large sums, with strictest injunction to keep her name, and even the locality of the donor, secret. I called these gifts my Trust Fund, and made grants from it to working allies all over the world. I also spent a great deal of it in printing large quantities of papers. Of course I began by sending her a balance sheet of my expenditure; but this she forbade me to repeat, so I could only from time to time write her long letters (copied for me by my friend as my writing taxed her sight), telling her all we were doing. At last she came to see us here in answer to our repeated invitations, but could not be persuaded to stop more than one night. Talking to me, out walking, she asked me: " Would I take charge of some money she wished to leave for protection of animals *in Liverpool?* " I answered that I could not engage to do this, and begged her to entrust it (as she eventually did) to some friend resident in the place. Then she said shyly: " Well, you do not object to my leaving you something for yourself — to my making you my residuary legatee? " adding to the question some words of affection. Of course I could only press her hand and say I was grateful for her kind thought. She did it all so simply, that, being prepossessed with the idea that she was in rather narrow circumstances, and that she had already given me the savings of her lifetime in the trust fund, it never even occurred to me that this residuary legateeship could be an important matter, after she had provided (as she was sure to do) for all legitimate claims upon her. Nothing could exceed my astonishment when I found how large was the sum bequeathed in this unpretending way. My friend thought I must be ill, from the difficulty I seem to have found in commanding my voice to tell her the strange news when she came into the hall, a quarter of an hour after I had read that epoch-making letter!

Certainly never was a great gift made with such perfect delicacy. Mrs. Yates had taken care that I should have no reason, so long as she lived, to suppose myself under any personal obligation to her. Since then, it may be believed that my heart has never ceased to cherish her memory with tender gratitude, and to associate the thought of her with all the comforts of the home which her wealth has secured for me.

Mrs. Yates, at the time I knew her, had been for thirty or forty years the widow of Mr. Richard Vaughan Yates, a Liverpool merchant. The following obituary notice of her appeared in the "Zoöphilist," November 2, 1891. I may add that beside her personal legacy to me (given simply by her will to "her friend Miss Frances Power Cobbe," without comment of any kind) Mrs. Yates gave £1,000 to the Victoria Street Society, as well as £1,000 to the Liverpool Society for Prevention of Cruelty to Animals; both bequests being over and above legacies to her executors, relatives, and dependants.

OBITUARY.

THE LATE MRS. YATES.

THE Victoria Street Society and the cause of antivivisection have lost their most generous supporter in Mrs. Richard Yates, of Liverpool; a good and noble woman if ever there were one. Born in humble circumstances, she was one of the truest gentlewomen who ever lived. Her wide cultivation of mind, broadly liberal but deeply religious spirit, and sound, clear judgment remained conspicuous even in extreme old age. The hearts of those whom she aided in their toil for the poor brutes, with a generosity only equalled by the delicacy of its manifestations, will ever keep her memory in tender and grateful respect.

A warmly-feeling article in the "Inquirer," October 10th, 1891, known to be by her friend and pastor, Rev. Valentine Davies, gave the following sketch of her life. It is due to her whose generosity has so brightened my later years that my autobiography should contain some such record of her goodness and usefulness.

MRS. RICHARD VAUGHAN YATES.

On Thursday evening, October 1st, there passed peacefully away one who was the last of her generation; bearing a name honored in Liverpool since the Rev. John Yates, in the latter part of last century and the early years of this, ministered in Paradise Street Chapel, and his sons took their places in the first rank of the merchants and philanthropic citizens of the town. Anne Simpson was born November 10th, 1805, and to the last retained happy recollections of her childhood's home, a simple cottage in the pleasant Cheshire country. She married, in the mid-summer of 1832, Mr. Richard Vaughan Yates, having first spent a year (for purposes of education) in the household of Dr. Lant Carpenter, at Bristol, of whom she always spoke with great veneration. Richly endowed with natural grace and delicacy of feeling, true nobility of heart, and great simplicity, sustained by earnest religious feeling and a strong sense of duty, there was never happier choice than this, which gave to Mrs. Yates the larger opportunities of wealth and freedom in society. She shared her husband's interest in many philanthropic labors, his care for the Harrington Schools, founded by his father, and for the Liverpool Institute, his pleasure and his anxieties in the making of the Prince's Park, opened in 1849, as his gift to the town. She shared also to the full his delight in works of art and in foreign travel. The late Rev. Charles Wicksteed published some charming reminiscences of

one of their Italian journeys; and still more notable
was that journey through Egypt, Sinai, and Palestine,
recorded by Miss Harriet Martineau in her "Eastern
Travel."

Since her husband's death, in 1856, Mrs. Yates has
stood bravely alone, living very quietly, but keenly
alive to all the interests of the world, with ardent sympathy for every righteous cause, and generous help ever
ready for public needs as for private charity. No one
will ever know the full measure of her acts of kindness,
her care for the least defended, her many quiet ways of
doing good. She was a great lover of dumb creatures,
and felt a passionate indignation at every kind of
cruelty. Four-footed waifs and strays often found a
pleasant refuge in her house, and for many years she
was an active worker for the local branch of the Society
for the Prevention of Cruelty to Animals. The cab-
men and donkey-boys of Liverpool at their annual sup-
pers have long been familiar with her kindly face and
gracious word, and many a time has her intrepid protest checked an act of cruelty in the public streets.
The friend of Frances Power Cobbe, she took a deep
and painful interest in the work of the Victoria Street
Society for the Suppression of Vivisection, and sustained its work through many years by generous gifts.
Herself a solitary woman in these later years, it was to
the solitary and defenceless that her sympathies most
quickly went. She desired for women larger powers to
defend their own helplessness, to share in government
for the amelioration of society, and to share also in the
world's work. She had a surprising energy and persistence of will in attending to her own affairs and
doing the unselfish work she had most at heart. With
a plain tenacity to the duty that was clear, she went
out to the last, whenever it was possible, to vote at
every election where she had a vote to give, and to attend meetings of a political and useful social character.

Hers was a life of great unselfishness and true humility. Suffering most of all through sympathy with
others, she longed for more light to dissipate the
darker shadows of the world. And she herself,
wherever it was possible to her patient faithfulness and
generous kindness, drove away the darkness, praying
thus the best of prayers, and making light and gladness
in innumerable hearts.

After only a few days of illness she fell asleep. A
memorial service was held on Sunday last in the Ancient Chapel of Toxteth, where for many years she regularly worshipped. The Rev. V. D. Davies preached
the sermon, and also on the following day, at the Bir-
kenhead Flaybrick Hill Cemetery, spoke the words of
faith at her grave. — "Inquirer," October 10th.

I have erected over her last resting-place (as I
learned that she disliked heavy horizontal tombstones)
a large upright slab of polished red Aberdeen granite.
After her name and the dates of her birth and death,
Shakespeare's singularly appropriate line is inscribed
on the stone : —

"Sweet Mercy is Nobility's True Badge."

On receiving that eventful Thursday morning the
news of the unlooked-for riches which had fallen to my
lot, our first act was naturally to telegraph to the
would-be tenant that "another offer" (to wit mine!)
"had been accepted for Hengwrt." The miseries of
house-letting and home-leaving were over for us, we
trust, so long as our lives may last.

There is not much more to be told in this last chapter
of my story. The expansion of life in many directions
which wealth brings with it is as easy and pleasant as
the contraction of it by poverty is the reverse. Yet I
have not altered the opinion I formed long ago when I

became poor after my father's death, that the importance we commonly attach to pecuniary conditions is
somewhat exaggerated (so long as a competence is left),
and that other things — for example, the possession of
good walking powers, or of strong eyesight, or of good
hearing, not to speak of the still more precious things
of the affections and spirit — are larger elements, by
far, in human happiness than that which riches contribute thereto. Of course I have been very glad of
this unlooked-for wealth in my old age. I have felt,
first and before all things else, the immense satisfaction
of being able to help the anti-vivisection cause in all
parts of the world while I live, and to provide for some
further continuance of such help after I die. And
next to this I have rejoiced that the comfort and repose
of our beautiful and beloved home is secured to my
friend and myself.

One step naturally suggested itself to me early and
was carried out at once. I made over the annuity of
£100 a year which the testimonial had given me to the
funds of the Victoria Street Society; feeling sure that
the generous donors would be pleased at this appropria-
tion of their gift directly to the cause nearest to all our
hearts. My debt of gratitude to them each and all is
not paid off, but doubled.

The friendly reader who has travelled with me
through the journey of my three-score years and ten,
from my singularly happy childhood in my old home
at Newbridge to this far bourne on the road, will now,
I hope, leave me with kindly wishes for a peaceful
evening, and a not-too-distant curfew bell; in this dear
old house, and with my beloved friend for companion.

The view of Hengwrt, which forms the frontis-
piece of this volume, gives a good idea of the house

itself, but can convey none of the beauty of the rivers, woods, and mountains all round. No spot in the kingdom, I think, not even in the lovely Lake country, unites so many elements of beauty as this part of Wales. The mountains are not very lofty — even glorious Cader, where the giant Idris (so says the legend) sat in the rocky "chair" (*Cader*) on the summit and studied the stars, is trifling compared to Alpine height, and a molehill to Andes and Himalayas; yet is its form, and that of all these Cambrian rocks, so majestic, and their *tilt* so great, that no one could treat them as merely hills, or liken them to Irish mountains which resemble banks of rainclouds on the horizon. The deep, true, purple heather and the emerald-green fern robe these Welsh mountains in summer in regal splendor of coloring; and in autumn wrap them in rich russet brown cloaks. Down between every chain and ridge rush brooks, always bright and clear, and in many places leaping into lovely waterfalls. The "broad and brawling Mawddach" runs through all the valley from heights far out of sight, till, just below Hengwrt, it meets the almost equally beautiful stream of the Wnion, and the two together wind their way through the tidal estuary out into the sea at "Abermawddach" or "Abermaw," — in English "Barmouth," eight miles to the west. On both north and south of the valley and on the sides of the mountains are woods, endless woods, of oak and larch and Scotch fir, interspersed with sycamore, wild cherry, horsechestnut, elm, holly, and an occasional beech. Never was there a country in which were to be found growing freely and almost wild, so many different kinds of trees, creating of course the loveliest wood-scenery and variety of coloring. The oaks and elms and sycamores which grow in Hengwrt itself are the oldest and some of the finest in this part of Wales; and here also flourish the largest laurels and rhododendrons I have ever seen anywhere. The luxuriance of their growth, towering high on each side of the avenue and in the shrubberies, is a constant subject of astonishment to our visitors. The blossoms of the rhodos are sometimes twenty or twenty-five feet from the ground; and the laurels almost resemble forest trees. It has been one of my chief pleasures here to prune and clip and clear the way for these beautiful shrubs. Through the midst of them all, from one end of the place to the other, rushes the dearest little brook in the world, singing away constantly in so human a tone that over and over again I have paused in my labors of saw and clippers, and said to myself: "There *must* be some one talking in that walk! It is a lady's voice, too! It *can't* be only the brook this time!" But the brook it has always proved to be on further investigation.

Of the interior of this dear old home I shall not write now. It is interesting from its age — one of the oak-pannelled rooms contains a bed placed there at the dissolution of the neighboring monastery of Cymmer Abbey — but it is not in the least a gloomy house; altogether the reverse. The drawing-room commands a view to right and left of almost the whole valley of the Mawddach for nine or ten miles; and just opposite lies the pretty village of Llanelltyd, at the foot of the wooded hills which rise up behind it to the heights of Moel Ispry and Cefn Cam. It is a panorama of splendid scenery, not darkening the room, but making one side of it into a great picture full of exquisite details of old stone bridge and ruined abbey, rivers, woods and rocks.

Among the objects in that wide view, and also in the still more extensive one from my bedroom above, is the little ivy-covered church of Llanelltyd; and below it a bit of ground sloping to the westering sun, dotted over with gray and white stones where "the rude forefathers of the hamlet sleep," together with a few others who have been our friends and neighbors. There, in that quiet enclosure, will, in all probability, be the bourne of my long journey of life, with a gray headstone for the "*Finis*" of the last chapter of the Book which I have first lived, and now have written.

I hope that the reader, who perhaps may drive some day along the road below, in the enjoyment of an autumn holiday in this lovely land, will cast a glance upon that churchyard, and give a kindly thought to me when I have gone to rest.

INDEX.